LADY HOLME

G J BELLAMY

ISBN: 9798848251340

This publication is a work of fiction. All names, characters and events in this publication, other than those clearly in the public domain, are fictitious and any resemblance to real persons, living or dead, or actual events is purely coincidental.

Copyright © 2022 by G J Bellamy. All rights reserved.

The moral right of the author has been asserted.

No part of this publication may be reproduced, stored in a retrieval system, or transmitted in any form or by any means, without the prior express written permission of the publisher.

G J Bellamy

gjbellamy.com

Contents

Cast of Characters	V
1. At home, at sea, at work Monday, 4 October 1920	1
2. Party	8
3. After the party	17
4. Research	22
5. Lady Holme, and how to get there from here	36
6. Private communication	45
7. Everyone's going	56
8. Names and trickery	65
9. It's not all plain sailing	76
10. Arrivals and a small bedroom	87
11. More arrivals	102
12. Loose Toffee	115
13. The day darkens	130
14. A question of suspects	144
15. Conversations and ideas	160
16. Old, old stories	176

17.	Someone oversteps the mark	187
18.	A secret and a confession	203
19.	Horses are only human, too	216
20.	Dancing divinely	231
21.	Revolution in the night	244
22.	Getting through it all	257
23.	Aha!	271
24.	Mutual aid	282
25.	Wet through	293
26.	What were you doing?	306
27.	Unbelievable	316
28.	Showdown	324
29.	You can't do that	333
30.	Roughly on the same page	344
31.	Kensington	367
32.	Smugglers	380
33.	Convoy	389
34.	Old Paradise Street	402
35.	Double-decker	413
Epilogue		424
Also by G J Bellamy		432

Cast of Characters

Sophie Burgoyne / Phoebe King
Henry Burgoyne, vicar - Sophie's father
Lady Shelling (Elizabeth Burgoyne) - Auntie Bessie
Ada McMahon / Nancy Carmichael - Sophie's friend
Flora Dane - Sophie's long-time friend
Archie Drysdale - Sophie's second cousin

The Agency
Miss Jones, typist
Elizabeth Banks, researcher and office helper
Nick and Alfie, errand boys
Fern / Dora, between maid with photographic memory

White Lyon Yard
Hawkins, butler
Mary Roberts, maid
Marsden, footman

Hazlett Family at Lady Holme
Lord James Hazlett (Horse - Chieftain)
Lady Jane Hazlett (Horse - Primrose)
Maude Hazlett, daughter, unmarried (Horse - Marmalade)

Staff of Lady Holme
Mrs WIlliams, housekeeper
Mr Isembard, butler
Mrs Chiverton, cook

Nelly, scullery maid
Mabel, scullery maid
Daniel, footman
Old Joe, general help

Hazlett family not living at Lady Holme
Basil Hazlett, oldest son and heir
Fiona Hazlett, née Simpson, his wife
Constance Reid, née Hazlett, youngest daughter
Oscar Reid, her husband
Reginald Hazlett, youngest son, unmarried

Guests at Lady Holme
Martin Scrope, MP, family friend (Horse - Fanfare)
Helen Scrope, wife, non-rider
Amelia Scrope, daughter (Horse - Kaleidoscope)
Vanessa Scrope, daughter (Horse - Shangri-La)
Adrian Benson, friend of the Scrope daughters
David Rand-Sayers, son of Lord Hazlett's friend (deceased)
Daphne Rand-Sayers, wife
Richard Smythe, young lawyer
Maria Smythe, wife, non-rider
Horace Digby, Colonel (retired), Lady Jane's brother (Horse - Claude)
Sandra Digby, wife (Horse - Mercy)
Dr Albert Beaton (Horse - Scotty)
Belinda Beaton, his sister (Horse - Conker)

Scotland Yard
Superintendent of Special Duties (Inspector) Penrose
Sergeant Daniels, Special Duties
Inspector Morton, CID
Sergeant Gowers, CID

Hampshire police
Colonel Warde, chief constable
Detective Inspector Talford, Portsmouth
Detective Clark, Portsmouth

Chapter 1

At Home, at Sea, at Work

Lady Holme Hall was, without doubt, the most picturesque Tudor house within a hundred miles — a few might venture to say, the finest in the entire country. This, however, was rarely stated, for Lady Holme was famous for not being famous. Hardly anyone had ever heard of the place, let alone visited it.

Built in 1567, the half-timbered hall, a stunning and intricate confection in black and white, was a big, rambling structure, possessing some eighty rooms — thirty principal bedrooms, six reception rooms, and a host of smaller spaces, ranging in size from small closets and pinched attics, to the uncommonly long, narrow gallery where, on rainy days, there might arise the temptation to play cricket or shoot arrows. Binding all these various places together was the bewildering, maze-like network of corridors, stairs, and ramps. A newcomer venturing away from the main staircase required a map.

The house spoke with a distinctive voice, for one step in three in any direction produced a creak from the broad, time-worn planks or narrow stair treads, or a rattle from the lozenged-paned windows or some china in a cabinet across the room. As for overhead noises - in some rooms they boomed while on the ground floor there was barely a peep to be heard. And withal and throughout, Lady Holme Hall possessed a faint, complicated scent of lavender and wood smoke, salubrious sea air, and, sometimes, a dry tang from the ancient wattle and daub walls.

Four ghosts are said to inhabit Lady Holme. One is Lady Holme herself. The second is a sea captain, supposedly Lady Holme's secret lover. The third is Sir Hazlett, the husband of Lady Holme. Sightings have been rare - usually experienced by the household staff who, if they did not actually relish the sightings, as some did, would faint, scream, or leave the house for good. Those are old ghosts and beside the point. The fourth, like a ghost and yet extant, is the Rt Hon Viscount Hazlett. Lord James is very much alive and vigorous, haunting his house for a secret reason known only to himself.

At seventy-three, he had left his 1,700-acre estate only once in thirty-nine years. At least annually, Royal invitations arrive at Lady Holme requesting the presence of Viscount Hazlett at this or that occasion. Just as frequently, his lordship declines attending the proposed event. In the past, Lord James had successfully avoided Queen Victoria and King Edward VII for a combined total of fifty-three times. He is currently avoiding King George V for the fifteenth time.

"I shan't go. London is too far these days." He was sitting at the breakfast table, absent-mindedly cutting up a kipper. A light rain pattered at the window. Outside, it was a day blanketed in grey and green. The usually visible sea had disappeared into the fog that had crept in from the Channel.

"I am quite certain," replied the Rt Hon Viscountess Hazlett - Lady Jane - with some acidity, "London has not moved an inch. It has grown, but it hasn't moved. How then is it too far? The train service is excellent, as you well know... It is a Royal invitation, for goodness' sake."

"You know what I mean... I'm just not going."

"Of course, you're not. Keep your secret. I don't care about that anymore. You will be buried with it one day. I hope you take some satisfaction in such a prospect."

"You know it's a private matter which we do not discuss."

"No, we never do."

"See here, Janey, I haven't denied you a thing. You go where you please. We have receptions at home. What more could you want?"

"Must I explain the expectations usually gratified within a good marriage after all this time? There is something wrong with your brain."

"There's nothing wrong with my brain... But what do you mean by expectations?"

"Oh, really! Haven't you considered that I might wish to go to Court? Just once! Has it ever crossed your mind?"

"My dear, it's always the same old argument every time one of these blessed invitations arrives. You'd think they'd have the hang of it by now, but no, not them. Anyway, it is never from the King himself, it always comes from some clerk working to a list."

"It is from Sandhurst, the Lord Chamberlain, and he is not a lackey. His lordship is a charming gentleman."

"I didn't say he was a lackey. Didn't even use the word."

"You implied it."

"But he didn't write it himself, you know. He got hold of somebody else who instructed a clerk, who then did the deed by having it printed."

"But he signed it."

"I haven't even met the man... Oh, let's stop this bickering... And me kipper's gone cold... I tell you what. We'll have a big party here instead. You can invite anyone you please. As many as you like - and we'll get them because we're ahead of the London season. How does that sound?"

"You're buying me off... You always do this. It is highly irritating."

"I do it because it works. I say, Carpenter, bring me another kipper."

Through the bank of fog spreading over the water, a motor launch slowly made way its way eastward to the Solent in the channel between the Isle of Wight and the mainland. Two men sheltered in a pilothouse open to the stern, vainly trying to keep the heavy, chill air off themselves.

"What's the matter with the engine?"

"I don't know," said the pilot. "It's running a bit rough, though… Might be dirty petrol."

"I s'ppose… Can't see a thing in this muck… I could do with some dry clothes… Are we getting anywhere?"

"Take a sounding with the lead line."

"I don't like this," said the man, approaching the side to drop the line. "Sailing in fog's a mug's game." He threw the lead forward and stared as the coiled line disappeared over the gunwale.

"Good money in it, though. Otherwise we wouldn't do it, would we…? What you got?"

"Four fathoms."

"Four! We've drifted too close to the mainland since rounding the Needles. Hurst Point has to be close now."

"Shh, shh… Is that surf I hear? To port."

"Dunno… I can't really tell. I'll put out further."

The engine responded to the controls - its revs increasing noisily while noticeable vibrations shook the pilothouse. The man carefully recoiled the lead line.

"What's going on? We're barely moving."

"Take the wheel and hold to starboard. I'll have a look."

As the changeover was being made, black smoke started to billow from the engine compartment. A red glow cast a brief strange light over the men and the tarpaulin, which covered their cargo stashed neatly in packing crates. With a soft boom, several large flames sprang up amid the smoke.

"We're done for!" shouted the pilot. "Grab a life belt and over the side!"

The two men wasted no time in abandoning the launch and soon plunged into the cold water even as the fire blazed.

"It's f-freezing."

"Swim! When that l-lot goes up…"

They stayed together as best they could and swam towards what they hoped to be the shore. The men bobbed about more than progressed in the direction whence had come the uncertain sound of surf. Soon they wearied in their water-logged clothes while the cold threatened them with cramps. The glow of the burning boat soon disappeared behind them, enveloped by fog. Several minutes later, they heard staccato ripples of minor explosions of varying intensity followed by an immense dull, booming thump.

"No. Soup spoons go on the right," said Ada, whose patience was running out.

"Oh, silly me. I always get meself muddled between left and right," answered Fern.

"You'll have to cure that pretty sharpish, my girl."

In the spare office in Burgoyne's Agency, Ada attempted to teach a young trainee for domestic service how to set a place for dinner. Progress was proving to be slow.

"Pick it all up and let's 'ave another go, shall we? You're right-handed. Set the cutlery that goes down on the right with that 'and. Use your other to place the cutlery that goes on the left. That should sort you out."

"You mean... like this?"

"Right. Simple, ain't it? Now, try again, only faster this time."

Once Fern acquired the basics of laying place settings, Ada began teaching her the proper way of serving drinks to guests. Fern was to carry a round tray of ten dainty glasses and observe the proper decorum while serving. This part of the instruction had to be halted as soon as it started.

"Stop! You're slopping it everywhere."

"As soon as I carry anything delicate with liquid in it, my hands shake. Also, I don't like being watched. I'm ever so sorry."

"How do you manage tea in a cup and saucer? It must go everywhere."

"No, it don't. We always have mugs at home. I'm fine wiv a mug."

"Fern, how do you get on? Where 'ave you worked before?"

"I've been a milkmaid. I'm really good with cows." Fern smiled.

"That'll help you out in milady's Drawing Room, won't it? She'll be right 'appy to have her cocktails served in buckets and mugs."

"You're joking, aren't you?"

"Oh, no, I wouldn't do that to you. What else 'ave you done?"

"Kitchen maid, laundry, tweenie and... let me see. Oh, yes, and seamstress. That only lasted a day."

"I wonder why that was. Look, you stay put. I must speak to Miss Burgoyne about something... Just keep practising with the cutlery while I'm gone. Forks closest to the window, remember?"

"How could I forget that?" Fern smiled again. "I've got a picture of it now."

On her way to Sophie's office, Ada walked through the Agency, which was alive with the sound of several typists hammering out their work. They did so at a minimum average rate of eighty words per minute up to Miss Jones' sustained frantic speed, which rarely dipped below 110. Behind her back, the typists referred to Miss Jones, manager of the stenographers, as 'Old Fury'.

"Come in," called Sophie when Ada had knocked on her door.

Ada marched in and shut the door behind her.

"Hello, miss. I'm 'ere to report on Fern's progress. Or, rather, the lack of it."

"Not doing well, then? Sit down, please."

"No, she's not," said Ada as she took a chair. "She's a nice girl and I've nothing against her personal but she is not ready and I don't think she ever will be."

"I haven't anyone else for Wednesday night... There must be six of us."

"Is her having a photographic memory that important? Because I could ask a friend if not. She's done waitressing and what 'ave you."

"I don't know. I thought Fern's special ability might come in useful in the gambling den. How bad is she?"

"Doesn't know left from right. Spills drinks if you so much as look at her. Stands like a puddin' waiting to be told what to do. If she's doing all that while watching how the croupier fixes the game, I think she'll get herself noticed, I do an' all."

"She had better not go... I must find Fern a job, however. I more or less gave her my word. Could we pass her off in a big private house or mansion somehow?"

"That wouldn't be so difficult... She's done laundry and between maid, so she could do those. I think Fern'd be 'appier working the udders on a cow. She brightened right up when she said she'd been a dairymaid."

Sophie smiled. "I've done that job. I'll give Fern a chance, but it will have to be elsewhere. Your friend, can she come in today so that I can explain the more delicate parts of our operation?"

"Yes, if Nick takes a message to her. Her name's Betty and she works in a clothes shop in Shoreditch, right across the road from the Old Blue pub. Nick will know where that is."

"Write out your note. Can Betty be here at half-past six?"

"If she flies, she might. But it's no problem about Wednesday, that's her 'alf day."

"Tell her to come as soon as possible. Here, give this sixpence to Nick. That will stop his grumbling about going outside his usual route."

"Right-o, miss. What do I do with her?" Ada nodded towards the room containing her student.

"Send Fern to see me. I can't lose my photographic memory... That didn't sound quite how I meant it. I mean, I believe she can be useful under the right circumstances."

Chapter 2

Party

"How reliable are weather forecasts?" asked Lady Jane at breakfast. "I've invited a few people for the weekend after next and promised them some riding... as if I knew the weather would be fine."

"Living dangerously, aren't we?" said Lord James, emerging from behind his newspaper. "It will probably be mild with a strong chance of rain. That won't bother me... unless it's windy. Who's coming?"

"There will be about twenty of us. The Scropes and their children."

"Oh, Martin will buttonhole me over some issue or other about the railway. *He'll* ride in any weather... Probably young Vanessa will, too. I'll telephone him to make sure he brings his horses in a van."

"All our brood will be here."

"Including Constance and Oscar?"

"Yes, dear."

"Oscar rides ponies when he visits Kenya on business and he used to be in the Lancers, so a little rain won't stop him. Might not get any, anyway."

"My brother Horace is coming with Sandra."

"Ah, are they? He won't bring their horses from Cheltenham."

"Dr Beaton and his sister. Oh, and of course, David and Daphne."

"Why ask the Rand-Sayers?"

"Because it is *October*, dear, and not everyone would want to come riding with the weather being so erratic. Anyway, we always invite them. I need to make up the numbers and we want a few of the younger set."

"We won't have mounts for all of them. They'll have to take turns. If you must ask the young uns, give me a list of their names or I'll be forgetting who's who... Do you think Beaton will pop the question to Maude?"

"I sincerely hope so, since our daughter is now thirty-eight."

"She doesn't care much for men. Prefers horses and dogs... Have you had a word with her?"

"Maude and I have had many words over the years but, regarding Dr Beaton, I've decided to stay out of this one. You know how difficult she can be at times."

"I like Beaton. A no-nonsense chap. An excellent rider, too. If there is anyone in this world who appears entirely suitable for Maude, I would say it was Beaton."

"We'll contrive to throw them together as much as possible. So don't go hauling him off anywhere on your own."

"That's the plan, is it? I'll steer clear of both of them."

"There's just one problem. We're under-staffed since our housemaid, Maureen, left to get married, and we need extra help with so many guests... It's very difficult to find good servants on short notice."

"Yes, I suppose it must be. Never mind, I'm sure you'll manage something... Twenty people coming, is it? How many extra servants do we need?"

"At least four, even if they have experience. Most of them are dreadful, you know. There's nothing worse than being embarrassed by one's poorly trained servant."

"Surely, you and Mrs Williams will fix something up between you." Lord James resumed reading his newspaper.

"Can I have your attention, please...? I see everyone is well turned out... Betty, your hem is crooked."

"Sorry, miss." Betty, Ada's friend, quickly wriggled and smoothed her dress.

It was seven in the evening and six women had assembled in the main office of the Agency. Sophie was facing the other five to give a last-minute run through of their mission. Two taxis were to arrive shortly to take them to an elegant house at 8 De Vere Square in Kensington.

"As you know, Inspector Penrose is interested in De Vere Square because of the distribution of forged bank notes. However, he has given us specific instructions about tonight. We will work among a crowd of wealthy socialites. There are three matters to attend to. The first is the sale of cocaine and heroin. As you are now aware, the Dangerous Drug Act is working its way through parliament and will become law next year. The people running this place hold lavish parties hoping to get many wealthy people addicted to narcotics before the Act becomes law. Afterwards, this operation will supply drugs to the addicts at higher prices and in more clandestine ways. That is what I am told. Our task is to observe and report on the numbers of people involved. This is what they sell... The clear bottle contains cocaine in tablet form and the brown is heroin. Pass them around."

Flora put her hand up after she had examined the bottles. "Do they sell these openly?"

"Yes. I understand they dispense the bottles in a separate room on the second floor. A man stands guard outside. He knocks on the door when a customer approaches. One person is admitted at a time, then the door is closed. After the transaction has finished, the customer comes out again. How many bottles each has purchased is anyone's guess. Betty, Marion, and Alice will monitor the door to the room while they are serving drinks. We've worked out a system to keep a count for the entire night. It includes winks, blinks, and raised eyebrows... Our faces have never had so much exercise before, don't you think?"

"It's good for the complexion, miss," said Marion, with a self-conscious smile.

"Let's hope so," said Sophie, returning her smile. "Now, the next objective belongs to Ada, who will be working exclusively in the gambling room. She will attempt to find out if the house, which I am told is the proper term, if the house has fixed the roulette wheel or if the Baccarat croupiers are cheating in some other way. We're assuming any cheating is for the house and not for themselves. A croupier may work alone or in association with a confederate who is also a player. Ada, how did your training go with Benny the Palm?"

"Very well, miss. I didn't know there was so many ways to cheat, but I do now."

"That's good. We had all better be careful when playing cards with you in future. The third objective is Flora's. She will monitor Steven Cooper, the manager of the establishment. She will gather as much intelligence as she can. Intelligence seems an odd word to use but is, I understand, the correct terminology.

"Now, I'm concerned that Ada's activities might be noticed, so Flora will also watch the staff, spotters they're called, stationed near the gaming tables. She will alert Ada if a potential problem arises. A cough means someone's watching. A sneeze means leave the room immediately. I have a police whistle. If a dangerous situation arises anywhere, I shall blow the whistle and we all leave immediately and *together*." She took the article from her pocket and gave it a gentle peep.

"Finally, as we are able, we are to observe gamblers who have extraordinary losses or winnings or ones who are playing for extended periods of time. They may receive or spend forged notes as they pay for or cash in their chips. All rather exciting, isn't it? Are there any questions?"

"What will you be doing, Miss Burgoyne?" asked Flora.

"I will come over to receive information from you when you signal me to do so. Generally speaking, I will keep watch and investigate anything that has not been already assigned. In particular, I will keep interesting individuals under observation. Remember, we want to collect as many names and pertinent details as possible, including complete descriptions of people and their behaviour — just as we have practised. The police shall keep the front and back entrances under observation. On the inside, we are their eyes and ears. Questions…? No? Then the watchword is *discretion*. Stay alert. When you notice something, turn your eyes and not your head. While we're doing all of that, let's hope we don't spill anything on a customer." She smiled warmly.

The sound of a horn outside in the street alerted the women that their taxis had arrived. Laughing and talking excitedly, the secret agents descended the stairs to embark upon their mission.

"Rien ne va plus!"

The roulette wheel had not stopped spinning. It had taken Ada many trips past the table, carrying trays of drinks, before she saw how the wheel was rigged.

Benny the Palm, while no expert where roulette was concerned, did tell Ada of a ruse known as ball tripping. The croupier presses a button which causes a tiny concealed pin to protrude at a certain point in the ball track. This battery-operated pin deflects the moving ball, causing it to land in a certain part of the wheel head. When the croupier correctly times the ball's pace to the spin of the wheel, he can get the ball to land into the group of numbers he wants - where no big bets have been placed. Or, conversely, he will time it to land on or near to a confederate's large bet.

Ada had seen it happen, only she saw it piecemeal, in fragments, as she passed back and forth, attending to customers and taking away used glasses. What first alerted her were the croupier's actions. He typically spun the wheel at one speed but, occasionally, he spun it at a slightly slower speed and watched intently a fixed point on the wheel track.

Eventually, she caught him discreetly pressing what must have been a concealed button beneath the table while the players' fixed attention was with the ball and wheel. She heard Flora's cough and felt alarm. Had her observation of the croupier's behaviour attracted the attention of a spotter? Ada approached the nearest person whom she knew worked for the house.

"'Scuse me. 'Ow much are those black chips worth?"

"'Undred pounds, lovey."

"Blimey," said Ada, "there's a gentleman over there who's just plonked down three of them. If I 'ad an 'undred pounds, I wouldn't be puttin' it on that little ball. It could land anywhere."

"Well, as they say, know your limit and play within it. Some people don't learn, but they've got plenty of money. And it's payin' our wages, ain't it, doll?"

"Doll, indeed. You're a bit too familiar."

"I am that. Fancy a drink later?"

"I'm seeing someone."

"Lucky fella. If you change your mind, you know where to find me."

"I do, now, you cheeky man."

They both laughed and Ada carried on working.

Flora ran into difficulties. Firstly, she saw an actor she knew from the theatre, which forced her to keep out of any room he and his lady friend occupied. Annoyingly, the couple did not stay in one place for more than a few minutes. Secondly, she gained a devoted and rather tipsy middle-aged admirer who actively followed her. For a time, Flora avoided the one and attempted to lose the other, all the while serving guests and keeping watch on those staff nearest to Ada. For almost two hours, she could not observe the manager's behaviour. Sophie, responding to Flora's raised eyebrow signal of distress, intervened to divert the admirer's attention by accosting him. The intervention brought Flora a temporary respite from the man's persistence.

Both problems finally resolved themselves. Flora's acquaintance began dancing with his companion to soft music performed by the small band in a separate room. Twenty minutes later, they left. The admirer, frequently outdistanced by Flora who resorted to speed to avoid him, eventually tired and fell asleep in a chair. The management left him dozing comfortably until it decided he had been there long enough and sent him home in a taxi. After that, Flora was at liberty to continue her official and unofficial duties.

Betty, Marion, and Alice successfully covered the door to the drug dispensing room. An initial setback had occurred upon arrival when Alice was assigned a station behind the buffet table in another room. She was stuck there for several hours. After her release from the captivity of helping guests to food, she joined Betty and Marion in the freedom of their more mobile assignments. Between them, they logged sixty-three probable customers entering the dedicated room.

Sophie, too, was free to busy herself, confident in the abilities of the staff she had brought with her. She watched Steven Cooper, the manager, while Flora could not, and helped from time to time with the drug dispensary headcount. Steven Cooper seemed to do nothing out of the ordinary. He toured the rooms, spoke to customers and staff, and seemed to be at ease - pleased with the night's work. The only place he avoided was the drug dispensary, which gave Sophie a clue as to the establishment's organization. It was obvious that the selling of heroin was not Cooper's business.

Sophie found eavesdropping in a crowded, noisy place unsatisfactory. Most things she heard were rendered inane by being just the scraps of conversation. Avoiding mere pleasure seekers, even the men and women who looked as though they might say something of importance failed to live up to the promise of their appearance. Gamblers left behind crumpled Baccarat score cards, but these yielded no notes or clues.

At about eleven, Marion gave Sophie a signal and surreptitiously pointed to an elegantly dressed young man in an impeccable black evening suit. Sophie began following as he drifted from room to room. He was an attractive man with graceful mannerisms and slick, dark brown hair. Sophie judged that his natural hair colour must be light brown — close to her own colouring — as one effect of brilliantine was to darken hair by several shades.

She served drinks to a seated couple. The man, in his fifties, had a roving eye. It roved appreciatively over Sophie. The woman beside him was barely twenty and looked thoroughly bored until she turned back to the man, whereupon she instantaneously became vivacious and playful. As Sophie turned away, the young man she was keeping under surveillance offered his gold cigarette case to another, older gentleman. They both took a cigarette. There followed a moment of confusion as the older man patted his pockets in search of his lighter, but without success. The young man lent his lighter to the other. Then, as an afterthought, he produced and gave his companion a book of matches. They both spoke and laughed as the older man suddenly found his own lighter in an inside pocket. Nonchalantly, the young man tossed the book of matches onto a nearby table. The two men began talking again.

Sophie came over to clear an empty glass from the nearby table and replace an ashtray with a clean one.

"He's a good man," said the older gentleman.

"Yes, I dare say he is," said the younger.

That was all Sophie heard before her meagre activities became stretched to the implausible. The older gentleman was a Londoner while the young man sounded as if he came from a southern county, possibly her own native Hampshire. When she had a moment, Sophie carefully examined the matchbook she had retrieved, holding it by the edges. Three matches had been used. On the cover it read Londesborough Hotel, Lymington, Hants. She congratulated herself in having placed the young man's accent so accurately.

Ada informed Sophie of a suspected crooked dealer at one of the two Baccarat tables. Sophie was, therefore, present when a very flamboyant woman at that table had a phenomenal win. The woman, larger than life in both manner and physique, made a great show of delighted surprise, and went on to play a further couple of desultory games before cashing-in about seven thousand pounds in chips. The immediate staff, Sophie noticed, did not seem at all bothered by this event. Neither did Steven Cooper look upset to any degree when he had briefly stopped to watch. Later, Sophie learned from Flora that Cooper had appeared, all along, totally indifferent to the woman's winning streak.

Sophie wondered about Steven Cooper and the part he played. It was through him that Penrose had got Burgoyne's Agency into the house. If he was helping the police, he could not be involved in the drugs, rigged gambling, or the passing of forged notes. Alternatively, he had such good connections that he felt himself to be immune from prosecution. However, she could not see how that was possible. Sophie decided she would ask Superintendent Penrose about Mr Cooper's seemingly charmed existence.

Chapter 3

After the Party

Sophie visited Superintendent ('Inspector') Penrose at Scotland Yard early the next morning.

"Well, Miss Burgoyne, you're looking lively for a person as has been up half the night." He was settled comfortably in an oak swivel chair in his office.

"I don't feel very lively, Inspector."

"Ah... Is that the report you have with you?" His accent had a trace of Somerset.

"Yes. Here you are. I hope we accomplished something."

"We'll find out. Give me a summary of what happened."

"As you wish. It was difficult keeping track of people because there was so much coming and going the whole night. I estimate the total number of guests to be about three hundred."

"Three hundred and twenty-seven. Go on."

"Of those, sixty-three went into the room to buy drugs."

"Hmm, that seems like a lot to me... About one in five."

"It's a similar ratio for those who gambled. We estimated seventy-five gamblers. It was difficult to count accurately without drawing attention to ourselves. By the way, taking drugs in the house is forbidden, and the rule strictly enforced. I saw two people asked to leave."

"That makes sense. They're trying to run a business and attract custom. People talking gibberish or taking an overdose would spoil their reputation. The people who bought drugs, what did they do afterwards?"

"Difficult to say. I followed a few of them. Most stayed, although one couple left immediately. None of them had much interest in gambling or watching it, but they may have done so earlier. I got the impression they were two different sets of people."

"I suppose they must be. That's something to bear in mind."

"Do these drugs sell for a lot of money? I mean, you used to see heroin and cocaine in preparations sold in chemist shops."

"Not a great deal because there's still a tremendous quantity out there — they are still legal at the moment. The new Dangerous Drugs Act will change all of that. Opiates will become illegal substances, available only when prescribed by a doctor. The price will then go through the roof for those of them addicted to the stuff." Penrose indicated the direction with the stem of his pipe. "It's like this outfit is providing a service of convenience at present, making drug-taking seem like normal, accepted behaviour. They're biding their time, as we all are. The laws and regulations will have a sharp set of teeth in the next twelve-month. That's when we'll start arresting these people."

"And the gambling?"

"At best, we'd get a conviction with a few months' hard labour for a couple of their more expendable people. Those who are the brains behind the operation would spring up elsewhere quick enough. The potential risk is always worth it to them."

"Then what about Steven Cooper? Why is he helping you?"

"He's sublet the house. Cooper has separate agreements with the man who runs the gambling and the other selling the drugs. Only those two gentlemen used false names. We think we know who they are, but we need evidence. As it stands, Cooper would get fined for a misdemeanor, for permitting such goings on, and told not to allow it to happen again."

"Then why is he helping you by letting us in there?"

"That's a secret. Let's say because he's been helpful in this matter, we won't be looking at another matter so carefully."

"Ah, yes! That type of horse-trading goes on, I suppose. They do indeed rig the gambling. Two croupiers are involved. One was at a baccarat table and the other at the roulette wheel. As far as we could tell, they're working for the house. However, one lucky player at roulette was at the table the whole night except for when he cashed in his chips, which he did about once an hour. We estimate his winnings to be some three thousand pounds. Another winner was the Baroness Von Koller of Austro-Hungary. She won at the fixed baccarat table. Although she had an accent, I doubt she's Austrian. Besides, they have revoked all titles of nobility in Austria. She won about seven thousand pounds."

"You have descriptions of these two?"

"Yes, they're in the report."

"They might be cardsharps, hired to make the game look fair. Ha, what a filthy racket. Was anyone losing heavily?"

"Um, no... Well, except nearly everyone. It's quite beyond me why they do it when the odds are so against them, but it's their money. I saw one gentleman lose twenty pounds straight off in three rounds... He didn't win a thing, looked bored the whole time, and then just walked off afterwards. Most mystifying to me."

"Right, I should look sharp. I've to follow up on the Baroness and the roulette man. If forged notes were being passed, the chances are that it was those two big winners who received them."

"Before I go, there was one curious incident I should mention. A young gentleman, possibly from Lymington, entered the drug dispensary without knocking. The guard outside treated him with respect, I'm told. I followed him and, although he acted normally, he seemed neither to be a patron nor a manager. He left a matchbook behind him, so I picked it up." Sophie handed Penrose a sealed envelope.

"I was careful about fingerprints," said Sophie, looking pleased with herself. "You must show me how they identify them one of these days."

"I can arrange that when you have some spare time. Just let me know when you're ready. Is there a description of this chap in the report?"

"There is."

"Lymington's close to Southampton. It's a small port, I believe."

"Yes, it's on the Solent, too," said Sophie.

"Now, that's funny, that is. A report landed on my desk on Tuesday. Someone was smuggling weapons and explosives on the Solent. Only they were doing so in fog, which seems a foolish notion. Their launch blew up, practically on the beach in front of the artillery fortress of Hurst Castle. A colossal explosion it was. I bet that made the lads in the Royal Artillery jump. They had to have thought they were under attack. Anyway, they were German weapons, and the debris and bits of packing crate were scattered along the beach and in the surf. The launch was so burned and smashed to pieces we're unable to trace the owner. The crew disappeared and we can't say if they're dead or not."

"My goodness. I didn't read about that in the newspapers."

"It's a War Office matter and they're a tight-lipped bunch. They don't like reporters at the best of times and likely they're scared the launch might have been accidentally destroyed with some of that artillery of theirs in the castle. Ha ha."

"I've often sailed past Hurst Castle. The beach is very narrow just in front of it. The launch must have exploded right under the walls."

"Ha ha, do you really think so?" Penrose derived great satisfaction from this knowledge. After a few moments, he continued, saying,

"Something's going on in those parts. There's always been smuggling along the coast, but usually it's tobacco, spirits, and luxury goods. Not machine guns, grenades, and high explosives. That's something quite different. How well do you know the area?"

"Fairly well. I know Christchurch better. But on the mainland coast of the Solent, there are many suitable places for smuggling between Hurst Point and Lymington. They'd need to sail on high tides, though, because of the mudflats. If they do that, there are many bays, rivers, and lagoons for them to use that lend themselves to such ventures."

"My goodness, Miss Burgoyne, you're a regular mine of information... How long a stretch of interesting coast are we talking about?"

"All the way from Hurst Point to Southampton Water, I should say, about fifteen miles. Lymington used to be notorious for smuggling."

"Ah, that's interesting. I want to know who was to receive these weapons. It's a nasty bit of business and no good at all."

"Well, should a country house be involved, don't forget about Burgoyne's Agency for domestic staff."

"Ho, I shan't do that... Wait a minute, that's given me an idea. Ordinary smuggling, and we're dealing with a gang of fishermen, or the like, bringing goods to shore and storing them in farms or other hideouts. Weapons be a different proposition. You don't sell grenades under the counter in a pub, do you, Miss Burgoyne? There's organization behind this. It means they have money to spend and a network to take care of handling the cargo. The launch was taking the weapons to a spot along the coast when it ran into trouble. They may well have been heading for a country house or other big estate. That's the kind of place most likely to house people with both enough money and enough peculiarity of political motivation to undertake such a thing. I'll pass this along to Mr Drysdale, seeing as the weapons are from abroad. Got to keep him busy, haven't we?"

"Yes, we can't have him idly drinking tea and nibbling digestive biscuits all day in the Foreign Office. But you've suggested something quite extraordinary. I wonder what estates are down that way...? Oh, well, I mustn't hold you up."

"Goodbye, Miss Burgoyne, and thank you for the report."

"You're most welcome. Goodbye, Inspector."

Chapter 4

Research

The increase in typing work arriving at the Agency had not abated since the end of the dismal summer slump. Miss Jones had worked full-time now for several weeks. Temporary typists were also a fixture. Sophie, when not working for the Foreign office or for Scotland Yard, actively promoted her business and such promotion was paying off. This was an immense relief to her. The influx of work kept her two office boys, the outgoing Nick and his small, depressed-looking, shy friend and subordinate, Alfie, very busy on their bikes, flying about the City, picking up and dropping off typing assignments.

The employment agency side of the business ticked over. Applicants for domestic servant positions came to the office in a predictable pattern. Monday and Tuesday were the busy days, while Friday was extremely slow. The requests for domestic staff came in batches. The start of the month was lush with enquiries, while the end was a desert. It surprised Sophie that, with the London season soon starting, there had yet to be a surge in requests.

After meeting with Superintendent Penrose, he who, for his own strange reason, preferred to be called Inspector, Sophie took the Underground. She ascended the stairs at Monument and emerged to walk along King William street. Sophie was no longer the visitor from the country, unsure of her surroundings in London; she had become a part of the city but, being a new part herself, Sophie had yet to lose her sense of magic at being in the world's largest metropolis. Today, she was surprised to find herself walking along considering weapons and smugglers, explosions, and roulette, and who she knew living south of the New Forest and west of Southampton. There was only the Rudge family. She had missed seeing them this year because of starting the agency. She thought she might write to them, but then stopped herself from pursuing that avenue. How could she? It was impossible for her to ask the Rudges about near neighbours because they, naturally, would ask why she wanted to know. And that she could never tell them. She could not say 'I'm a spy, so is my cousin Archie. At present, I'm trying to discover if any of your neighbours are smuggling arms into the country for revolutionary purposes. Whom do you suspect who lives nearby? I'll relay whatever you tell me to the Foreign Office and Scotland Yard.' No, she could not ask. Sophie now lived a life separate from her friends and family.

"Good morning, Elizabeth," said Sophie as she entered the agency.

"Good morning, Miss Burgoyne."

Although Elizabeth was not a receptionist, she often fulfilled that function. An employee of less than a month's standing, the sixty-year-old woman had already become an office fixture. A shy, retiring lady, she could easily be imagined as the maiden aunt of somebody's family. Sophie had hired her out of compassion more than for any specific reason — although Elizabeth's research work experience might someday be of service.

"May I see you in my office in a few moments? I must speak to Miss Jones first."

"Yes, of course."

Ten minutes later, the women had settled themselves in Sophie's office. Elizabeth always seemed shy to Sophie.

"Are you conversant with the south Hampshire area? I'm wondering if any of our sort of people own property there." Sophie looked slightly embarrassed because of her phrasing.

"Oh, um, no. I have relations and friends in Portsmouth and Bath, but no closer than that, I'm afraid."

"How does one find out, then? I'm looking for a list of large properties and their owners in a particular area."

"It's necessary to compile your own list. There's no work I'm familiar with that does that, unless one goes to the area itself and looks up county records. If all you wanted was a list of landed gentry and their country seats, that's easy to obtain. It would be a very incomplete list, though."

"I suppose it would."

Sophie looked out of the window. If she explained her reasons for wanting such a list to Elizabeth, she would need to take her into her confidence. She was against doing that for several reasons - Penrose's motto of 'Trust nobody', being one of them. For police work, it did not matter so much. Sophie's test for staff she employed in police work was that they must be firm believers in upholding the laws of the land. With espionage, however, knowing whom to trust was of prime importance. Espionage was an invisible war fought against a shifting, sometimes nameless enemy, who used unorthodox methods.

"Just an idea I had, nothing more."

"May I say speak? I hope you don't think it rude of me."

"Please go ahead." Sophie was curious about what she would say.

"Do you remember us discussing the research I did during my war work?"

"Yes, I recall it."

"For a time, the government made a concerted effort to capture German agents. This had nothing to do with the pre-war hysteria. This was a wartime hunt for active agents. I'm under the Official Secrets Act. Without doing violence to it, I may have seen the name of Penrose before."

Sophie's eyes widened. "My goodness me."

"We never met, but I knew who he was when he visited a few weeks ago - I recognized the name. I'm a researcher, that is all. Your dealings with him are private, and none of my business. However, I noticed a marked change in the office after he had left, so it wasn't difficult for me to surmise that something unusual and important was contemplated. I tried to mind my own business but, without meaning to, I overheard several things that led me to conclude you were doing work for Scotland Yard."

"I suppose it would become apparent to an observant person. Is Miss Jones aware of this?"

"I don't believe so. She devotes herself to her typing. As you are aware, Miss Jones keeps up the same hectic pace from the moment she arrives until her day ends."

"Typing makes a lot of noise, too," observed Sophie. "What do you think of my initial question of finding a property?"

"When someone asks for information not commonly available to the public, it means there is an uncommon reason behind it. If this is ill-mannered, I can stop, for I certainly do not wish to overstep the mark. You have been very kind to me."

"Please, continue."

"In my career, I have met a wide range of individuals with an even wider range of interests for which they seek information. People want information according to patterns. Your looking at properties in a certain area suggests you are seeking a person about whom you know little. Perhaps not even their name. Should you discover a person who fits the bill, so to speak, you would then investigate them. It is best I stop there."

Her abrupt halt caught Sophie by surprise. She was unsure how to proceed, and so lapsed into silence, pondering how she could be sure of Elizabeth.

"Elizabeth, if I took you into my confidence, would I be disappointed?"

The older woman looked embarrassed.

"I sincerely hope not. However, I've not spoken to win your confidence or... or build myself up. It was just that for me to remain quiet seemed unfair. You would labour under a false impression of what I understood. Because you have been friendly and very kind, I thought you should know my view of things. I hope I've caused no offence."

"No offence taken. Trust is of vital importance to me... That report I asked you to prepare explaining the reasons behind the Greco-Turkish war was thorough and informative. Could you prepare a list of estates, farms or large commercial buildings on or close to the Solent between Hurst Point and Southampton?"

"Yes, I could. Although we would need reference materials. A visit to the area may also be required."

Sophie nodded. "What materials would you need?"

"An Ordnance Survey map of the general area and such twenty-five inch larger scale maps suitable for specific areas of interest. A Kelley's Directory, both Debrett's and Burke's Peerages, local newspapers - I should make a list. There are quite a few things."

"Could you start at once?"

"At once? Is this urgent?"

"The only urgency is my impatience. A matter came up which requires immediate attention."

"Yes, I can make a start. I'll have to visit libraries and possibly the Land Registry Office in Lincoln's Inn Fields."

"You'll need money for the project. When your list is ready, we will discuss what is required."

"I will begin immediately. Thank you, Miss Burgoyne." Elizabeth left the room looking pleased.

After she had gone, Sophie indulged in reflection. Her conjecture led her to consider whether Lord Stokely might be involved in arms smuggling. It would not be him directly, but were his agents involved? If not Stokely, then there was someone else who needed to be stopped. What broke her train of thought was remembrance of Elizabeth's mention of a telephone directory. Sophie realized she may well soon need a telephone in the office. Sophie went to see Miss Jones.

"Excuse my interruption," said Sophie. To her astonishment, Miss Jones' hands ceased typing the instant she spoke.

"Yes, Miss Burgoyne?"

"How important is having a telephone to the business of this office?"

"I would say it is vital. At the factory, the salesmen conducted a great deal of business by phone. It expedited many matters."

"Customers would call here to have their typing picked up?"

"Yes, exactly that. Also, I think you would see more placements in the staffing business. The phone is much more convenient than writing and waiting for a reply. I had thought to mention it, but it wasn't my place to do so."

"Miss Jones, I would welcome any suggestions."

Something like a smile hovered about Miss Jones' lips, but it failed to come to fruition.

"I will bear it in mind, Miss Burgoyne."

"Now, typewriters. We'll need an extra should we get busier and one of the Royals needs overhauling or replacement. What do you suggest we do?"

Miss Jones' smile blazed forth. "Best to replace it - there are better models available now. I know just the place to go. They sell new and reconditioned models and are the cheapest place in the City."

They talked over the relative merits of typewriter brands and ribbons for some minutes.

"I'm going out and won't be back until after lunch," Sophie informed Elizabeth as she was about to leave.

"I have the list ready."

"Do you? May I see it, please?"

Elizabeth gave her the list. Sophie scanned it.

"There are quite a few things. A lot of them will be useful in the future. Where do you want to start?"

"Foyle's will carry the Peerages and is closer than the Haymarket. Perhaps Nick or Alfie can be sent to get them. I must attend to the maps myself."

"We'll leave the boys out of this. You manage it all and go by taxi for whatever you need."

"Goodness, I never use taxis... It's the expense. We never take them in my family."

"My immediate family has the same attitude. You must overcome your aversion just this once. What do you think? Does the office need a telephone?"

"Well, I marvel at how busy your office is without one. For research work it saves an immense amount of time when dealing with institutions. In my experience, a telephone call followed by a letter usually expedites the matter."

"Does it make such a difference?"

"Oh, yes. It's a remarkable little phenomenon in its way."

"I must remember that. You will need money. Let us go to my office."

An officious door-keeper was intent upon denying Sophie entrance to the Foreign Office. They were just inside the main door — the small man with the bored, disdainful attitude sat at a desk while Sophie stood in front of it. She had wished him a good morning and informed him that she was here to see Mr Archibald Drysdale.

"Do you have an appointment?"

"I don't."

"Name?"

"Phoebe King."

"I'll look you up in the lists… King… King… Phoebe. No entry for you. You're not on the Admissions List nor the Daily Appointments, neither."

"Could you send a message to him, please? I know he will see me."

"I can't leave my post and there's no one to send, it being near lunch. You should have come earlier."

"Then allow me to go to his office and neither of us will waste our time. I know my way because I've visited before."

"I can't let you do that. It's more than my job's worth."

"Why not use that telephone to find out if he will see me?"

"Can't be done. It's not allowed. That's for appointment arrivals only."

"You *could* make an exception."

The man shook his head. Sophie placed a half-crown on the desktop and held it in place with a gloved finger.

"Make the exception — just this once."

The man gave a quick nod. She slid the coin across the table. The door-keeper, without a word or change of expression, deftly moved it to a pocket.

He picked up the telephone receiver, looked down at a list of extensions, then dialed a number.

"Hello, Mr Drysdale? Albright downstairs, here. There's a lady wanting to see you... a Miss Phoebe King... Send her up...? Oh, and add her to the list. Very good. I'll do that at once, sir."

"You can go straight up," he said after replacing the receiver. He gave her a wan smile.

"Thank you," said Sophie, and off she went with her head held high.

"To what do I owe this unexpected pleasure?" Archie, standing, drew out a chair in front of his desk for Sophie to sit in.

"Hello, Archie... thank you." Sophie sat down. "I'm here about two matters." She watched as Archie seated himself behind the desk.

"Two matters, eh?"

"Yes. Did Inspector Penrose talk to you earlier?"

"He did." Archie became guarded.

"Was it about the boat explosion?"

He hesitated before speaking. "We can't discuss the matter."

"Of course we can. I have an idea how they're doing it. I think it's worth investigating."

"Sophie, I understand your zeal, but it is I who must initiate the action. Then I ask you to perform certain tasks. There are boundaries that cannot be crossed in how these matters are to be handled."

"Hmm. What task do you want me to perform?"

"I'm nowhere near that point in the process. I've put out some feelers and I have to wait for responses. When I hear back, then we can decide what needs to be done."

"Oh. That's a disappointment. May I explain my idea to you?"

"Is this to do with property owners on the Solent?"

"Our Inspector is quite thorough, isn't he?"

"And fair — he gave you the credit."

"He rises even further in my already high estimation of him."

"You've taken the trouble to come to see me, so tell me your idea."

"Thank you. The boat was sailing for a landing place to unload its cargo of weapons. Wherever it was had to be a hidden, out-of-the-way spot because they were sailing during daylight... Although, it was foggy. There are many places for smugglers to land, but not all of them are suitable for unloading packing crates full of weapons and bombs and... things. I tried visualizing the type of place I would choose. I'd bring my boat in on high tide and anchor at a small bay or a small, navigable river and tie up there. The site must lend itself to easy unloading. Nothing must overlook it, which means it can't be on public property or in a town. Now, because the goods are in crates, a lorry might have to be waiting. Alternatively, the crates would have to be *carried* into a house or barn, storage shed or even a factory building."

Archie raised his hand to speak. Sophie raised her eyebrows.

"This is very good. Have you considered this? The weapons may have been going out of the country. We don't know which way the boat was sailing."

"Ah, no, I hadn't... However, if they were going to France, that's more their problem than ours."

"Of course, your scenario also works in reverse order. To load a boat with contraband is almost as risky as to unload it. The weapons might have been heading for Ireland, of course."

"Oh... Archie, I had the impression you were against me meddling."

"No. It was just a flash of proprietary jealousy on my part. I'm supposed to come up with the ideas. Believe it or not, the government pays me to do that. Anyway, enough of my silliness. What happens next?"

"My sincere apologies for stepping on your toes."

"Don't mention it. Please continue."

"Let's assume the weapons were to be landed in this country. Once landed, they must be secured in storage or transferred elsewhere for safe-keeping. Also, a buyer could have purchased them. That means the sale and delivery have to be arranged. My suspicion is this. The weapons were to remain on the coast for a short time before being transported elsewhere. They wouldn't stockpile such things at the point of landing. At least, I don't see why they should, because each new delivery only increases the risk of discovery of all their stored shipments."

"I'm not so far behind in this line of thought as you might think. It is possible a large weapons cache is being made. But where o where do you see multiple shipments among the scanty information you have?"

"I made that bit up. But should the smugglers have a safe landing place, surely it would see frequent use?"

"It would. I don't disagree. There are a lot of assumptions being made, however."

"Yes, there are. That's why I'm doing something about it. We have undertaken to investigate the matter."

"Have you, indeed? Please clarify this 'we' business."

"I have found a research assistant. I have high hopes for her."

"What is her name and address?" Archie picked up a pen.

"I hadn't thought of that. I suppose you have to check her background."

"Yes. Flora had a background check and has a clean bill of health."

"You didn't investigate, Flora, did you? But you've known her for years."

"People change, you realize. It's a required procedure, anyway. The chaps smuggling weapons were twelve-year-olds once upon a time. How is Flora these days?"

"She's very well... I don't think she's fully over my brother's death in the last week of the war."

"Yes, what an unfair blow it was when they were to be married. And you?"

"Not a day passes without my thinking of my dear Shining Boy... I miss him. Ah, well..." The cousins were pensive for many moments, until Archie pulled himself out of his reverie.

"Name, please."

Sophie gave the name and address for Elizabeth Banks. "She is a very shy, quiet lady. As a researcher, she worked for the government during the war."

"That makes my job easier, thank you." He wrote a note. "Whatever was on that boat packed a wallop but, in the scheme of things, it was a relatively small shipment, suitable to arm heavily for battle a group of forty or fifty. Now, apart from research, what is it you are proposing we do?"

"Identify likely properties in the area. Then get in them and have a look around. If there are country houses down that way, I would pay special attention to them. That's my self-interest speaking."

"Here's one to start off your list, only don't mention it to Miss Banks just yet. Lord James Hazlett."

"I don't recall the name."

"It's an old family in the Lymington area. Been there for centuries. We're interested in Lord Hazlett for several reasons. He's in his seventies now but, when he was young, he had connections with what we term 'suspicious characters'. Next, he is a self-imposed recluse. He hasn't left his estate in over thirty years. Although curious, we're not interested in him presently for either of those things. What has drawn Hazlett to our attention is a letter. Someone I cannot name received one last week from a local lawyer — local to Hazlett, that is. The correspondent is concerned about late-night activity on country roads. Lorries, to be precise, travelling country lanes close to Hazlett's estate. He finds the activity suspicious and mentioned smuggling. The lawyer, a young man, referred to Hazlett's estate purely to give a geographic context. He did not name his lordship as being connected with the activity.

"On top of this, Penrose mentions Lymington to me, and then we have a boat, laden with explosives and guns, choosing Hurst Castle as a place to shipwreck. Do you see a hazy picture forming?"

"Most certainly, I do."

"All I can say is conduct your research and, if Miss Banks' bona fides are as they should be, collect your findings and thoughts. Then come and tell me about them. Did you have to slip Albright some money?"

"Yes, half-a-crown."

"I'll have a word with him about that. By rights, he was supposed to turn you away. It's ridiculous... some of the absurd procedures in this place defy reason." Archie reached into his pocket for some change.

"No, please don't. I found it rather fun, actually. And, ah, business is better these days."

"As you say. Business improving, what? Excellent. I haven't liked to ask in case, well, you can imagine."

"You helped save the agency, Sweet Boy. For that, I am eternally grateful. But, of its own accord, the agency suddenly resurrected itself. At least, the typing service side has. That neatly brings me to the other purpose of my visit. How do I get a telephone line without waiting months and months? Also, I don't want it to be a party line. There's one in my building already. I can't tolerate the thought of people being able to listen in on other people's conversations."

"I've managed to pull the occasional rabbit out of a hat, but never a telephone line. The GPO is a law unto itself. However, leave it with me, and I'll see what I can do."

"Thank you. Now, how is Victoria?"

"Extraordinarily well, thank you for asking."

"Any softening in Mr Redfern's iron will?"

"Very droll. Unfortunately, no. In fact, he's more obstinate than ever about cutting Victoria off, even after her getting the submarine steel contract."

"Ungrateful man. I take offence with him because he has taken offence with you. How dare he? You and Victoria are well-suited. Does he not see that?"

"Not when he can't get past his assumption that I am a mountebank, looking to marry a rich heiress. I don't know. All we can do is give him time to get used to the idea."

"Let me know if I can help. Promise me you'll do that."

"I promise to keep you informed of our trials and tribulations, such as they are. It's not as bleak as it looks. We'll just have to economize."

"I've had much experience with economy. It's nothing as bad as it sounds. I'm sure, as long as you have each other, you will have a lovely life. Having dispensed my little rays of sunshine, I must be off. By the way, if you get me a telephone, I'll call you first. Now there's something for you to look forward to. Goodbye Archie."

As soon as she had gone, he picked up the phone.

"Hello, Howard? It's Archie. How's the Admiralty today?"

"Hello, old man. Can't complain. What's the bother now?"

"Just a small thing. Know anyone who can get a telephone line installed without the wait?"

"Oh, GPO. They have the stare of a basilisk... Abandon hope all ye who entreat the GPO. Where's it to be installed?"

"Burgoyne's Agency, 14 Sack Lane."

"Where in the world's that?"

"Near the Monument."

"Right. A telephone line is more of a Home Office matter, I would have thought. I'll ask around. Someone's bound to know the right person."

"Thank you. I believe I owe you a lunch."

"Yes, you do, and I choose the restaurant. Au revoir."

After Howard at the Admiralty hung up, he placed a call to the Home Office.

"Tony? Howard. I need a telephone line put in promptly."

"Good grief, man. I'm just toddling off to put the feed-bag on. Can't it wait?" said Tony.

"No, it's urgent. I'll give you the party involved."

"Very well, go ahead. Where's a pencil when you want one? Ah, found it. Go on."

After making notes, Tony called a more exalted official at the Home Office.

"Sorry if it's inconvenient, Sir Gerald, but a very urgent matter has come up."

"It better be urgent. I'm halfway out the door. It's lunchtime, man..." He then sighed. "Tell me what it is."

Tony did so.

"It takes a grand pooh-bah in Downing Street to manage that sort of thing. Do you know what they're like at the GPO? You can't get a favour from them unless willing to sacrifice your first-born. I'll deal with this after I've eaten. Never call me again so close to lunch. It ruins me appetite."

"I promise not to, sir."

The matter rested there for a while.

Chapter 5

Lady Holme, and how to get there from here

The postman from Lymington cursed under his breath at the thick layer of fresh-laid gravel on Lady Holme's tree-lined driveway. He muttered as he got off his bicycle at the large estate.

"Can't cycle upon that." His countryman's drawl put three undulations in the 'A' of the word 'that'. "And mustn't cycle upon the grass. Daft — they should make up their minds what they want."

Through the colourful landscape where the lawns remained lush and green while the trees had begun producing their palette of golds, browns, reds, and yellows, he pushed his bike towards the glorious Elizabethan house — a patterned mosaic of black and white, topped by a brown-tiled roof from which sprang seven large complicated, decorated chimneys constructed in orange-red brick. It looked splendid against the blue sky, adorned with puffs of white cloud. The postman did not view the house as splendid because he had cycled or pushed his bike along the same drive six times a week for fifteen years — holidays excepted. He called it The Old Place. He trudged around to the tradesmen's entrance, knocked, and waited.

"Hello, Bert," said the housekeeper when she had opened the door to his knock.

"Morning, Mrs Williams. Not much today." He handed the post to her.

"So, I see." She skimmed through the envelopes. Her education had not entirely displaced the rural accent of her Hampshire roots.

"Reckon you're hoping for summ'at special."

"Is it that obvious?"

"Ha, well, tis that. I've come to know, you know. There's always tomorrow." He paused. "I've been thinking. That new gravel's a perishing nuisance. Can I be cycling on the grass?"

"You understand that I can't approve such a request. His lordship is most particular about his front lawns. Speaking for myself, I'd be tempted to cycle next to the drive where the grass doesn't matter, but only while unobserved. But I cannot possibly say that I permit you to do such a thing. Good day, Bert."

"Good day, Mrs Williams." He pushed his bike back across the drive with a grin on his weathered face. At a point he found suitable, Bert looked about him before mounting his machine to begin cycling. Before he had got to the gate, he was whistling - a tuneful chirruping that pierced the solemn silence beneath the sycamores, beeches, horse chestnuts, ash, and great oaks.

In the house, Mrs Williams crossed the wide, flagstone hallway, where dark wooden panels, relieved by wide battens forming a simple, heavy square pattern, ran up some fourteen feet to a richly patterned, moulded-plaster ceiling. As she approached the small study at the front that served as an office, Lady Jane emerged from the room.

"Ah, Mrs Williams. Has anything arrived?"

"It doesn't look like it, your ladyship."

She held out half a dozen envelopes. Lady Jane went through them.

"No, nothing. I recognize most of the return addresses. What are we going to do?"

"Well, I had high hopes for the advertisement in the Lymington Chronicle, but it's utterly failed us. A laundress and a scullery maid were all who applied. To answer your question, my Lady, I don't know."

"Dear, dear... Getting *good* servants *is* difficult nowadays but not getting any of any calibre?"

"Shall I speak to Mr Isembard, to ask if he has any connections?"

"I spoke to him earlier, and he doesn't. He only suggested trying agencies in Southampton and Portsmouth, which we already did. And apart from polite replies, they've yet to do anything."

"Perhaps, my Lady, we could try borrowing servants from other houses, just for that weekend."

"I've tried. One maid was half-promised me but, in general, I sensed resistance to the idea among my acquaintances. You're busy, but if you can think of *anything*, let me know at once."

"Very good, my Lady."

Elizabeth returned in triumph to the agency. Alighting from the cab, her face had a suffuse glow of excitement. She tipped the taxi driver. But while she worried the amount was too much, he thought it woefully insufficient after he had carried a heavy box of books upstairs, besides his having been her driver. Settled once more in the office, Elizabeth unpacked her purchases as though it were her birthday. Each book she held and map she unfolded meant a beginning of research and the start of a reference library. Although a microscopically small start, it was still a definite start. That meant much to her.

"Oh, Miss Burgoyne! I've had tremendous success — particularly with the maps. I've put everything in the spare room."

Sophie was barely through the door when Elizabeth had spoken.

"I'm glad it went well. Give me one moment and then tell me all about it."

"Please excuse me, I should have waited until you had settled. I confess an impatience to begin."

"I also have that, so don't worry."

They went to the spare office. Elizabeth had arranged everything in the room and it was ready for use. She gave Sophie the change and receipts from her expedition. They then set to work.

"May I suggest we start with the small-scale map and work from there?" said Elizabeth.

"That would be a good starting point. We are looking primarily for a place where smugglers can land contraband unseen during daylight hours and at high tide. Then they will transfer it to a secure place or onto a waiting lorry."

"Ah, that is interesting." Elizabeth opened a map of the Hampshire coast.

"It's something different."

They scrutinized the map together.

"Already I notice several likely places that lend themselves to such an enterprise," said Sophie.

Elizabeth picked up a pencil and wrote in a notebook. She stopped and said,

"Please point out the places of interest."

After lunch, the matter of the telephone line began moving again. A Downing Street assistant answered a telephone call from the Home Office. He hurried to find someone who could help with the Home Office request, returning with a very dapper gentleman who picked up the receiver.

"Sir Gerald, how are you? It's Franky Baker."

"Hello, Franky, I wasn't aware you had a billet at number ten."

"Only been here a few months. We should meet and catch up."

"Yes, we should. First, I've got to find the Home Secretary. He isn't there, by any chance? I've been looking all over for him, but he's vanished."

"He's in with the Prime Minister. They're in a long discussion... they have even longer faces."

"Oh, that's nothing new. All politicians look glum once they're in office. Think you could break into their meeting? I've received a request for a telephone line that must be installed at once. It's of vital importance."

"Is it? I suppose it would be. You'd better give me the details."

"Burgoyne's Agency, 14 Sack Lane. Don't ask me where it is because I don't have a clue. My assistant found it and then started blithering about the fire of London."

"Near The Monument, then?"

"That must be the place he meant. Do what you can, will you?"

"I'll deal with it at once and call you back."

"Good man. I'll wait be waiting to hear from you."

"Excuse me, Prime Minister, a matter of some urgency has arisen." There were six people in the room.

"Well, what is it?" said David Lloyd George, leaning back in his chair.

"A telephone line needs to be installed at once. The hope is the GPO can start work immediately."

"Then it must be a secure line."

"Oh, yes, I should think so. I understood it to be urgent in the extreme and, er, hush-hush."

"I see. Where's Jack Pease?" He addressed the man sitting across the table from him.

"He was in the House before lunch," answered Edward Shortt, Home Secretary.

"I'll write out a note. Edward, you write one, too, authorizing and accepting the expense. You'll take the notes to him, Baker, and impress upon Jack the need to expedite the matter. Though why they can't plan these special operations ahead of time, I'll never understand."

"Just a moment, David. To which department do I charge it?"

There was a momentary silence before Lloyd George answered.

"Do you have a department that's still within budget?"

"That's difficult… There is one, come to think of it. The Registrar of Friendly Societies. I read their report last week and they're in a robust position."

"There's your answer. Give us the details, Baker."

"Yes, Prime Minister. If I may, I took the liberty and wrote out a note. You need only sign or amend it as you deem necessary." Franky Baker slid a memorandum, written in an elegant, flowing hand, across the polished table to the Prime Minister.

The PM read it, added the word 'secure', signed it, then slid the note across to the Home Secretary, who wrote out his own note.

"Debrett's doesn't have a list of peers by county," said Sophie. It was now approaching four o'clock. She had been searching through peerages and was now studying a map. "Are you up on peers and their family seats?"

"Not in the slightest, I'm afraid," replied Elizabeth. "Although I know someone who is. Shall I ring him up…? Oh."

"You must write to him instead."

Sophie looked at another map.

"We have eighteen likely properties so far," said Elizabeth. "The areas around both Pitts Deep Lane and Sandpit Lane look promising."

"As does Saltgrass Lane… It's flat land there… as is the entire stretch of coast, for that matter… except for Marley Mound. Where was that?" Sophie leafed through the maps and extracted the one she sought. "Ah, here it is. A disused mine — that makes one think, doesn't it?"

"Yes, that is interesting. There's also Frog's Hole." Elizabeth pointed at a large, nearby pond on the same map. "See how the river finds outlet in the sea at the southern end? There's a track north of the pond. A small boat might go upriver, into the pond, and then moor on the north shore. From there, they transfer the cargo to the waiting lorry."

"They could do that." Sophie noticed many tracks and lanes presented possibilities. "Nothing for it, Elizabeth. We must go to look for ourselves. Although we'll hold off for the moment, as I'm expecting some information."

Sophie was waiting upon Elizabeth's background check before taking her into any further confidence.

"Excuse me, Lord Gainford, I bring important messages from Number Ten."

Franky Baker had tracked down Jack Pease, 1st Baron Gainford, Postmaster-General, MP, in the lobby of the Houses of Parliament. He was conversing with several others.

"Just a moment... What is it, Baker?"

"These signed notes are from the Prime Minister and the Home Secretary concerning a delicate and critical matter."

"What do we have here, then?" He took the proffered notes and read them.

"Friendly Societies? Edward's becoming a right comedian. Thank you, Baker. I'll attend to this at once." He turned to the others. "I've been called away on business. We'll talk again soon."

A private conversation on a bench near the Hyde Park Lido was taking place between two men. They wore hats and buttoned-up overcoats — one brown and a grey.

"Not what you'd call park bench weather today," said the younger man in the brown overcoat.

"We get complete privacy, though, and it's in a mutually convenient place... The next shipment is ready." The middle-aged man in the grey overcoat lowered his already deep, insistent voice when annunciating his second statement.

"Then I'll send another launch over to you. There was nothing left of the old one."

"I hope it's of a more recent construction. We need to land the cargo and soon. We were already behind before this setback. Can your men be ready, let's say, on the twenty-first?"

"Oh, yes. You know, this is getting pricey. While the men waited, they heard the explosion. Now they want more money, even though the engine caught fire and it was an accident, pure and simple." The young man offered a cigarette to the older, who declined.

"Then make them see that's how it was and that they've nothing to worry about. Buy 'em a drink, but don't pay 'em more. Anyway, that comes off your cut, so it's your lookout."

"We know how to handle the men, thank you."

"Yes, I suppose so. How do we know the coast is not being watched?" The older man turned to his companion.

"It's not. I've got it on good authority, too. Besides that, we're taking extra precautions at our end and leaving nothing to chance. When the launch is lowered from the ship mid-Channel, we'll have another boat already on the Solent. That one will scout the landing, but they'll be coming from the other direction, you see. They'll look ahead and if HM Customs or the Royal Navy are in the area, they'll signal the launch. You needn't concern yourself, because they won't be about but, if they are, the launch turns back and goes to the secondary landing place. If it's all clear, they'll signal that, too. See, it's foolproof. Nothing for you to worry about."

"I hope you're right. But let me tell you something. We can't have another mess-up or you know who will come and sort it out for you. You don't want him doing that."

"Tell the well-dressed gentleman that I can ensure our service runs as smoothly as it ever has. It was just an unfortunate incident."

"Yes, well, I s'ppose these things happen. I'll be seeing you."

Chapter 6

Private Communication

After the agency closed for the day, Sophie walked home to her aunt's house at White Lyon Yard. She had her own key now but rarely used it because Marsden, the footman, seemed to possess second sight and always opened the door before she had her key out.

"Good evening, Miss Burgoyne." He had done it again.

"Good evening, Marsden." Sophie entered the elegant hall of the spacious Regency townhouse.

"May I?" he asked.

They went through a ritual in which the tall, thin footmen helped Sophie from her coat to hang it up in a closet. Although thin, Marsden, according to Mary, Sophie's maid, ate like a horse - she had almost said pig but refrained because she liked the footman — and, so Mary further stated, he ate enough for three normal men. By his appearance, one could be persuaded to believe Marsden ate but twice a week.

"Where will I find Lady Shelling?"

"She is in the lounge, Miss Burgoyne. The Colonel and Mrs Simpkins are with her. Mr and Mrs Lund, Sir Robert Dalrymple, and his son Eustace will arrive shortly for dinner."

"I had better go up and change. Send Mary to me if you see her."

"Yes, miss."

Lady Shelling — Sophie's Auntie Bessie — always gave excellent dinners because her chef of choice for dinner parties was Pierre Benoit, who was an exceptional artist. His real name was Donald Wilkins, but his expertise in the kitchen was so great that his pseudonym was the preferred usage in polite society. An invitation to dine at Lady Shelling's house when Pierre was in the kitchen was never one to be declined.

Long after dinner and once the guests had gone home, Sophie and her aunt sat in the Drawing Room talking.

"Pierre's rich sauces are going to be the death of me," said Aunt Bessie. "Still, there are worse ways to go. The doctor will put Béchamel poisoning for cause of death on me certificate."

"Auntie, please stop. You're hale and hearty. There's nothing wrong with you."

"Clock's running down. Get to my age and then you'll understand exactly what I mean. How did you find young Eustace?"

"Are you matchmaking again?"

"You must marry, dear. He already has five thousand a year in his own right and more when his father dies."

"I wish you wouldn't do this. It's unseemly."

"Well, he's not much to look at it… He'd do better if he had more chin. Yes, that's what letting him down. A chin isn't everything, Sophie."

"I have not the slightest interest in Eustace's chin or his five thousand a year. Apart from the English language, I can't tell what else we had in common. I've played golf, but he's obsessed with it. I couldn't get him off the subject."

"Nerves that's all. He's in love with you and talks about things he is sure about because he's nervous."

"I just met him tonight. He *can't* be in love with me."

"Oh, Sophie, he is at that highly malleable stage that young men go through. When it strikes them, and it does so quickly, they can do nothing but drool like idiots. If you showed some interest, you could marry next year."

"That's the farthest thought from my mind."

"What is the nearest thought?"

"Nearest…? The agency, I suppose."

"No, not that. There's something else. Perhaps it's someone else."

"There isn't anyone."

"What are you doing, then? Or can't you tell me?"

"You are perceptive, but I must decline to answer your question. I hope I'm not being rude, because you have been very kind to me. In fact, I am extraordinarily grateful to you for letting me stay in your beautiful house. But there are subjects to which I can never refer."

"Yes, you are being rude. It's because you think you can't trust me. You cannot imagine the massive quantity of secrets I have kept over the years. Some of them are such corkers you would hardly credit them as being true. When I'm on me way out, I'll tell you one or two. "

"I'm sorry, Auntie, if I've offended you. I would never want to do that."

"Yes, dear, I know or I wouldn't even raise the topic with you. Let's clear the air, shall we? I met my first cousin once removed and your second cousin, Archibald Drysdale, last week. Although he's in the Foreign Office, when I expressed an interest in what his job entailed, he tried to pass himself off as a vague person occupying an inconsequential post with no particular duties... a Eustace-like character, only tall and handsome. But that's all wrong. His character was never vague and I could tell he isn't vague now. It was a show he put on. Because I asked some harmless questions, as if I were his aunt, he tried to divert my attention with non-answers.

"I puzzled over it. He's always been intelligent and was remarkably brave during the war, although he will never speak of those deeds. That's the manner of most gentlemen who were at the front. The obvious conclusion to me is that he's a spy. What do you say?"

"He probably is, Auntie. He's not likely to tell you, though, is he?"

Auntie Bessie looked cross.

"What's the matter?" asked Sophie.

"I didn't expect you to agree with me."

"What are you up to?"

"What are *you* up to?"

"I asked first," said Sophie.

"I'm your elder and you should show me some respect."

"I have great respect and profound fondness for you. But foisting Eustace upon me means you have to pay a penance. So answer my question first."

"I will not."

"Then we *will* sit in silence."

"You're making up rules as you go along!" exclaimed Aunt Bessie.

"Somebody has to make the rules. I simply got in first."

"Ha, I do not subscribe to that statement or your rules. However, if we sit here arguing or silent, I'll go to bed grumpy and I don't like that at all. You're doing secret work for someone. I'm sure Archie is, too. I've met spies before, so I know exactly what I'm talking about."

"Where have you met spies?"

"Yes, we're interested now, aren't we? But I will tell you. They can be quite transparent once you develop an eye for their type. Some are furtive and jumpy. Their shifty eyes give them away. Others are so taciturn they may as well be dead. They're scared to speak in case they let the cat out of the bag and their tension is quite palpable and very different to those who are shy or poor conversationalists. I suppose I've never noticed the good ones because they would seem normal or be entertaining."

"It's hard to believe you've met so many. How did you confirm your suspicions?"

"Apart from those I found frankly dubious, one was arrested, two were deported, and I remember a particular man at a large dinner attracting the eagle-like attention of a British naval officer whom I knew to be a man of action and proven heroism. There, Sophie Burgoyne! What do you make of that? Furthermore, I've seen you daydreaming about the house and you're simply *miles* away, thoroughly absorbed by something. It's not about business - I'm familiar with that strained look. Shelling was afflicted by it often enough. Then, by your own admission, it isn't an *affaire de coeur*. What does that leave? Spying, of course. M'lord, I rest my case."

The elegant French clock in gilt, and pink and sky-blue porcelain, with a cartouche containing an exquisite hand-painted romantic scene, stood on the mantlepiece and had a pleasant, quiet tick. Sophie stared at it, hoping for guidance.

"Well, Auntie, you have put me in a difficult position. Very difficult... Yes, Archie is a spy, and he recruited me, but that's all I'm telling you."

"Ha ha, marvellous! I *knew* it...! Now, how can I help?"

As Sophie ate an early, solitary breakfast - her aunt rarely rose before eleven - she wondered if she had done the right thing. Within Burgoyne's Agency was the Secret Agency, comprising herself, Ada, and Flora. As of last night, there was now a fourth and new auxiliary member of the select band in the form of Aunt Bessie, of all people. Sophie and she had talked, resulting in her aunt being all set to gather intelligence on Lord Hazlett, the recluse. It was the sources of that intelligence - Sophie thought the word peculiar and one she could not get used to - that caused her to doubt the wisdom of involving Auntie Bessie. Looked at in one light, it was intelligence gathering, which is how she had thought last night. Viewed in the cold and revealing light of day, Sophie's aunt would gossip with her friends and acquaintances, making a muck of it, and causing trouble. Her aunt, insistent about helping, had wrung an agreement from Sophie in a moment of weakness.

The weather was dry, therefore Sophie walked to Sack Lane. As she walked, she thought about the substantial sum of money Sir Ephraim had sent because of her involvement in one of her only two cases to date. She held that money as sacrosanct - funds for a specific purpose, that purpose being to wage war against Lord Stokely, the most popular man in Britain. Sophie despised him and wanted to see his downfall because of his wickedness. This idea, this combat yet to be, did not consume her thoughts. Neither was it far from them. At present, as she headed south through the City, she could not yet see how to manage it. While journeying, she saw several thousand people, so congested were the streets with pedestrian traffic heading to offices. Not one of them, she thought, knew what she knew about Stokely. If she stopped any man or woman to get their opinion, 'He should be in charge of the country' would probably be the response as often as not. Having knowledge that nobody else possessed, she found to be a lonely business. But, and she cheered herself with this fact, Auntie Bessie could not stand the man either, for the right reasons, and not from anything Sophie had said. There were others who knew the truth, too — Archie, Penrose, and, of course, Flora and Ada. Too few to battle someone as wealthy, powerful, and beloved as Stokely, the murderer and extortioner.

Miss Jones always arrived first at the office. Sophie thought she might be the world's most efficient typist, although she was not exactly a likeable woman. Miss Jones devoted her waking hours to work and no hint of her personal life ever intruded. It was 8:45 when Sophie arrived.

"Thank goodness you've arrived," said Miss Jones with a mournful, desperate look. "It didn't seem right to send them away. I didn't know what to do."

As she was speaking, Elizabeth emerged from the spare office, looking bewildered.

"Please, tell me what has happened." Sophie sounded calm, but felt much less so than she appeared. Then she heard a man's footsteps on the stairs.

"I hope it's him coming back!" said Miss Jones.

She spoke with such warmth, it surprised Sophie.

The possessor of the footsteps hoved into view. He was that middle-class type of Englishman one saw on any street throughout the land. His shoes were polished, his dark trousers pressed, and one assumed they formed the lower half of a suit. He wore a light-coloured raincoat and everything was topped off with a bowler hat — neither new nor old, but well cared for. Above the detachable collar and hint of a dark, conservative tie was an English face that had about forty years on it. The face would have been bland, except it was relieved by a toothbrush moustache. All else around his jaw had been scrupulously shaven. And, although he had nicked himself shaving, a noticeable trace of lime from a styptic pencil signified how the flow had been staunched and bore testament to the stoic manner in which he conducted his daily toilette.

"Good morning," he said, removing his hat. His light voice was one of strangulated politeness and he enunciated his words with clipped, middle-class precision. "Do I have the pleasure of addressing the proprietor?"

"Good morning. I am the proprietor, Miss Burgoyne."

"Ah, good. Perhaps we may now proceed with the business at hand. Here is my card. Crouch is the name. And it's a pleasure to meet you... On account of the fine work you're doing for the country... And you being a lady, as well."

"Thank you, Mr Crouch. I'm not sure..." She read the card and received a puzzling shock. "You're from the GPO?"

"Yes. If we may talk in private, I can explain the matter as it stands."

"Ah, yes... yes, by all means. My office." Sophie indicated the room.

"After you, Miss Burgoyne."

They settled themselves.

"I am responsible," began Mr Crouch, "for supervising the special installations in the area. We received an order late yesterday afternoon and began laying the extra line last night. This neighbourhood has had many installations with access to the operator-assisted circuits, but you're situated just beyond the edge of the Whitehall Automatic Exchange area. Nevertheless, because the order was such an urgent one, no expense has been spared in getting you patched into the system as soon as was humanly possible. So we ran a separate line just for you. I apologize if there has been any delay, but it certainly wasn't on our end. They had to work throughout the night."

Sophie tried to hide the stupefaction she experienced. She sought for the right words or any words.

"May I see the order, please?"

"Of course. I have a copy with me." He took it from his breast pocket. "The installation gang is waiting outside in a van. You must have walked straight past them without realizing they were here for you." Mr Crouch appeared to find this speculation highly amusing. He unfolded and then handed her the order.

"Yes, I saw them... This order... it says you're putting in a telephone?" If Sophie had been in a stage rehearsal where the director had asked her to register astonishment, her performance would have amply fulfilled his expectations.

"That's correct. No doubt you're surprised how quick we've been. I think we've arrived here before you were notified a line had even been ordered. Oh yes, we can move right smartly when we need to. It came from the top." Crouch nodded with a knowing look. He leaned forward to speak confidentially. "The very top." He gave a nod of great significance.

"My goodness." There was nothing else for her to say.

"The, ah, standard equipment for a secure line is two model 124 telephones with a direct connection to the Private Automatic Branch Exchange. What with the anti-sidetone circuitry installed, you will have conversations of exceptional clarity... And no operators until you get to the call recipient's local exchange. When you speak to a party on another secure line, there will be no operators involved. It is very edifying the way the technical specifications are being improved continuously. One day, you'll be able to see the caller, at the rate it's going."

"See them? I'm not sure I would care for that. Please, I must have a straightforward answer. Who is paying for all of this? It sounds very expensive."

"It says it in the order. The Registrar of Friendly Societies. They're paying for the installation, the equipment, and the ongoing costs in perpetuity. Or the end of the world, whichever comes first. Excuse my little joke, but I find some humour makes life more pleasant."

"Mr Crouch, that is the best joke I have heard in ages. You have positively made my day."

"That's very kind of you to say... Um, where shall we put the phones?"

"Hello... It's me." Sophie spoke in a soft and tentative voice on the telephone. Using the instrument made her nervous and self-conscious.

"Hello, who's there?" said Archie. "Speak up, I can't hear you."

"It's me, Sophie!"

"Soap...? No need to shout, my dear old thing. Where are you calling from?"

"On the phone you had installed."

"I had installed...? No, I'm drawing a blank. Try again."

"The GPO finished installing a phone half an hour ago. Two phones, actually. And I have a secure line. They were so efficient and obliging. I don't know how you did it, you darling, but I am impressed that my dear Sweet Boy has such pull."

"Honestly, I had nothing to do with it."

"You're so modest and so kind."

"No, all I did was ask a fellow for a favour."

"I don't believe you, my self-effacing chappie. Thank you a thousand times, thank you."

"Let's leave it like that, then. I'm shocked they were so prompt. Just shows you what they're capable of, doesn't it?"

"Yes. I'm quite amazed. And that it's all free — toll charges, as well... Just too, too wonderful for words."

"What!"

Later in the conversation, Sophie learned from Archie that Elizabeth Banks had once had a high-level security clearance. Archie gave provisional consent to her working on police matters, but not yet on any other issues. Archie trusted Sophie's discretion, and so the smuggling issue could now be mentioned to Elizabeth. While he was speaking, Sophie had a guilty feeling because of Auntie Bessie. That, she felt, required meeting Archie face-to-face to explain what had happened.

An hour later, the story of the line's installation had reached Franky Baker. All contributors to the success responded in varying degrees of shock in differing volumes, but every hearer of the news ended by feeling rather pleased with the part he had played.

Elizabeth and Sophie studied and discussed Lord Hazlett. They realized that Marley Mound, containing the disused mine, lay substantially within his very large estate.

"How can we get into Lady Holme?" asked Sophie.

"Well, I don't know. You might if you had an introduction."

"I'm sorry. I was thinking of how to get *inside* the household as a domestic servant."

"You were...? How odd." Elizabeth looked puzzled.

"Do you think we should write or telephone?" Sophie frowned. "I've got it! We'll send them a sales letter and include our telephone number. You know, I think it's a very nice telephone number. Whitehall 2121... It sounds quite *distinguished* to me... When they get the letter, they'll call here if they've a need to employ staff... Then, as per your dictum about letters and telephone calls — only reversed, I will follow up with a telephone call to see if they received the letter and ask directly if they need Burgoyne's services. I'll type it at once to catch the first collection."

Sophie marched out of the room, taking Debrett's with her for the correct titles and address. She was soon clacking away on a typewriter, using her best Whatman rag paper. Her missive, addressed to Lord and Lady Hazlett, extolled the virtues of choosing Burgoyne's Agency — for peace of mind in all matters relating to domestic staff, whether permanent or temporary. She added that the rates were competitive and reasonable, and the service was second to none. Her last line stated that, to expedite matters, a call today saves delay. She had borrowed the line from a typing assignment, but felt it was memorable and succinct. Sophie signed the letter, typed the envelope, and hurried to the post box.

Chapter 7

Everyone's going

"Heaven has sent an answer," said Lady Jane in near disbelief. She held the Burgoyne letter in her hand.

"I thought it looked promising," responded Mrs Williams, smiling.

"I must phone at once. It says I may." She waved the letter. "Who do we need?"

"We don't need a footman because there's Daniel and the others, and Old Joe's a help when needed. The kitchen is not too bad. It's maids, really. Could do with a between maid and three or four who can look after guests and serve at table."

"Right. I'll call. Stay in the room, please, in case I forget anything."

"Very good, my Lady."

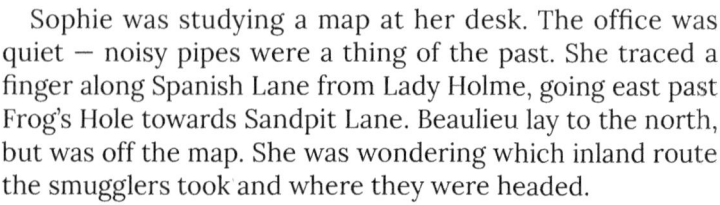

Sophie was studying a map at her desk. The office was quiet — noisy pipes were a thing of the past. She traced a finger along Spanish Lane from Lady Holme, going east past Frog's Hole towards Sandpit Lane. Beaulieu lay to the north, but was off the map. She was wondering which inland route the smugglers took and where they were headed.

"Ahh! What on earth…?"

The phone rang with the first telephone call to the office and took Sophie completely by surprise. She looked at the instrument in fear. Then she snatched up the receiver.

"Hello...? Burgoyne's Agency. Miss Burgoyne speaking."

The operator spoke, and Sophie accepted the call from Lady Jane Hazlett.

"Good morning, your ladyship," said Sophie, her composure in partial recovery.

"What an absolute relief," said Lady Jane. "There are four of them coming."

"I hope they're all right, my Lady. I have my doubts about some of these London businesses. And what type of characters are they?"

"Miss Burgoyne sounded most competent and was very obliging. She assured me she will send her best staff and guaranteed complete satisfaction."

"It's funny, her writing to you like that."

"They are trying out a pilot programme. She's written to a select few houses in different counties to see what market there is for her agency. Miss Burgoyne said that with the excellent train service, travelling presented no problem for her staff. I find that a most commendable approach. Miss Burgoyne went on to say Lady Holme was selected by virtue of its being one of the foremost estates in southern Hampshire. I'm glad we've not been entirely forgotten here, but that is another matter. Well, Mrs Williams, we have our staff for the weekend. Four of them will arrive next Thursday morning and stay until Monday afternoon."

"Are you sure we should take her?" asked Ada.

"I gave my word, and they asked for a between maid," replied Sophie.

"I don't like it, miss. It's a bit risky."

"Perhaps. We shall see. Her photographic mind might come in handy. She was already primed about police work, and this is no different. If our behaviour appears odd, we will have already countered her suspicions by telling her it's an investigation."

"Fern will want to know what the case is about. What will you say?"

"I think I will tell her we are at Lady Holme because of a fraud case that is… top secret. There, that should do it."

"All right, we don't tell her about the smuggling and we're down there on our own account."

"Correct. We can't say if smuggling *is* taking place through Lady Holme, anyway. But it's going on somewhere along that coast. We can't allow these people to bring weapons and explosives into the country. It has to be stopped. No, we'll avoid telling Fern the true nature of our mission until we know she can be trusted. Which reminds me, I must tell Flora to be careful of what she says in front of her. Fern is just to do her work and tell us if anything out of the ordinary happens or looks suspicious."

The phone rang, causing Sophie to start.

"I hope I get used to that soon. It makes me jump every time it goes off."

The operator connected the parties, and Auntie Bessie was on the line.

"Hello, Auntie, isn't the telephone marvellous?"

"Wait until you get the bill for the calls. That'll change your tune. I'm calling because I have some intelligence… Ha!" Aunt Bessie roared with laughter on the other end. "Oh, dear me, what a *peculiar* thing to say. I have information on you know who about you know what."

"Excellent. My pencil is ready. By the way, we're in."

"That's why you're my favourite relation. You don't let the grass grow under your feet. The reason for the solitude of Mr X stems from his once having opposed a group of very influential people. It was explained that should he step one foot outside of a certain place, it would be the last step he took. Don't know if it's true or just a story, but it sounds frightfully dramatic. I'll fill in one or two blanks later. It was difficult getting that much. I must ring off to see what else I can find out. Remember, dear, keep all the calls short or it will cost you a packet. Cheerio, as they say."

Ten minutes later, the phone rang. Sophie jumped once more, but not quite so high.

"Me, again," said Auntie Bessie. "Do you possess a superstitious nature?"

"I would say I don't."

"That's good. The place is haunted. Real ghosts, I'm told. That's all I could get on that subject. Bye-bye."

Sophie frowned at the telephone. "She only drinks sherry or a glass of wine with dinner," she said to herself.

In the afternoon, Sophie had satisfactorily placed a footman and a butler at different London houses. Auntie Bessie telephoned with her third and final call of the day.

"I have it on good... No, no, I need to start over. I have it on reasonably accurate and rather malicious authority from two quite spiteful independent sources that a certain female personage has not always been the dutiful wife one might imagine her to be when she's away from home. Of course, my sources may have been informed by the same person. They couldn't remember where they heard it, but they were convinced it was true. Neither could name the co-respondent. Take that for what it's worth. This is rather amusin', don't you think? I can understand why you do it. See you at dinner. Oh, yes, I was also told something thoroughly scurrilous about a certain general. That will be for dessert unless your scruples put a stop to a good story again."

"Mummy! What possessed you to fill the house with atrocious people and promise them riding? It's bad for the horses. They don't enjoy meeting strangers and they *hate* poor riders."

Maude was an energetic and abundantly healthy woman — big-boned and strong-featured. She had not had a day's illness since she was seven. Brown-eyed, with short, brown curly hair that shook when she moved, everything about her spoke of vigour. Much of her determined character and bodily strength had been formed by controlling horses weighing better than half a ton and training a variety of dog breeds. Her one genuine regret was that people were not as easily controlled as animals.

"I understand, Maude. But it's lovely to have some festivity in the house. Offering riding, weather permitting, was the incentive for many to come. This get-together was your father's idea, and it's his way of making amends to me for him being a *complete* fool over royal invitations."

"Oh, he got one of those, did he? That's why he's been looking down in the mouth the last few days. This is for you, is it? Then I won't spoil your party, darling... I heard the Scrope family is coming. Vanessa's all right — at least she can sit on a horse. But really, Mr Scrope talks about nothing but railways while his wife sits by him totally *mute*. It's too, too dreary for words."

"Did you see the list?"

"No, I didn't. Anyone interestin'?"

"Uncle Horry and Sandra, the Rand-Sayers, Basil, Reginald, and Constance, and their spouses. There's a new face, Adrian Benson. He's a friend of Amelia Scrope, but I've also met him. He's rather a creature of the drawing room."

"Humph," she snorted with derision, "the way you describe him, I doubt he hunts or even rides."

"I don't know if he does. Dr Beaton and his sister Belinda are coming. Oh, and the Smythes."

"Old Smythe? How did you get him to come out?"

"No, no. Not him. His grandson, Richard, and his wife, Maria. He's virtually running the law firm now. Poor old Smythe. He does little these days. Richard will take over the practice soon, I'm sure of it."

"Doctor Beaton's coming, is he? Well, it doesn't sound so bad after all. I'm off to the kennels. The lazy beggars need some exercise."

Lady Hazlett watched Maude stride from the room with a red setter trotting at her heels. What had been for some time a forlorn hope sprang up with renewed strength in her ladyship's mind. Maude had actually hinted about liking a man — Dr. Beaton. She could not recall her daughter expressing a similar sentiment ever before. Dare she nurture this fledgling hope?

At evening time, in a delightful living room with chintz curtains, within a very pleasing and respectable five-bedroomed house in Lymington, there sat a young, active lawyer and his young, charming wife. Upstairs, two small, active, and often charming children were asleep.

"I wish we weren't going," said Maria Smythe. "They're all such horsey people. It amounts to a club and I'm not a member."

"Well, it's a pity you don't ride, otherwise this would be a lovely weekend for you... That's it! Take Sheba with you."

At the mention of her name, a dozing border collie at Maria's feet lifted her head to inquire into the meaning of it.

"That's a thought..." She stroked the dog's head. "Only Maude *will* make such awful comments about how to train dogs. I don't like being bullied and I don't like how she bullies Sheba."

"Yes, she's a bit much sometimes. But, Maria, the place is enormous. You can avoid her with ease."

"I suppose so. If we must go, I'll put a brave face on it."
Richard smiled at her before speaking.

"Maude strikes me as a *type* of person rather than her own character. I don't mean to be harsh or critical, but we have several outdoorsy clients who are just like her. There's probably a Maude or two or ten in every town in England."

"What type am I?" A certain archness had crept into Maria's voice.

"Oh, you're one in a million, of course."

"If I'm that special and so *thoroughly* unique... let's not go. I have a funny feeling about this weekend."

"We must. The Hazletts are old and important clients. It just wouldn't do to refuse an invitation. Besides, I've already accepted and it would look even worse to back out now."

"I know... What's the matter?"

"It's that business I was telling you about. I'm sure there's a smuggling gang working in the area. Two farmers on Spanish Lane have heard lorries passing in the night. It's happening with some regularity and yet when I rang up Lord Hazlett about it, he knew nothing and showed not the slightest interest. The lorries are going right past Lady Holme. It's so quiet out there that they must have heard them. But I couldn't get him interested enough to question the servants. I shall try asking again."

"You wrote to the Customs people and spoke to the police. What more can you do?"

"No action has been taken, that's the issue. Once a week or twice a month, a mysterious lorry travels late at night. There's nothing around there to warrant such activity. There's no through road to anywhere. It's all lanes and tracks. Farmer Voyles is convinced they're smugglers, and I'm inclined to agree with him."

"You're so serious sometimes. Does it matter if someone sneaks in a case of spirits once in a while?"

"No, that's not the attitude to take. Frankly, I'm surprised at you. If it were a minor matter, I would ignore it. They may be filling those lorries with contraband, and that amounts to a serious crime committed by an organization. Also, some forms of contraband are a lot more dangerous than others!"

"Don't be so grumpy. I take it seriously, too. I simply believe it's a matter of a few crates of brandy and some rounds of Brie."

"I hope you're right, but it looks highly suspicious to me."

"Have you spoken to that man nobody likes?"

"Oh, you mean Roland Phelps, Hazlett's next-door neighbour. No, because I'm not the police, dear. It is up to them to make the proper enquiries. I, in the capacity of a private citizen, can only draw their attention to the matter."

"When you talk to Lord Hazlett, be diplomatic. He is a client, after all."

"Of course, I shall… Sorry, my love, but I just can't help it once the bee is buzzing in my bonnet."

"I think you would make a splendid barrister, you're so… so dogged."

"Perhaps… It would mean my starting all over again in training, pupillage in chambers, and then building a reputation afterwards. At present, I'm a country solicitor, a junior partner in a respected firm, and a well-contented husband."

He got up from his armchair to kiss his wife.

At another Lymington house, a prestigious, seven-bedroomed building, a thirty-one-year-old man in a well-tailored suit, and a handsome, thin, tall, dark-haired woman, wearing a conservative, dark blue dress sat in the same room. She was twenty-five and looked irritable.

"We should go," said Daphne Rand-Sayers. "At least we'll eat decent food among decent people for a few days."

"We're not that badly off." He spoke with an airy, dismissive lightness.

"Aren't we? Tell me, how much is it you owe the bookies and where is the money coming from to pay them? I am *not* taking another phone call in this house. I can't bear listening to their demands."

"Look, we can scrape by on your income until things improve. And they will."

"You make me sick sometimes, David. You have done *nothing* except lose money at cards or terrible investments. Ha, you are everyone's friend, the life and soul of any gathering. Somebody at the golf club gives you a tip and you believe what they say... You told me, you *promised* me, it would all change. I'm done with your lies. I want a divorce."

"Oh, see here, Daphne, don't talk wildly. I have ideas, so all is not yet lost. I've just invested in the wrong companies, that's all. It could have happened to anyone... Has happened to many others. As for the cards... I admit, that was stupid of me and I'm sorry. I will make it up to you."

"Without telling me, you've gone through your fifteen thousand pound inheritance as though it were water and have nothing to show for it. Why should I trust you? It's better we separate."

"No, Daphne. I shall not give you a divorce. We can work this out."

"You like games of chance. Then let us play a game, you and I. We'll do this for old times' sake, in memory of when, as a naïve young woman, I believed in you, and before spending money had gone to your head. There will be several businessmen present at this party. You've worked in business before; you can do so again. If you get a job through someone at Lady Holme, I will reconsider the matter. But if you are unsuccessful, then divorce or separation it is."

"You've become quite hard, my dear."

"That's your doing," replied Daphne in a sharp voice.

David shook his head and took on a look of reluctant resignation. "Very well, I accept the wager."

Chapter 8

Names and trickery

The train puffed its way out of Waterloo station early Thursday morning. Four women had a corner of a third-class compartment to themselves.

"Here we go again," said Flora Dane.

"I love it," said Ada, grinning broadly. "There's nothing I'd rather be doing."

"Do you think this will become regular work?" asked Flora. "I mean, can it be our careers?"

"It's too early to tell," replied Sophie. "I suppose it might... I hope so."

"I ask, because I'm fed up with being an actress. The acting is fine, and it's what I love. The camaraderie with the cast is beautiful. It's producers I loathe. The other day, I auditioned for a part that was absolutely perfect for me. And, modesty aside, I played the part well. Four of us tried out and then the wretched producer gave it to his current lady-friend. She is so unfit for the play... Can't act, can't project her voice, and she's a catty trouble-maker. It's all very depressing."

"Cheer up, Miss Flora. You'll be puttin' in a star-turn this weekend."

"Ada, you are such a nice person. I humbly thank you for your kind, supportive words."

"Oh, dear me. I've just realized something." Sophie was frowning. "You must all call me Phoebe King this time."

"Sophie, what are you talking about?"

"I spoke with Lady Hazlett on the phone as Sophie Burgoyne. She mustn't know I'm one of the staff, too. Bad for the agency's reputation, don't you see?"

"Oh, of course."

"Yes, then I'll be Nancy Carmichael," said Ada.

"You both have *noms de guerres*? You've done this before, I can tell. I'm not being left out of this. Now, what name shall I give myself?"

The steam train sped on, swaying and sometimes rattling over points.

"Nothing," said Flora. "I'm ashamed of myself. I've played countless parts, read hundreds of books, and I can't think of a single name."

"Do you want suggestions?" asked Sophie.

"No, I must conquer this metaphysical challenge alone."

"Please, Miss Burgoyne, what do I call you?" Fern had been quiet during the journey and now looked puzzled.

"I'm Phoebe. If it's easier, call me Miss King, but I'd prefer you use Phoebe this weekend."

"I'll do that, Phoebe. Takes some getting used to, dunnit?" Fern's face clouded over. "Should I have another name?"

"You can if you wish. What name would you choose?"

"Oh, Lillie Langtree. I think it's a beautiful name."

"Yes, it is, but it's rather a famous one and I believe she's still very much alive. It might cause comment. Try to find something less spectacular."

"I was born in Datchet near Windsor, but we moved when I was little, so my name... will be... Dora Datchet. How's that?"

"Perfect, and easy to remember, too."

"That's so nice of you, Phoebe. It's a right lark, ain't it?"

"I wish I could follow suit," replied Flora, "but you can't make a surname out of where I was born - Itchen Abbas. Itching Abbot of the Holy Flea is what we called it as children."

"Where's Itchen Abbas?" asked Ada.

"It's a village near Winchester. Lovely country in that area."

Sophie knew the story of how the Dane family lost their title and beautiful house through an entailed estate and a chronic lack of money. After the Danes moved to Winchester,

Sophie met Flora at a local school they both attended when they were eight years old.

The train slowed as it approached a station.

"That's what I'll call myself!" Flora pointed to a large station sign.

"You can't call yourself Walton-upon-Thames," said Sophie.

"No, of course not. I shall be Gladys Walton. How does that scan?"

"Sounds good to me."

"Hold on a mo," said Ada. "Every Gladys I've ever met got called Glad."

"Glad…? Oh, I'm sure I can live with that…
>   *Gladys is my nice new name, 'tis no passing fad.*
> *Flora sadly leaves the stage, I'm happier being Glad…*
Needs polishing, I think."

Stopping at Brockenhurst, the secret agents had to disembark to catch a train to Lymington. They sat in a row on a bench in the empty station.

Flora looked about and breathed deeply. "It's so peaceful here. I always like returning to the country."

"I agree. It's such a restorative," said Sophie. "Twenty-three minutes until our train arrives. Let's go over what we shall be doing. We must remain incognito, as no one at Lady Holme must discover we're investigating."

"What's incognito, please, Phoebe?" asked Fern.

"It means to remain unknown with one's true identity concealed. For us, it further means undetected while we investigate people and events."

"Oh… How do you spell it?"

"Fern!" exclaimed Ada. "Do that later. We've got to know what we're doing so we can get on with the job."

"I was only asking."

"The owner of the estate is Viscount Hazlett. Lady Hazlett is a viscountess. When answering them, say, yes, your lordship or ladyship. My Lady or my Lord is also acceptable. Don't look any family member or guest in the eye. Stop to let them pass you on the stairs or in a corridor. Work to the best of your ability and remember what you overhear. Write it down as soon as possible, if necessary. We must work unseen in the background. We cannot draw attention to ourselves.

"Now, I understand the immediate family will be present. According to Burke's and Debrett's, there are four children. Basil..."

"Who's Burkes and Debretts, Phoebe?"

"They are separate reference works known as peerages. If you're interested, I will show you back at the office, but Dora, you must let me finish."

"Oh, sorry, miss... No! Phoebe, Phoebe, Phoebe! I'll remember it proper."

"That's right. Basil Hazlett, 39, is heir to the title and married to Fiona, whose maiden name was Simpson. Maude, eldest daughter, is 38 and unmarried. Reginald is 30 and unmarried. Constance is 28 and married to Oscar Reid. Mr Reid is a coffee importer of some substance. I received the impression they all will be attending, but of the other guests, I have no knowledge."

"How we goin' to divi them up?" asked Ada.

"That depends on what duties we're given. Let's assume it will be general service and we're not specifically assigned to individuals. I have planned it like this. Ada, you stay close to Lord and Lady Hazlett. Flora, you concentrate on the Reids and Reginald, while I watch Maude, Basil and his wife Fiona. My idea is that, as the guests arrive, they will naturally form cliques. As they do, the clique that forms around a person one already has under observation also becomes one's responsibility. We'll see how it goes and adjust the plan as necessary. Can any of you think of another way of dividing the tasks?"

"I can't," said Flora. "What's the place like?"

"I don't know. No one does beyond it being an old estate."

"That doesn't sound good," said Ada. "I hope they give us decent beds and some privacy. I worked in an old place once; falling down, it was. At night from my bed, I could see stars through a hole in the roof. It was November, mind you, so I froze, and the rain come in. I stayed a week, and that was enough for me. What I've noticed is if they give you a decent bed, the gentry treat you decently in all other ways. It all goes hand in hand."

"That sounds horrible, Nancy," said Fern. "See, I remembered." Fern looked pleased.

"You must have run across it, too," said Ada.

"Sort of... I know exactly what you mean. They gave me a room in a cellar once and it was horribly damp. I felt like I'd been buried alive. I like winders, I do... Phoebe, what's *my* job at this place?"

"You are to observe the other servants. We shall, too, but you will be better positioned as a between maid. Observe the butler and the housekeeper to see if they do or say anything that indicates they might be involved in the fraud. If there's anything suspicious, then tell me at once."

"I will. If they're criminals, I'm going to catch 'em."

"Good. I hope you do. Just make sure they don't catch *you* watching them. Be discreet."

"They won't... What's discreet mean - and fraud?"

Sophie explained both words.

"Usually," began Ada, "when a butler or housekeeper is 'elping themselves, they 'ave an arrangement with the grocer or butcher. The trades mark up the bills and give a backhander in cash. Happens all the time. Not wines and spirits, though. If there's one thing a lord knows in this wide world, it's the price of wines and whiskey. Hard to diddle him on that. Of course, the butler drinks it as well as his lordship. Housekeepers all have their little bottle of something by 'em... Sometimes, I think the whole country's alcoholic."

"I have an aunt in the Temperance Movement," said Flora. "You should hear her wax lyrical on the demon drink."

"I've an aunt like that," said Ada.

"So have I," said Fern.

"Are you odd-man out, Phoebe?" asked Flora.

"No, I have two aunts — sisters on my mother's side. With my father being a vicar, they are forever preaching at him to do more to spread the temperance message. Some things they say are sensible, but it's the virtuous vehemence in their attitude that's so off-putting."

"I only ever have two drinks. Any more and I get woozy," said Ada.

"That's my limit as well." Flora smiled.

"Let's return to business. Lord Hazlett is a recluse. He has not left his estate in nearly forty years. I'm interested in finding out the reason for his behaviour. An informant," Sophie's Auntie Bessie came to mind, "has told me there was an incident. He upset some powerful people and has confined himself to his estate ever since. Who they are or what Lord Hazlett did to upset them all those years ago remains a mystery."

"I bet he did something disgusting," said Ada. "Otherwise, he'd go to the Old Bill."

"I'm not sure about disgusting," said Sophie, "but it must be illegal, whatever it was."

"How beautifully mysterious," said Flora. "Does he wear an iron mask or anything similar?"

"Wouldn't it be marvellous if he did? When speaking to Lady Hazlett, she didn't alert me to anything peculiar like that... But I wonder what she makes of it all? He must have told her his reasons for separating from the world. Surely, the family knows the history."

"Could it be to do with the fraud?" asked Fern.

"I don't think so. The fraud we're investigating is against His Majesty's Government and is recent. The past incident seems more like a personal or business matter to me."

"I don't get how me having a photographic memory is going to help."

"An opportunity might present itself where it will come in useful."

"Dora, how does that work, exactly?" asked Ada.

"I can do the tray trick easy. Pull the cloth back for two seconds and I can remember every object, its size, colour, everything. Put fifty items on it and I remember 'em all. Don't know how I do it, but it's like a pattern to me. I see it in a moment. Take one object away and I know it's gone and what it was when you show me the tray again."

"That's true. I tested Fern quite rigorously," said Sophie.

"Have you ever considered going on the stage?" asked Flora.

"Lots of people say I should, but I don't want to. I couldn't get up in front of people. I just couldn't."

"Ah, I see." Flora gave an understanding nod.

"I like it how we are now, talking friendly, sitting on this bench. If we had a tray, I'd do the trick for you. But if there was a crowd or even one stranger, I'd keep me mouth shut."

"Glad. How did you handle stage-fright?" Ada turned to ask.

"That is a very interesting question. I used to be dreadfully shy as a child. I can't answer fully, but speaking in public becomes much easier the more frequently one does it. Once having spoken in public, fear of the next occasion is halved. Then it halves again until one begins to enjoy the experience. At least, that's how I found it."

"It's strange you should mention that, Glad," said Sophie, suppressing a smile while Flora bit her lower lip. "You should all know that Lady Holme is supposedly haunted."

"Haunted…? I don't believe in ghosts." Ada spoke rapidly.

"I do. I'd like to meet one," said Fern.

"Why would you like to do that?" asked Ada.

"I think it would be nice. They must get very lonely."

"That's a curious way of looking at it," remarked Sophie.

"Do you believe in ghosts?" asked Ada.

"I'm prepared to believe in them, but I'm rather doubtful. What do you say, Glad?" Sophie directed the question to Flora.

"Stop teasing me… Why don't we tell them the *embarrassing* story? I don't think I mind now."

"We took an oath, remember?"

"So we did. I know… We'll suspend and extend the oath just this once."

Sophie considered for a moment.

"Very well, we shall. Nancy and Dora, what you are about to hear must never, ever be repeated. Cross your hearts and hope to die."

They both crossed their hearts.

"Good. Flora and I were thirteen when this, um, incident occurred," began Sophie.

"We were at Martingale, the Duke of Hampshire's estate," said Flora.

"They were having a gala party and had invited hundreds of guests."

"Sophie's father was invited because he's an old friend of the Duke's."

"He couldn't go because, as vicar, he had parish duties at the time of the party. However, the Duke and my father arranged for me to go and to bring a friend along for company."

"That was me." said Flora. "It was a glorious, glorious house party. The best, grandest, and loveliest I have ever been to. It was like a dream, a fairy tale."

"Many influential and famous people were there."

"And their wretched children."

"It was only one of them who was so awful, Flora."

"One bad one and a gaggle of non-entities following him, then."

"There was a bad, wicked boy of fourteen. He took against Flora and me. He called us the poor relations and made fun of our clothes, amongst other things."

"And my buck teeth."

"No, he didn't."

"Yes, he did," said Flora. "I heard him."

"You can see how thoroughly rotten he was. So, after getting over our upset, we plotted our *revenge*."

"Martingale is haunted by Anne Boleyn, so they say. She stayed there once."

"The headless ghost has been seen dozens of times, so they say."

"We decided to become the ghost and frighten the wicked child."

"Flora tossed a coin, and I called heads," said Sophie. "As luck would have it, I was to be the head."

"Which meant I was the headless body - dressed in a white sheet. I was relieved to be Anne Boleyn's body because I wouldn't have a speaking part. I was so shy."

"We borrowed old clothes we found in a trunk and I dressed in black so that, in the dark, when I tucked my head underneath Flora's arm, I completely disappeared. I put white powder on my face and looked a frightful sight."

"Most corpse-like, in fact. And we used a small torch to illuminate the dreadful, fearful undead visage."

"We took up our position at the end of a hall in the east wing near the wicked boy's bedroom."

"From our gloomy niche, we would surprise him and become his grisly nightmare."

"When our victim neared his room," recounted Sophie, "we were to step out of hiding. I would groan first, then say, 'Can you help me?' in a dreadful, graveyard voice. He was to run away screaming instead of helping me to put my head back on."

"That was how it was supposed to be," said Flora.

"As we were setting up, we caused a maid to jump out of her skin. We explained we were playing a trick, and she left us to it, though she was rather gruff about it."

"Behind a dark corner, we waited and waited. Then we heard approaching footsteps."

"Certain it was our victim, I started groaning while Flora started shaking with laughter."

"Sophie exaggerates. It was a slight tremble, nothing more."

"We stepped from our hiding place and turned. There we were, a white shrouded figure and a detached head under an arm. In the murky gloom, I switched on the torch beneath my face. I said, just like this, 'Please, can you help me? Oh, do help me!' Then I made a light gurgling noise."

"It was a totally convincing performance," said Flora. "Even I was frightened."

"But I realized, by size and shape, it was not the wicked boy at all. It was a large man facing us. He shrieked and exclaimed, but he didn't run."

"Instead, when he recovered his voice, he said, How may I help you? That was a shock for us, let me tell you."

"I said, 'Sirrah, I have been as you find me for many long years.'"

"Sophie was perfect and kept in character. He asked, 'Are you Anne Boleyn?'"

"'I am she,' I answered."

"He said, 'I fear it is beyond mortal power to aid you... Unless, unless you tell me of a way in which flesh and blood can assist immortal spirit.'"

"I couldn't think what to say next," laughed Sophie. "If we owned up, he would be furious with us."

"Then someone screamed further along the corridor. It was the wicked boy. He had seen us, too. I found his shrill wail *most* satisfying."

"When the man turned to see who it was, we ran away and didn't stop until we got to our room."

"You'll never guess who we had been speaking to," said Flora.

Fern and Ada looked blank.

"It was..." Sophie and Flora looked at each other and nodded. Together they said, "Sir Arthur Conan Doyle!"

"Oh, my godfathers!" exclaimed Ada. "The Sherlock Holmes man."

"What happened next?" asked Fern, her face alight with excitement.

"That's a long, involved story," replied Sophie. "Bunny Warren, who is Duchess of Hampshire, heard Sir Arthur's story. He was convinced he had spoken to the ghost of Anne Boleyn and was making a *tremendous* fuss over the incident. Also, the wicked boy supported his account. Her ladyship is such a lovely woman. However, she noticed two young girls unhappily skulking about. She wondered why we looked sad while the entire house was in excited uproar and merriment. Bunny had a word with us and she cleverly discovered our guilt."

"Confession *is* good for the soul," said Flora. "She got our entire story out of us and laughed like anything. Bunny Warren forbade us to mention it to anyone because Sir Arthur was thoroughly enjoying himself. He had recounted his experience to all who would listen, and she neither wanted him robbed of his pleasure nor to appear gullible. And that incident helped me overcome my shyness and stage fright."

"And we crossed our hearts and hoped to die if we ever publicized our girlish prank to which the great Sir Arthur had fallen victim... Here comes the train!"

Chapter 9

It's not all plain sailing

The train puffed its way into Lymington Town Station. The next stop, which was the terminus at Pier Station, was somewhat closer to their final destination, but not within walking distance.

"Excuse me, porter. Will we find a taxi here or at Pier Station?" Sophie had opened the carriage door to speak.

"No taxis at Pier Station."

"Thank you. Quick, everyone off."

The secret agents, with their cases, descended to the platform, then made their way out of Lymington Town Station.

"We missed them all," said Sophie, as they watched the only cab in view driving away with a fare.

"I can smell the sea," said Fern. "Lovely, ain't it?"

"We've only seen the river so far. The sea is a mile from here," said Sophie.

"I've never seen the Channel before."

"From Lady Holme, you can look across the Solent to see the Isle of Wight, about three miles distant."

"I can't get it straight, Phoebe," said Ada. "It feels like I've come down here on holiday, it do an' all."

"Perhaps, one day, we shall. I think that would be rather nice. We could go sailing."

"Who, me go sailing…? Yes, I'd give it a go."

A taxi came into view and Sophie hailed it.

"Where to?" The taxi driver was about fifty, with a huge, drooping moustache, tanned face, and country accent.

"Lady Holme, please."

"Very good, miss."

They climbed into the passenger compartment while the driver dealt with their luggage. When they set off, Sophie tapped on the glass. The driver slid the partition open.

"Excuse me, driver. We're new to the area. What can you tell me about Lady Holme?"

"The Old Place? Well, it's right fancy if you like that type of a thing. Be you visiting?"

"No, we're maids working there this weekend."

"You're from London, I reckon."

"That's right. Lord Hazlett is having a party."

"Is he now?"

"Yes. Is it true he hasn't left the estate for years and years?"

"Ah. It be true."

"What, not even to come into town?"

"No… We're coming to the causeway across the river and there's a toll to pay."

"Oh, wait a moment… Here's a shilling. You keep the change."

"A whole shilling? Right, you are."

The gatekeeper emerged from the tollhouse, received a penny from the taxi driver, and waved them on.

"That's most inconvenient — having a toll road by the town."

"You can blame Captain Cross for that, curse him. Begging your pardon, miss. He built this here causeway and nigh on silted up the river down to the sea. Caused trouble in the port, it did. He got took to court, but he won. Years ago it were, and we've suffered ever since."

"I'm sorry to hear that. It's like highway robbery."

"So it is."

"You were saying about Lord Hazlett."

"Right, I was. Well, the story goes, 'cause it's afore I was growed, that although he be confined for thirty-nine year to date, he did leave once in the first year of his isolation. Went to buy a thoroughbred hoss up Newbury way. That's where his groom died. Accident it were - drownded in a river."

"My goodness, that's dreadful… I should think that was the River Kennet."

"Well, 'tis believed he were drunk at the time and fell in of his own accord. So I doubt he knew much about it till it were all over. I'm acquainted with the man's son. He owns a baker's in the High Street. They bake the best sticky buns of anywhere I know."

"That's interesting… How did he become a baker?"

"His lordship set him up in business when he come of age. Somehow, 'ee must have felt responsible for the boy's father a-dying like that. That were a decent thing he did. There's many as wouldn't have bothered themselves."

"Yes, that's all too true… Does Lord Hazlett farm?"

"No, hardly nothing at all outside the little home farm. No tenants. They be riding mad where you're goin'."

"Have you ever ridden?"

"I tried it. When I fell off, I gave it up. I was nothing but a little kiddy on a pony, but were enough to make up my mind."

"You prefer motor cars, I suppose."

"In a way, I do. I like to see the hosses about, but they're going now. Be there many in London?"

"Still quite a few, but nowhere near as many as before the war."

"It's all a-changing. I hope it's for the good."

"So do I… Now, tell me something. Is it true there are smugglers still along this coast? I got it from a friend who swore there were."

The cab driver laughed loudly. "I reckon there be a few things that gets landed as missed the Excise man. But it won't be much. Don't axe that question down in the harbour. They won't take to it kindly. Now, in the public houses, they'll spin you yarns by the hour if you're buying them drink. But you can't believe the tithe of what they say, with their tunnels under taverns and what not."

"That must be where my friend heard the story… There's a lot of forest about here."

"Ah. You can still walk under New Forest trees from here to nigh on Salisbury... Them's the gates to Lady Holme ahead of us."

The taxi driver dropped off the secret agents on the gravel driveway in front of the house. Sophie paid and tipped him again, which he greatly appreciated. She joined the others. They stood together, gaping at the beautiful house.

"Pinch me, someone," said Flora. "I want to know if I'm awake or not."

"Well, I never," said Fern.

"If good Queen Bess," began Ada, "was to come out them doors, I wouldn't be at all surprised."

"How unexpectedly glorious... and such symmetry. This has to be the right place, don't you think?"

"Even if it isn't, Sophie, I must see inside," said Flora.

"That's Phoebe, remember?"

They knocked on the front doors and the footman who answered directed them to the servants' entrance on the eastern side.

"Look at that stained glass," said Fern, as they crunched over the gravel.

"Rather fine stained-glass windows, too," said Sophie. "That has to be a chapel."

They came to the corner.

"Oh, my goodness, there's more of it," said Ada, as the long side came into view. "The place is huge. It must take an army to keep it clean."

"Fifty people could live here," said Flora. "They must have shut up some rooms."

"If this was in the East End, there'd be five-hundred dossing down in here for the night. There's the door."

"That fabulous doorway looks as though it belongs in a fairy tale," said Flora. "What lies behind it? Heart's-ease, treasure, or a dragon?"

"That might depend on the 'ousekeeper," said Ada. "Oh, look at this. I'm getting dust all over me shoes from the gravel."

"We must smarten ourselves up before knocking," said Sophie.

Mrs Williams, who had been expecting their arrival, admitted the four maids from London into the passage. She had an honest face, yet there was a hesitancy in her manner. It deepened and amounted to suspicion as she looked them over.

They entered into a corridor. If it had not been for a telephone mounted on the wall, they could well have believed they had gone back in time to the Elizabethan age. The flagstones were worn, and the floor sloped. Overhead, the low blackened beams sloped. On each side, the white distempered walls bulged and sloped. The dark corridor started out wide and then narrowed until it met another corridor at right-angles.

"Come in. Welcome to Lady Holme. I'm Mrs Williams."

"Good morning, Mrs Williams." Sophie put on a bright, brisk London accent that almost made Flora raise her eyebrows in surprise. "Pleased to meet you. I'm Phoebe King, I am. And this here's Dora Datchet, the scullery maid, Gladys Walton, and Nancy Carmichael."

"Well, you're on time, I'll say that for you. How was the journey?"

"Very nice, Mrs Williams, thank you. There were no hold-ups or anything."

"Good. You're here a day early to get used to the place. Dora, you'll start at five-thirty tomorrow to fire the stove in the kitchen and light the fire in the Breakfast Room. Cook, Mrs Chiverton, to you, will give you the rest of your duties. The rest of you start at six. You have your own breakfast at seven-thirty and lunch is at eleven-thirty. You'll find the Servants' Hall quite pleasant, I believe. We get along very well in the main, and there's no room for airs and graces or fanciful notions."

"I'm sure it will all be perfect, Mrs Williams. Miss Burgoyne said that we must do our best work. Client satisfaction is of prime importance. I remember her saying that just yesterday."

"That is an excellent view to hold. Now, then, it's easy to get lost. You're in the servants' quarters and everything here is on the ground floor. The two floors above are closed, as the rooms aren't needed. In the west wing, the two floors above are also closed. Come with me, and I'll show you your rooms."

The party left the crazed passageway to step into parts that were solidly built and much straighter and level. That was not what caught the attention of the visitors, however. All four young women were entranced by their surroundings. The decorative plastered high ceiling gave a spacious airiness. Light streamed in through a myriad windows. Ancient, lovely furniture was dotted about - small tables, an upholstered chair with barley twist legs, and heavily carved and figured cupboards.

"That's the Chapel and we have a Sunday service. We call this staircase Chapel Stairs. The Pantry is behind you." The four turned to look and saw the words 'The Pannetry,' painted in gilt lettering on an ancient door. "Other side of Chapel doors is the Buttery. Around the corner is the Dining Parlour. That's where the family eats in the evening. This weekend they'll be in Great Hall. Follow me."

Mrs Williams pointed out the extensive kitchen and the Breakfast Room opposite before they exited this more spacious area. They walked down a corridor that was a wall of diamond patterned windows on one side and doors, rooms and short passageways on the other. Outside the windows lay a path, a strip of grass, and flowerbeds up against an old, high brick wall. Inside, at the far end of the corridor, was a door leading to the gardens.

"That's my suite there." She pointed to the first room on her left. "This part is the Old Manor House, which was built before 1520. It was remodelled for servants' quarters while Lady Holme was being built."

"When would that have been?" asked Sophie.

"They finished it in 1567 and it has been in the Hazlett family ever since."

"Miss Burgoyne said that Sir Walter Hazlett was an admiral."

"That's right. He was the first baronet... She explained that to you, did she?"

"Yes, and about him capturing a Spanish galleon carrying silver. It was the prize money from that which paid for the building of Lady Holme."

"I'm pleased you're taking an interest. Not many people know of Lady Holme's existence."

"How did it get its name, Mrs Williams?"

"Cicely Holme was Sir Walter's second wife, his first having died shortly after their marriage. Cicely's brother, John Holme, was the Duke of Exeter, although he died without issue and the title ceased with him. As an honour to his new wife, Sir Walter named the place Lady Holme, even though she was really now Lady Hazlett. Sir Walter and his wife were devoted to each other."

"It's so romantic. This is a really beautiful house."

"Yes, we very much love the place. And you're right, Phoebe, it is a romantic story."

They came to their rooms — one a-piece — which were more similar in size to cells, although the pretty curtains at the windows and the narrow beds with thick mattresses and colourful blankets did much to dispel any sense of confinement.

"I'll give you a few minutes to arrange your things. Come together when you're ready and knock on my door. Then I'll take you to meet Mr Isembard, the butler... A word of warning, you must take some of what he says with a pinch of salt."

Mr Isembard was in his sixties. He was six feet tall with a slight stoop. A fleshy man, he had pendulous jowls, rheumy eyes, and a perpetual sneer on his face. At least, that was how it seemed as he reviewed the four London maids while they stood for his inspection. He spoke slowly, in a low, breathy rumble.

"Pretty maids all in a row... From the Big Smoke, eh? You'll have to work while you're here. I won't have any of your snooty London ways. And no followers... Ha. Don't s'ppose you'll be here long enough to get into trouble. If I find any of you making eyes at the men, you'll be out on your ear and I'll give you a bad reference. Do I make myself plain?"

"Yes, Mr Isembard. You're quite easy to understand," said Sophie.

"What's your name?"

"Phoebe King."

"Did I ask you to speak?"

"Yes, you asked a question."

"I did...? No matter. Say yes or no in future. I need no more than that from the likes of you. Do your work and keep your nose clean. I think I've seen enough, Mrs Williams."

"Yes, Mr Isembard," she replied and then addressed the maids. "Come along and I'll explain your duties."

They entered the Breakfast Room which was empty.

"I apologize for Mr Isembard's manner - he has not always been like that. I'm afraid you will have to tolerate his behaviour. He was born on the estate. As a young man, he joined the army. While a corporal at a supply depot, he had an accident, rendering him unfit for duty. Afterwards, he came into service at Lady Holme. He started as a footman and has been the butler for twenty-seven years. Within the last five years, he has become difficult, particularly with female staff. He has reverted to his army ways. Your stay is brief, so I'm sure you can accommodate his peculiarities."

"We'll do our best, Mrs Williams," said Sophie.

The housekeeper explained their duties to them.

Lady Jane and Lord James sat at lunch in the Breakfast Room. They preferred this room because it was a smaller and more intimate space with an extensive view over the walled garden and down to the sea.

"Horry's arriving this afternoon," said his lordship. "He's bringing his horses from Cheltenham, after all. Said it was worth taking the trouble, what with this nice weather we're having. He wants them to settle down after the journey so they'll be fit tomorrow."

"That's nice, I haven't seen my brother for quite a while... Oh, dear, the new maids have just arrived. I wanted them to become familiar with the place before the guests came."

"You mean get used to Isembard, I think?"

"Well, that, too... Isn't it time he retired?"

"He does his job well. He's been here so long I'm reluctant to cast him off just like that."

"But he's nasty to the maids."

"Oh, he means nothing by it, I'm sure... How do you find these maids?"

"They're smartly turned out. Mrs Williams will tell me what their work's like later... I must say... No, it doesn't matter."

"What were you going to say?"

"Well, I'm surprised by their looks, all of them. One of them is an absolute beauty... Dark, and gipsy-like. You'd swear she had just stepped out from one of those pre-Raphaelite paintings."

"Really? Well, that'll make a change. I liked Maureen when she was here. She was a cheerful soul, but she looked an absolute gorgon."

"Let's not discuss this anymore, thank you. Passing comments on people's looks... They're not horses, after all. I shouldn't have mentioned the subject, but then you'll see for yourself soon enough."

They ate on in silence.

"I heard another lorry in the middle of the night," said Lady Jane. "I forgot to mention it earlier."

"Did you? Amazing how sound carries at night," said her husband.

"No, it drove right past the gates," insisted Lady Jane.

"Probably a farmer with livestock. I doubt it'll happen again."

"I don't like my sleep being disturbed. Could you ask someone to make them stop doing it?"

"I can ask… I doubt it will go anywhere. I'm sure it's just temporary. Some people live next to train tracks and they don't complain."

"But they expect the noise… Why aren't you on my side?"

"Of course I am, dear. Though there's little or nothing I can do to prevent lorries travelling at night. Take a sleeping draught, then you won't be disturbed."

"You can be quite tiresome sometimes."

"I don't mean to be, but we are powerless in the matter."

"Ah, Mrs Williams. What is the report?" asked Lady Jane.

"I'm very pleased, my Lady. They do excellent work. Dora, the scullery maid, she works well and has a happy disposition no matter what task she's doing. Nancy… All I can say is I've never seen the like. She's so quick and I can find no fault. As for Phoebe and Gladys, they are efficient and competent. Both of them have very nice manners."

"Which is which of those two?"

"Gladys is the, um, dark one, and Phoebe has light brown hair… I did think we might have trouble, but I'm more settled in my mind now."

"That's good. And Mr Isembard?"

"I'm afraid he's getting worse, my Lady. Although he doesn't seem to have upset them unduly — yet."

Two maids stopped as they passed one another in the square, high-ceilinged Entrance Hall.

"That man is absolutely insufferable," said Flora.

"He's an old git, that's what he is," said Ada.

"Don't let Phoebe hear you say that."

"I won't. I bet she's thinking it, though."

"Oh, I don't think so."

"I've come across other high-ranking servants just as bad. But not right at the start."

"Ah, here she is."

"How's the work going?" Sophie had a stern, determined look on her face as she strode towards them as if the house belonged to her.

"All finished," said Flora.

"Same here."

"By your faces, I know exactly who you were talking about. Put up with him as best you can. However, I have drawn a line and *when* he oversteps it, he will regret it. Unspeakable, ill-mannered, jumped-up boor."

"Does that mean the same as git?" asked Ada.

"Yes, it does. Though I wish you would not use that distasteful word. Let's find Mrs Williams and see what needs doing next."

Chapter 10

Arrivals and a small bedroom

"Uncle Horry! How lovely to see you!" Maude shouted across a short distance as she approached along the west side of the house, heading to where a horse was being led down the ramp of a van.

"Hello, Maudie!" called her uncle, Colonel Horace Digby, who watched as a groom walked the horse. "How have you been, my dear girl?"

"Perfectly spiffing. And how are Claude and Mercy?"

"They journeyed well, as you see. Claude will probably crib a bit and kick the boards tonight, but he'll soon settle in. We'll give him a light feed and a good brushing. That should settle him down. By the way, what's this shindig about?"

"Didn't Daddy tell you? Yet another royal invitation came, so he's paying his penance by placating Mummy. Usual nonsense. Still, it got you out of your shell, didn't it?"

"It did, indeed. If this weather holds, we'll have a marvellous time. The rides here are the best anywhere in England."

"You always say that. Is Aunt Sandra in good health?"

"Yes, she is, thank you. She's inside with your mother. I'm staying out here until they've finished talking, which should be in about two hours. Heaven only knows what they find to talk about. I can't take more than ten minutes of teacups and polite conversation."

"Neither can I. Here comes Mercy... She's such a good-tempered animal. Looks in excellent condition... Come on, you," Maude linked her arm through her uncle's. "The grooms will take care of them. Come and see the dogs. I've got a few new ones, including a pair of whippets. They're not overly fond of horses, but they're so funny, tearing about all over the place. Then they plonk themselves down and don't move for hours and hours."

"Lead on, Maudie, lead on."

"I don't — I don't *understand* why he has never explained his behaviour." Mrs Sandra Digby was three years younger than Lady Jane. They sat in the spacious Drawing Room where they could enjoy the view through the windows.

"Apparently, he gave his word he would never leave the estate, and that's as much as I have ever got from him."

The two women broached the subject about once a year.

"Yes... Of course, men are so obstinate, aren't they? Quite imbecilic sometimes, I would say."

"You mean, my brother Horry's like it, too?"

"Not all the time. Just often enough for it to be trying. He's too regular in his habits to do anything so dramatic as James. It must be most aggravating for you — that James refuses to speak. I do confess to having an inordinate curiosity concerning his great mystery."

"I've long since ceased to wonder. What I fear now is that he'll tell me and the reasons will be so thoroughly asinine and commonplace that I'll never be able to take him seriously again! A lost wager or something equally ridiculous of that sort. What I used to fret over was who he had made the promise to or whether it was his own conscience that impelled him to this form of self-punishment."

"It can't be a wager. I refuse to believe it. I always thought it was connected with the groom who drowned, although I might be mistaken."

"No, that was nearly a year afterwards. It was the only time he left the estate after he had astonished me with his declaration. That unfortunate death, more than anything, allowed me to accept James would never leave Lady Holme again. It made me quite superstitious and nervous for a while."

"Well, it would. One doesn't like to give way to primitive thoughts and attitudes, but they're there, under the surface. Thirteen of anything always makes me think twice. If James broke his self-imposed prohibition and a man died... well, it rather appears as though he's under a curse. Not that I believe in curses, but one can't help one's thoughts sometimes."

"No, one can't... Are you riding this weekend?"

"Yes. We've brought Mercy. I must say, it's lovely weather we're having for October. I really had my doubts about coming, but I'm so glad we did."

"Do we have to go tomorrow?" asked Fiona Hazlett, wife of Basil, heir to the title. They were eating dinner in their London townhouse.

"Yes, we must... I don't understand, Fiona. When we were first married, you were happy to spend time there. You wanted to take up riding and enjoy country life. Good heavens, we even talked about living at Lady Holme, you were so enthusiastic."

"That was then, before Michael was born. Naturally, we will live there in due course, but although I can now ride, I don't much care for it. Particularly when the weather's so iffy."

"You'll change your mind once we're there."

"Possibly. I don't mean to be difficult... Oh, you know what the real problem is."

He sighed. "They don't dislike you."

"That is an anaemic way of putting it, isn't it? Because I'm not county and they are — and extremely so — your brother and sisters look down on me."

"They don't. Anyway, Constance can hardly say anything when she's married to Oscar Reid."

"You seem oblivious to the problem. They don't *say* anything. But I see their glances and hurried whispers, which cease when I come into a room. It puts me on edge and on the defensive."

"They're snobs and they can't help themselves. When you become Lady Fiona, believe me, that will all change."

"I wish I *could* believe you. It's the difference between being born into it and marrying into it. It's all about bloodlines for horses and people alike."

"Oh, come, come… I'm not like that, am I?"

"No, you're not. And I don't think they can help it, either. Besides, you are also doing particularly well as a broker on the stock-exchange and, while they may not begrudge you that success, they don't mind airing a few choice remarks in front of me… Well, they were just unpleasant last time, that's all."

"Why didn't you tell me…? I haven't mentioned this to you before, but you're not alone in that belief. I've been made aware of a little undercurrent of envy running through the family."

"And yet, even if only out of a sense of family duty, we will go tomorrow."

"Yes, we will go."

"Good afternoon, Mrs Chiverton," said Sophie.

She had gone to the kitchen and found Mrs Chiverton and two kitchen maids busy preparing for tea. She approached the cook.

"Good afternoon," she replied, her voice a rich, warm country purr. "Who might you be?"

"My name's Phoebe King. I'm in charge of the maids from Burgoyne's Agency."

"From London?"

"That's right, Mrs Chiverton. I was hoping you could tell me how Dora is settling in. She's new to the agency and I've to keep an eye on her."

"Ah... Well, too early to say, yet. I'm satisfied with what I've seen so far."

"That's very good... Is there anything I can do for you? That looks like a snack for the grooms."

"That's right, only in this house they call it a peck. If you wait a minute, you can take it to them. They make their own tea."

"I've always found grooms eat more than their horses."

"That's right, an' all!" Mrs Chiverton smiled. "I never know how such thin, wiry men can tuck it away as they do. I think they've hollow legs." She laughed.

"That's a good one. I must remember that."

"You weren't born in London, were you?"

"No. I was born and lived in and around Winchester."

"Oh, you're a Hampshire lass, then... I'm from Ringwood."

"I know where that is, but I've never visited."

"It's a nice enough place... There you go."

"How do I get to the stables from here?"

"They're back of the west wing. You'll know 'em when you see 'em. Go out the door and along the path aside the servants' quarters. Carry on past back of the walled garden and you'll see the stables ahead. Go to the main entrance and ask for Ronald. He's second groom and has the best manners. The stable master is old Mr Harkley, but he won't want you bothering him."

"How many are there? There are so many sandwiches and pies."

"There's the three grooms and three stable boys. They're all working on account of the visitors. Leave the can there. A stable boy will bring it back."

Sophie grasped the bail handle and lugged from the kitchen a round metal cylinder with a locking cap. On the sheltered stone path between the tall garden wall and the long rank of pretty windows, she formed the impression that she walked in Tudor England, following the innumerable steps of countless maids taking cannisters of food to hungry grooms. It was a long, inconvenient journey - required in all weathers — that no one had ever thought to change. Soft sunlight warmed the walk, and the novelty of her situation struck Sophie. This hidden, peaceful nook and prosaic, simple task spoke to her. When she recalled Lady Holme in the future, she would remember this time-worn duty as part of the quintessential life and history of the place and, of course, the lovely scent in the house.

Greenhouses and fenced vegetable gardens lay ahead of her. A gardener, dressed in brown shapeless clothes, was at work - bent over his task. He did not look up. Her mood changed when she rounded the corner of the walled garden and as the full extent of the estate came into view. It was a soft gentle land sloping to the sea. Across the Solent lay the Isle of Wight, floating in autumnal air rendered misty by the distance. The sun reflecting from the water made the air bright under the blue sky. The trees were advanced in changing colour and lay in isolated clumps and copses amid an extensive flat grassland as broad as it was long. There were no other buildings, no neighbours in sight, from Lady Holme down to the sea, more than a mile away. Recalling her study of the map, Sophie realized how large an area seventeen hundred acres encompassed. She remembered there lay a large section of forest and marshes to the east. She looked in that direction and located the bald grassy dome of Marley Mound rising above the trees. It was not overly high, but it was prominent — a gentle rounding of pale green against the blue sky above and which also nestled into the darker greens and burgeoning browns and golds of the forest canopy below.

As Sophie resumed her walk, the stables ahead of her became apparent, at least the small part she could see, as she skirted the southern wall of the garden. Everything she had observed about Lady Holme so far was in an excellent state of repair. The appointments within the house, whether old or new, were of excellent quality. The Hazlett family, she surmised, had to be in good financial health to maintain the upkeep of such an enormous property.

The nearer the stables, the more her anticipation increased in expectation of what was to come. The stables were massive. A high wall of rosy bricks supported a half-timbered section of equal height above it. A pattern of curly strapwork, suggestive of horses' tails, lay stark black on white. The tall tiled roof peaked at some forty to forty-five feet above the ground. She kept expecting the building to end, but it did not. She could see a tall, stone-arched doorway which permitted entrance for a mounted rider. A porch came into view — one with an oriel room and gabled roof above. It proved to be in the middle of the façade. Finally, she saw the whole building and stopped again. Two more stone-arched entrances had appeared — one, much taller, was wide enough for a carriage to pass through. The stables stood, shaded and quiet, a purpose-built structure of surpassing beauty. Sophie hurried across the stone pavement to the porch.

She met a boy of fourteen or so coming out, who stopped and stared at her.

"Where will I find Mr Ronald?"

"Him be inside." The boy nodded towards the interior and walked away.

Sophie went in and the warm smell of horses, barns, and straw greeted her like the chance meeting of a near-forgotten friend.

A man, an inch shorter than herself, and wiry, came around a corner suddenly. He was wearing a comfortable tweed jacket, trilby, jodhpurs, and riding boots.

"Whoops, sorry, love." He was a Londoner. "You're new here... and a sight for sore eyes." He glanced meaningfully at the cannister.

"Yes, just temporary, though. Are you Ronald?"

"That I am and at your service, Miss...?" He had expressive eyes and a lively, ready-to-smile face.

"Phoebe."

"Lovely name. Suits you perfect."

"Oh, I think I need to be careful around you," she said.

"No, I'm harmless, I am. I just like to keep cheerful, you know what I mean?"

"Yes, I do... Um, where do I put this?"

"I'll take care of that," he said confidentially in mock-seriousness. He took the cannister and put it on a table.

"I was wondering, how big are these stables?"

"Beautiful, aren't they? I don't have the exact measurements, but I paced it out once. I calculated 47 yards by 22. If you're not busy, come and have a look see."

They went further inside and immediately entered a recently raked sanded area where the horses could be walked or ridden. There, the eye was invited up into the beams and roof trusses high overhead. The floor above terminated in railings on either side of the open space. One side was a hayloft.

"Quite the article," said Ronald. "A real bit of history and the largest stables in Hampshire."

"I'm amazed… How many horses?"

"We have eleven, including the two old Shires, Flo and Ben. There's room for thirty-five, but if the floor above was used, fifty. It's storage up there now. Do you know horses?"

"A little."

"Come and see his lordship's horse… It's all right, no one's about."

"I've got work to do."

"Won't take a minute. Blame it on me if anyone says anything."

"Oh… very well."

They walked into a wide but dim aisle with a sixteen-foot-high ceiling of boards which also formed the floor above. Ronald stopped to switch on the electric light.

"Much better… That's his nibs over there." They walked to a large stall. "King of the stables, and he knows it. Don't you, Chieftain?"

A black, glossy horse came to the stall door and put his head over.

"Best not to touch him until he lets you… He's quite particular. He's his lordship's horse first, but we're good friends. Aren't we, old man?"

The horse gave a soft whinny.

"Yes... Big, ain't he?" He began stroking the horse. "Eight years old, seventeen and a quarter hands. Completely black save for a white tuft on his right hind fetlock and some dark brown in his mane and tail. Chieftain, say hello to Phoebe."

The horse turned slightly towards her.

"There you go. His Royal Highness has acknowledged your presence. Give him a stroke."

Sophie stepped up to the horse and gave him a light, sweeping caress along the length of his nose. Chieftain whinnied again.

"Ooh, he likes you all right. Only his lordship and me ride him. Lord James is out here every day, rain or shine, to visit Chieftain... You like your exercise, don't you? He's a good galloper."

Sophie could plainly perceive the strong mutual affection between horse and man.

"I best be going. Goodbye, Chieftain.... He's a lovely horse. Thank you... Something I've been wondering about. A friend told me there were smugglers in these parts. It made me quite nervous when I heard that."

"Oh, don't you worry about them." They began walking back. "They work out of Lymington and they're harmless, I reckon, unless you meddle with them. It's not like pirates, you know. That's what I thought when I first come down here... But it's funny you should mention smugglers. I've heard a lorry going along the road at night. The noisy object woke me up. I sleep in one of the coachman's rooms, you see. When I got my wits about me, I said to meself, Ronald, I reckon those are smugglers driving that lorry. They're travelling at night so as not to be noticed."

"What time was that?"

"Oh, er, about four because I didn't get back to sleep and I get up at five."

"Might be anything if it was just the once."

"Ah, but it wasn't. It's not regular... about once a fortnight and on different days. I don't suppose it is smugglers — like proper criminals, I mean. But in the dark, it was easy for me to think that."

"We'll probably never find out... Something else, Ronald. What's this talk about ghosts?"

"What in the house? I'm not decided either way. But a word of warning. Whatever you do, don't bring up that subject in the Servants' Hall. There's a division of opinion. It's like Catholics and Protestants discussing who goes first entering the Pearly Gates. I don't eat my dinner there anymore because of that... Goodbye, Phoebe. It was nice you taking an interest like you did."

"Goodbye, Ronald. Your stables are wonderful and Chieftain is magnificent. I found everything fascinating."

For the rest of the day, the London maids scattered throughout the house and learned some of its bewildering layout as they began their duties. They had started with a tour. The house, having four staircases, three pantries, four dining rooms, and dozens of bedrooms, required the maids to pay strict attention to what they were told. Sophie drew maps for the two floors they were shown. The various dining rooms were named the Breakfast Room, the Dining Parlour, Great Hall, and the Alcove. In some less-frequented corridors, they saw ancient rush matting and discussed among themselves how it could be cleaned. They were thankful they had not the cleaning of them. They gaped in the Great Hall - at its size, the array of heraldic devices in glass windows and the shields hanging on walls, but mostly they stared at the monstrously tall, wide, intricately carved and fluted-columned stone fireplace that could accommodate five foot logs in its hearth. Within the Great Hall, lay the Alcove - a quarter sectioned off by tall carved and panelled wooden screens, thus creating a more intimate dining area in one corner. This, they learned, was where the family entertained guests.

Finally, the feature of this singular house, that had them whispering in amazement to one another, was the Long

Gallery at the rear on the first floor. It possessed a tremendous view of the sweeping landscape from its myriad windows, but the length frankly astonished them - more so, when they learned that, in times long past, children used to ride their ponies up and down the gallery. Mrs Williams pointed out several marks made by horseshoes dug into the wide, old boards that were now mostly covered with long, pretty-patterned runners of deep red and pale blue.

The housekeeper took pride in Lady Holme. It was difficult to tell if her attachment was to the family or the place itself, but it was probably because she viewed them as one intertwined entity.

In meeting Lady Jane, the maids found her to be quite reticent. Sophie, in the guise of Phoebe, received a mild and embarrassing shock when Lady Jane suddenly began praising the business acumen and overall manner of Sophie Burgoyne. She did not know where to look. The meeting was mercifully brief, and the maids were soon attending to their assigned duties in different areas.

Flora, Ada, and Sophie served the family at dinner in the Dining Parlour rather than the Great Hall. This was Lady Jane's idea - as a try-out of their skills before the big dinners of the coming weekend. It was an odd atmosphere at first. Lady Jane passed a shrewd eye over each of the maid's actions for several minutes before completely relaxing, evidently satisfied by what she saw. Maude virtually ignored them. His lordship and Colonel Digby were both surprised. Partially so, by the efficiency of all three women. More so, by the pleasing aspect all three presented. Specifically so, by Flora's striking dark beauty.

"Did you hire them for their looks or their skills?" asked Mrs Digby. "They seem to possess both in abundance... What is the name of the agency?"

At this comment, Colonel Digby attended to his meal more assiduously than before while the maids stood silently at their stations.

"Burgoyne's Agency. It's near the City, I believe. It's an up-and-coming firm."

"I shall remember the name. Do you think they would go out to Cheltenham? I ask not for myself, but for friends who are looking for competent servants."

"I don't know, Sandra. I'll give you the telephone number later and then you can enquire directly."

Earlier, at dinner in the Servants' Hall, Mr Isembard had been absent. The food was good and plentiful. As the staff sat together in common, the talk was relatively free of the conventions that once would have held the youngest junior staff in a thralldom of silence unless spoken to. Even so, the two youngest maids had been quiet - all eyes and ears - intent upon the exotic newcomers from London.

The talk among the servants had turned to matters of lesser and greater houses and families. Those of Lady Holme showed an interest in those from London. Fern and Ada recounted their actual experiences as domestic servants, while Sophie and Flora told of their fictitious ones. Flora had the table spell-bound with several fanciful, highly coloured anecdotes.

"Have you noticed the floor's warm in 'ere?" asked Ada.

With their work finished for the day and everything from the Dining Parlour cleared away, the four secret agents were crammed into Sophie's bedroom to compare notes on their observations. They were keeping their voices low so as not to disturb the other servants in adjacent rooms.

"They've got some funny sort of flue system," said Fern. "The gardeners look after a little furnace outside and it heats all the floors from underneath."

"That's highly unusual," said Sophie. She had a notebook and pencil ready as she sat in a chair while the others sat on her bed.

"The Romans used to do that sort of thing," said Flora.

"Very sensible of them, too," said Sophie. "I was curious why it felt so pleasant throughout the house."

"Saves me and the sculleries a lot of work," said Fern. "We don't have to make up fires in every room what's occupied. There's a few a bit draughty that want a fire."

"Now that we know why we're all so comfortably warm, I need your reports. Dora, you go first."

"Well, I've spent most of today gettin' the hang of things, Phoebe. Mr Isembard's very peculiar, and I think he's nicking stuff like what Ada explained. I think it was a butcher who I answered the door to, only he wasn't delivering goods, so I don't know for certain. The butler come along, puffing away, and ordered me off. It was all in that old corridor we came into first off. I hid around the corner and listened. I heard them say their hellos and the butcher, I think he was a butcher, he says, 'Here's your usual and here's the bill, which includes the extras you ordered'. Then Isembard says, 'Prices have gone up again, I see.' The butcher says, 'Can't do a thing about it. The costs keep rising'. Isembard says, 'We can't kill the golden goose or we'll have no more eggs.' He laughs - horrible laugh he's got. They say goodbye, and he shuts the door. I hid in the kitchen until he passed, but then I popped out to watch him. He limps badly, you know, and one shoulder's lower than the other. He was carrying a paper, but then he did something in his inside jacket pocket. Smoothing down a pound note, I reckon." Her face was alive with the novelty and excitement of her experience.

"That's most excellent work, Dora. Keep it up." Sophie had been writing in shorthand as she spoke. "Nancy, what do you have?"

"Lorries in the night. I don't know how often, though."

"Oh, no. I have that one, too," said Flora. "And I was so pleased with myself."

"I have the same," said Sophie. "They pass by about four in the morning once a fortnight on different days. What do we make of it?"

"I think," Ada gave a signal with her eyes towards Fern, intimating not to mention smugglers, "that the fraud… the fraud… What do you call someone who does fraud?"

"A defrauder," said Sophie

"But wouldn't a defrauder be doing a defraud?" asked Ada. "Who does the fraud?"

"That's right, they would," said Flora. "If we are investigating fraud, then we are after a fraudist. That's what I say."

"Perfect. But not like in artiste with an e," said Sophie.

"Right. I think the fraudists are diddling the government regular. All we need to do is find out where they're coming from," said Ada enthusiastically.

"I know! I know!" said Flora in a whispered shout. "The lorry drives up from the shore on a track leading towards Frog's Hole and then turns onto Spanish Lane, eventually making its way past Lady Holme."

"How on earth did you find that out?" exclaimed Sophie in a repressed, earnest whisper. "That's quite similar to what Elizabeth suggested."

"Oh, it was simple. I've gained an admirer. He's an elderly gardener named Wilfred. Unfortunately, he has very few teeth, but he is observant and delightful in his forthright, rustic fashion. Cutting through his extraordinary accent and bold professions of admiration, I gleaned that, when they had reaped the field for the last haymaking of the year, they had a merry celebration. He told me, freely and proudly, that he had drunk, in company with other like-minded gardeners and field-hands, a stupendous quantity of beer and cider. After these libations, he wobbled homeward on his bike along Spanish Lane, only to get as far as Frogs Hole. There, he decided, he may as well as sleep in a hedgerow as in his bed. I suspect he fell off his bike, but was too bashful to mention it. Anyway, this hardy Hampshire native found a comfy, retired spot among the herbage for himself and his bike. He lays himself down and sleeps. He did not say when, exactly, but the noise of a lorry, first approaching along a track from the sea, disturbs our gallant scout into a wakeful state.

"He listens and thinks. He thinks some more when the lorry turns onto Spanish Lane. His conclusion? Here I shall try to do his accent justice... 'It be the ahhrmee. None be so foolish as they! Arrrgh.' That last noise signifies the accuracy and truthfulness of his preceding statement. Sort of like his own amen. And I *must* tell you this one. We had only just met and said hello, and he immediately asked, 'Be you married? I be'ant.' After that, it took great fortitude on my part to withstand his irresistible charm. Another half an hour in his company, and I might have been on my way to becoming Mrs Turnip. Had we married, our part of the hedgerow would have been the envy of all our neighbours and pointed out by passing traffic."

Flora smirked at her handiwork, as she watched her companions convulse with stifled laughter — intensified by their having to remain quiet. Fern was definitely on the verge of bursting out when someone tapped lightly on the door. Sophie cleared her throat and hid her notebook.

"Come in."

The door opened and a small plump, rosy-cheeked maid, a girl of fourteen, put her head in — a pretty mob-cap over her curls. She smiled and said in a soft voice with a pleasant burr,

"Are you having a party? It sounds ever so lovely."

"You're Nelly, aren't you? No, we're just talking," said Sophie. "Come and join us."

"Oh, thank you, Miss King. I *knew* you wouldn't mind. It's quiet and a bit lonely here sometimes. Can Mabel come? She's too shy to axe for herself."

"Yes, of course," replied Sophie. "There's just enough space for six."

"Shall us'n bring our own chairs, miss? Your bed's already took."

The secret agents made room and welcomed the two youngest maids. They all sat and talked — six little maids in a snug Tudor room, swapping gentle, occasionally funny, anecdotes for half an hour. Then it was time for sleep.

Chapter 11

More arrivals

Lord James was behaving like an excited boy. By always remaining on the estate, he had become isolated and sometimes craved company. Sometimes, the advent of visitors to Lady Holme produced a more abrupt manner.

An early riser, he usually ate two breakfasts - a sandwich he took with him to the stables and, weather permitting, ate while walking. When he arrived, he drank tea with the grooms. Hours later, he would eat his second breakfast. Today, that changed. Lord James ate a full, early breakfast alone because there was much for him to superintend where the horses were concerned.

"Carpenter, bring a cup of tea to the office. I have to ring somebody."

"Yes, my Lord," replied Ada. He called her Carpenter, as this was the ancient Lady Holme nomenclature for the Breakfast Room servant.

When she took tea on a silver tray to the office, Lord James had papers on the desk in front of him. He picked up the telephone receiver.

"Who's this...? Get off the line, Isembard. I want to place a call. I'll hang up."

Isembard had been speaking of codfish on the extension to a fishmonger in Lymington.

"Yes, my Lord." Isembard was standing, using the telephone in the eastern passage. "I will ring back later," he said to his party. He depressed the hook, terminating his call. He waited with the receiver to an ear, then he released the hook to listen in to Lord James' conversation.

"Put the tray there... Why did you bring biscuits?"

"Well, my Lord, I asked Mrs Chiverton if you was partial to anything with your cuppa tea, and she said you was, and that you preferred Garibaldi biscuits once in a while. So I brought them on the off-chance you wanted to nibble something, your lordship."

"Ah... What is your name?"

"Nancy, my Lord."

"Very good, Nancy."

"It's a pleasure, my Lord."

She bobbed and left the room. As she closed the door, Lord James began dialing while obtaining the number from a paper in front of him.

From the Entrance Hall, Ada wanted to listen at the door, but other servants were passing. So she walked away swiftly into the corridor by the Grand Staircase. She turned the corner by the Chapel and, with the coast clear, moved quietly past the Pannetry. She crossed the passage to the side door. Isembard was listening to the call. Her face took on an 'I knew it' look. Ada continued to the Breakfast Room to put it back in order.

"Psst, Phoebe." When she turned at the sound, Ada beckoned her with quick waves of her hand. She was standing in the doorway of the School Room that connected to the Great Hall. Sophie had been dusting furniture in the School Room, which was now a lounge. It contained large sofas, covered in patterned material of open, flowered chintz on a creamy white ground. The many easy chairs, small polished tables and lace curtains made it a comfortable, welcoming room. The paintings here were more decorative. The gloomy or serious portraits of ancestors found elsewhere gave way to several horse portraits, decorative garden scenes, and landscapes.

"What is it?" she whispered.

"I can't stop. I've got so much to do. I've got news, I have. Isembard listens in to his lordship's telephone conversations, but that's not the big thing. I got a squint of a letter on his desk."

"You mean his lordship's desk?"

"Yes, in his office. I saw it when I was putting the tray down, but I couldn't read much. I got past the hello-how-are-you business and it said, 'With your incarceration' but I couldn't read no more 'cause his Lordship was right there."

"That's wonderful, Nancy… It might mean it has been imposed upon him. Someone else knows why he's a recluse."

"That's what I thought. I wish I could have read it all."

"Um… We'll get Dora to read it. Or I could copy it, but Dora would definitely be faster."

"Right-o."

"Was there anything else you noticed?"

"Yes. It looked rough around the edges, like old books. And it had a funny stamp at the top."

"That might be handmade laid paper. What did the stamp say?"

"It looked worn out and splodgy. In an oval, there were these right old-fashioned letters. I only remember, P-W-P, but there was little uns an' all. It wasn't like an address or nothing."

"So a person in the authority of the organization has written to Lord James referring to his incarceration. It seems to me as though it might be coming to an end."

"I don't know about that. I 'ave to go, Phoebe."

"Yes, of course. Well done."

The guests started arriving as Sophie was finishing up her work in the School Room. Lady Holme began to speak. Part of the Long Gallery lay overhead, and Sophie heard faint footsteps, accompanied by petty creaks and squeaks. She stopped to listen intently and perceived two or three people walking together — slowly progressing along the gallery. One of them laughed, and she heard it plainly.

Lady Holme had garages. But the grand old dame appeared to be embarrassed by the advent of the twentieth century and the wretched motor car it insisted upon hauling with it and depositing in her presence. The red-brick and rather plain four-stall garage had been reluctantly built and hidden away among trees near the front of the house on the west side. The garage was completely screened except its immediate front.

Lord James did not drive, although he possessed a splendid pre-war Vauxhall A-type. Ronald, the groom, performed the infrequent chauffeuring of Lady Jane while Maude sometimes hurled the car around the country lanes like a maniac or, more often, drove sedately into Lymington.

The Scropes arrived early. Mr Martin Scrope, Member of Parliament for Portsmouth East — although he lived in Southampton — was a rotund, talkative, and direct person. A man of business, he was also a director and a significant shareholder in the London and South Western Railway, as was Lord Hazlett. That was how they befriended one another. Years ago, Martin Scrope had come to see Lord Hazlett about an upcoming shareholders' meeting. They then discovered, in matters concerning railway business, they were of a similar, if not single, mind. From that day, Mr Scrope exercised Lord Hazlett's proxy at meetings, as they always voted the same way. This brought Mr Scrope to Lady Holme regularly as he liked to talk about railway matters, which Lord Hazlett often liked to hear. In their fashion, they grew comfortable with each other. This was Lord James' lifeline to the world outside and a method of exerting influence on affairs.

If prosperous and extraordinarily well-preserved at age sixty-five, Martin Scrope did have one gripe in life. It was that he did not have a son. Instead he was, as he once put it to Lord Hazlett, "... besieged by females. My life's not my own." His wife, Helen, had stopped bothering to air her own opinions in public, drowned out as they were by the quantity and volume of her husband's opinions on any given subject. But in private, without an audience to be won, control of the air shifted. Later at night, after jointly attending a public gathering, Helen would often review Martin's behaviour — beginning with words like, "Martin, I don't think you should have said..." The list was sometimes long. Martin Scrope, MP, listened, and learned, once more, that while he might fully possess the public stage, his wife possessed the Scrope household. When first married, he raged and blustered at his severest critic. She defeated such outbursts by never once losing her temper. She did this by first hearing and subsequently ignoring everything he said. Then there were his daughters.

Vanessa, 23 and unmarried, owned a car that was much too fast for any road anywhere, had climbed in the Alps, flown a plane, sailed, played golf at par, spoke of deep-sea diving, played a competitive game of tennis against male opponents, and had already left a trail of broken hearts in her wake. She besieged her father with demands for money and responded with delightful laughter when he told her that living beyond her means would catch up with her. Her means — an allowance from her father, a moderate income from a trust set up by her maternal grandfather, and gifts from admirers — always struggled to keep pace with her pursuits.

Amelia, 26, also unmarried, was different again, yet still representative of much that was opposite to Martin's way of life. From the books she read, he was convinced she was a socialist and free-thinker. It annoyed him that, after eating no meat for five years, she was still alive. Not that he wanted her dead. But he could not believe it right or normal for a human not to eat meat at least twice a day, as he himself did. Besides that, she wrote poetry and hung about with artists and intellectuals who needed a bath and a haircut. Her remarks to him, spoken in tones of patient condescension, frequently began, "But you don't understand, father. Let me explain..." What she then related caused his eyes to roll and him to sigh with deep feeling.

Martin Scrope was happy to go to Lady Holme. Sometimes he envied the serenity of Lord Hazlett's isolation.

The first of the Scropes to appear was Vanessa, who roared up the driveway in her Sunbeam Coupé de l'Auto and skidded to a halt, spraying gravel everywhere.

"What ho!" she cried, lifting her goggles. She wriggled out of the green, single-seater that came to a sharp point at the back. Vanessa removed her gauntlets.

"Hello, Vanessa," called Maude, who had dressed in tight-fitting riding clothes. "Kill anyone with that thing on the way over?"

"No, not this time. Father's taking it slowly, but he's not far off with the gees and the family." Vanessa, a small, active woman, was good looking and self-possessed.

"Excellent. I want to get riding as soon as poss."

"Don't we all." Vanessa removed her driving cap and goggles to reveal short, blonde hair. She unbuckled her driving coat, revealing riding clothes, except for a jacket, beneath.

"Where do you keep your luggage?"

"Oh, there's hardly any storage. Father's bringing my togs. Would you like a gasper?"

"Why not? Daddy doesn't approve of women smoking, but I rather like it."

Vanessa lit their cigarettes with her lighter.

"Good grief, these are strong."

"It's a Turkish blend... Live life to the full, I say."

"Too many of these and life may be full, but quite short."

Vanessa laughed.

"How are you doing, Maudie?" she said affectionately. "I haven't seen you in ages."

"Life's good..." They chatted for several minutes.

"Oh, look who's here." A pleased glow surmounted Maude's face.

Vanessa turned and saw a man in tweeds and bowler hat riding a grey horse.

Dr Beaton was a square, heavily built man, with dark hair and a dark moustache that had a touch of grey in it. Not exactly handsome, he was filled with life and purposeful energy, whether speaking, quiet, or at work. He rode into Lady Holme on his great, grey stallion named Scotty. The doctor wore dark tan riding boots, light tan jodhpurs, and a green jacket. With an easy manner, he rode slowly, a brown gloved hand resting on his hip while holding a long rope. Had he worn armour, he would have been a paladin, a warrior of surpassing calm, nonchalantly walking his horse to or from a battle. Behind him, he trailed the chestnut horse, Conker, belonging to his sister.

"Maudie!" His bass-baritone voice rang out under the trees.

"Dr Beaton seems extraordinarily happy to see you," said Vanessa, smiling. "I must say, he looks quite heroic."

"Yes," said Maude vaguely, as she waved to him and he waved back.

"A proposal in the offing?"

"There'd better be or I'll propose to him."

"How daring of you, darling… But where will you live?"

"I don't care."

"Then I *think* I'll say hello to Lady Jane."

"Good morning, Vanessa. How are you this fine day?" enquired Dr Beaton, as he drew nearer. He touched the brim of his hat.

"Good morning, doctor. I'm very well, thanks. You must excuse me. I believe I'm wanted in the house. I'll see you both later."

They had not heard her. Dr Beaton and Maude, with smiles, had begun to discuss the most ordinary things imaginable.

"Belinda's bringing the car with our luggage."

"And how is your sister?"

A taxi drove into the grounds, bringing London visitors, Oscar and Constance Reid. Daniel, the footman, came out to get their luggage.

"Where is everyone?" asked Oscar, who had stopped to look about while Daniel had gone inside. He was in his mid-thirties, had pointed features and was wearing glasses. Of average height and average build, his pallor betrayed his profession of office worker, although he was also the manager of a successful business. When he went to Kenya to visit coffee plantations, he had to guard carefully against the fierce sun or he would go uncomfortably pink before burning.

"At the stables, of course," replied Constance. At twenty-eight, she had held on to her youth and favoured her father, who had the look of a patrician. She followed in length of nose, but to a lesser degree. However, it was through a bright pair of intelligent eyes that she viewed the world. She continued speaking, "Except for Mummy. She's probably waiting to do her grand entrance when everyone has arrived. Let's go in. Another taxi's arriving. It's bound to be Basil and his awful wife, Fiona. They will have travelled on our train."

"Certainly, but what have you against her? She seems all right to me."

"Oh, she's a frightful woman." Constance lowered her voice and spoke in a sibilant whisper as they began walking. "She doesn't love Basil at all, you know. Fiona trapped him because she's just a common fortune-hunter who married him for the title. He was too besotted with her to see what everyone else plainly saw."

Oscar shrugged. They stepped smartly inside the house.

"Where have we been put, Daniel?"

"In the Blue Room, madam."

"Lead on. Come along, Oscar, we must change."

"This house always impresses me," her husband said as he gazed up at the ceiling in the Entrance Hall.

"Let it impress you later," replied his wife.

"I'll bring the luggage if you can get the door for me, please." Basil Hazlett, heir to the title, had to carry his own luggage.

"Let me help. I'm not feeble, you know." said Fiona.

"No, I insist... just hold the door open."

"You're so stubborn sometimes." They smiled at each other.

"Oh, Fiona's got you working as a footman now." The voice came from within. The figure descending the stairs resolved itself into Constance.

"Hello, Constance," replied Basil. "Where have all the staff got to?"

"I don't know. Daniel took our cases upstairs, but where he went afterwards, who knows? How are you, Basil, darling? You're looking peaky. Some gentle riding and rest will do you good. Really, you need some proper looking after."

"Hello, Constance, remember me?"

"Where *are* my manners? It's so good of you to let Basil get away for a few days. I'll see you later when we go out... Oh, but of course, you don't care much for riding, do you? I'm afraid you will find it dull by yourself."

As she walked away, Fiona mimed the words, 'Basil, darling' in ridicule of her sister-in-law.

"Good grief," said Basil in great annoyance. "She's starting in early... Yes, it's just as you said." He set the cases down in the hall and bawled, "Hoi! Footman!"

"Coming!" called a voice somewhere in the chapel corridor. An old, bent, bearded man emerged.

"Bless my soul. It's Mister Basil and Miss Fiona."

"Hello, Joe." Basil smiled warmly. "I was calling for Daniel, actually."

"Him be busy somewhere's about. He's a good lad. But no, you be Mr and Mrs Hazlett now. I'm that sorry I didn't answer the door to you. I was just helping with a delivery. Bootiful flowers, but never mind that. You come right in an' Old Joe'll take care o' these luggages."

"How are you, my old friend?"

"Fair to middlin', thank 'ee, sir. Every extra day's a blessing o' the Lord."

"Can you manage?" asked Fiona with concern.

"I can manage, never you mind, mum."

He was slow at picking up the cases.

"Excuse me, sir." Sophie had approached and spoke to Basil. "Allow me, Mr Joe." She now picked up the two heaviest cases.

"Who be you?" asked Joe.

"Phoebe. It's the Rose Rooms, isn't it?"

"Arh."

Before he could say more, Phoebe carried away the cases.

"Well, I never," said the old man, staring after her.

"Phoebe is a new maid?" asked Fiona.

"House be full of new maids. All temporary, though. Come down from Lunnun and they rush about summat fierce. I'm ready now. If you'll kindly follow me, I'll show you to your rooms... It's good to have you back, and no mistake."

"Oh, blast it!" Reginald Hazlett came out of the station and found no taxi waiting. He was quite tall with light coloured hair and wore tweeds. He had a strong face, with prominent features, blue eyes and a placid air when not irritated by the lack of a conveyance.

"There seem to be only two taxis in service." A man's smooth voice came from someone seated on the bench.

"I beg your pardon?" Reginald glanced at the speaker.

"Only two taxis on duty, I believe."

"Ah, I see." Reginald saw, indeed. He saw he was further inconvenienced by being second in line. He had noticed that the man had new matching brown leather cases and a square box. Reginald put down his two mismatched cases, knowing that, where he stood, everyone could see he was properly next in line. In true British fashion, he declined to engage further in conversation with the seated man and stared into the distances along Station Street and Mill Lane, hoping two taxis would suddenly and simultaneously materialize.

"It's a pity the Britannia's not open," the seated man had approached Reginald, "but then it is a little early for a drink. And we'd lose our places if we left."

Reginald, slightly shocked at being addressed so familiarly when he felt their relative positions were settled, and further shocked at the suggestion of alcohol in the morning, said,

"But it's only half-past nine?"

The man smiled. "Care for a smoke?"

He was dressed in excellent tweeds and, with elegant movements, produced a gold cigarette case and offered it, open. Reginald recognized the Bond Street cigarette maker. He also noticed the man's expensive white cuff secured by a gold cufflink. The man's nails were manicured. Reginald had never been to a manicurist. He felt he had no need of such a service and that no man did.

"Why, thank you."

As they smoked, the stranger said,

"Um, in which direction are you heading?"

"Across the river."

"I'm going that way, too. Perhaps we can share a taxi."

"Oh, yes, I suppose we could."

Two competing thoughts vied in Reginald's mind. Economy saw eminent sense in the proposition. Reserve did not care for the fellow's look. Reginald economized more by personal taste than by necessity. Living in London was expensive, but he also saved for the future, which left little over for pleasure. His income was decent, although his job with the London Port Authority did not pay as well as he would have liked. Worse was the fact that there was no prospect for advancement in view, which had him always looking for other sources of income. Also, he was loath to ask his father for an increase in his allowance. Being the second son of a peer, he felt, was quite difficult sometimes, with the estate and the money for its upkeep going to his older brother, Basil. On top of this, his father was little help because, having withdrawn from society, Lord James had no useful connections. Basil felt he might as well be the sixty-second son.

Reginald's reserve was the last fortress of his self-respect — his single characteristic that prevented him from being middle class, which, in every other material respect, he was. His reserve flowed out from his character more than from his public school education, although he would point to the latter as being the making of him. This self-contained composure of his rested on his confidence in the superior training he had received. He had manners and breeding and an assumption of his innate rightness in all things. While he held on to his reserve, he could suffer his office-worker life, and the other concessions he made to make ends meet.

He had enjoyed school. His childhood had been enjoyable. Reginald felt he had done important work during the war and he now missed that work. Since then, the uniformity of his habits threatened him with shabbiness. Why should he, a Hazlett, endure such a life? Reginald chose not to endure such a life and had already made his own useful connections, which should, in time, prove to be lucrative. However, he was all set to ride at Lady Holme, and that prospect brought back many fond memories. But to share a taxi with a man who suggested a drink at nine-thirty? Reserve rallied.

"Although we're probably not going the same way."

"I'm going to Lady Holme. Do you know it?"

"Yes... I'm going there, too."

"Excellent. I'm Adrian Benson." He offered to shake hands.

"Reginald Hazlett." They shook hands.

"You must be one of the family. I'm told it's a remarkable place," said Benson. "I jumped at the chance when I got the invitation. And the weather's co-operating. It should be fun."

"Yes, I daresay... Who, er, who was it who invited you?"

"Lady Hazlett... Although I know both Vanessa and Amelia Scrope very well."

"You do?... Have you met mother?"

"Oh, I'm sorry. I didn't appreciate you were so closely connected. Yes, we've met."

"Ah," Reginald said, seemingly quite affably.

The single syllable cloaked a growing distrust and distaste for the elegant Adrian. How was it mother knew him? This man oozed charm — too much of it. Clearly, he had not gone to a proper school.

In that assumption, Reginald was incorrect. Although not as prestigious as the one Hazlett had attended, Adrian, twenty-seven, had gone to an excellent school. His middle-class family had scrimped and saved to send him there. Unfortunately, an awful mistake had occurred. Some confusion over a boy's missing money. Adrian left at about that time. However, the three years he had spent at the school instilled in him a strong, ambitious drive, especially since he had there observed, displayed among the families of his fellow pupils, the evidence and effects of wealth and privilege.

He grew to be a clever man, succeeding where others saw no opportunity. Adrian had been a secretary, had worked in various offices in the City, and had avoided the war entirely. Where his success lay was in being so thoroughly useful to wealthy or powerful men — sometimes in covering up their indiscretions. Equal to that were his engaging ways in London drawing rooms. Younger women found him dangerously fascinating or wonderfully sympathetic. Older, wealthy, widowed women found him particularly delightful, feeling flattered by his attentions, and, occasionally, more than flattered — overwhelmed. At present, Adrian was riding a tall wave of success and yet he had no visible means of support.

The two men shared the taxi. Adrian leaned back at ease, friendly, not overly talkative, while Reginald had the growing urge to stop the car and walk. He could not have said why he felt that way.

Chapter 12

Loose Toffee

"Come on. 'urry up," whispered Ada as she peered around a corner into the Entrance Hall.

"Why's it called Hoover Baby? This vacuum weighs a ton and needs emptying." said Fern, who was holding the little monster.

"Shush."

The maids scurried furtively across the hall while it was clear. Ada carried a broom, a brush, a bucket, and a feather duster. She opened the office door, and they hurried in.

"You watch. I'll set up the vacuum cleaner," said Ada.

"All clear." With the door slightly ajar, Fern surveyed the hall.

"Anyone comes, plug it in."

"Nancy, why was you so annoyed with Phoebe?"

"No, I wasn't angry. But I'm not having her do this when we can do it. If she gets caught, we're all sunk. It don't matter about us. So I was adamant, that's all."

"Oh."

Ada searched Lord Hazlett's desk.

"Where's he put them…? Hmm, that's where. He's locked 'is desk."

There followed a momentary silence followed by slight noises.

"Are you picking a lock?"

"You keep a lookout and never mind what I'm doing… I've *never* done this with criminal intent before… There, got it…

Now then, what do we 'ave...? Ooh, there's a lot of interesting stuff in 'ere... How many pages can you remember?"

"I'm all right with three. But with the fourth one, I start forgetting the first. You mustn't talk to me afterwards, either."

"Right you are... This should do you. There's three short letters ready for you... Dora, don't 'ang about."

They changed positions. Fern began reading the letters carefully. Ada's eye was peering around the door. She gripped the feather duster in one hand and the plug to the Hoover in the other. The socket was within reach; envelopes and other rubbish lay in the bucket. A clock ticked. A board creaked on the floor above. The perfume of Lady Holme became more pronounced. The hall was empty, silent. Fern muttered the occasional word. Ada dared not look at her - remembering how Fern had slopped drinks while under observation.

Mrs Williams crossed the hall, her heels clicking on the flagstones. Ada slowly squatted, preparing to jam the plug into the socket as the Hoover had no switch. As the danger receded, she relaxed and stood up again.

After a while, Ada thought Fern was taking a long time. She glanced over and was shocked to find the young woman standing upright, staring at nothing, with her cheeks bulging as though she were holding water in her mouth. Ada supposed some photographic memory development process was taking place, so she hurriedly put everything back in order and locked the desk, using one of her special tools.

Then, as stealthily as circumstances permitted, she struggled with the vacuum, broom, bucket, brush, and duster, while dragging a still bulging Fern by the hand. It was a miracle that no one discovered them and that Ada did not drop anything before they reached the safety of the Dining Parlour where Sophie awaited their return.

Surprised by the spectacle the two presented, yet warned by Ada's shaking head not to speak, Sophie said nothing. She took charge of Fern's hand, leading the maid around the side of a tall cabinet. Ada guarded the door, ready to intercept intruders. Behind the cabinet Fern spoke and her face returned to normal. The contents of the three letters poured out while Sophie scribbled away in shorthand.

When she had finished writing, Sophie leaned against the wall and said, "Good grief."

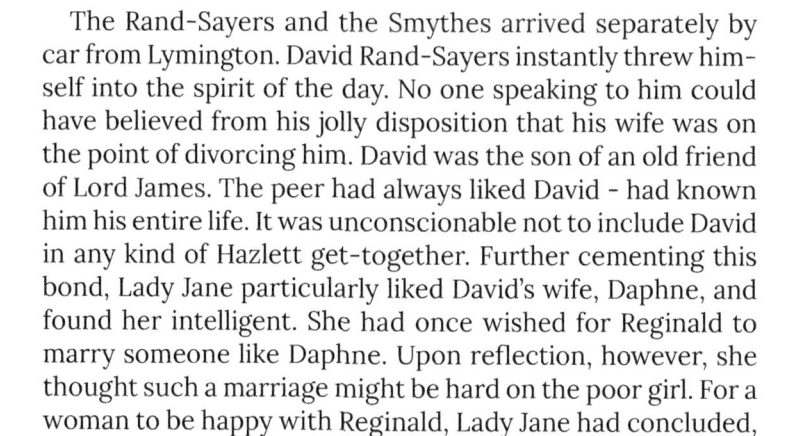

The Rand-Sayers and the Smythes arrived separately by car from Lymington. David Rand-Sayers instantly threw himself into the spirit of the day. No one speaking to him could have believed from his jolly disposition that his wife was on the point of divorcing him. David was the son of an old friend of Lord James. The peer had always liked David - had known him his entire life. It was unconscionable not to include David in any kind of Hazlett get-together. Further cementing this bond, Lady Jane particularly liked David's wife, Daphne, and found her intelligent. She had once wished for Reginald to marry someone like Daphne. Upon reflection, however, she thought such a marriage might be hard on the poor girl. For a woman to be happy with Reginald, Lady Jane had concluded, she needed to be not quite so clever. Daphne also liked Lady Jane and so sought her out in the house, leaving her husband to make of their desperate wager what he would.

The Smythes arrived last but were by no means late. They drove up in an old car. Colonel Digby, who had been loafing about outside, talking to whoever passed by, espied them and approached the newcomers as their car came to a stop.

"Hello, hello, I don't know you, do I?" The Colonel opened the door for Maria.

"Ah, no. We haven't met before," said Richard. "This is my wife Maria, and I'm Richard Smythe."

"Then you must be old Mr Smythe's...?"

"Grandson."

"Ah, got it. I'm Colonel Digby. Sorry to pounce on you like this, dear lady. Please."

"Thank you." She smiled as he helped her from the car.

"What brought me over was your old bus. I had a Rover 8 before the war. Marvellous little machine until I pranged it. Steering went at an awkward moment and I ran into a stone bridge. Then me old Rover was like Humpty Dumpty… Couldn't be put back together again, what?" He roared with laughter. Daniel came out to collect the luggage. "Anyway, I'll let you get settled in and see you both later."

"We look forward to it," said Maria.

Once installed in their room, Richard first took Sheba to the kennels and then searched for Lord Hazlett. He returned to his wife without having found him.

Maria asked, "Is anything the matter? You're very tense."

"I seem to be stopped at every turn. It's this stupid smuggling business bothering me. I wanted to speak to Lord Hazlett about it."

"Don't worry, dear, you have the whole weekend to discuss it. But really, you must change now or they'll be riding off without you."

The family and visitors assembled in the stable yard. They had broken into small groups to chat. The grooms were ready to bring out Lord James' horses. Eight horses belonging to Lady Holme were suitable for riding. When added to the visitors' seven horses, it made a total of fifteen available mounts, which meant three riders had to sit out the first ride. Another three guests did not ride.

Richard Smythe took the opportunity to speak to Lord Hazlett, who was temporarily standing by himself and unoccupied.

"Lord Hazlett, I wonder if I might have a quick word with you?"

His lordship saw the determination in the young man's eyes and the anxiety on his face.

"Oh, it's not about the lorries and that smuggling business again, is it?" he said irritably.

Richard nodded.

"They're just about to bring Chieftain out."

Realizing he had spoken with some emotion and had caused several glances, Lord James then smiled.

"Richard," he said in a patient tone, "we'll discuss it later, at our leisure."

"Thank you, sir. I shouldn't have presumed."

"Don't give it a thought. Just enjoy yourself."

Everyone to mount had mounted. Three riders remained behind to take their turn later. They watched the festive troop, accompanied by an assortment of dogs, leave the stable yard via the worn main track. This track soon branched in several directions. A wide, grassy ride led south to the seashore, while other, narrower paths ran easterly, either branching again or disappearing into the forest to the east.

As horses and riders warmed to their exercise, some began changing position in the column of horses to converse with a particular person. Laughter arose and many, with bright, animated faces, exchanged comments or cajoled one another. Soon, the troop, without conscious planning, resolved itself into several natural groups. Vanessa Scrope, Lord Hazlett, Dr Beaton, and Maude formed the vanguard, and the distance between them and the rest lengthened. Next came the doctor's sister, Belinda Beaton, a tall, angular woman with a pleasant disposition, chatting with Colonel Digby. Next were David Rand-Sayers, who believed he had struck a goldmine of potential jobs while talking to Martin Scrope, since the MP and railway director had many other business interests. Furthermore, Martin Scrope, on his part, felt strongly inclined to help his attentive riding companion.

The largest party, trotting along last of all, centred around Lady Jane. Her riding habit was of an older style. She wore a low crown top hat with a gauzy veil secured to protect her complexion from the elements. On her left rode Sandra Digby, while on her right was Adrian Benson. He was keeping them amused with stories. On his right was Constance Reid, who was finding Adrian more fascinating than she should have, liking the sound of his voice and the nonchalance with which he controlled his horse. Close behind and bringing up the rear were Basil Hazlett and Richard Smythe. The latter, now relaxed, was finally enjoying himself. The two men spoke intermittently, both drawing contentment from their surroundings, their conversation, and their well-behaved horses.

Sophie seriously needed to collect her thoughts, and so privacy was required. She ascended the staircase in the Great Hall, pausing briefly on the first floor to ensure she was unobserved. Then she climbed to a small landing on the second floor, the whole of which was in the roof. This was a part of the house she had not seen before. It was fairly dark because, even though the doors to many of the rooms were open, inside the gable windows were small and grimy, allowing in only a little light.

The first room into which she peered was not much bigger than a large kennel. The roof's pitch pinched the space and the ridge beam was a mere five feet above the floor. It had been a servant's room. Several ageing, split, and dusty sacks of straw lay piled on the lowest bed she had ever seen — a tiny structure of planks. From a nail above the bed hung a faded scrap of parchment — a prayer written in Latin. Sophie guessed it to be centuries old.

Sophie turned away. The floor of rough pine boards was not as dusty in the passage as it had been in the tiny room. The single passageway proved to be so twisting and erratic that Sophie was made to think of a staggering drunkard, lurching this way and that. Intrigued now, she followed along, tip-toeing to minimize the inevitable creaks. The sun's warmth radiated through the roof tiles, inches above her head. The air felt close, heated, smelling of dust, but dust resting on a more profound smell — the perfume of Lady Holme. As if answering her question of what produced the smell, she found an old, massive lavender bunch hanging from a beam. Sophie sniffed it but there was no scent to the brittle, faded, and very dusty sprays. She stifled a sneeze.

All the rooms were gabled. A few were larger, cleaner, and used for storage. It became clear that she had ascended the least frequented staircase. In about the middle of the house, towards the back and above the Long Gallery, was a room distinct from the rest due to its obvious much greater size. She pushed open the panelled door, which was five feet by three. The door swung with a squeak. To enter, Sophie had to step over a high ledge while ducking under the lintel. She was reminded of an old sailing ship. The effect proved to be intentional. The layout of the room was approximately twenty feet wide by ten deep, with a row of windows facing the sea. This room was clean, but had the air of infrequent use.

The furniture was plain, heavy, and old. A large brass telescope on a stand pointed seaward. On a four hundred-year-old table were several more articles that indicated the room had belonged to some old seadog or sea captain. There were several smaller telescopes, a pair of ancient dividers, rulers, a pewter tankard, and a lidded, salt-glazed pot with the word 'salt' embossed upon it. Sophie lifted the lid and was surprised to find the jar full of off-white salt crystals that had fused together into a single lump. The word 'salt' brought Sophie up short and back to the reason she was looking for privacy. She sat in a chair and opened up her notebook.

Fern's recapitulation of the letters she had viewed sounded accurate, although the young woman had mispronounced a few words. The letter writers referred to Lord James Hazlett as Salt (retired). Three different people had written to him. Each letter was dated the first of October.

The first, from Iron, was from the year 1882. Summarized, it said that now the incident was closed, Iron hoped Salt (rtrd) had drawn the intended lesson from the council's prompt response. Reports from observers showed that, since that time, Salt (rtrd) was abiding by the terms of his incarceration. Iron encouraged Salt to keep his spirits up and enjoy the quiet life.

Sophie counted years and supposed the incident referred to was the one of the groom drowning in the river.

The second letter, signed Poppy and dated 1894, also referred to observation reports. This letter said that if Poppy, who was soon to retire with a new Poppy already nominated, should happen to meet Salt, he sincerely hoped they would behave as gentlemen, putting the past firmly behind them.

The writer of the third letter, dated 1919, signed himself Iron but mentioned that a former Iron was now retired because of advanced years and failing health. Sophie presumed the Iron of 1882 was the one who had now retired. This letter specified that, with the retired Salt's incarceration ending on 20 September, 1921, the council considered the entire matter finished. When the term ended, the council had determined that Salt (retired) would be a free man to go where he wished. They had further decided that certain emoluments and benefits befitting a retired council member would be restored to him. Each letter bore the same stamp. Fern had described the violet stamp as being oval, two inches at its widest, and containing the letters t-P-W-o-P.

Sophie wrote out a narrative trying to string the events together. Lord James had offended a council - that much was obvious. The council members had various titles - Iron, Poppy, Salt. In punishment for the offence, the council had sentenced and sanctioned Lord James. The sanctions had taken the form of Salt being confined to Lady Holme for forty years. But Salt had flouted these imposed sanctions and had left his estate early on. Sophie had learned from the taxi driver that Lord Hazlett had gone to look at horses around Newbury where his groom had died. Sophie surmised the observers who reported on Salt's movements had to be nearby — possibly in the house — to be able to report such a matter.

The most recent letter meant Lord James would be free of the sanctions, prohibitions and, perhaps, the observation, too, in a year's time. She had much to think about.

She stood up and noticed, hanging on the wall, a small, round tapestry of a falcon with wings and claws extended. She decided it was quaint, but ugly, and that only a man would think to want it hanging in his room. She thought to leave, but not before looking through the large brass telescope. The image was dark, suffering from distortion around the edge of the lens. She did not dare to open the window in case someone saw her. Sophie trained the telescope on some riders who were leaving the stables at a trot. She recognized Reginald and his sister-in-law, Fiona. She did not know the third rider. Further away, she espied Lady Hazlett galloping her horse. Needing to get on with her duties, Sophie left, retracing her steps to the inhabited areas of the house.

Lunch was ready in the Servants' Hall. Isembard sat at one end of the long table while Mrs Williams sat at the other. Sophie sat near to Mrs Williams and, as the meal progressed, struck up a conversation with her.

"Mrs Williams, I noticed a lot of suitable farming land on the estate."

"It used to be farmed but hasn't been now for fifty years," replied the housekeeper. "There's just the small home farm left."

"Has there been any industry here?"

"There used to be a marlstone mine. That's at Marley Mound. The old name for it is Rodden Top. But the mining stopped about two hundred years ago. Some tunnels collapsed afterwards because they had burrowed so far and wide. You can see where it fell in from the top of the Mound."

"That's interesting... What is marlstone, exactly?"

"They used to use it in churches and important buildings. It comes out wet and soft so they can carve it for fancy pieces. Once the air gets to the stuff, it goes hard. But mostly it went to improve the soil."

"You seem to know so much about Lady Holme, you should write a book."

"Who, me?" She laughed at the thought. "What an idea! But old Lord Hazlett had a history of the place printed about fifty years ago. There are copies in the library. I'll show you when we get a moment."

"That would be lovely."

"'Course, the real business of the Hazlett family has always been salt. They had two salt pans here, going right back to the Domesday Book, but they closed them. After that, they had salterns between Lymington and Hurst. It was a prosperous business for many years. Then they were involved in foreign salt... Shipped it all over the world."

A voice boomed from the far end of the table.

"That's private, family business," said Isembard. "Not something to be aired at the table."

"Mr Isembard, this is all public knowledge," answered Mrs WIlliams. "Why, every child of ten in Lymington knows of the salterns and the Hazletts."

"Nevertheless, these here London maids don't need to be told about the family's affairs."

"Oh, that *is* a pity," said Sophie, turning her sincerest expression upon Mr Isembard. "I was going to ask next about the ghosts. I'm very interested in them."

The table fell markedly silent. Isembard grinned back at her.

Mrs Williams said in a quiet voice, "We don't talk of such things."

"Very good, Mrs Williams," said Sophie.

"There be ghosts all right," said Daniel. "Aren't there, Mr Isembard?"

"Oh, yes. There be ghosts." The butler had a thin, unpleasant smile.

"A lot of strange things happen when they walk at night," said Daniel. He was almost laughing and kept glancing towards Isembard for confirmation. "People can die of fright," he continued, but this time he looked at Sophie.

"I wouldn't," said Sophie, remembering something Dora had said. "I think ghosts might be lonely. I'd like to talk to them."

Daniel's smile faltered. "You what?"

"Eat your food and do the job you're paid to do," said Isembard to Sophie.

"Very good food it is, too. Mrs Chiverton makes excellent pastry." Sophie addressed Mrs Williams.

"Yes, she does, Phoebe. You should tell her so, yourself. But do so after lunch has been served to the family."

Richard Smythe had been in the company of others for an hour, but now he rode Toffee, a brown five-year-old, along a less-frequented track beneath Marley Mound. This track lay among brush and trees and its course skirted the sea. The turbid water lay fifteen feet below where the tide, now just beginning to ebb, lapped at the piled bank of pebbles it had cast up over the years. At low tide when the water went out, flats appeared while the sea receded a distance of some two hundred yards.

Riders met riders and formed different groups or pairings - all of them, at some point, riding to the top of Marley Mound. Richard decided he would rejoin them later. First, he thought he would examine the coast on the off-chance of discovering something interesting, such as a landing place or a bay or something to further his knowledge of the smugglers. He hoped they had left traces of their activity, or that a land-form or feature would present itself as worthy of closer inspection.

He was in no hurry as the horse picked its way carefully along the narrow track, avoiding roots and large rocks embedded in the ground. Richard gazed across the Solent to the island and then along the shore. Nothing he saw met his expectations. He rounded an extensive but stunted clump of blackthorn full of ripening sloes. On the further side, he found the track ahead overgrown. He had to turn back. Being hemmed in, he dismounted Toffee to turn the horse around. As he did so, he heard slow hoof-beats beyond the blackthorn.

"There's no way through," called Richard to the unseen rider.

The hoof-beats came to a stop. Richard led Toffee around the bushes and saw who it was.

"Oh, hello," said Richard.

The rider on the horse stepped forward.

"What are you doing?" asked Richard irritably.

He was being crowded. Something struck him on the head. He fell down senseless. Toffee backed away, free of restraint.

The rider dismounted and struck again at Richard as he lay on the ground before pulling his body to the bank and rolling him into the sea below. The tide struggled to lift Richard, but a larger wave pulled him free of the surf for the sea to claim.

Maria Smythe allowed herself sufficient time to take Sheba for a good long walk and be back for lunch at one. The border collie believed she was in heaven. She wasted no time in following the rich and interesting profusion of tracks left by so many dogs and horses. Although Sheba darted this way and that, she remained close to Maria at all times. They walked and walked. Maria hummed to herself, her coat open, hands in pockets, and a lead draped around her neck. She tried whistling — something she had not done for years. Maria had never been good at whistling. Now, she thought, if she practised enough, she might whistle commands to Sheba. The dog cared little for Maria's efforts as the young woman struggled before admitting defeat. She could not make a tuneful note of any strength.

Instead, Sheba brought Maria a good throwing stick. So they progressed down to the sea in the sweet air of a gentle breeze — the stick flying forward — the dog bringing it back. At the coastline, Maria stopped to take in the view. She sighed deeply with pleasure and began counting the red-sailed fishing smacks and white-sailed yachts. In the distance were larger vessels, but none of any great size.

As she looked, she saw two riders atop Marley Mound. They were unrecognizable dots in the distance. Along the shore path, coming towards her, she saw a galloping horse. She continued to watch because something struck her as odd. It was moving fast, but somewhat erratically. It came closer, and Maria realized the horse was riderless.

"Oh, dear, Sheba. Someone has fallen off their horse... Come, Sheba... Heel." She hurriedly put the dog on its leash. They hid behind a nearby tree to keep out of the path of the oncoming horse.

The bolting animal soon raced past — foam-flecked and wild-eyed — its hooves thumping hard on the turf. It barely slowed when turning up the grass path leading to the stables.

Already unnerved by the fierceness of the sight, Maria gaped as she realized this was the same erstwhile, placid animal she had watched her husband mount two hours earlier. "Richard?" She could not believe it. "Richard... Richard!" Louder and louder she shouted. She started running with Sheba in the direction from where the horse had come. Repeatedly calling her husband's name, Maria ran until her mouth was parched and she stumbled.

Ronald saw the riderless horse approaching. "Davey, get me a lunge line and cavesson!" he shouted to a stable boy as the groom began walking, arms spread wide, cap in hand, to block the horse's path. Another groom, recognizing what was happening, did the same. Maude hurried from the stable to join the men.

Toffee slowed upon entering the stable yard as the three formed a loose semi-circle in front of him.

"Not too close, anyone," said Ronald. "Leave him to me." He took a step forward towards the distressed, hard-breathing horse with heaving flanks and frightened eyes.

"Toffee." Ronald began speaking in a low, soothing tone. "You're home now... Nothing to fear... You're home... Toffee, it's me... your old friend, Ronald." The groom started making a soft clicking sound. "You're safe... Don't be frightened... No one's going to hurt you." He clicked again and inched forward. "Can I hold your rein? Let me hold your rein and everything will be fine... There, old boy, it's me, Ronald, your friend." He reached slowly for the rein, gripped it hard but without pulling.

"There, there... You're in a muck sweat... You'll soon be nice and clean... It's all over..." He tentatively stroked the horse, then addressed the stable boy standing behind him. "Pass me the line slowly and fetch a bucket of water."

The horse nervously shivered and twitched - exhausted but ready to bolt, even as he responded to the groom's touch. Ronald slowly attached the cavesson and adjusted the bridle, moving the reins out of the way. He stepped back when the horse was secure.

"There you are, Toffee, you're among friends. Got some scratches, I see. We'll put those to rights." He clicked more authoritatively and snapped the line gently. The horse hesitated before walking in a slow, small circle. Ronald kept talking, giving hand signals, and encouraging the horse as they turned together.

It would take time to restore Toffee's equanimity. When Ronald felt the horse was in a less fractious state, he relinquished control of the line to the other groom. He spoke to Maude, who had just mounted her own horse.

"Toffee has seen blood, miss. That's what's upset him. Something terrible has happened."

"Richard Smythe was riding Toffee." Her horse was turning, made restive in the tense atmosphere. "I'm going to look for him. I'll press-gang anyone I meet. When riders return to the stables, send them straight back out. If you see Dr Beaton, tell him to get his tackle from his car."

"Understood, miss. I'll organize a search party here and inform the house."

"Good man." Maude had barely uttered the words before she galloped from the stable yard.

Chapter 13

The day darkens

Lady Jane Hazlett could not run the house as usual in the face of such extraordinary demands. The lunch was converted to a buffet, and a commissary established in a hastily erected tent. Tea was brewed by the gallon, food was laid out for the search parties, and supplies brought from Lymington to feed the extra mouths.

The grounds of Lady Holme were being searched continuously by riders in pairs. Neighbours came in to help. A line of beaters, organized by Ronald and made up of farmhands, gardeners and servants, scoured section after section of the open country. The police arrived and wrested control of the proceedings from Ronald. They searched methodically, extensively and repeatedly, but could discover no trace of Richard Smythe.

Dr Beaton insisted the exhausted and nerve-wracked Maria Smythe go to bed. A nurse from Lymington arrived to take care of her. She arrived in the ambulance that now awaited Richard Smythe.

The secret agents gathered for an impromptu meeting in the servants' quarters because of Richard Smythe's disappearance. Their first order of business was Sophie giving the newly discovered details of Lord Hazlett's seclusion.

Sophie looked at each of them as she asked her question. "Who is keeping Lord Hazlett under observation on behalf of tPWoP?"

"Isembard," said Flora.

"Oh, yes, definitely 'im," said Ada.

"He's not very nice," said Fern.

"I suspect him, too, so that makes it unanimous," said Sophie. "But we must keep an open mind. There may be other observers."

"What are we to do about this dreadful situation with Mr Smythe?" asked Flora.

"As servants, whatever we are told," replied Sophie. "Let us each state what we believe has happened to him. I suspect he was assaulted. If Mr Smythe fell off his horse, he would lie by the side of the track, whether injured or dead. He wouldn't crawl away and hide. He's been missing for over three hours now with a hundred people looking for him. Surely, he would have been found by this time?"

"He might have got lost and his horse might have run away," responded Flora. "Or does it all mean we have a murderer in the house?"

"Possibly... Though it's just as likely Mr Smythe may have fallen into a rock crevice. I wish we had something definite to go on."

"Maybe the fraudists done him in," said Fern.

"Again, possibly... We're calling them smugglers now, Dora, because we've found out more about them - but they're still fraudists at heart. I think calling them that will be easier for us all."

"Yes, Phoebe. I think smugglers sound more romantic, but not if they're murderers."

"It still could be an accident," said Ada.

"Yes," said Sophie. "We're guessing at present. I wish we knew what the police make of it."

"There might be a way of finding out," said Ada. "When sitting quiet in the Chapel, I could hear the coppers talking next door. I tried it for a minute when they first started poking about in the house."

"Which side of the Chapel?" asked Sophie.

"Not the Pannetry wall, the other one."

"That's the Armoury," said Flora. "It contains bits of armour, pikes, muskets, and more modern weapons, too."

"How did you discover that?" asked Sophie. "The door is always closed."

"Ah, yes. You must be careful around Mr David Rand-Sayers. The Armoury door was open, and he was inside, looking at the displays. As I passed by, he saw me and called me in, and then shut the door. I turned to see why, and it became apparent he was about to make a fool of himself. He had this species of grinning idiot smile as though he had hit upon a perfectly brilliant romantic idea, when, in fact, he was about to be sordid and irritating. I marched out again before I made a scene. Mind you, I could have stayed and picked up a sword."

"Hat pin time," said Ada, "although a sword would be even better."

"To get the point across," said Flora. They laughed.

"What do you mean?" asked Fern.

"To scare off them who want a cuddle and more," said Ada.

"Oh, them silly beggars. They're not all like that, though. Have you seen that lovely looking man?"

They all shook their heads.

"He must be in films. It's the way he moves about... like a Greek god."

"I shall keep an eye out for this phenomenon," said Flora.

"Let's return to the police," said Sophie. "If they use the Armoury for interviews, we could take turns at listening... I'm not sure that will prove satisfactory... Also, there's the matter of the Chapel being consecrated ground. Does anyone know if it has been consecrated?"

They all shook their heads.

"Oh."

"If we're praying," said Ada, "and we just happen to hear what's going on next door, wouldn't that be all right?"

"We can fool people, but we can't fool God."

"No, I suppose we can't," said Ada.

"Perhaps God would approve or, at least, not mind?" suggested Flora. "Considering the circumstances."

"Well, he might approve... Ask first before listening. That's the polite thing to do," concluded Sophie.

"Very good," said Fern.

"This reminds me, there are some strange acoustics in this house. While in the attics, I stood at the top of the Great Hall staircase, and I could clearly hear Daniel speaking to someone at the front door."

"It is funny, isn't it?" said Fern. "Early this morning, I was in the Drawing Room cleaning and I heard you and Nancy whispering in the School Room."

"My goodness, we must be careful. I hope no one is listening now..." Sophie lowered her voice. "Right, this is what we shall do. Nancy, when you can, continue following Lord Hazlett and find out what he knows. He's bound to have to explain the situation to others. Gladys, question the police. Find out what they make of the disappearance. Dora, keep close to Mrs Williams and get her opinions on what has happened, but don't overdo it. If she won't talk, leave her be. As for Isembard, we'll keep him under surveillance. It wouldn't surprise me if he turns even more peculiar after today's events."

They stared back at Sophie expectantly.

"Yes, Phoebe?" asked Flora.

"Of course you want to know what I'm doing. I'm going to Marley Mound to find out how the search is progressing. I'll leave by the back door and go past the farm. Then I'll be safe under the trees. Should anyone want me while I'm gone, be vague as to my whereabouts. If you can, cover any work for me. I will be gone for about an hour."

"What if someone catches you?" asked Fern.

"I'll say I'm searching for Mr Smythe, which is true in a sense."

They separated, with Sophie going to get her hat and coat.

The walk was pleasant. The small dairy farm she passed was pretty, with its ancient cottage and barns. This was obviously the home farm Mrs Williams had mentioned earlier. As she walked along the lane, a friendly Guernsey cow followed her on the other side of the fence. Sophie stopped and bent down to pull a tuft of juicy grass to give to the cow. The cow crunched the offering. Continuing on past gorse bushes, she heard the fast chirruping song of a warbler before entering a wooded area of ash and beech trees. In the shade, and to one side of the path, a low uniform understory of brown ferns suggested a vast palliasse of moderate lumpiness.

For half a mile, as she headed south along the shady forest path, Sophie did not meet another person. As she approached a crossroads, a policeman on a bicycle came towards her along the western track. He stopped.

"Good arternoon, miss. We're looking for a gentleman who's gone missing. Did you pass anyone?"

"No, I didn't. I'm searching for Mr Smythe. Are you?"

"Yes, I am. Does that track lead to the farm?"

"It does, but there's no sign of him."

"Ah. I'll take the east track, then. Where are you going?"

"To Marley Mound. Is this the right way?"

"So it be, if you stay on that path. I best be moving along. Good hunting, miss." The policeman set off.

The track rose, the trees gave way to bushes, and the bright sky dappled the path through the thinning canopy. She emerged into open grassland, studded with gorse and with very few trees. The incline became steeper and the curving dome of the mound lay crisp against the sky. A small clump of trees grew on its flatter apex. On her left, Sophie noticed a great wedge-shaped depression which tapered towards the top of the hill. This proved to be full of whitish boulders, patches of grass, and a few bushes thriving among the debris. She realized this feature had resulted from the collapsing marlstone mine. The disused galleries beneath had caved in and brought down the land above it. Since then, nature had been healing the man-made wound.

Sophie gained the top, and the glory of the land about her struck her forcibly. From below, glinting lights reflected from the rippling Solent which was dotted with small vessels. The great arch of heaven above her produced a sense of exultant freedom. An uninterrupted view presented the whole countryside — the great swathe of Lady Holme's pale grassland; the encircling forests of warm browns and dark greens; and the New Forest to the north. She gazed towards Lady Holme — she of the intricate black-and-white pattern and many roofs, chimneys, and windows. The distance turned her into a little grey cottage — a sweet doll's house of a place. No matter where Sophie looked, no area presented itself above another as a spot suitable to search for a missing man.

She turned towards the sea and noticed a collection of small vessels congregated at the edge of the flats, where surf and sand met. The biggest was a fishing smack — its red sails furled. It stood off from the shore in deeper water. A launch was between it and the surf. Two rowing boats lay very close to the water's edge. At first, she could not determine what they were doing. They worked at something in the water between them. At last, she sadly came to the realization that they had found Richard Smythe and were hoisting his body into a boat. She looked away.

Sophie more carefully scanned the landscape. She picked out a rider coming up from the shore. He approached a man who was part of a beater's line. They conversed. She heard a shout, or imagined she had. The line of beaters stopped, slowly turned about, and gave up their work. The wind gusted, and she shivered on the exposed hill.

Sophie had gone to Marley Mound for two reasons. The first, to assist in finding the missing man or, at least, discover how it was possible for him to have disappeared. Her second purpose was to seek out landing sites suitable for smugglers to use. At the start, she had carried a slowly fading hope for Richard Smythe's return. Knowing he had drowned, that hope had been taken from her. Earlier, she had seen him and his wife, Maria. Sophie thought of her. The news Maria was about to receive would be devastating.

An eastern path seemed to her the most promising choice. The track descended and soon narrowed into an area of tall bushes and short trees. Horse droppings told her that riders had passed by recently. She stopped when she met with a wider north-south trail, which was annoying because she could not see what lay ahead to the east.

She pushed through an overgrown gap between tall bushes and came close to dying. Her foot slipped and she clung on to branches. Immediately before her was a steep slope of loose rocks leading to a cliff with a fifty-foot drop. Another step and she would have fallen. Sophie watched with horror as pebbles slithered and rolled off the edge. It was a near miss that made her catch her breath. She calmed her beating heart, and, once restored, took stock of the view. A name came to mind from what she saw.

Sophie thought of it as Smuggler's Cove. There were no smugglers in sight. It was more an elongated trench than cove-like, and the sheltered river-mouth was not picturesque. At its northern end, it disappeared into a swamp. However, the navigable stretch was serviceable — that was the main thing. Opposite and lower was an unremarkable headland — perhaps half the height of Marley Mound. Between the two lay a channel. She could not see the water immediately below her, but a little further inshore was a narrow lagoon wide enough for a twenty-foot boat to navigate and she assumed the lagoon was tidal. This meant a vessel coming in on a tide could tie up somewhere without scraping the bottom. She knew the Solent to have ten-foot tides — double tides at that, which meant this channel would frequently fill with an extra three or four feet of water. Beyond a doubt, she must come back to investigate further, but, for now, she needed to return to the house before anyone noticed her absence. She smoothed her coat, straightened her hat, and marched back.

"Miss King, where did you go? I've been looking for you."

The housekeeper had caught Sophie upon her return.

"Ah, Mrs Williams, I've finished my tasks. As I had time, I went to see how the search was going. I'm very sorry to have inconvenienced you..."

They looked at each other. Mrs Williams saw Sophie had made a discovery.

"It's bad news, I'm afraid," said Sophie.

"Is it? Oh, dear me. What has happened?"

"They had boats out. They've recovered Mr Smythe's body from the sea."

"God preserve us...! That poor woman upstairs."

"Indeed, it is dreadfully sad. My heart goes out to her... What would you like me to do?"

"Yes. Her ladyship wants to have the dinner as planned. Mrs Chiverton is run off her feet with the changes to lunch, the dinner, and providing for the volunteers. See what help you can give her. She's in the tent."

"At once, Mrs Williams."

Sophie followed the path around the walled garden. She considered the likelihood of Mr Smythe's drowning being an accident. There was nothing else it could be, surely, although it seemed to her a very odd notion — to fall off a horse and into the sea. What a *freak* accident! It also occurred to her that this was the second drowning death connected with Lady Holme — a groom, years ago, and now a young lawyer. She suddenly remembered what Archie had told her. He had not stated a name, but mentioned a young, local lawyer complaining of lorries in the night. The situation at once became pregnant with possibilities.

She walked with too much conjecture and too few facts racketing about in her mind. Sophie rounded the corner but immediately stepped back out of sight. There was someone in the stable yard whom she recognized. He definitely had to be Fern's lovely man, for he was handsome and wore his expensive riding clothes with great poise. He was also the suave gentleman Sophie had followed in the De Vere Square gambling house - the man who had entered the drug dispensary unaccompanied. This man might recognize her. She was unsure what she should do next.

Considering the matter, she reasoned that Burgoyne's Agency had been legitimately hired to provide service at the gambling house. That the man's matchbook had started a sequence of events leading to Lady Holme was a fact of which he was totally unaware. However, should he remember her being at De Vere Square, he might suspect he was being followed, even though he should neither know of the police presence at De Vere Square, nor be aware of Burgoyne's connection. Everything should be all right, she assured herself. What and who was he, though? Why was he here? Sophie knew already that he somehow had connections to gambling and drugs. Why not smuggling, also? She concluded he was bound to see her about the house eventually, so she might as well grit her teeth and get it over with.

In attempting to walk normally within the man's field of vision, Sophie's self-consciousness insisted she possessed two left feet, wobbled, blushed, and that the man knew her thoughts, having recognized her immediately. He was talking to Vanessa Scrope. Perhaps he had not seen her. She reached the safety of the tent, feeling flushed and hot.

Sophie became a barmaid. She served beer or cider to the men returning from the search. Servants brought jugs of ale filled from barrels in the cellars. Within the tent, a strong smell of beer and old canvas had established itself. As always, the pouring of beer was a delicate matter. Some liked a head on their ale and some liked it flat. She asked before pouring. When there was a lull in demand, she made inquiries.

"He wor' drowned in the sea," said a young man named Tom who, more than willing to give his opinion, was doing so with elaborate gestures. "Head bashed in, an' all."

"He must have hit against a rock," suggested Sophie.

"T'weren't that. Proper bashed in. T'ain't no rocks to speak of on that stretch of shore."

"Where did they find him?"

"Below Marley Mound. I was there afore they took him by boat to Lymington. His corpus was stuck in the mud a hundred yards out and his head didn't look right... Next tide would 'ave sucked him out to sea."

"Would you like more beer?"

"I won't say no, thank 'ee."

Sophie half-filled his tankard.

"Are you saying it wasn't an accident?"

"I don't know about that... I'm not saying it wor' deliberate, neither. No, I wouldn't go that far. But I think it needs investigatin'... Maybe the hoss... Ah, now that's possible... It might ha' been the hoss. He fell, the hoss struck him mightily with his hooves... You mark my words, that's what happened... Good beer, this. Got a drap more in your little jug?"

"A tiny one. Others are coming and they'll be thirsty, too."

A group of men approached the tent.

"Ah, they look fine to me, lass," said Tom, "whereas I worked perishing 'ard and I'm right parched."

"No. You're not parched. You've had plenty to slake your thirst!"

"Can't blame me for tryin'."

Lord Hazlett dismounted in the stable yard and plodded to the office, deep in thought. He found Lady Jane there, sitting, staring out of the window.

"James? What has happened?"

"I'm very sorry, my dear. It's bad news, I'm afraid."

She caught her breath. "What...? Tell me."

"They found Smythe on the edge of the beach... His, ah, his body had become entangled in some old rope or the tide would have swept him away."

"He drowned, then? How is that possible? What could he have been doing?"

"The police don't think he drowned. He had head wounds... They think Smythe was already dead before he fell into the sea, but they won't know for certain until the medical examiner has performed an autopsy. They've taken him by boat to King Edward Hospital. It was easier than bringing him to shore. The ambulance has gone ahead to meet them at the pier. "

"I don't understand. What are you saying?"

"They took him away by boat. The sergeant who informed me was very cautious, but he left me in little doubt that they suspect foul play."

"You *cannot* be suggesting murder?"

"I don't know. I suppose I am. They haven't said as much. But they're going over the Armoury."

"What could interest them in the Armoury? This is intolerable."

"We must be patient while they examine the matter. An inspector will arrive soon. Let us hope it's all a misunderstanding. However, there's no escaping the fact that Richard Smythe is dead."

"This is truly dreadful... I suppose I must speak to Maria Smythe. I can't imagine how she will take the news."

"He's dead, isn't he?"

Maria Smythe's words came quick as she lay on the bed in her room. The drawn curtains produced a low light in which her face appeared white and pinched. She was anxious, nervous, yet there lay a driving force behind her words demanding she be told the worst.

"I'm afraid so," said Lady Jane. "Leave us for a moment."

The nurse left the room. When she had gone, her ladyship approached the bed.

"What happened?" demanded Maria. She was dry-eyed and staring fiercely.

"They are not completely sure. The only certain part is your husband hit his head and somehow tumbled into the sea. I'm terribly sorry that this tragedy has occurred."

"Dead... I told him we shouldn't come... I felt odd about it... Where's Sheba?"

"In the kennels."

"May I have her in here, please? She's an excellent dog. She won't lie on the bed."

To Lady Jane's ear, the childish request was unusual — something she would not have allowed for her own children during sickness. However, she could plainly see Maria's strained and exhausted state.

"I don't see why not. I'll have someone bring your dog to you."

"Thank you."

"Is there anything else I can do? Anything you need?"

"I don't know... I don't think so."

"It is probably best to rest, my dear. Try to sleep. The nurse will stay tonight."

Maria understood that Lady Jane had done her duty by visiting and now wished to leave.

"Thank you, your ladyship."

"Ah, please, don't mention it. These sad trials come upon us all. I wish I could lighten the burden for you."

She smiled faintly, but with compassion, then left the room.

As the enormity of Richard Smythe's death fully sank in — it was being referred to as an accident — the inhabitants' behaviour became more muted. The staff had received a severe shock and was now discharging its duties in silent distraction. The visitors and family were quiet but tried to carry on as though nothing had happened. All thought of riding ceased. Most of them had gathered in the School Room.

It was now late afternoon; several still wore riding clothes, but most had changed. They talked in small groups.

"What I don't understand is where did he fall in...? Does anyone know?" Maude raised her voice. Having failed to find a satisfactory answer in her immediate group, she hoped to get a response from someone else in the room.

"The consensus among those that found him," replied Basil Hazlett, "is that he fell from the path below Marley Mound."

"That's all overgrown and doesn't lead anywhere. Hasn't done for years, since the sea washed out the path," she replied.

"I'm afraid Richard must not have realized such was the case. Has he been riding here before?"

"Not that I can recall."

"Then he was probably trying to get through, and met with an accident."

"We're calling it an accident," said Oscar Reid, "but is it? If it is, the police are making more of this incident than they need to. To be frank, they're acting as though a crime has been committed."

"Of course, it's an accident," said his wife, Constance. "A bizarre and upsetting accident that probably needn't have happened if he'd only kept to the proper paths."

"I'm only making an observation, Constance. Answer me this: why are the police still in the house? And why such interest in the Armoury?"

"They had to be put somewhere so they could ask their questions."

"Shall I take a peek and see what they're up to?" suggested Adrian Benson.

"Good idea," said Vanessa. "Bring us back a full report."

Adrian put down his cup and saucer. "I shall spy out the land."

When he had left the room, Reginald Hazlett said,

"Should he be bothering the police when they're busy?"

"Why not?" asked Constance sharply. "If they're making an unnecessary fuss, the sooner we find out, the sooner we can get rid of them. He's doing us all a service."

Martin Scrope entered the room.

"Any news, sir?" asked David Rand-Sayers.

"Ah, yes there is, David. An Inspector Talford arrived a short time ago. The interesting thing is, he's a plain-clothes man. A detective. You know what that means, don't you?" The MP for Portsmouth East nodded significantly, as though addressing a crowd of five hundred to intensify their expectation of his answer. Constance obliged him.

"What does it mean?"

"It means the police are suspicious concerning poor Smythe's death. A very bad business all round. Life is so fleeting and precious... They have sent an inspector because they're not happy with ruling the incident as a mere accident. You can take it from me, the police are searching for something in the Armoury connected with the death of Smythe. God rest his soul..."

Martin was on the point of continuing when Adrian returned.

"We're in the soup now," said Adrian. "I saw they had the whole place dusted for fingerprints before they asked me to leave."

Ada carried a tray over to Martin Scrope. He took a cup of tea and stirred in milk and sugar. "Yes, as I was saying, and as Mr Benson has now confirmed, I fear a police inquiry is already under way. It reminds me of a situation I had to endure some years ago..." Martin Scrope reminisced at length because either he had not noticed the warning glance from Helen, his wife, or he had ignored it.

Chapter 14

A Question of Suspects

The Armoury was reached by a short separate corridor near the front of the house. This corridor ended at the main entrance to the Chapel - great wooden doors that were always kept locked, there being another smaller door elsewhere to use. The Armoury was situated to the left and was a plain and narrow room — some twenty-five-feet long. It had a sturdy door at one end and a barred window at the other. The left wall was decorated with muskets from different eras and countries, ranging from a plain Brown Bess to an elaborate Ottoman miquelet, heavily decorated with mother-of-pearl, gemstones, silver, and gold. Beneath the muskets were several glass cabinets crammed with flintlock pistols and daggers. A suit of armour stood in a corner by the window.

The crowded wall on the right disappeared behind many ancient banners, lances, spears, and shields. Standing on the floor, tall racks supported sheaves of upright halberds, spears, and pikes, while shorter racks held swords, axes, and maces. Some of these items pre-dated the building of Lady Holme.

The maces ranged in length from eighteen to thirty-six inches and had several styles of head. They all held one thing in common: they looked ugly and lethal. This Friday, however, they all possessed another commonality - every mace had traces of fingerprint powder on it.

By the window was an oak table. Upon sheets of newspaper on the table top lay a single mace and it, too, was covered in fine white powder. In the chair behind the table sat a Portsmouth CID man, Inspector Talford. He had a thin face, thinning hair, and was close to retirement. He looked like he wanted retirement to come early. In front of him stood a young, uniformed police constable — a Lymington man, named Collins. Another CID detective was examining some other weapons a few yards away.

"Collins, what possessed you to cover everything in powder?"

"When I observed the body, sir, I said to myself, Hello, he's been murdered. I examined the wounds and, straightaway, I remembered Lord Hazlett's old collection of weapons. So, then..."

"Hold on. Are you even trained in collecting fingerprints?"

"In a manner of speaking, sir, yes. I taught meself until I was..."

"You mean you're not trained? You aren't professionally trained, whereas I am. Detective Clark, here, is a bloody expert while you, sonny, are an amateur. A meddling amateur who's overstepped the mark."

"Sorry, sir. Won't happen again, loike."

"No, it won't."

"But that there's the murder weapon, right enough, sir."

"Let's hope it is for your sake. Now buzz off. Keep out of my way unless I ask you to do something. You behave yourself, and maybe, just maybe, it won't go any further. Dismissed."

"Thank you, sir." Constable Collins left the room. They watched him shut the door behind himself. The detectives looked at each other.

"Enthusiastic blighter," said Talford.

"He did a nice job," said Detective Clark.

"I'm not saying he didn't. He's saved us work, but I'm not allowing these young upstarts to do what they want. Self-taught... he probably fingerprinted his mum, dad, and the neighbour's cat."

"Likely, he did."

"Right. Here's the mace with four fins. Is that what they're called?"

"Flanges. There are books over there describing these types of weapons."

Inspector Talford amended his notes. "Flanges... Weighs about two pounds, twenty-one inches long, has a residue of fresh blood on the head. Someone tried washing it off but missed some. And the handle's wiped clean of prints. But, our boy scout, who's after his forensic badge, found us a nice thumbprint on the shaft. It could be recent, too."

The inspector thought in silence. After some seconds, he whistled tunelessly.

"I hate this, Clark. We must fingerprint the lot of them. Have we got enough cards with us?"

"It crossed my mind, so I checked. Thirty-seven."

"May not be enough with the servants. Ask Collins if he's got any spares. We'll get a list of who's in the house. First thing, though, nobody leaves the estate."

"Yes, sir."

"They won't take kindly to the request coming from me, so I'll ring up Major Warde. He'll be able to handle these people."

The searchers from outside the estate had gone home, and men were folding up the tent. It was five o'clock. Sophie took a bucket of scraps away from the area, going around the back to get to the rubbish heaps near the greenhouses.

She recalled what Ronald had said about Toffee.

"That horse doesn't have it in him to do harm. He's as sweet-natured as they come."

For her, Ronald's opinion settled the matter. The horse did not strike Richard Smythe. As she emptied the bucket behind a tall wooden fence, she heard a youthful voice on the other side.

"Oh, fiddle-faddle!"

"Who's there?" asked Sophie.

"It's me, Nelly. Be that you, Miss King?"

"Yes, it is. What are you doing?"

"Mrs Trout, the laundress, sent me to see if the sheets were dry. And they are, but I can't manage by mesel'."

"I'll come and help after I've washed my hands."

"Will you...? I'll wait."

Sophie went to a pump and got the water flowing.

"That water's cold," she said as she came around the fence, drying her hands on her apron.

"That's nice of you to help me fold," said Nelly.

"It's easier with two. I'm surprised Mabel's not here to help."

"She's washing up... What a busy old day it's been... That poor gentleman."

"Yes, it's very, very sad."

"I was shocked when I heard, but now I don't know what to think. Some say one thing and some another. What happened to him?"

"All I can tell you for certain is they took him from the sea."

"That seems silly. You can't drown when you're on a horse. I suppose he fell off."

"Yes. There are a lot of sheets here."

"Ah. Mrs Williams thought more would be staying, what with the police an' all. These were kept in a big press, but she said they were musty. They had to be rewashed, and that put Mrs Trout in a right tizzy."

"Because of their having to be washed again without being used? Yes, I can see how that would annoy her... Tell me something. Why is the subject of ghosts forbidden at table?"

"Well you might ask! It's Mrs Williams, really. She kicks up an awful fuss when the men talk about it."

"Does she?"

"Oh, yes. It's about Lady Holme hersel', you see."

"How do you mean?"

"Mrs Williams has all the history of the family. She's looked in the books for it. But the men, they've the story from the taverns. Mrs Williams says there's never been one sensible word ever spoken in a tavern since they built the first one. She reckons Cain built it arter he went into the land of Nod."

Sophie smiled. "Mrs Williams could be right. What are the two stories, then?"

"Well, they take some tellin' and we're nearly finished. Can I tell you tonight?"

"That would be lovely. I'm sure Nancy, Gladys, and Dora would very much like to hear them, too."

Mr and Mrs Scrope had gone upstairs to change for dinner.

"This is outrageous. I shall speak to Chief Constable Warde," said Martin.

"Don't let your outrage spoil your dinner. Mrs Chiverton is a superb cook."

"It is the principle of the thing, my dear. While I'm quite ready to assist the police over the weekend, I find it intolerable to be told by that man Talford that we have to stay until the matter is settled. Heaven knows how long that will take."

"There's no law keeping you here," said Helen.

"Oh, yes, there is. There's the unwritten law of doing the decent thing amongst one's peers. Once one has been asked to stay, it would look frightful to insist upon leaving."

"We were staying until Monday, anyway. They'll probably have finished by then."

"You do not seem to grasp the gravity of the situation. That little bounder suspects one of us."

"Why wouldn't he? I know I would."

"What a thing to say. I can't believe you said it."

"Can't you, Martin? Now you have something interesting to put in your diary for today. Are you ever going to publish your memoirs?"

"Of course, I am. As soon as I've won the next election."

"Then I sincerely hope the electorate facilitates you in the matter. Pass me my shoes, dear. They're in the wardrobe behind you."

"Shoes... Which ones?"

"The black ones."

"What, these?" He held them up. Helen nodded. "We're getting away from the main point," he continued as he brought the shoes to his wife. "I'm absolutely innocent and the police are infringing upon my rights — all our rights."

"You're usually pro-police, aren't you?"

"Of course, I am. But in this instance, they've gone too far with their insinuations."

Helen looked at him. "Why are you taking this so personally?"

"I'm not. As I've already said, it's the principal I'm defending."

"Defend all you want but, please, do so quietly. We're not at home and other guests may take your blustering as a sign of domestic instability."

"Helen, I do not bluster."

"That's good. Then stop doing it now."

"I say, Beaton. What do you make of this show?" Colonel Digby, having dressed for dinner, was in the School Room.

"It's too early for me to say. After dinner, I'll telephone the hospital and find out what I can. They must have finished the autopsy by now."

"Yes, that would be a help. Police are obviously acting as though Smythe was murdered."

"So, it seems."

"You know what I've been thinking? They'll question us to find out who saw him last. When they've established the time of death, whoever was with him closest to the time will become their prime suspect."

"They will be more thorough than that. At least, I hope so. I'm sure Inspector Talford knows what he's doing. But I must correct you on something, Colonel. The autopsy will suggest only a time-range. Smythe was in cool water on a warm day which would retard or advance the effects of various processes, such as rigor mortis."

"Ah, how much of a range?"

"Two hours or so."

"That doesn't help much. We could do better amongst ourselves."

"Perhaps, but we don't possess the entire picture, whereas the police soon will."

"Well, I don't know. My idea was to discuss the matter privately to discover if we could come up with something."

"What are you suggesting? We find a suspect without an alibi and hand him over?"

"No, of course not. I simply believe we can cut down police involvement by airing the matter between us."

"It might work. Though it would be hard upon anyone who is innocent but who doesn't happen to have an alibi. Without meaning to, we would all condemn him."

"I agree there's a risk. But there's also a guilty party among us. By stating where we went riding and who we were with, it will narrow the field to just a few. I'd feel better if we did that."

"The situation is best left to the professionals. You wouldn't want me telling you how to run your regiment. I would not appreciate you advising me how to deliver a baby. By the same token, the police will not want our help in their investigation."

"You're right, of course. Mind you, I suppose if we're forced to stay a week, it couldn't be in a lovelier place than Lady Holme."

"I doubt they'll take that long."

"You never know. Martin Scrope has a low opinion of Inspector Talford. He's going to call the chief constable... Poor fellow."

"Phoebe," whispered Flora from the doorway. She had found Sophie in the Alcove of Great Hall. Sophie stopped what she was doing and came over.

"Just listen. Isembard's irritable and on the prowl, so we must be careful. The police have found the murder weapon. A mace was used to kill Mr Smythe."

"Good Heavens."

"Shh. But, yes, and that's not all. Everyone's staying here until further notice while the police investigate everything and everyone. They're going to be taking our fingerprints... Isn't it exciting? I feel like a criminal. Last item, some guests are cutting up rough about it. That's all for now. See you later."

"Before you go, Gladys," whispered Sophie, "Nelly has ghost stories to tell about Lady Holme. We'll hear them tonight."

"Ooh, how lovely! Must go."

After she had gone, Sophie returned to her task of setting the table. She considered what she had heard, realizing that a person had taken a mace from the Armoury, killed Richard Smythe with it, and then put it back afterwards. *That*, she thought, *was an extraordinarily peculiar thing to do.*

"So, that's that," said Inspector Talford. He had replaced the receiver.

"What did he say?" asked Clark.

"Cause of death was by a heavy metal object. Deceased was struck twice and died immediately. I suggested a mace. The doctor said it had to be something of the kind. If we bring the article to him, he'll have a better idea and might be able to confirm it's the murder weapon."

"So he was dead before he went in the water. Did he give a time, sir?"

"He was cautious. Said the death occurred between nine and one. That's hardly helpful. We know that already... What time are they sitting down to dinner?"

"Seven-thirty."

"In half an hour. The servants will be busy, so we can't interview them now."

"I asked the butler a few questions. Isembard's his name. A closed-mouthed gentleman he is. None of the staff wanted to stop working, except for one maid. Her name's Gladys Walton and she was most helpful. Took an interest in what we're doing. She and three others travelled from London. Apparently, they were hired out from Burgoyne's Agency. Gladys said it was one of London's foremost agencies for domestic servants, and I can quite believe it."

"Taken with her, were you?"

"Oh, no, sir, no," he said hurriedly. "It's just nice to meet people who are willing to assist us."

"Well, that's true enough. I've a bad feeling she'll be the only one who is helpful. We've got to handle them properly. Let them know we won't stand for any nonsense. We're here to do our duty and can't let them stop us. Upper classes... Always the same. Someone in that dining room will eat dinner as though nothing happened and yet they've killed a man... No port and cigars for that lot. We'll start interviewing right after they've eaten. The servants can wait until tomorrow."

Nineteen sat down to dinner in the panelled Alcove, within Great Hall. Maria Smythe remained in her room. The electric lights from Great Hall produced shade within the Alcove, so corner lamps were used. Four Georgian three-light candelabra on the table created warm pools of light and gave an intimate feel under the high ceiling and within the screens of dark brown wood. Occupying much of the room was a long table set with an old Minton dinner service in turquoise and gold. The immense tablecloth — pure white in daylight — became amber under the illumination. This combined effect of lamps and candles extended to the silver, turning it a pale gold, and warmed the appearance of the old crystal glasses. It went further, and gave a tanned look to those seated, while the candlelight caused jewels to glint with subtle gleams. Occasionally, eyes flashed and laughs sparkled. This effect usually made a dinner at Lady Holme appear more witty, more full of gaiety, but, under the current circumstances, these chance reflections of light from the diners' eyes seemed like glints of suspicion or insincerity or a fear of danger.

To start, the family and guests observed a silence. Then Lord Hazlett spoke briefly of the tragedy, careful to avoid characterizing it as anything more than an unhappy and regretful occurrence. The first course followed. Sophie, Flora, and Ada served the table along with Daniel, another footman, and a Lady Holme maid. They did so under the direction and critical scrutiny of the butler, Isembard.

As the dinner progressed, the mood became less constrained around the table. Several groups conversed. Seated at the middle of the table, two people had been silent for some time. Amelia Scrope sat next to Reginald Hazlett. While those on either side of them engaged with their other respective neighbours, Amelia and Reginald began talking to each other.

"I don't think I've seen you since the last time I was here," said Reginald. "That must be six months ago."

"That's correct... Odd, isn't it? At one time, we almost lived here. I used to feel quite embarrassed about our frequent visits. Father insisted we tag along, and Lord James was very pleasant about our staying. I always got the impression we were imposing ourselves upon you. The feeling got worse as I grew older."

"Did you think that? We never did. I don't believe it ever even crossed my mind. In fact, I was always glad you came."

"Oh, that's nice of you."

"What I meant is, you in particular."

"Me?"

"Yes, because I thought we had much in common."

"Oh, Reggie, how can you say that? I'm a socialist and you're... so very much not one."

"That's how it seems to you, but I beg to differ. I'm quite apolitical, so I don't mind hearing both sides to an argument. I think it must be satisfying to believe in a cause that one feels makes a difference. I only wish I had one."

"That's a way of looking at it... If you hadn't noticed, I'm also a vegetarian."

"I think that's admirable, living according to your convictions, as you are."

"You do?"

"Do I surprise you?"

"Ra-ther. I've known you for years and I don't ever remember your being so open about things. I had often wished you were."

"Perhaps my attitudes have changed... I could try being a vegetarian."

Amelia was about to say something when Colonel Digby burst out laughing close by, derailing her comment. She looked at Reginald as he ate. He was thirty and she twenty-six. Throughout the years, she could not recall their having much to do with each other. He had been older, remote, and interested in the pursuits of growing boys, while she had been quiet, withdrawing into her own world. Amelia was uncertain, but she believed her acquaintance of twenty years was taking a personal interest in her. She found it pleasing.

"We can talk after dinner," said Amelia.

"I look forward to it."

"What I'd like to know," asked Constance Reid, her voice carrying far down the table, "is what did Richard mean when he mentioned smuggling?"

She was sitting near her mother, Lady Jane. All other conversations at the table ceased except for the one Lord James was having with Martin Scrope. When his lordship looked up, someone repeated the question for him.

"I wish I knew, my dear," he replied. "Mr Smythe was convinced that passing traffic in the night constituted a smuggling ring. I think he was mistaken."

"Surely it bears investigation?" asked Basil Hazlett.

"Possibly," said Lord Hazlett.

"See here," said Martin Scrope. "We're all placed in an invidious position. I haven't liked to mention the subject at dinner, but as it's come up, what are we going to do about being detained?"

"I don't feel detained," said Helen, without looking at her husband.

"What we need to do is present a united front. Yes, we should give our statements and answer the questions the police put to us. But shall we also see our freedom impinged upon when forced to stay while they conduct their investigation? Who knows how long they will take? I suggest talking to the chief constable to see what can be arranged."

"It's hardly an imposition," said Lord Hazlett.

"No, no, it isn't. Not at the moment. But give these fellows an inch and they'll take a yard. I happen to know something the rest of you don't. Inspector Talford voted Labour in my ward last election."

"We mustn't hold that against him, dear," said Helen Scrope. "I nearly voted Labour myself."

This produced a great deal of laughter as Martin Scrope was a Conservative MP. He looked sharply at his wife but, upon realizing the rest of the table found her joke amusing, he gave way to laughter himself.

"Martin's got a point, though," said Colonel Digby. "You know they're going to fingerprint us after dinner?"

"Not with black ink?" asked Lady Jane.

"Afraid so. But it washes off, I'm sure."

"Wears off, more likely," said Maude.

"Ha, possibly that's true," said the Colonel.

"I'll have to wear gloves for my next robbery, or they'll know who I am," said the younger Scrope daughter, Vanessa.

"What is your speciality? Jewellery shops or banks?" asked Adrian Benson.

"Banks are the best. You must join me on my next raid. They're such fun."

They both laughed while Lady Jane, observing them, did not.

"That demonstrates my point," said Scrope, picking up his theme once more. "Have they spoken to us? Did they introduce themselves? No, in both instances. But all at once, they must fingerprint me, and I'm to wait upon the pleasure of a police inspector who might not even be diligent or efficient."

"Can one refuse to be finger-printed?" asked David Rand-Sayers. His wife Daphne watched him out of the corner of her eye.

"I believe you can, unless they've laid charges or you're under arrest," answered Martin. "That's the issue right there. Each of us knows we had nothing to do with poor Smythe's accident, so why should we submit to being treated as felons? Hmm?"

"I hadn't thought of it in that light," said Dr Beaton. "Still, I mean to accommodate the police to the best of my ability."

Maude smiled to herself, not for anything Beaton had said, but because she liked the sound of his deep, measured voice.

"Any idea who saw him last?" asked Colonel Digby.

Everyone exchanged looks before anyone replied. Several answered at the same time.

"You go first," said Rand-Sayers.

Constance thanked him. "I was up on Marley Mound at, oh, about ten o'clock, I would say, and saw him coming up the west path. He didn't come to the top, so he must have turned back."

"I believe I saw him on top of the hill at about ten-fifteen," said David Rand-Sayers.

"I saw him later than that, but I'm not sure when - about ten-thirty. He was by the sea below the hill." It was Belinda Beaton, the doctor's sister, who had spoken. She looked slightly embarrassed.

"Ah, yes, that's more like it," said the Colonel. "Sooner or later, Smythe had to be on the shore. Can you be more precise with the time?"

"No, not exactly. Amelia and I were together, though."

"Once we left the stables... I thought it was about eleven when we saw him last." said Amelia, the elder Scrope daughter.

Lady Jane seized the opportunity of a momentary silence to say,

"I think we are precipitate, particularly as we have yet to finish dinner."

"Excuse me, Jane. All my fault... As usual, what?" Colonel Digby laughed.

Lady Jane nodded, accepting her brother's contrition.

At a signal from Isembard, the serving staff started clearing away to prepare for the next course. Sophie grudgingly gave the man credit for running the dining room efficiently. He kept a close watch on the progress of the slowest diners, as well as taking his cues from Lord and Lady Hazlett. When Sophie went to pick up a plate near to Adrian Benson, she knew Benson was watching her. She had to remind herself to keep her eyes averted. It was a relief when Sandra Digby asked him a question.

"Do you work in the City, Mr Benson?"

"I have worked there in the past, but at present..."

Sophie missed his answer as her duty took her away from the table.

Very close to the end of the dinner, Isembard approached Lord James and whispered in his ear. The viscount looked at his butler and nodded. Waiting a few moments, he said,

"The police are ready for us now. They have asked to see me first. Might I suggest that we all adjourn as we would do normally."

At this prompt, Lady Jane rose from the table. The ladies followed her to the Drawing Room.

"Isembard, if you would serve the gentlemen anything they desire in my study..." and Lord James went dutifully along to the Armoury. The gentlemen adjourned except for Martin Scrope, who rushed away to call the chief constable.

"Thank you for seeing me, Lord Hazlett," said Inspector Talford, sitting across the table from the peer. Sitting unobtrusively in a corner, Detective Clark was ready to take notes. "I'm sorry to have interrupted your house-party but, considering the circumstances, I had no choice."

"I quite understand, Inspector."

"How long have you known Richard Smythe?"

"I've known him his entire life, although I've had little to do with him until recently. He's the grandson of Peter Smythe."

"Ah, yes, he's the solicitor in the High Street."

"Yes. Richard was to take over the firm. We have dealt with Smythes for more than a century."

"Was he here today for some particular reason?"

"He was invited because we always invite the Smythes to our larger gatherings. He was here for the riding."

"Then it wasn't for something like writing a new will?"

"No, not at all. Nothing like that at all."

"You hinted at having had more to do with him recently. Was that over business matters?"

"No."

"I see. What time did you go riding this morning?"

"The main party set out shortly after nine."

"Main party, sir?"

"I have horses and some guests brought their own mounts. There were more riders than horses available. All the horses went out about nine. After a while, several riders returned to the stables to allow a turn to the three who remained behind."

"What are the names of those three people?"

"They are Fiona Hazlett, Oscar Reid, and Reginald Hazlett."

"I see. Forgive me for not being up on all the members of your family."

"Fiona is married to my elder son, Basil. Reginald is my younger son. Oscar Reid is married to my younger daughter, Constance."

"And you say these waited for others to return. Would you have their names?"

"Oh, I wasn't present at the time, but I believe Colonel and Mrs Digby returned."

"Who would have been the third?"

"There you have me. It could have been Constance or Basil, or it may have been Belinda Beaton. She has a marvellous filly named Conker, suitable for inexperienced riders, and I remember her saying she would loan out her horse."

"We'll get to the bottom of that as we go along. Now, as to your movements, sir. At what time did you learn of Mr Smythe's disappearance?"

"I had just joined Lady Hazlett on top of Marley Mound when we noticed Maria Smythe in a state of distress. That would have been about eleven."

"Could you be more precise, sir? Before eleven, after eleven...?"

"I really couldn't say."

In the Chapel, Sophie stood against a wall with her pencil poised over her notebook. Listening in on interviews was fraught with difficulty. Eventually, Isembard or Mrs Williams would notice the London maid's absence or, as seemed inevitable, catch one of them in the act of eavesdropping.

Chapter 15

Conversations and ideas

"Excuse me, I'd like a quick word with you." David Rand-Sayers pleasantly beckoned to Flora as she crossed the Entrance Hall. When she came over, he drew her to one side. He had stepped out of Lord Hazlett's study to find her.

"Yes, sir?" asked Flora.

"I must apologize for what must seem my very forward behaviour towards you this morning." When Flora did not reply, he continued. "I called you into the Armoury because I simply wanted to ask whether Lord Hazlett needed a secretary."

"A secretary, sir?"

"Yes, that's all it was. I didn't want to approach his lordship directly just yet. I was sure the servants here would know everything going on in the house and if a job's available. That's all I was going to ask. I realize now, I probably appeared a little strange, shall we say?"

"Oh, that's what it was about, was it, sir?"

"Yes, absolutely it was. I'm sure you receive unwanted attention from time to time, but believe me, that was the furthest thing from my mind. As soon as you left the Armoury, I left, too. Do you remember my doing so?"

"I'm not sure, sir."

"Oh, aren't you? What's your name?"

"Gladys, sir. My friends call me Glad."

"That's a very nice name. Now, Glad, this is for you. It's just my way of saying sorry for the misunderstanding."

"Ooh, I'm *really* not supposed to... but thank you very much, sir. And, I've just remembered, you did leave the Armoury right after me." She put two one-pound notes in her pocket.

"There, I was certain you would remember."

"I must go, sir. It's been *such* a pleasure meeting you proper." Flora gave a feather-brained giggle before hurrying away.

"Anyone know what port this is?"

Oscar Reid asked his question in the study. Martin Scrope was absent, ringing up the chief constable while Lord James was being interviewed by the police.

"It's Fonseca 1908," replied Reginald Hazlett.

"Jolly good stuff... I should familiarize myself with port wine. I feel it's a topic I should know more about. I'm better with French wines."

"It can become an expensive hobby if you're not careful, especially with the older vintages."

"So I've heard. Are those older vintages worth the money, though?"

"Not in absolute terms. To a connoisseur, the value lies in the wine's unique characteristics, which may only be marginally superior in a great year over a good one. Add to that scarcity, competition, a little history, and the wine's worth to the avid port drinker is incalculable."

"Are you a connoisseur of port?" asked Oscar.

"In theory only, I'm afraid," answered Reginald. "The best strategy is to buy recent vintage ports from a reputable merchant. One can still get a 1904 Grahams at a reasonable price."

"You've hit upon Reggie's hobby horse," said Basil Hazlett.

"So it seems. I had no idea."

"Father has a 1797 vintage in the cellar that we hope he will bring out one day," continued Basil. "He's waiting for that special occasion. To date, he has not deemed marriages, births of grandchildren, or the end of war special enough."

"I won't bore you too much," said Reginald, smiling, "but right now, sitting in a bonded warehouse, are four hundred cases of 1815 Ferreira. Can't give you certain details because of my job, you know. Apparently, when Portugal had its civil war beginning in 1832, someone at Ferreira hid their valuables in case there was looting. They did so in a cave and blocked its entrance. When the danger had passed, they disinterred the valuables. It seems the chaps who had actually hidden the wine had all died beforehand, so some three thousand cases from various years were forgotten because they were hidden in a separate blocked alcove. Last year, they found the wine which had lain, undisturbed, for nearly ninety years. The 1815 sold for a considerable sum of money to a London merchant."

"How could the company misplace three thousand cases of port?" asked Adrian Benson. "Surely their records would have shown its existence?"

"I cannot say," replied Reginald coolly, nettled by Benson for critiquing his story.

"That's a marvellous tale," said the Colonel. "I think I'll poke about in my cellar when I go home. Tap the walls, don't you know?" He laughed.

"Makes you wonder, doesn't it?" Dr Beaton sipped his port appreciatively. "Any chance of hidden treasures at Lady Holme?"

"No, I don't believe so. Do you remember, Reggie, how we used to hunt for buried treasure?" Basil turned to his brother. "We drew maps but found nothing except broken harrow tines." Basil, at 39, was nine years older than Reginald.

"I imagine you were just indulging your six-year-old brother," replied Reginald.

"Perhaps, but it's a fond memory."

The study door opened. Martin Scrope entered and began speaking.

"Just got off the telephone with Major Warde. He says he'll speak to Talford and put him straight about keeping us here."

"Very good," said Rand-Sayers. "Let me pour you some port, sir. It's excellent stuff."

"I believe I've earned it... Where's Hazlett? He's not still in there with them, is he?"

"I'm afraid so."

"Oh, really? What *can* they be asking him?"

"I should imagine they will establish an overall timeline," replied Dr Beaton. "They need to know where each of us was, and when."

"And who saw whom doing what," added the Colonel.

The men became quiet over their port. Several smoked. A few reflected on what they had seen while riding.

"I feel we must do something for Maria Smythe," said Lady Jane. She was conversing with Helen Scrope and Sandra Digby in the Drawing Room. The arrangement of the comfortable upholstered chairs allowed several conversations to be conducted simultaneously.

"How do you mean? She has a nurse with her and Beaton's on hand." Mrs Digby looked at her quizzically.

"I'm not so concerned about that as her financial security. She has a young boy, you know. With Richard gone, old Mr Smythe will have to sell his practice."

"Surely he only needs to hire a law clerk or whatever they're called," said Sandra.

"Yes, but that's a little beside the point. Maria may be provided for somehow, but I doubt it will be much."

"Wouldn't she receive income from Richard's share of the practice?" asked Helen.

"I'm not privy to their arrangements. But, as is often the case, I doubt Richard's dying at a young age was seriously contemplated as a possibility. Not after the war, anyway."

"He may have had life insurance," said Helen. "If he didn't, put me down for ten pounds... You are raising a subscription, I take it?"

"I'm still in the planning stage, but thank you, Helen."

"Put me down for the same. Only, please, don't mention it to Horry," said Sandra.

"I won't. And thank you."

Maude came over to them.

"What are you cooking up?"

"We are not *cooking* anything. This slang will be the death of the English language. We were discussing Maria Smythe's plight."

"Yes, yes... poor thing. It's a simply rotten outlook for her. What does one say? I mean, it's bad enough with war widows, but with Richard being murdered. How do you console someone in such a predicament?"

"With patience, gentleness, and some practical help. There's very little else to be done," said Lady Jane.

"I'm not good at comforting people, but I can chip in on the practical side. Just let me know."

"Thank you, dear. I shall remember that when the time comes."

Belinda Beaton sat with a puzzled Amelia Scrope.

"Amelia, I can't understand why you said we saw Mr Smythe at about eleven."

"But I did. I thought you did, too. He was, oh, two hundred yards away, walking Toffee. He crossed right in front of us just before we turned east by that big flat rock."

"Yes, I know where you mean... I must be going blind, then. But I definitely saw him earlier close to that place, about ten-thirty, and you say you didn't see him then."

"Belinda, if they put me in the witness box, you'll have to prompt me."

"I can't do that." Belinda looked comically shocked. "I have wondered about the exact time myself. I just thought it was earlier."

"Oh, I can't recall, either. Ten-thirty. Eleven-thirty. I lost track of the time."

"So did I. It couldn't have been later than eleven. Afterwards, when we had been in the forest for ages, Basil told us of Richard's disappearance. That means we'd left Marley earlier rather than later."

"Does it matter?"

"Of course it does. The police thrive on such things. We, or I, may have been the last to see him alive."

"Second to last. The murderer saw him last."

"That's true... It's hard to credit that it's someone in the house. I suppose it might be a tramp or one of those wretched smugglers that keeps popping into the conversation. Do you think there's any truth in Mr Smythe's suspicions?"

"Lord Hazlett doesn't seem convinced. I believe it's possible. There's always been smuggling along this coast, so it wouldn't surprise me if Richard had been right."

The rest of the ladies formed a third group.

"Wherever did you find Mr Benson?" asked Constance Reid.

"Adrian's a beautiful creature, isn't he?" replied Vanessa. "He was easy to find because he goes to all the right parties and is friends with all the right people. How we met is quite absurd. Amelia dragged me along to one of her Marxist meetings. You wouldn't believe the rot some of them talk, but that's beside the point. Well, I was there and so was Adrian, although, naturally, I didn't know who he was at the time. I'd seen him at some party or other, but we hadn't been introduced. He came over and we started talking. Can you imagine it? Silly little me, serious Amelia, and lovely Mr Benson talking among a throng of working class roughs and intellectual revolutionaries. It was super. So delicious. Anyway, Adrian's not all looks. He has a brain, too, much to Amelia's surprise and delight. They engaged in a deadly earnest conversation about socialism that I barely followed and that bored me to tears." Vanessa laughed. "When we decided we'd had enough, we all went dancing instead. Let me tell you this, my dears. He's an absolute dream on the dance floor. Even Amelia enjoyed herself. I think he floated her up to the moon and back."

"My word," said Constance.

"Yes. Adrian has brought some of his gramophone records. He has an assortment of dance music, including Ragtime from America. I had hoped we'd all be doing Turkey Trots, Grizzly Bears, and daring Tangos, but I suppose we can't now under the circs."

"Not tonight, of course," said Constance. "What's your opinion, Daphne?"

"Perhaps we should consider our hosts' wishes." Daphne Rand-Sayers found Constance's attitude amusing. She had noticed her attraction to Benson.

"We must consider," said Fiona Hazlett, "that Mrs Smythe is still in the house and there is, of course, the police investigation. What would they make of us Turkey-trotting about the place?"

"It doesn't matter what the police think, Fiona," said Constance. "As for Maria, I'm sure she will leave tomorrow."

"I see... Will Oscar dance?" asked Fiona.

"Yes, he's quite good."

"Will you persuade him to attempt the Grizzly Bear?" asked Fiona innocently.

"Perhaps. Why do you ask?"

"No particular reason. I find these dance crazes quite fascinating. I didn't realize that you do, too."

"Oh, I'm ready to try anything once," said Constance quite seriously.

Daphne had to stop herself from smiling. Both she and Fiona supposed Constance was ready to try a tango with Mr Benson.

After nine, the entire party assembled in the School Room lounge.

"How *does* one get rid of it?" asked Lady Jane. She was rubbing at the dark grey stains on her fingertips - the result of fingerprinting. "It looks like I've got a disease."

"Mrs Williams will know," said Maude.

Sophie cleared her throat pointedly.

"Yes, what is it?" asked Lady Jane.

"Excuse me, my Lady. Scrubbs' Ammonia at half strength will remove the stain the quickest, but it must be washed off within a minute or it will yellow the skin. Dara's or any hair removal product will lift the stain in two or three minutes. Gently scrubbing with toothpaste or powder takes several minutes and is the least deleterious, or so I've been told. Thank you."

"How about that?" said Maude. "You have three choices, Mummy. What's your name?"

"Phoebe, Miss Hazlett."

"You seemed to be prepared for this."

"Yes, miss. We assumed the ink would stain, so we discussed dealing with it among ourselves. Another maid knew of the toothpaste trick."

"Very good... What's the name of your agency?"

"Burgoyne's Agency, Sack Lane, London near the Monument."

"I shall remember it," said Maude.

"What are we doing about riding tomorrow?" asked Colonel Digby in a voice loud enough for everyone to hear.

"The police will return tomorrow morning," said Lord Hazlett. "They will finish their interviews and clear up any outstanding points. As long as we make ourselves available to them, I don't see why our riding should present any difficulties."

Martin Scrope entered the room in a foul mood.

"This ink will never come out." He was rubbing at his fingers as he walked. "Well, I don't like that man's sneering attitude and intrusive questions. Did anyone else find him unpleasant?"

"I didn't care for his approach at all," said Constance. "I found him rather rude."

"It's just his manner, dear," said Lady Jane. "One learns to put up with it these days." She smiled at her daughter.

"He was rude to both of you, was he?" asked Lord James, looking from his daughter to his wife, who said,

"To be blunt, he inquired if our marriage was sound. I found his questions smacked more of sensational journalism than what one would expect from a professional policeman. It's past, so please don't make a fuss."

"Good grief... Martin, may I trouble you for Colonel Warde's telephone number?"

"By all means. Shall I come with you? I have his number in my book."

"Yes, please do." They left the room together.

"Oh, Lor, Daddy's very annoyed," said Maude.

"Serves the blackguard right," said the Colonel. "I hope he gets hauled over the coals. I haven't seen him yet, but when I do…"

The School Room simmered for several minutes over the sad lack of standards to be found among the police.

"If we can knock off a few more tonight, we'll be ahead of the game," said Inspector Talford. He stretched himself and stood up. "Who's next on the list?"

"David Rand-Sayers," replied Detective Clark.

"I wonder what his secret is. They nearly all have one. But it's so difficult getting anywhere with these types. You could tell Lady Hazlett has been indiscreet in the past. The way she blushed when I asked about her frequent trips to London… You know, it's always bothered me why Hazlett confines himself to this place. Before meeting him, I would have said he was mad. Simple as that. But he doesn't come across that way. What do you reckon?"

"He seemed perfectly reasonable and natural to me."

"That's what I thought. Now Martin Scrope, my MP, if you please, is a man I'd like to get on a drunk and disorderly change. I'd get the press with their cameras waiting for him when he came out of the cells in the morning. That man gets my goat — his politics and his attitude. Anyway, let's have what-his-name in."

"Rand-Sayers, sir."

"Yes. Send the footman to find him. There you go, Clark, we're lords of the manor, ordering servants about - for a couple of days, anyway."

Reginald and Amelia walked slowly together in the Long Gallery. No one else was present.

"Did you ever play Squeak Piggy here?" asked Reginald.

"You mean seeing how far one could get before making a board creak?"

"Yes, and if you creaked, then you got oinked into oblivion."

"Oh, yes, I remember. You were one of the loudest oinkers, I recall."

"Probably. By staying close to the windows, you can get half-way without creaking."

"I see... Um, Reggie, why the sudden interest?"

"In you, you mean...? I find it rather difficult talking about such things, but here goes... I've always liked you as a friend. I've been thinking, lately, that it might blossom into something more if we started seeing each other... Away from our respective families, I mean."

"What an interesting idea. So, in a cool, rational manner, you have thought this over."

"I suppose I have... You're not offended by the lack of romance, are you?"

"No... It's unexpected, to say the least. I'm not offended because it makes sense to me. The idea reminds me of those old newspaper advertisements where people sought spouses based on economic considerations. After an interview and a few favourable meetings, they married. That might work for us. You and I both live in the shadow of other family members. That leaves us no space for ourselves. In my family, I have to squeeze myself in between three over-sized personalities. Not that I mind. It's just a fact. It's one reason that made me look into the various causes I've attached myself to."

"Is it? I can see why. Some of your views could not be more divergent from those your parents hold."

"They say I'm seeking attention. That's true in a way, but I could hardly admit it to them. I'm sincere in my beliefs, though. Yet, I'm a bit of a hypocrite because I've yet to leave home. I still depend on the very things I say I despise. Mother has reached her wit's end in trying to pair me off with someone, to the point of giving up."

"That can't have been easy for you. On my part, I'm like a blank slate upon which a story has yet to be written. It's difficult to say why... I believe my father's odd behaviour has much to do with it. Going through school, his seclusion caused me some embarrassment. There was occasional trouble over it, too. It sort of trained me to keep my head down."

"Yes, I can see that it would. Anyone who doesn't conform gets picked on. Yet, it's strange that people like Maude and Vanessa get away with non-conformity and are accepted and cheerful. I tried in my own way, but I'm not content and I meet with disapproval. It's a little unfair."

"Maude and Vanessa fall within the conventions of society in ways I don't properly understand. However, they don't challenge the existing order of things, whereas socialism does. You, espousing that, cannot expect a different reaction to the one you get."

"That's a good point."

"I feel the time has come for me to do something. That's my reason for speaking to you. I knew you would understand what holds me back, because the same forces are at work in your life. If we align our interests, we might do well. I'm sure it will be enjoyable, too — I would dearly like having an ally and confidante. We may even come to mean much more to each other. I hope so."

"What do we do next? You're in London and I'm in Southampton."

"My lodgings are guarded by a watchful landlady who doesn't permit female visitors. You live at home, where they will ask a multitude of probing questions should I knock on the front door. Difficult, isn't it? Any suggestions?"

"Then why don't we go to places together before we decide anything? Art galleries, museums, concerts, that sort of thing... If you don't mind my asking, how are you off financially?"

"My job's a bore, but the pay's adequate. I get an allowance from father. Together, that's a little over three hundred a year."

They reached the end of the gallery and turned about.

"I've always loved this place. This gallery in particular... I have a hundred a year. So, four hundred and we'd need to live in suburbia because of your job."

"You seem to be planning rather far ahead."

"It's what we're talking about, isn't it? Marriage or living together is the natural extension of the subject we're discussing."

"I think marriage, if things work out between us."

"That would be my hope, too. Father would make a decent settlement. I'm sure your father will do something as well. Perhaps it would be enough for us to escape suburbia. If money were no object, within certain bounds, what would you choose to do?"

"Well, I did have an idea to paint to earn extra money. I would become a painter of landscapes — dreadful daubs that sold for the cost of the materials."

"Ah, yes! But I can trump that. I'd churn out third-rate poetry that nobody wants to hear. Sounds quite idyllic in its way."

"It does, doesn't it?"

"You must give me your London address. I'll get an accommodation address in Southampton for your letters."

"What a practical mind you have. Amelia, have you ever been in love?"

"Once... And you?"

"Twice, fleetingly."

"We could discuss or forget them. Which do you prefer?"

"Forget them. We must concentrate on our future and not our pasts."

"That suits me... Do you have any vices?"

"I can't afford them. If I could, I doubt I'd bother."

"I tried cocaine, but I didn't like it. I smoke sometimes."

"You do?"

"When you go to a socialist meeting, you'll discover it is de rigueur for all women to smoke. I'll take you to a get-together one day. Everyone talks a lot and tries hard to be impressive with their intellect."

"This may sound strange. You are Amelia, whom I've known forever, but whom I don't know at all."

"It's the same for me. You're a stranger, but one I can talk to... Reggie, I am learning what you're thinking, but what are you feeling?"

"Relieved and very pleased... Regretful we've wasted time in not talking like this before. And you?"

"Surprise with you and myself... I have a rising feeling of delightful anticipation... Here we are. I suppose we must go back down. We'll ride together tomorrow, but not for too long or they'll notice. Since when have you entertained the notion we might have a chance?"

"For quite some time... since we last met, in fact. The idea didn't quite coalesce until we saw each other today."

"Quite the experiment, isn't it? Will love spring forth?"

"I don't see why not. If it does, I hope it does so simultaneously."

The party broke up. Most were early risers, but all were glad to get the day over and done.

"Maude, just a moment, please." Dr Beaton sounded hesitant.

"Yes, what is it?"

He waited for two people to pass them before speaking hurriedly.

"I, um, I've had little chance to see you today with everything going on. We haven't been able to talk. Could we ride together tomorrow?"

"That would be lovely."

"Ah, good, good... You see... Yes, I think I'd better keep it for tomorrow when we're alone. Good night, Maude."

He left her abruptly. Maude smiled, and felt happiness welling up inside, for she was certain of what he would say when they were by themselves.

"Lord Hazlett, may I see you for a moment?" Adrian Benson had found Lord Hazlett sitting in his study.

"Mr Benson, I'm about to go to bed. Can't it wait?"

"I would not presume to trouble you under normal circumstances and I apologize for doing so now, sir, but it is rather important."

"Sit down, then."

"Thank you."

Lord James watched the elegant man gracefully seat himself. When ready, he said,

"I believe if I tell you I have a message from Poppy, it will make plain my reason for bothering you."

"Yes, it does, indeed."

"The message is simple. Poppy would like to meet you at your convenience when the term has expired."

"I see. Any reason in particular?"

"The desire is to restore good relations among the Council. To that end, it is felt a face-to-face meeting would help settle matters. The intention is to be generous in material terms, too."

"Is it?" Lord Hazlett felt surprise but did not show it. "You seem well informed about this business."

"I have the honour of being entrusted by several council members to facilitate in delicate matters. This is another such matter."

"So you're here to sound me out and report back."

"That is one way of putting it. It's natural under the circumstances that all council members should wish to maintain a co-operative and collegial atmosphere among those who are active and those who are retired."

"Let bygones be bygones, eh? Tell Poppy I shall meet with him."

"Excellent, sir. Poppy's secretary will telephone you in the coming days to arrange the details."

"Is that everything?" asked Lord Hazlett when Benson did not move.

"There's another matter entirely unconnected with the message. Smythe's murder is a very unfortunate incident. While riding, it so happened I saw you alone several times. Once, you were on Marley Mound above the shore path. No one has actually stated where Smythe was killed, but there on the shore path seems a logical place for it to have happened. It occurred to me that should you or any of your family require an alibi, I could probably help with something in that direction."

Lord Hazlett stared at the young man. He had openly opposed the Council in the past and had been subjected to its ire. Here was evidence of how low the society and its council members had sunk. His lordship held his disgust in check.

"I will remember that."

"Good. I must point out, I would be rendering a personal service to you. Such a service would involve risk to myself."

"Of course it would. How much do you have in mind?"

"That's difficult for me to assess."

"Then let us say a thousand pounds - once, and never a penny more."

"Lord Hazlett, that is a most generous offer. Those restrictions you mentioned allude to a pattern of behaviour that is abhorrent to me. Taking advantage of this situation is the farthest thing from my mind. Let me know, sir, if my services are required. Good night."

"Good night, Mr Benson."

The young man left the room. Two minutes later, Isembard stepped in.

"What is it?" asked Lord Hazlett.

"May I speak to you, my Lord?"

"Yes, of course."

"I've been your butler for many years. My retirement will come up soon." He coughed. "That is to say, I doubt your lordship will keep me on a year from now. I have reported fairly in all matters and always in terms favourable to yourself, my Lord. Still, you'll not want to see my face when it's all over and done with. As I will be retiring, I'll need to do so with some dignity and a sense of security in my declining years. There's less than a year to run on the term and I've still to report on matters. Believe me, my Lord, this is very difficult for me to say. I had hoped we could come to an arrangement. A settlement, my Lord, so that everything is wound up to the satisfaction of all parties."

In disbelief at the proximity to Benson's suggestion and for the proposal itself, Lord Hazlett surveyed his butler with revulsion.

"Why speak to me today about this? There's plenty of time."

"Ah, well. What with the murder and all, it appeared to me I'd best speak now before the murderer is found. It's because we don't know who it is, you see, my Lord."

Hazlett stared again. Was his butler suggesting he had killed Smythe? Benson had done something similar. Hints that he, Lord Hazlett, had murdered Smythe! Did they believe this, or was it a ploy? Were they acting together? Was the Council behind this? The truth was, Hazlett realized, Isembard held his future in his greasy palms, whatever the situation. With police in the house, these two men could destroy him in an instant.

"How much were you thinking?"

"Three thousand pounds, my Lord." Isembard spoke with confidence as, for him, money was a far more certain subject for discussion.

"That's rather a lot... I'll have to think this over." Lord Hazlett had feared a higher amount. Isembard might come back for more later. If there was to be a settlement, Lord Hazlett determined it would be on his terms, to keep Isembard's greed in check. He must do everything to keep his repugnant butler content and restrained. Lord Hazlett felt tired.

"You may go, Isembard. We will talk again soon."

"Yes, my Lord. Good night."

Chapter 16

Old, old stories

The four London maids were once again in Sophie's bedroom. They had each contributed final reports for the day and were ready to assess what they had.

"We must be quick," said Sophie. "Nelly and Mabel will be here soon."

"What do I do with the money Mr Rand-Sayers gave me?" asked Flora.

"Hold on to it because we really should give it back."

"We could all go to a lovely restaurant," said Flora.

"That remains to be seen. He obviously wants you to provide him with an alibi, so he goes on our suspect list."

"I don't know when he left the Armoury, but it seemed important to him, so I took his money. He was relieved I did. But, you know, he didn't ask again about the secretary's job, which makes his excuse seem like utter nonsense."

"He's feeling guilty over something. Although he might be innocent of murder, he obviously hasn't an alibi and feels he needs one. As for the servants, I think we can rule them out, unless one rode a bicycle."

"But you walked down there, Phoebe," said Ada. "Did you meet anyone?"

"A policeman... Oh, dear. I'll probably be a suspect. They're bound to ask me some awkward questions. Mrs Williams knew I had gone, too."

"Well," said Ada, "we know you weren't carrying a mace when you left. Did you have your cosh with you?"

"Yes, I did. I look quite criminal, don't I? However, my little blackjack won't match the wounds made by a mace."

"Why do you carry a blackjack?" asked Fern.

"We all do. In case of danger, we can protect ourselves."

"May I see one, please?"

"Here you are," Ada passed her blackjack to Fern.

"Oh, it's a proper little cosh." Fern began swatting the air with it.

"That's enough, Dora. Who else do we suspect?"

"Isembard," said Ada.

"No, he can't have done it. Who else?"

"What about the beautiful Benson?" asked Flora.

"He doesn't really look the type to me," said Sophie.

"I'm not so sure about that. He might be vain, in which case, he'd be sensitive to being slighted."

"True, but then I'd expect him to use a dagger or poison, not a mace. He's interesting in his way, yet completely out of place here. He looked at home in the gambling den."

"Vanessa Scrope's friendly with him, and she's of the same set."

"That's a point. Oh, I forgot to mention an interesting item," said Sophie. "There's something brewing between Reginald Hazlett and Amelia. They were alone in the Long Gallery. I heard footsteps overhead, so I decided to see who it was. I couldn't hear everything because they spoke in low tones, but Amelia clearly said, 'What do we do next? You're in London and I'm in Southampton.' It's remarkable the way sound carries in that room."

"How tantalizing and romantic," said Flora.

"And we're all waiting for Dr Beaton to pop the question," said Ada. "The female staff are on tenterhooks, hoping he'll marry Maude and get her out of the house. They say she can be very difficult sometimes."

"Totally believable of her," said Flora. "People that hale and hearty are often intolerant of weakness in others. I played a character like Maude once and it was really quite fatiguing."

"Back to Benson. I've noticed a curious *something* between him and Lady Jane. Any ideas?" Sophie gave them an inquiring look.

"It can't be you know what," said Ada. "Could he be 'er son?"

"I hadn't considered that... Anyone notice a resemblance?"

"They're different," said Flora. "He has a darker colouring... But Phoebe, how could she get away with an illegitimate child?"

"From what we understand, she couldn't. But there might have been an estrangement between the Hazletts which we know nothing about. I'll see if Mrs Williams can shed any light on the matter. If not that, then what is going on between them? After all, it was her list of guests, not Vanessa's. Why invite him?"

"Perhaps the sinister tPWoP is involved," said Flora.

"Can we call them PWP? It's a bit of a mouthful, otherwise," said Ada.

"That's much easier," said Sophie. "I can't see why Lady Jane would be in league with either PWP or Benson against her own husband. It's only a simple invitation, after all, but what's the explanation for his inclusion?"

"I'm losing count," said Fern. "How many mysteries are we trying to solve?"

"Let me see," said Sophie. "Smuggling, murder, PWP, Lord Hazlett's secret, Isembard's behaviour, Benson's secret — including Lady Jane inviting him, and the ghosts of Lady Holme. That's seven and we're ignoring the counterfeit money."

"Counterfeit money?" exclaimed Fern.

"Don't worry about that. It has no bearing on why we're here."

"I think Reginald and Amelia count as a mystery," said Flora.

"Dr Beaton and Maude do an' all," said Ada. "I like romances."

"Nine, then. That's all for the moment."

"I prefer round numbers," said Flora. "Surely we can find a tenth? There are plenty of others to investigate."

"Let's remain objective. Murder first and smuggling second. A few other things will be cleared up as we go. Listen, this is an extremely important question we must consider. How did the murderer carry the mace without being observed?"

"Oh, yes."

"Down his trousers?" asked Fern.

"Most of the men and several women were wearing riding breeches or jodhpurs. It would be impossible to conceal a mace in those. Loose trousers... I don't remember anyone in loose trousers."

"The other women were in riding habits," said Flora. "Plenty of room under those skirts and easy to manage with side saddles, I should think."

"That's true, although they'd have difficulty keeping a mace under their skirts as they mounted."

Ada laughed. "That'd be funny if a lady dropped a clanger like that. 'Scuse me, miss, your mace, I believe.' How about under a jacket, then?"

"I prefer jackets as the most likely place of concealment. I noticed Vanessa's close-fitting outfit and I doubt she could hide a thimble anywhere without it being noticeable. Other smaller women, like Fiona Hazlett, would have trouble concealing something that long. The mace is twenty-one inches in length."

"Being taller, both Maude and Belinda Beaton could get away with it," said Flora.

"Yes, they could. I would say all the men, too, except for Oscar Reid, who's a slightly built man."

"I do believe we're getting somewhere," said Flora.

"Mode of transporting the mace. I can't get to grips with this part. Was it down a sleeve or tucked in a waistband?"

"Waistband's no good, miss... Phoebe," said Ada. "I reckon down a sleeve. Oh, I know! Tie it in a loop of string over the shoulder, using a simple bow knot. It'd come right to hand, then."

"Very good, Ada. Now, this is what we shall do. We'll inspect as many men's riding jackets as we can, looking for signs of blood, recent stains, tears in the lining, burst stitches, or other marks commensurate with carrying and concealing a lumpy iron bar under a jacket. It must have been difficult, but someone managed it. Hopefully, it left a trace."

"Just to clarify," said Flora, "that's Maude, Belinda, and all the men, except for Oscar."

"Yes, to start with, anyway. If the opportunity presents itself, examine the ladies' riding habits. We may also have to consider the non-riders at some point."

"I can find out who used the bikes yesterday," said Fern. "I was talking to the friendly boy who looks after them."

"Excellent, please do that."

There came a knock at the door, which then opened.

"Hello, it's us," said Nelly. "We got our chairs."

The maids briefly discussed the tragedy, but as the shore was more than a mile away, it felt remote to those in the snug little room. All six were looking forward to discussing the ghosts of Lady Holme and so the subject of conversation was soon changed to satisfy that expectation. As Nelly began to recount what she had gleaned from the male servants, it soon became apparent that she, at fourteen, was a born story-teller. By turns, her face registered shock, horror, surprise, impudence, and delight. The curls peeping under her cap often shook. Her voice explored a wide tonal range, and she punctuated important points with a varied array of sounds:-

"There are two stories about the ghosts of Lady Holme... Two." She raised her eyebrows significantly.

"The first'n is this and it be the favourite of the tavern drinkers. Long ago, in the reign of Queen Bess, when this house was built, there lived here Sir Walter Hazlett and his wife, Cicely Holme. She was a great beauty. If you don't believe me, her picture hangs in Great Hall. She wears a dark brown dress with all that lace at her neck."

"Is that the pale lady with auburn hair?" asked Sophie.

"Yes, that's her. Lovely she was. And this house be named arter her, though she be Lady Hazlett by rights. Sir Walter Hazlett was a daring man and a great sailor so they made him an admiral in Queen Bess' navy. Tis said he was quiet and good - beloved by his men. But when roused to anger and in the heat of battle, he was the devil hisself. He took three ships to the Spanish Main and came back a rich man, a favourite of the Queen. With the prize money, he built over the old house here and got knighted into the bargain. That was when Lady Cicely was presented at court.

"Him being a sailor, Sir Hazlett was away for long stretches. His new wife did find hersel' lonely more often than not. Here she be, a beautiful lady, all alone in this great house, a-waiting, waiting, waiting for her husband and she with no children to care for, no friends a-visiting, and her family in Exeter.

"Lady Cicely had a cousin by the name of Captain Ben Beaumont, a sailor. He was a handsome man and a favourite with the ladies wherever he went."

"That's like Mr Benson," said Dora. "Their names are similar."

"I know who you mean," said Nelly. "Maybe Captain Beaumont looked just loike Mr Benson and made the ladies sigh and swoon with his soft talk. No one knows if the Captain and Lady Cicely knew each other before, but they say he settled in Lymington while Sir Hazlett was away at sea.

"Next, Captain Beaumont rides his horse eastward every day and disappears for hours on end. Then he was gone for days at a time. Back then, there was nothing east of Lymington except this house. Soon, the wagging tongues must have it that the handsomest man in the county was visiting the most beautiful woman in the south. The rumour spread.

"Sir Hazlett's ships were forced to return from cruising the Indies because disease among the crew had left him short-handed. The ships come back early with little to show for their sufferings. He was in a black humour.

"They docked at Portsmouth. By night, he rode through a great storm that crashed and rumbled about him. He pushed his horse hard — on and on — for he was eager to see his lovely wife, his beautiful treasure, she who possessed his heart.

"He comes to journey's end. Sir Hazlett opens the door of the Entrance Hall, wet through, covered in mud. He throws his hat down upon the stones and stamps his feet. No servant comes, and he wonders why. Why is the house so quiet and so dark? Up the stairs he goes, happy at heart, but he does so quietly, for he wishes to wake Lady Cicely gently and tenderly.

"At his wife's bedroom door, he grips the handle and opens it softly. He stands there in the pitch black. The lightning flashes and he can't believe his eyes! He sees them both... Together. But they've not seen him. He goes to the dresser and lights a candle. Now they see him by flickering flame. He frightens them, for they see the black rage upon his face and the sword in his hand. He strides across the room. Lady Cicely starts to speak, but he runs her through the heart and she dies. Captain Beaumont tries to stop him, but Sir Hazlett cuts him, wounding him sorely. There's blood everywhere. He gets a chair for hissel', to sit down so he may watch the Captain bleed to death before his eyes.

"When he's dead, Sir Hazlett leaves the house, taking a fresh horse back to Portsmouth. He speaks to no man. The next day, he puts to sea on a ship. By evening, the ship was wrecked with all hands lost.

"Ever since then, the unhappy ghosts of Lady Cicely and Captain Beaumont walk the halls of Lady Holme, searching desperately for each other but doomed never to meet again. On stormy nights, many a visitor has seen Sir Hazlett staring at them through the window, with a sword in his hand. The sight drives them near mad with fear."

"Good grief," said Sophie.

"I won't get to sleep tonight," said Ada.

"Is it all true?" asked Fern.

Flora smiled at Nelly. "You have a gift. Thank you."

"Did you loike it? I'm ever so pleased." Her cheeks dimpled as she smiled.

"Now thisn's the true story of the ghosts of Lady Holme. Sir Walter and Lady Cicely loved each other with a great love. An undying love. They're newly married when Lady Holme is built. The first thing Lady Cicely did upon becoming mistress of the house was plant great beds of lavender. Row upon row upon row. She planted other things besides, but it's the lavender her garden's known for. She tended her plantings with her own hands and the place was so pretty it was the talk for miles around. When people came to visit, they remembered the scent as long as they lived.

"When Sir Walter went to sea in his ship, the Falcon, his sea-chest had many sprigs of lavender in it to remind him of home and she whom he loved. What with the bunches that Lady Cicely put in his cabin and below decks, he wrote of his worry that the enemies of England might be warned of his approach with the scent wafting before him on the breeze.

"Whenever he returned after a voyage, it was no use for visitors to come to the house. The loving couple would shut themselves up and think of no one else but each other. The longer he's away, the longer they'd spend time together without a thought for family or friends. When they did go abroad to the town, and everyone saw them, it was as if the King and Queen of May blessed the land, such a delight to see was their joy and their deep devotion to each other.

"Sometimes he was gone for weeks or even months at a time. He gave her a day when he would return, but warned that winds, storms, and enemies might delay him. At the top of this house, there's a special room. The Crow's Nest it be called and, to this day, there's the very telescope through which Lady Cicely used to look towards the sea. Sir Walter promised that no matter where he had been, when he returned he would sail along the Solent within sight of Lady Holme. He did so because when he landed, he often had to attend to other business or go up to London before he came home. This early sighting saved her days of anxious waiting.

"When she thought her husband was due back, Lady Cicely began to visit the Crow's Nest to keep a sharp lookout. As the hopeful day grew nearer, she'd stay more often, knowing she was more loikely to see'un and anxious to do so. Perhaps she had second sight, for she was always there a couple of days before the Falcon appeared and never missed once. Sometimes she ate and slept in the room to rise early, for she loved him so.

"They were happy as happy could be for four years. Then Sir Walter must sail down to Spain. Said he'd be gone a month. After three weeks, Lady Cicely started her vigil, going to the Crow's Nest once in a while. At four weeks, every day she woke, her heart leaped for joy, for she was certain she would see the Falcon upon the Solent and her heart's desire returning to her. But it was not to be.

"By the end of the second month, she wouldn't leave the room. No, not for anything. All the while, she pressed her eye to the telescope or walked up and down looking, always looking. Then she hoped to see him coming at night. Whole nights she stood at the window. Ah, whole days, too. The weather grew colder outside.

"One night, there was a dreadful storm. She thought to spot the Falcon, as if her sight could pierce both the dark and rain, though it was impossible. She opened the window, leaned out, and got soaked through. She screamed at the servants when they tried to reason with her. Lady Cicely caught a chill because of that soaking. It turned into a fever and she took to her bed. She died three days later.

"No more than a week afterwards, Sir Walter returned home. The Falcon had been damaged in battle and many of the crew were killed or wounded. The ship was forced to sail south with half a mast to escape its enemies. Somewhere on the coast of Africa, they repaired the Falcon as best they could, then limped home. Sir Walter was wounded hisself and come near to death. Upon returning to Lady Holme, he learned of the tragedy and it sent him almost mad. He wrote in his diary. It's so sad to read his thoughts. There was nothing he wouldn't have done to bring her back, and he cursed himself for ever having gone away. Mrs Williams read some of it to me and I cried. A month later, he was dead, too. Died of a broken heart, I reckon.

"Sir Walter's ghost has never been seen, no, not once. But the house smells of lavender to this day, even though the lavender beds have been gone for years and years. They were never replanted once they were let go, though they always keep a few plants in the walled garden. Tis thought that Lady Cicely is still here, but I've not seen her."

"What a sad tale," said Flora, brushing away a tear.

"Oh, dear me," said Sophie.

"Excuse me." Ada darted outside to blow her nose.

"Is that story true?" asked Fern.

"I believe it is. Most of it come out the books, but I did tickle it up with the bit about the May Queen. And Captain Beaumont was real, only he was Sir Walter's cousin, and his full name was Beaumont-Hazlett. He got Lady Holme and then was knighted afterwards and raised to a lord or summat. I don't remember it well - it's that confusing."

Ada returned. "That's better."

"Do you know," said Sophie, "ever since we arrived, I've had the tune to Lavender's Blue in mind."

"So have I," said Flora.

"Me, an' all." Ada hummed it.

"I know that one," said Fern.

"Let's sing it, shall we? Ready...? One... two... three."

All six sang quietly but when they came to a certain verse, they found they knew different versions which had them laughing at the muddle they made. After sorting out their verses, they began again.

> *Lavender's blue, dilly dilly, lavender's green.*
> *When I am king, dilly dilly, you shall be queen.*
> *Who told you so, dilly dilly, who told you so...?*

They were quiet so as not to disturb anyone. By one of Lady Holme's eccentricities, the song - soft and clear - reached into Mrs Williams' room. She was lying in bed, propped up on pillows, reading Pilgrim's Progress by the light of an oil lamp. She put down her book and removed her glasses. Her childhood, when she had first learned the song, rushed back to her forcefully. She sang along with the maids. When they had finished, Mrs Williams lay staring into the shadows, smiling. She recalled her little daughter, long gone, to whom she had sung Lavender's Blue. She remembered her husband, lost at sea. They came vividly to her mind. The housekeeper smiled because, she believed, she would see them again one day. Reaching over, she turned down her lamp.

The maids were about to leave Sophie's room to go to their own beds. Mabel had sung along, but now she uttered her first words at their gatherings.

"I seen her." Mabel spoke in a flat, emphatic way. She was quite child-like, a slim figure, with large brown eyes.

"Have you?" said Sophie. "Please tell us about her."

"I seen her on the top floor."

"Were you scared?" asked Sophie.

Mabel shook her head vigorously. "She was wearing a silvery dress with lace at the front. And she wore pearls in her hair."

"She must have looked lovely."

Mabel nodded.

"What was she doing?"

"I was at the stairs this end when I saw her come out of the Crow's Nest and walk away. She held her skirts. I ran arter her. She got to the top of Great Hall stairs and stopped. So I stopped. She turned and waved at me before going down. I ran arter, but she had gone... She had a lovely smile."

"Ah, it must have pleased her to see you."

Mabel nodded. She stood up but, before picking up her chair, she impetuously hugged Sophie and rushed out of the room.

Chapter 17

Someone Oversteps the Mark

The early train left Waterloo station. In a separate compartment by themselves, Detective Sergeant Gowers neatly occupied a corner with his back to the engine. Sitting across from him, Inspector Morton gave the impression he required the whole bench seat to be comfortable. He sprawled, his long legs taking up much of the floor space, too.

"I was going to watch Fulham play today." Gowers looked mildly annoyed.

"Who are they playing?" asked Morton.

"Cardiff City. They've just joined the League this year. Fulham's bound to win, but I'd have liked to see them do it."

"Think they'll be promoted to first division?"

"They've got a chance. Five wins, a draw, and two losses from eight games played so far."

"That's a good start."

"Last season was better, but they faded mid-way through. Oh well, with Fulham, you get used to disappointment."

"And you a lifetime supporter?"

"Just facing facts, sir. Disappointment builds my character. Makes me stoical." Gowers smiled briefly.

"I also had plans for today. Now we're going to be stuck in the wilds of the New Forest."

"I recall someone telling me about a decent local brew. Carter's, if I remember correctly."

"Unfortunately, this won't be a pub-crawl. The place is outside Lymington. Lady Holme, if you please."

"Who'd choose a name like that? Sounds quite pretentious. Didn't you say it was Lord Hazlett's estate?"

"That's right. I'd better fill you in. The chief constable for Hampshire, Colonel Warde, called Scotland Yard late last night because Hazlett and his guests started getting bolshie. They took against the local man, Inspector Talford. He obviously wasn't wearing his kid-gloves, so Warde called us in as a favour to him. We must calm the troubled waters and find the murderer."

"How nice for us. It was a murder, then?"

"Oh, yes. They're old-fashioned around Lymington — the deceased male was whacked with a mace."

"A mace! Sorry, go on, sir."

"And in daylight, mind you. It appears it was a fellow rider who did it. Can you ride?"

"Does a donkey at the seaside count?"

"That's been my experience, too. We've got a house full of people, all county, all bonkers about horses. One of them is the killer. If we knew how to ride, we'd get on better with them."

"Sounds like a very interesting set-up we're walking into. Where was the body found?"

"In the sea. He was dead already."

"That means the assailant fatally struck the deceased, then pushed him into the water to have the tide take the corpse away. I hope they haven't trampled over the crime scene."

"We'll see," said Morton gloomily. "That's everything I've been told."

"What puzzles me," said Gowers, "is why we were picked for the job?"

"The Super won't tell us that. But we've done a couple of these out-of-town cases in the past. Then we got Dorking last month and now this. Perhaps we're considered experts in the field. I don't feel like one, though. A body in the Thames, and it's a piece of cake without the headache of country house politics."

"Yes. Although it's nice seeing different places. All the same, sir, this case can't be as bad as Abinger Mansion. We'll catch whoever did this. How can you hide a mace in your pocket?"

The boot-boy worked his way along the winding passages, leaving pairs of clean riding boots outside of their owners' bedrooms. As he approached Constance Reid's room, Sophie came out and closed the door.

"Mornin', miss."

"Good morning, Benjamin. You've done a good job on those boots. "

"Oh, thank you, miss."

On the stairs of the Grand Staircase, she met Ada coming up. They stopped.

"Phoebe, there's something going on."

"What is it?"

"I gave his lordship his breakfast, and he looks right depressed. Like his last shilling just rolled down the drain. I reckon 'e's 'ad bad news, I do an' all."

"What can it be? A letter, perhaps?"

"I dunno... No, it can't be. He went through his post yesterday, and it's too early for the postman."

"Wait! Did you notice Isembard?"

"Yes, he's smiling like a Cheshire cat. It's a hideous sight, but 'e looks well pleased with himself today, whereas he was grumpy yesterday."

"If we're correct and Isembard is a PWP spy, what does it mean if the servant is happy and the master is sad?"

"Money? What else would it be?"

"If the assumption's true, then Isembard got a windfall and Lord James doesn't want to pay... Blackmail?"

"That's right! It has to be something like that."

"Could he be threatening to send a bad report to PWP?"

"He's the sort of - person - who would do that. I nearly said it, but I didn't."

Sophie smiled. "Yes, he is. I wonder if Dora can keep a close watch on him?"

"Ow, streuth, here 'e comes. He's caught us good and proper."

Isembard ascended the Grand Staircase.

"I'll deal with *him*," said Sophie. Her lips compressed into a line.

"What do we have here?" said Isembard in his barracking tone when he stopped in front of them. "A couple of stupid…"

"Mind your manners! We came here to work. That's what we were discussing, so we shan't take any lip from you. Call yourself a butler? Your conduct is disgusting. One more insult and I go to her ladyship to tell her we're leaving. All four of us. Do I make myself clear…? I'll take your silence as an affirmative. Come along, Nancy."

The maids started down the stairs. The stunned Isembard found his tongue.

"You're under contract, so you can't leave."

"That's no concern of yours," said Sophie, who had stopped, turning to face him several steps lower. "Tell me something. How are you still employed here?"

"What do you mean?"

"Your appalling behaviour is so apparent it's a miracle you haven't been fired."

"Look, you just do the work and keep quiet or I'll…"

"You'll what?"

"Never you mind." A grin spread across his face. "Go to her ladyship if you want. Then we'll see what happens."

"Are you finished? We're busy."

They continued downstairs while Isembard glowered after them. When the maids rounded a corner, Ada said,

"That was brilliant, but you've made an enemy there. He'll tell Mrs Williams."

"We shall destroy him… Something useful came from that. He does have a stranglehold on the Hazletts."

Sometimes, sound carries in Lady Holme. The conversation of distinct, slightly raised voices on the Grand Staircase entertained some, and astonished a few, while delighting several servants. Those guests still asleep learned later of 'The Row.'

"I just don't believe it," said Inspector Talford. "The chief's called in Scotland Yard. They'll be here by noon."

"Oh, dear. Why'd he do that?" asked Detective Clark.

"Hazlett and that bloody Scrope used their pull. I got a tongue-lashing from Warde."

"Why have they taken us off the case?"

"I wish they had. No, we're to assist the Yard. We've to interview the servants and leave the upper crust alone. That's a terrible way to treat your own men. I'm too old for this."

"There are three and a half hours until noon. What if we crack the case before then?" asked Clark.

"Dream on... Mind you, we could process the beggars before the Yard gets here and find out who the thumbprint belongs to. Let's get them in here sharpish, then, before they all go galloping off."

"Yes, sir. Adrian Benson's next."

"Give the footman a few names to find. They can wait on us for a change."

The stable-yard was active. Instead of Friday's grand procession, the riders departed in twos and threes. Inside the stable building, Maude waited while a groom brought out her dark bay horse from a stall. Doctor Beaton entered the aisle and saw her lifting a saddle onto the horse's back as he approached.

"Good morning, Maude," said Doctor Beaton.

"Albert, how marvellous to see you!"

"I thought to shout to say I'd saddle your horse, but it was a pleasure watching you. You're such a capable woman."

"Am I?" Maude expressed more archness than ever before in her life.

"Oh, yes... And particularly radiant today."

"My word, Albert, what will you say next?"

"I'll save it for when we're alone. And how is Marmalade today?"

"She's in fine condition and wants to be out and about."

"Scotty is looking forward to meeting her again. They get on perfectly together."

"Yes, they do, rather, and I feel that's so important."

"Where shall we go? Along the lanes, Marley Mound, or into the forest?"

"We'll see. It very much depends on who is riding with us."

"Does it, indeed? I *was* thinking of Cupid's Ride."

"It's Cowper's Ride, as you well know."

"I don't believe Cowper will be there today. Cupid, on the other hand..."

"Oh, is that so? Then why are we standing here talking?" Maude turned to the groom. "Bring out Dr Beaton's horse."

As the groom left, Daniel, the footman, arrived with a message.

"Excuse me, sir. Inspector Talford is wanting to see you."

"What *now*?" A mild form of fury distorted his features for a moment.

"Tell him Dr Beaton shall see him later, Daniel," said Maude.

"Well, I would, Miss Maude, but the Inspector's anxious loike."

"Why?"

"I dunno, but he's calling for others, too."

"Huh, I'd better see what he wants," said the doctor.

"This is too bad... I know, I'll see him as well."

"I don't think he asked for you, miss," said Daniel.

"I'm seeing him, whether he likes it or not." Without warning, Maude bellowed to the groom. "Leave Scotty in his stall!

Take Marmalade for a walk!" She smiled at Albert. "Come on," she took him by the arm, "let's meet this blighter, together."

Basil and Fiona Hazlett stood on Marley Mound with a sparkling countryside about them.

"This is so lovely," said Fiona. "The wind sweeps everything clean... All one's thoughts, I mean."

"Yes, it's refreshing. The weather will change any day. It feels like we're living on borrowed time in more than one sense."

"Who do you think killed him?"

"I haven't a clue and I don't really want to know."

"The police believe it's one of us, don't they?"

"So it seems. Mr Scrope's bluster and father's anger hide their fears. We all have the same worry."

"All wondering who it was, and someone hoping not to be discovered... I lost sight of you yesterday. Did you stay behind after we exchanged horses or did you come out again?"

"I was with Uncle Horry, drinking a whisky. He and I can give each other an alibi."

"Ah, that's good for both of you. And a relief for me. I get the impression that I'm exempted from suspicion because I was not with the main party."

"You were with Reggie and Oscar... You didn't notice anything odd, did you?"

"About them, you mean? No, I don't believe so. We left the stables shortly after ten. I caught up with Lady Jane and those two galloped off somewhere."

"I suppose they can vouch for each other. What a ghastly business it all is."

"Yes... Maria Smythe returned home. I shall stay in touch with her... poor woman. She clung to her dog as though someone was going to take it away."

"Mother is planning something for her."

"Yes. I put us down for a hundred. I hope you don't mind."

"No, I want her looked after," said Basil.

"It seems we can't escape even high up here."

They were quiet for some moments until Fiona spoke again. "What was that row about? I missed it."

"Quite the shocker," said Basil. "It appears one of the London maids tore a strip off Isembard."

"Good for her. I'm sure he deserved it. That man is most peculiar."

"Yes, he is. But what's interesting is she didn't sound like a maid. Uncle Horry said she was more like a duchess, and he heard them."

"That can't be Nancy, not with her accent."

"Which one's that?"

"The one with reddish curls. She's so funny. Nancy told me a story that had me in a fit of laughter."

"What did she say?"

"I'm not telling you, it's private."

"Who's the dark one, then?"

"Gladys. How anyone could be so beautiful and still be a maid, I have no idea. Apparently, she's brainless. Vanessa loathes her."

"Does she?"

"Competition, dear. Vanessa has to be the centre of attention, so she finds it hard to be outshone by a maid."

"And she's brainless?"

"It's what several have commented. But they don't fault her work, which is very good, I understand."

"There's the maid we met when we arrived."

"Phoebe. Yes, she's sharp. I can visualize her pitching into Isembard."

"What an interesting lot of maids."

"Far too interesting. When I'm able to choose the staff at Lady Holme, we'll employ dry old sticks who dither and then there'll be peace in the house. Come on, the horses want their exercise."

"It will go easier if you help us in the matter," said Talford. "We've got your thumbprint on the mace."

"As I told you, I handled several maces." Dr Beaton looked exasperated.

"You were selecting a suitable one for the job, no doubt."

"Lord Hazlett always keeps the Armoury open for visitors. It's a museum, after all. I couldn't have been the only person who came in here and picked up weapons."

"You were in here alone. Nobody saw you, and you left unseen. Why'd you do it?"

"I didn't do anything. What's the matter with you?"

"You've got no alibi."

"Ask among the servants. One of them must have…"

"What? That won't do you any good, even if they did see you. You had the mace under your jacket. You kept it there while riding. For some reason, which we'll discover, you had murderous intent towards poor Mr Smythe."

"Of course, I didn't. This is absurd. By profession, I'm a healer, a medico. I don't take life; I restore it."

"Is that the best you can do?"

The men in the Armoury were silent until Talford spoke again.

"Dr Albert Beaton, I arrest you for the willful murder of Richard Smythe. You need not say anything, but anything you do say will be taken down and may be given in evidence against you in a court of law."

"I'll wait to see a lawyer before I say anything more, other than that I am completely innocent of the charge. You've made a grievous mistake, Talford."

"Ring up Lymington." Talford spoke to Detective Clark. "Tell them we want a car and two constables, as quick as they can."

Ambling down a grassy path through the trees, Reginald and Amelia were enjoying their time together.

"Are you at all jealous about your brother getting the title and Lady Holme?"

"Not anymore. As a young man, it sent me broody for a while. I didn't begrudge it him, but I wished I could have had the same. It's not the title so much as the place."

"Did that change when you moved away?"

"Before that. It's when I realized the extent of the responsibility that came with the inheritance. I saw it was for the best. Being second fiddle has its advantages."

"I like Basil... I like all your family. He will be a kindly master, I think."

"He does well on the stock exchange, too. I want to invest, but I don't understand it properly."

"Here's an idea. Why not ask him to help you with your investments? You're his brother and he's kindly disposed towards you. If he does well, you'll benefit from his experience."

"How extraordinary. Do you know that while I've been, yes, I'll say it, a little jealous of him, asking for his advice has never once crossed my mind?"

"I'm the outsider peeking in. The arrangement of your family's attitudes looks somewhat different to me than it does to you. There's nothing clever about it."

"I think there is. You're very perceptive."

"One of my many talents," she laughed.

"Hold on a moment. You're a socialist and here we are, talking of stocks and profits."

"That must be puzzling for you. I shan't be tiresome, but I should give you some sense of what I believe. My idea is that all people should receive set minimum incomes that rise with inflation. If they can, they must work. Those working harder or more diligently should be rewarded for their efforts. For people to strive to better themselves and help the nation as a whole, there needs to be incentives, otherwise they simply won't do it... The exact details need to be thrashed out, but that's it in a nutshell. The stock market should continue because it's an efficient use of capital, if well regulated.

"Populations will always stratify into different classes. There are those that rule, those who make up the bulk of a population, and then those who are poor for various reasons. If this could be a land that shares more of its wealth and power instead of concentrating it into the hands of the few, it would be better, far better for many millions of people."

"That sounds sensible. I think our democracy, successive Labour governments, and the war have advanced some of those things."

"They have. There's a long way to go."

"So you don't espouse bloody revolution, or grinding taxation?"

"No, not at all. Threaten it, to wrest power away from where it's tightly gripped now, but never deliver on the threats. Whenever I reflect upon these things, I always keep Lord Hazlett in mind. It causes me difficulties sometimes. There is nothing I want to take away from him. Better would be is if he saw what was right, and yielded some privilege and control to others... His situation is unique, but I really mean the entire class. That's my outline for Utopian Britain. What's yours?"

"As a born stick-in-the mud, I'd prefer for things to carry on as they are. But if there has to be a change, I'll subscribe to your Utopia, if I may."

"That is very flattering. Is it sincere, though?"

"I said I was a blank slate. You've just written something."

"I understood you meant that metaphorically."

"Amelia, for anything to work between us, we should be of one mind. Why would we not pick the best thoughts that each brings and stick to those? I would have voted for your father if I resided in his riding. After our discussion, I'll vote for the candidate who benefits the most Britons."

"You'll change as quickly as that?"

"I must."

"I suppose so... You're starting to fascinate me."

"Then let's talk more politics."

"No. We'll race instead."
"All right... That oak tree. Last one there is a...?"
"Smelly pig."

"Beaton? Has Talford gone mad?"

Lord Hazlett, sitting on Chieftain, had just returned from a ride. Lady Jane, dressed for riding but yet to go, had told him the news.

"I fear he must have. I don't know what to do. Maude's in her room having a crying fit. They've taken Dr Beaton away in handcuffs. Come inside, James, and we'll discuss everything quietly, before the others make a fuss."

"Is Doctor Beaton a murderer?" asked Sophie. "Nancy, you go first."

"I wouldn't 'ave said so. He's too dotty about Maude to be bashing people over the 'ead."

"I agree," said Flora. "Remember, Rand-Sayers — he of the magnificent two-pound bribe — was in the Armoury. Why bribe me if he's innocent?"

"Well," responded Sophie, "the problem we face is that all we are doing is guessing. The major factor is that Richard Smythe was on to the smugglers and he was right. Guns and explosives are coming into the country. Which of the two men we were just speaking about is likely to have silenced Mr Smythe because he was drawing attention to a criminal network?"

"Before we go any further," said Ada, "I'd like to say it's getting risky... again."

"Yes, it is," said Sophie. "We shall be careful and watch what we say. However, if we can identify a suspect, then the risk diminishes."

"Thinking about it," began Flora, "the bribe Rand-Sayers gave only sufficed to cover an indiscretion, such as, don't let my wife know I was flirting with you, or please don't complain about my behaviour because I'm trying to get a job."

"He frequently talks to Martin Scrope," observed Sophie.

"Now you mention it, that's right. I heard them talking in the School Room, and Mr Scrope was giving directions to some railway offices. I thought it odd at the time."

"So if you kick up a fuss, Mr Scrope will not consider Rand-Sayers for a position. We need to check this point. It strikes me that a murderer would never draw attention to himself with either the behaviour of a bounder or a bribe to cover such behaviour."

"He's out then, is 'e?" asked Ada. "I hope so, because I'm tired of 'earing 'is name."

Sophie smiled. "I have a relative with a three-barrelled name."

"I can beat that," said Flora. "I've one with four."

"Do you? Who's that?"

"John Winslow-Pickett-Ayres-Caernavon."

"You mean John Pickett? I didn't know he carried all that baggage."

"I didn't beat you because you know him, too."

"No, you won, because you knew the name and I didn't. Mine's Anne Ponsonby-Forbes-Miller."

"Those two should get married," said Ada.

They all laughed.

"Do you realize that they're about the right age?" Sophie looked serious.

"How could we engineer a meeting?" asked Flora.

"I'm not sure... Yes, I am! Auntie Bessie would be on for that."

"Yes, she would. Do ask her and make sure we're both there. Ada and I can be maids."

"No, you won't. You'll both sit down to dinner. Ada will go as... What can you go as?"

"Oh, no, you can't do that to me."

"Yes, we can," said Sophie. "There's nothing to worry about and you'll enjoy it."

"I know, you can be a Music Hall entertainer," said Flora.

"Yes, brilliant."

"I don't know about that," said Ada, shaking her head.

"I'll coach you," said Flora. "You can definitely sing... or you could tell jokes. They'll expect something from you to earn your supper. Go on, be a sport."

"I'm going to pretend to be a music hall entertainer, sing in front of a crowd of people with titles just so you *might* get two people to fall in love and have the longest name in history? You're crackers... I must be an' all. All right, I'll do it."

"Ada, you're a darling," said Flora.

Sophie hugged her. "You'll meet my Auntie Bessie, and she is one of a kind... That reminds me, she knows I'm a spy."

"I'm astonished," said Flora. "How did she find out?"

"It requires explanation, so I'll tell when we go home. She's become a spy, too, by the way. A sort of auxiliary. Anyway, what were we talking about? Ah, yes, we must remain in character and get on with the job. Let's eliminate Mr double-barrel for the time being. Dr Beaton as murderer and smuggler... What do you think?"

"No," answered Ada and Flora.

"Then it's unanimous. The best way for us to get him out of hot water is to find the actual murderer. He's safe where he is; upset, no doubt, but he'll survive."

"I don't think Maude will," said Ada. "Did you 'ear 'er? She was lying on the floor at one point, banging, kicking, and screaming. Then she started wailing."

"That was her making that noise, was it?" said Sophie. "She should be ashamed of herself... Perhaps Dr Beaton would be safer to stay in prison."

Flora, laughing, said, "I think so, too, but look at it another way. She might need Dr Beaton to set her straight. He doesn't seem the sort of chap to put up with that nonsense."

"And they lived happily ever after. I wonder if we'll be here long enough to see him released." Sophie wrote some notes in shorthand.

"Now, riding clothes. Any signs of wear and tear from a knobbly mace?"

Both Flora and Ada gave several names while Sophie recorded their findings.

"Nothing interesting there. Dora says the laundress hasn't received jackets yet. It's difficult for us to get access to the rooms we're not assigned to... What about this for an idea? We put a note in everyone's bedroom saying they should leave their riding jackets on a hanger outside if they want them brushed."

"We could do that," said Ada. "The door 'andles are sturdy and high enough. Do we keep it from Mrs Williams?"

"I don't really like to but, because she might say no, I think we must. It's easily excused if she finds out and objects."

"I like Mrs Williams," said Flora. "She was humming Lavender's Blue this morning."

"Ah, that's nice," said Ada. "Poor soul, 'aving to put up with Isembard."

"I've heard all about what happened," said Flora. "I wish I'd been there."

"You should have seen 'is face. It sort of sagged as Phoebe was speaking. His jaw dropped so far it was resting on 'is stomach. Beautiful, it was."

"Sorry, I couldn't stop myself. I know, I'm supposed to be incognito, and I've jeopardized things."

"Don't be sorry in the slightest," said Flora. "I learned today that he bullies Nelly from time to time, but the beast's favourite target is Mabel."

"What! He bullies them... those little girls?"

"Mabel slept in Mrs Williams' room for a while. She was so frightened of Isembard she couldn't sleep by herself."

"Didn't Mrs Williams do anything about it?" asked Sophie.

"She informed Lady Jane, who went to Lord James, who spoke to Isembard. Matters improved afterwards, but Mabel's afraid of him. Now he teases her over her fears. She's an orphan, as I'm sure you've realized, and has nowhere else to go."

"It's because that wretch has a hold over Lord Hazlett," said Sophie. "Ada, did I say anything to you when we left Isembard earlier?"

"You said, 'We shall destroy him'. Sounded like you wanted to do it on the spot."

"Ah, so I did speak it and didn't just think it. We have duties now, but later, when we meet again, please bring ideas as to how we can see about the man's complete downfall and utter destruction."

Chapter 18

A Secret and a Confession

"Janey, I'm completely adrift."

Lord and Lady Hazlett had gained a temporary respite from maintaining appearances by hiding in her ladyship's bedroom.

"It's all so dreadful... Is there something the matter?"

Lord James looked pathetic when he shrugged in answer, remaining mute.

"No, tell me. It's not just Beaton and Smythe, there's something else... Please tell me."

"I can't... I can't say anything."

"What is it? You look so haggard. My dear James..."

They sat in silence. Lady Jane sat on the thick quilts of her four-poster bed while his lordship sat, as though whipped, in a chair with soft gold upholstery.

"If I'd not stayed on the estate for so long, I might meet the challenges that have arisen since yesterday, but I find I can't."

"How can I help if you don't confide in me?"

She asked again, "Who is it?"

James stared at her.

"Is it Benson?"

Jane watched as he struggled to understand and failed. A flush mounted to his face.

"Why did you invite him?"

"You have your secrets and I have mine. Before you leap to the wrong conclusion, I have always been faithful to you, so don't go ruminating in that direction."

"Janey! What secrets are these?"

"I can't tell you, just as you won't tell me yours. But I'll tell you this much. Never trust Benson for a minute. He is a snake."

James stood up. "I can't take much more. You must tell me."

"Very well, I will. It will do me good to unburden myself. I shall tell you the truth and you can probably bear it quite well, *if* you trust me."

"Go on."

"There was a time when we could not stand the sight of one another."

"Never."

"I'll rephrase it. You annoyed me so much with your refusal to go anywhere, that I was sick of this place and your attitude for some months. I believe you recall that time."

"I do."

"When I took Basil and stayed with my aunt in Eastbourne, it so happened that after a month I met a gentleman, the son of an acquaintance of my aunt. He was kind and quite charming and we got on well. I could not help but find his company pleasant. We wrote to each other. These were not passionate letters. However, you could not mistake the chaste fondness contained in them. They were mildly indiscreet, but you couldn't possibly read anything more into them. The gentleman departed and we both subsequently lost interest. We never corresponded again. I realized what a near miss I had had and how foolish I'd been. I regretted my attraction to him and that's when I came home. The letters themselves were innocuous. If I had one, I'd show it to you now. I'd blush over the connection, but not for the contents of the missive.

"About a year ago, when I travelled to London to stay with my sister, I attended a large party in Mayfair. I remember telling you about it. That was where I was introduced to Mr Benson, the snake. To be brief, he suggested we meet for lunch the next day because there was something urgent he wished to impart concerning you. Naturally, I was intrigued, because I thought I might learn something about your secret. In considering our age difference and my being some thirty-five years older than he, I assumed there was no harm in lunching in a public place.

"They say there is no fool like an old fool. I was not aware of Benson's reputation, which is that of a gigolo. My being seen with him got my name lumped in with those of his other victims, and victims they are, as I learned later. It was just the one occasion we met alone, and yet, it was sufficient for my reputation to suffer a slight tarnishing. That's all it amounts to, I believe."

"This is disturbing," said James. "Why did you invite him here?"

"I'm coming to that. Being seen with Benson and becoming a subject of gossip is not the main issue. While we sat at the table, he mentioned he possessed letters of mine - the letters to the Eastbourne gentleman. I have no idea *how* he obtained them, but it is certain that he did. He was repellently smooth in his explanations. He quoted from one and it sounded more or less as I recalled it, containing mild admiration, esteem, and a wish to meet again at some future date. However, he went on to say he had eight such letters. That was impossible. I wrote three. He said there were eight. I challenged him and he quoted something which had a truly gross and monstrous meaning. He further stated that no expert could tell the handwriting apart between any of the eight letters."

Lady Jane stared at the rug.

"I'm sorry. A moment's weakness and I've caused so much trouble."

"I suppose he asked for money."

"Not immediately. He gained a type of control over me. I couldn't have you find out. By arrangement, I attended a few larger gatherings where he was also present. Privately, he showed me one of the forged letters, for such they are." Lady Jane swallowed hard. "It looked like my handwriting." A tear dropped on her dress. "Excuse me." She dabbed her eyes with a handkerchief.

"How much have you paid him?"

"To date, almost four hundred pounds. He's asking for much more now. He wants to sell me all the letters, including my originals, for two thousand."

There was a long silence between them. It extended for so long, Jane was on the verge of pleading for her husband to respond. She would rather he raged at her or put his head in his hands and groaned than keep silent. Then she would know what he thought.

"I'd give a shilling for the lot. They're not worth more than that."

Jane started and gave him a hopeful look. James got out of his chair to sit on the bed beside her. He put his arm around her shoulders and she lent against him. He cradled her, kissing the top of her head.

"I'll deal with him from now on. If he approaches you, just say you can't get the money at the moment. He's a dangerous man, my dear. He will not always oppress us. A year from now, things will change. Believe me, they will change for the better. We'll go to London together. However, there's great danger for us both between now and then."

"Oh, I think I see… Ha, why is this happening to us? Someone has forced you to stay at home."

"I have been forced, but I can't tell you more. It's for your own safety. It is best you never know, but ask again in a year's time, and I shall tell you the entire history. Come, Janey, let's pull ourselves together and go downstairs."

"What a picture," said Gowers as the car entered the drive.

"Just stop a moment." said Morton.

The Morris came to a halt. Morton got out first. He stared at Lady Holme. His dark grey suit jacket was open, his hands were in his pockets, and a look of delight was on his usually serious face.

"They don't make them like that anymore," said Gowers, joining him.

"This is the prettiest place I've ever seen," said Morton.

"Look at the brickwork in those chimneys. Lovely. They knew what they were doing back then."

"And the stables... Well, let's knock and we'll see what's inside."

They got back in. Gowers parked the car, and the two men presented themselves at the front door. Isembard opened it.

"Morning," said the inspector. "We're from Scotland Yard. We'd like to see Lord Hazlett. Is he at home?"

"He is, sir. Please, come in."

The butler held the door while they entered.

"If you wait here, I shall find his lordship."

"Thank you," said Gowers. The two men removed their hats.

When he had gone, Morton said,

"I don't like his looks. If he hasn't got a record, he should have."

"He drinks," said Gowers. "Probably fiddles the accounts."

While they waited, they examined the Entrance Hall.

"It's funny. The house is so fancy on the outside but quite plain inside. But it's a nice, comfortable sort of plain... Something you could live with and enjoy."

"Would you rather have seen Fulham play or come here?"

"Must keep things in perspective, sir. This is a nice consolation prize."

The detectives waited. A maid crossed the hall. She stopped when she saw them.

"I don't believe my eyes," said Morton. His astonishment was complete. "What's she doing here?" His pale blue eyes smouldered with annoyance.

"Oh, it's Miss Burgoyne," said Gowers, smiling.

Sophie approached them.

"Gentlemen," Sophie bobbed. "Who are you waiting for?" She glanced behind her and then turned back to whisper.

"My name's Phoebe King. Don't forget it. Flora and Ada are here, too. I'll tell you their pseudonyms later. Please act as though we've never met."

"Would you mind telling me *why* you're here?"

"They hired us as maids. Inspector Morton, please don't be annoyed, it's all above board."

"I doubt it. The maid part might be. The fake names?"

"I'll tell you everything later. It's so lovely seeing you both again. I must go. Remember, you don't know us. Goodbye."

"Miss Burgoyne's a right gem of a lady, isn't she?" said Gowers, smiling, watching her walk away. He looked at Morton, who was scowling ferociously.

"You do realize," said Morton, "her presence here means there's more than murder going on?" He shook his head and looked annoyed. "I don't *believe* it!"

The Scotland Yard men met with Lord Hazlett and, after a brief discussion in which Beaton's arrest was mentioned, he took them to meet Talford and Clark in the Armoury. As soon as they were introduced, Hazlett left them to it.

Detective Clark and Sergeant Gowers conversed with each other. They spoke a little of the case, but more so of their mutual interest in the weapons in the room.

"Let's go for a walk," said Morton to Talford. The Portsmouth Inspector had a complacent air.

"If you like," he replied.

They stepped outside to stroll across the gravel.

"So you've nicked Doctor Beaton. On what grounds?"

"Evidence. His thumbprint's on the murder weapon, and he doesn't have an alibi."

"That's good... promising. And his motive?"

"Can't say yet. We're looking into that."

"Hmm, I see... They've given me the lead on the case. Is that your understanding?"

"Yes."

"Then why didn't you wait for my arrival? I'm sure Beaton wasn't going anywhere."

"Didn't want to trouble you. See, I don't understand why they called you in. Not in terms of the case. There's an MP named Scrope here. He took against me and made a complaint. Swayed the others, including Hazlett. They spoke to Major Warde, and the rest, you know."

"These types can be difficult to handle," said Morton. "You should have waited, but you've jumped the gun. Now, let's hope Beaton is the murderer, otherwise you've done a wrong 'un."

"No, I haven't. Beaton's the man." Talford sounded confidant.

"Any witnesses?"

"No. We haven't interviewed everyone. Now they know the murderer's identity, it will go a lot faster."

"Crime scene evidence? Anything tying Beaton to the place and time?"

"Not yet."

"If he's not the murderer, I'd say you've got yourself some trouble. I hope we can get along, but I see it this way - you wanted to make the arrest before the interfering Yard men arrived. Well, you've done it. You objecting to our being present is your affair. I didn't want to come as much as you didn't want us. I was told to come. We must work together and neither of us has a choice in the matter."

"That's a very nice speech, but it's unnecessary now. We've got our man, and that's it. Sorry, you had a wasted journey."

"Like that, is it? I gave you your chance. I want all your reports at once. Remove yourself from the Armoury and find another room. Confine yourself and Clark to interviewing the servants as instructed. Once I've reviewed everything, I'll consider whether to release Beaton from custody."

"You can't come in here…"

"Try me. Enough chat. Reports first, Talford, and get a move on."

Inspector Morton turned away and strode into the house.

"Name?"

"Phoebe King."

"Address?"

"27 Windermere Road, Mile End, London."

"Why are you here?" Talford looked bored. He was interviewing servants in a room off the Servants' Hall.

"'ired out as a maid, sir. Come down Thursday. I wouldn't 'ave come if I'd known anyone was gettin' murdered. And 'im a doctor, an' all. Makes you think, dunnit?"

"What does it make you think?"

"That you can't trust *nobody*." Sophie was serious.

"Yes. Now, tell me all the times you noticed Beaton. From the time he arrived until his arrest. I'm asking all the servants the same questions so I can put together a complete list of his movements."

"Coo, 'ow interesting. Let me see. The first time was when I saw 'im getting off 'is 'orse. Beautiful creature... Ha, ha, the 'orse I mean, Inspector, not the doctor. Whatever will you think of me?"

Sophie laughed loudly, without restraint. Talford stared as though something was the matter with her.

"But tell me something. What 'ave you got against 'im?"

"Just answer the questions, Miss King."

"I will, but go on, tell me, or I won't say another word. Fair's fair, ain't it?"

Talford sighed. "Got his thumbprint on the mace that was the murder weapon."

"Oh, well, then, that's that. He did it if you've got 'is thumbprint. Terrible state of affairs, it is. Anything else?"

Talford brightened. "He has no alibi."

"You'd think 'im being a doctor, 'e'd be clever enough to make one up. Silly man. I reckon it's a crime of passion. Dr

Beaton is taken with Miss Maude. That's worth looking into, that is."

"Yes, it is."

"What more you got? I'm really interested because you policemen are so clever. I don't know 'ow you do it. And the risks you poor boys take, lord love-a-duck, you're all so brave." Sophie fluttered her eyelids.

Ten minutes later, Sophie left, meeting Flora outside, who was waiting to be interviewed.

"I got everything," whispered Sophie to Flora.

"You should have left something for me to discover," she whispered back.

"Sorry."

"Next!" Talford shouted from the room. Flora went in and Sophie returned to her work.

"Name?" asked Talford.

"Gladys Walton."

"Address?"

"83 Cherry Blossom Drive, Wapping."

"Ah, you're from London, too."

"Yes, sir… I didn't do it! I swear, I had nothing to do with it." Flora put a handkerchief up to her mouth.

"Nobody's saying you did. Please calm yourself."

"I'm so afraid of your questions. I might make a mistake and you'll arrest me. My mother would disown me if I'm put in prison."

"We won't do any such thing. You're not a suspect."

"I'm not?"

"No, of course not."

"Did the doctor do it?"

"Yes."

"I'm being so silly. Please forgive me, superintendent. I'm sure you will."

"I'm *Inspector* Talford."

"You should be a superintendent. What a kind, dear man you are. You see, I have lived through so much tragedy. Ever since they arrested father for bigamy and we were forced to live in reduced circumstances, I've been afraid of the police. When I was twelve... Can I tell you my story? It's so heartbreaking, but it's *such* a relief for me to meet someone as sympathetic as you." Flora put a hand on the Inspector's sleeve. She gave him her imploring look, the one that had melted many hearts in London theatres - hearts often harder than Inspector Talford's.

He hesitated. Captivated by the lovely face before him, he felt gripped by the sudden, noble urge to aid Beauty in Distress. "Of course, my dear. I'm in no hurry."

By noon, the news items of Beaton's arrest, the arrival of Scotland Yard detectives, and Maude retreating to her room were known by everyone. Lord and Lady Hazlett's reserve was attributed to those events. As the guests returned from riding, they sought either of their hosts to express their regret over the events. Conventional phrases covered their sense of shock that Dr Beaton was a murderer, often expressed as "It can't possibly be Beaton," and their sense of relief disguised by, "What drove him to do such a thing?" Belinda Beaton was in the School Room lounge with some other guests who seemed to be avoiding her, not knowing what to say. Fiona Hazlett joined her.

"I can't accept Albert is guilty of the charge," said Fiona to Belinda. "Basil and I believe a terrible mistake has been made, one that will soon be cleared up."

"I hope you're right. It's impossible to take this situation seriously," said Belinda. "He would never do such a thing. Never. And why would he? He knew Richard. We both did. They were friendly but rarely met. Will the Scotland Yard men take him to London?"

"I'm not sure," said Fiona. "I don't think so."

"When can I see him?"

"Again, I have no familiarity with the way the police work. I'll get Basil to find out. He's very annoyed about this business."

"He'll want a lawyer..."

"Basil will see to it. He'll make sure that everything is done properly. Try not to worry, Belinda. It's a nightmarish mistake, that's all it is."

"You're very kind... I'm feeling rather awkward here. Some of the others, well, I suppose they're assuming there's no smoke without fire. It's awful how people can change so quickly."

"Yes, it is. Try to buck up. You've got a fight on your hands. You didn't ask for it, but you have it nonetheless. Face them down and tell them your brother is innocent. And keep on telling them. I certainly will."

"Thank you. You're being a good friend, and we've only met a few times."

"Then we'll know each other better in the future. Come on. Don't sit here by yourself. Go and talk to someone." Seeing the idea did not exactly appeal to Belinda, she said, "I know Maude is feeling as bad about all of this as you are. Why not go and find her and try to cheer her up?"

Belinda seemed to far prefer this suggestion and soon went off to find the daughter of the house. Fiona joined a small group comprising the Reids and Colonel Digby.

"I am devastated," Constance was saying. "Why would he do such a thing?"

"Oh, come on," said Colonel Digby. "Nothing's proven yet. They found his fingerprints, that all. Good heavens, it might have been mine they found. I've handled that mace in the past... Years ago, you understand."

"The police are not stupid," said Constance. "They consider Beaton killed Smythe. What a horrible thing he's done. He must have had a reason and they'll find it out. Inspector Talford knows his job and should be commended for acting with such alacrity. It saves us from the ghastly ordeal of not knowing whom to blame."

Fiona spoke.

"Last night you loathed Inspector Talford. Today you praise him. Which is your real opinion? Or should we await a third and definitive pronouncement?" She swept on. "I, for one, believe that Dr Beaton is innocent. I find it disappointing that those whom he would have counted as friends yesterday are now turning against him."

"Your opinion doesn't count, my dear," said Constance. "It's what the police say that does."

"Ah. You and Talford are kindred spirits then. Who could have guessed?"

"Excuse us, Colonel," said Constance, ignoring Fiona. "Come along, Oscar." Constance departed. Her husband smiled awkwardly, then followed her.

Colonel Digby leaned forward to say to Fiona under his breath, "Well done."

"Constance and I have never got along. I doubt we ever will."

"She can be a little unpleasant sometimes," said the Colonel.

"Sad to say, that's true. I can usually put up with her unpleasantness, but not today. It's too important."

"Quite right. But here's the thing. If not Beaton, and I sincerely hope it wasn't because he's a decent fellow, then who was it?"

"I wish I knew. It could be anyone."

"Ah, yes. Puts us all back to square one, doesn't it? Staring at each other and asking oneself, Was it you, old boy?"

"Or, old girl."

"Good point! Though one doesn't like referring to ladies as old girls, what?" He laughed. "Can cause serious trouble saying that sort of thing."

Fiona smiled.

After lunch, a bell in the Servants' Hall summoned Ada to the office.

"Nancy."

"Yes, my Lord."

"Where is Mr Benson at present?"

"About an hour ago, he was out riding with Mrs Digby, Miss Vanessa, and Mr Scrope. I haven't seen any of them since, so they must still be out. Would you like me to enquire further, my Lord?"

"That's unnecessary, thank you."

"Very good, my Lord."

"Wait a moment. Do you know anything about the disturbance on the stairs?"

"I do, my Lord. I was there."

"What happened?"

"Well, Mr Isembard was not being very nice and, er, he was put in 'is place."

"By whom? Was it you?"

"No, my Lord. It was Miss Phoebe King."

"That's all, you may go."

Chapter 19

Horses are only human, too

Early Saturday afternoon, Morton, Gowers, and Detective Clark cycled down to the sea and continued along the coastal track. They came to a stop below Marley Mound and got off their bikes.

Morton walked ahead, closely scanning the path on either side.

"What's the tide doing?" asked Sergeant Gowers.

"It's at full ebb now, so it'll turn soon and come back in."

"Whereabouts was he fished out?"

"See that rock? It was submerged when we got to him. He got fouled in a long bit of rope tied to it. Lucky, or he'd have gone right out."

"You got to him by boat, I hear. I wouldn't fancy traipsing through that lot to pull him in. What is it, mud or sand?"

"A bit of both. It's quite firm here, but it's dangerous elsewhere."

"Reminds me of the Thames Estuary. The muck there wants to pull your boots off. Where did he go in?"

"I'll show you."

Morton had found the place before Clark got there.

"Stay back," shouted Morton, standing by the clump of blackthorn. "It's been trampled enough." He then crouched down to examine the ground, disappearing from view. A minute later, he popped up among some low scrub at the edge of the bank leading down to the sea. He took off his bowler, smoothed his hair, and replaced the hat. Morton searched the mudflats and then gazed across the Solent. He turned, gazing up at Marley Mound. Carefully, he changed position, and looked again. He came out from the scrub and walked beyond the blackthorn bushes, which he examined minutely. He emerged after a while and returned to the others.

"See what you make of it," said Morton to Gowers. The sergeant left to perform his own examination of the scene.

"It's a dead end down there," began Morton. "This path's not used much and can't be overlooked from up top. For open country, he chose a most suitable spot to kill Smythe. The only risk he ran when he killed him was being observed by a passing boat while rolling the body down the slope. Have you asked at the port in Lymington?"

"No, we haven't, sir."

"Right. Uniforms can do that job. Know anyone on the Lymington force who can expedite matters?"

"I do."

"Good. Ring him and tell him to find anyone on a boat along this stretch yesterday morning. They have to be gossiping on the docks. The locals will remember which boats were in the area at the time. I want a list of those boats, whether they came from Southampton or Timbuktu. Got that?"

"Yes, sir. You want that right away?"

"No, next month will do."

"Oh, I see, yes, at once, sir." Clark left immediately.

A little later, Gowers, having finished his examination, returned to Morton.

"He followed Smythe," said Gowers. "He knew this was a dead end and saw his chance."

"Yes. See where that horse crashed about?"

"Couldn't miss it. The murderer's horse didn't, though. Ground's soft beyond that bush and there's plenty of hoof-prints but only from the one horse. It's all hard-packed and stony on this side. I don't think I can get a cast. There was one soft place we passed that looked promising, but it's mucked up with boot-marks and horse traffic."

"I reckon two dozen people walked through here. Go over the ground again. I'll ask around the stables about the horses."

"What do you mean, sir?"

"I don't know exactly. But if one horse was scared, why wasn't the other? We've seen street accidents where nearby horses get jumpy and have to be calmed."

"That's right, they do."

"After that, we'll start the interviews."

"Your name and address, please," asked Inspector Morton.

"Ronald Butterworth. I've lived here for seven years except for one when the Army was like a mother to me - until I caught a packet and got invalided out."

They sat in the stable office that looked more like a sitting room.

"Two ways of looking at getting wounded."

"I'm an optimist now. At the time, I wasn't. Bloody agony, it was. Anyway, how can I help?"

"At the moment, I'm interested in horses. Why did Mr Smythe's horse panic?"

"That's Toffee's way. He's a very nice horse. Perfect manners. But if he gets startled, he wants to bolt. And he did. He came back to the stables cause he knows he's safe here. Saw the blood, he did."

"Do you mean actual blood or a violent action?"

"Um, I suppose I mean the violence. He saw Mr Smythe being struck and when he fell over and didn't move, Toffee knew what was happening."

"I see." Morton wrote notes. "What about the other horse?"

"Other horse...? Oh, I see what you mean. I haven't thought about it."

"You'll have to help me here. The two horses were on a path below Marley Mound. You know it?"

"Yes, the shore path. I've been told it used to be a nice ride along there, but part of it collapsed. This was before my time. The sea undercut the bank until a section disappeared."

"Right. Now it's a dead end, travelling east. With two horses on the path, what happens when one tries to bolt but is trapped by the other?"

"Well, poor old Toffee went a bit mad. Got scratched, so he must have been backing and plunging a fair bit until he got free."

"That sounds fair. What about the other horse?"

"I get you. That depends. A similar temperament to Toffee and they'd both be off."

"The second horse didn't, though. At least, I couldn't see any signs at all that it had panicked. Smythe's assailant also had to dismount and must have tied up the horse."

"So you're trying to narrow it down by the horse's temperament. That's very clever. Puts me in a spot, though, don't it?"

"It does. It won't prove anything, but it's a possible line of enquiry."

"I suppose so. Very well, then. I know Lord Hazlett's horses as though they're family. Chieftain, his Lordship's horse, could go through a battle without twitching. Same could be said of Marmalade, Miss Maude's horse. Marmalade has a lot of energy, but does as she's told. Primrose, Lady Hazlett's horse, is on the flighty side, so I don't reckon her."

Ronald explained the temperaments of the various horses.

"So, by your estimation, three would have stood by while Toffee panicked. Who was riding Falcon?"

"Falcon was a change horse. Let me see, it was Mr Basil first, and then Oscar Reid."

Morton wrote the names in his notebook.

"What about the horses brought by guests?"

"The Scrope family has three. Miss Vanessa's horse, Shangri-La, is far too nervy. A nice, fast colt, but he needs proper training to get the best out of him. Both Fanfare and Kaleidoscope are quiet. Yes, they both might be placid enough for what you're thinking."

"Who rode which?"

"Kaleidoscope is Miss Amelia's and is a quiet horse… possible. Fanfare's Mr Scrope's mount. He's quite old now, but very sound."

"The horse, you mean?"

Ronald laughed while Morton smiled.

"What about Dr Beaton and Belinda Beaton?"

"Scotty, I'd have said no. Dr Beaton has trouble with him sometimes and it takes a while to get him settled again. Now, Conker, oh yes. She's a beauty."

"Is that all of them?"

"No, there's the Colonel's horses, Claude and Mercy. Claude's got a bit of a temper, but he settles down quickly. I don't know what to tell you about him. Mercy, I'd say she would stand calmly by while a murder's going on, but I'm not sure. You know, Inspector, even though I've said all that, a horse can be unpredictable, and do the exact opposite of what you'd expect."

"I wish you hadn't told me that last part. At least I've got something to go on. Thank you very much."

"I'm happy to help. Oh, something I've been thinking about. This murder wouldn't be connected with the smugglers, would it?"

"Smugglers? What are you talking about?"

"Don't you know? Of course, you've only just arrived. Mr Smythe was talking to Lord Hazlett about it before everyone went riding. His lordship was none too pleased with him bringing the subject up. Got quite sharp with him, he did. I'm not surprised, though, as they were all happy about setting off and Mr Smythe was spoiling it."

"Where was this?"

"Just outside here. First thing, it was."

"That's interesting. What have you heard about this smuggling business?"

Ronald told him his story.

Mrs Williams found Sophie putting some clean linen away.

"Phoebe, Lady Hazlett wants to see you. She's in the office."

"Yes, Mrs Williams." She observed the housekeeper's stiff attitude. "Is it about this morning?"

"I should imagine so."

"I'm very sorry if I have caused either you or her ladyship any trouble."

"No, don't apologize to me. We all know how difficult Mr Isembard can be. I can only reiterate that you put up with him as best you can while you're here. I wish there was something to be done." Mrs Williams appeared ready to say more, but did not.

"Yes, Mrs Williams. Are we to see Lady Hazlett together?"

"No, it's unnecessary. I'm sure she will just inquire into what happened. Nancy has already informed me about the incident when I asked her." A smile played about Mrs Williams' mouth. "She described it so well, I thought I'd been present."

"You wanted to see me, my Lady," said Sophie.

Lady Hazlett turned in the chair at the desk.

"Come nearer."

Sophie approached to stand on the Turkey rug. Lady Jane stared at her, as if seeing the maid for the first time.

"You had a fracas with my butler this morning, which disturbed some guests. What do you have to say for yourself?"

"I apologize for such disgraceful behaviour on my part."

Lady Hazlett waited. "Is that all?"

"Yes, my Lady."

"Extraordinary - that you do not try to justify yourself. It so happens that my brother, Colonel Digby, has given me a more or less verbatim report of what passed between you and Isembard."

"I regret subjecting the Colonel to such unseemly conduct."

"The Colonel is no shrinking violet. He was in the army for thirty years. I have not called you here because of your row with Isembard. I should apologize to you for retaining such a servant. That's beside the point. What I wish to know is what Isembard meant by saying, 'Go to her ladyship. We'll see what happens.' What do you understand he meant by it?"

As Sophie stood there, the ground seemed to shift under her feet as she thought rapidly. It seemed apparent that Isembard's hold over Lord James was a fact unknown to Lady Jane. Her ladyship was fishing for information. Should she speak or keep quiet? If she spoke, what could she say?

"I assumed he meant that his position being one of such importance, he would convince you to sue the agency for breaking the contract if we all left you in the lurch."

"It was unfortunate I was dragged into your contretemps at all, but if that is all you understood by his remark, no more need be said."

"The way he spoke was quite significant," said Sophie.

"Oh, was it?"

"His manner suggested he has a hold over you. Or, if not you, then Lord Hazlett."

Lady Jane stared again at Sophie before replying.

"Isembard is a peculiar person. He may not have full control over his features or his mind."

"His features, yes, my Lady, I agree. I believe his attitude results from his blackmailing Lord Hazlett over a serious matter that has nothing to do with infidelity."

Lady Jane's mouth opened slightly, although she did not speak. She looked stricken.

"The other servants are unaware of this," continued Sophie, hoping she had not made a mistake.

"How do you know?"

Sophie understood she referred to Isembard and not the rest of the household.

"By observation. Isembard is stealing from the household accounts through arrangements with the trades. I have evidence of one arrangement while I'm assuming the others. He eavesdrops on Lord Hazlett's telephone conversations. He makes himself unfit to be a butler through his conduct towards the staff. It's remarkable he has avoided being discharged. The question I ask myself is why is he kept on? My answer is he has a hold over Lord Hazlett. I understand that you would have discharged him, but it was his lordship's desire to keep him."

"You think it blackmail, then?"

"I can't think what else. As his lordship has not left the estate in thirty-nine years, either the blackmail must relate to his seclusion or his seclusion to the blackmail. When he left years ago, a man died. I suppose, should he leave again, another person will die. It is my conjecture, and it is only my opinion, my Lady, that Isembard is a spy, installed in the house to report to others on Lord Hazlett's conduct and movements."

"This is too far-fetched."

"It is highly unusual, although I would add this. With a murder on the estate, and Lord Hazlett, and yourself, of course, my Lady, being so unfairly troubled by such an event, it is quite remarkable that Isembard is walking about the house looking rather smug. Under these trying circumstances, he must have achieved something in which he takes pleasure and pride. As an avaricious man who steals from the accounts, it is easy to infer he has found financial success in another area. If he were merely a butler, he would adopt the mood of the house. As a blackmailer, he has triumphed and he cannot help but show it. I have no definitive proof of blackmail. Although I never gamble, I would stake all I have on my conjecture."

Lady Jane considered what she had been told.

"Phoebe, stay right here until I return. I will be gone for five minutes."

"Yes, my Lady."

Lady Jane hurried to the stables. She found Lord James talking to a groom. She did not hesitate.

"Please leave us for a moment. I wish to speak to his lordship privately."

Lady Jane stared after the groom as he walked away. Her husband gazed at the side of her face. She turned back to him.

"More bad news?" he asked.

"This is not about Benson. I'll not leave until you tell me one thing. Is Isembard blackmailing you?"

"My dear, really…"

"You shall tell me. Is he blackmailing you?"

He did not answer.

"Is he? I will not step from this spot. I'll spend the night here if I have to. Is he...? Look at me. Is he?"

"Yes."

"Thank you."

Lady Jane walked away. She returned to the office, regaining composure on the way.

"You were perfectly right," she said as she closed the door. "How you deduced all of that is beyond me. But, it seems, it is a matter of fact."

Sophie felt relieved even while an awkwardness arose between them.

"May I speak, my Lady?"

"Yes."

"I'm sure Dr Beaton is innocent."

"Are you? Do you have an idea who killed poor Mr Smythe?"

"Unfortunately, I don't. I trust the Scotland Yard men to discover who did."

"Let us hope they do. Thank you, Phoebe. You may return to your duties."

Sophie bobbed. As she reached for the door handle, Lady Hazlett said,

"Another thing. If you notice unusual behaviour in anyone else, would you keep me informed?"

"Certainly, my Lady."

Sophie closed the door, wondering to whom her ladyship referred. In the office, Lady Jane stared at the closed door, surprised and baffled by the character and conduct of the maid from Burgoyne's Agency.

At four, tea was served in the Drawing Room.

"How did the interrogation go?" asked Constance as she sipped her tea.

"Darling, it was positively indecent," said Vanessa Scrope. "Inspector Morton has these penetrating blue eyes that transfixes one. I felt he could read my innermost thoughts, and I was unable to withhold a thing from him. It was *absolutely* thrilling."

"Oh, was it?" replied Constance. "I'll be seeing him soon."

"What sort of questions?" asked Daphne.

"The usual rot they have to go through. I gave him my telephone number and asked him to ring me - simply begged him. I suggested dinner together. Do you think that was brazen of me?" By looks, Vanessa polled the others for their opinions.

At another table, Helen Scrope, Sandra Digby, and Lady Jane sat together.

"I despair of my children sometimes," said Helen, in a matter-of-fact voice. "Vanessa's the worst of the two. I used to be deeply concerned about her welfare. Now I'm simply embarrassed by my offspring. I wish she would marry and move to South Africa. Actually, I'd be content if she just moved, though I'd pity the South Africans. I wonder what they would make of her?"

"She certainly makes a splash wherever she goes," said Sandra.

"I've stopped following her antics in the society columns, otherwise my face would take on a permanent flush."

"Do her escapades affect Martin's position as a member of parliament?" asked Lady Jane.

"Surprisingly, no. It might if the Conservatives ever form a government again. As it is, it seems the electorate of East Portsmouth is quite proud of our wayward daughter and has taken her to heart — that includes Labour voters. I can understand how entertaining she must be to others, but, being her mother, I find her rather awful."

"Maude's being difficult," said Lady Jane. "She won't come out of her room."

"Shall I go up and have a word with her?" asked Sandra.

"If you could, it might help. I'm surprised at the depth of her affection for Doctor Beaton."

"It's a pity he was arrested," said Sandra. "They've obviously made a mistake, although, it makes one think, doesn't it?"

"Yes." Lady Jane watched as Sophie offered more tea from a tray to Adrian Benson. "Perhaps Inspector Morton will put matters right if he can find the time between corrupting our daughters."

"Don't you believe it," said Helen. "Vanessa dramatizes everything. A welcoming smile from the Inspector will be construed as a deep, hidden passion for her. She thrives on it."

"Despite all the frightfulness," said Sandra, "Amelia and Reginald are spending quite a lot of time together. It made me wonder if a romance is blooming there."

Lady Jane and Helen searched each other's face for a sign that they found such news agreeable. They were both reassured by what they discovered.

"What have you noticed?" asked Lady Jane of Sandra.

"I read in the paper, they're making hand signals compulsory," said Colonel Digby. "About time, too. Some drivers have a complete disregard for life and property."

"I'm about to purchase a car," said Adrian Benson. "I'd better learn what they are."

"Have you driven before?" asked the Colonel.

"Rarely. Only cars of friends to learn how. What are the hand signals?"

"I'll show you."

The Colonel put his cup and saucer down to show and explain the signals for turns and stops. Adrian followed his lead.

"Adrian!" called Vanessa. "You simply must put that in a dance routine!"

"Only for you, darling," he replied.

Vanessa giggled. Lady Jane glowered. Reginald sneered. Lord Hazlett turned away. Constance raised her eyebrows. Basil shook his head. Helen Scrope expressed nothing. Maude would have slapped Adrian on the back and laughed uproariously, but, at that moment, she was leaning out of her bedroom window looking towards Lymington. Up until luncheon, she had only had thoughts for Dr Beaton. Now, thoroughly bored, Maude was trying to gauge when she might safely return downstairs and how to minimize the fuss and comments her reappearance would cause. She was determined not to miss dinner.

After tea, the Drawing Room was restored to order in record time. The London maids astonished the other servants by their speed and dexterity. The reason for this alacrity was that the germ of an idea had first sprouted and was then whispered amongst them before tea. As one told another, the hearer's face lit up with extraordinary joy. She would then augment the scheme with her own input. Now that they had a plan, they wanted to prepare and rehearse for that which they would bring to pass. They needed every minute they could gain between teatime and their own dinner.

"A word with you, please." Inspector Morton had stepped out of the Armoury to block Sophie's path.

"Is this how you arrest people? It's so effective. I can only spare you a few minutes."

As soon as he heard her light tone and superior, friendly voice, Morton understood he would not receive complete answers from Sophie. He may learn something, but not everything. It annoyed him. They sat down among the weaponry of past eras.

"Right. You are here for an ulterior motive. Let's have it."

"I know I irritate you, but really, Inspector, please be civil. It's much nicer, and I'm sure you're not as gruff as you pretend to be. I'm not a criminal."

He stared.

"Every time I talk to you, Miss Burgoyne, you withhold information, and I don't like that. You may have your reasons for keeping mum, but I have my reasons for needing to find out what you know. Such as, I've a murder case on my hands."

"Anything useful I'll give to you freely."

"All right, let's see how far we get. Phoebe King? What's all that about?"

"It wasn't absolutely necessary for me to use my nom de guerre this time but, you see, I spoke to Lady Hazlett on the telephone as Sophie Burgoyne, manageress, so I didn't like to be SB, the maid, as well."

"Fair enough. The others?"

"They entered the spirit of the thing and chose names for themselves."

"Very nice. How did Lady Hazlett come to hear of Burgoyne's?"

"She received a sales letter advertising our services."

He paused, transfixing her with his pale blue-eyed stare.

"Don't you believe me?" asked Sophie. "It's true. Ask Lady Jane or Mrs Williams."

"I will. It's not the truthfulness of your statement so much as its potential incompleteness."

"In what way do you think it might be incomplete?"

"That's the problem, right there. I've no idea unless you tell me." He waited.

"Oh, well," said Sophie. "Shall we press on?"

"Your arrival pre-dates the murder. Are you here because you believed a murder might take place?"

"Absolutely not. I'm as shocked and outraged at the surprising turn of events as anyone else."

"What's the other reason for your presence in Lady Holme?"

"There is no *other* reason, as you put it. We are present because of the possibility of smugglers operating along this particular coast. I wanted to confirm my suspicion."

"So you were aware of the smuggling?"

"It's possible Mr Smythe was killed because of it," said Sophie.

"You think so...? How did you hear of it? And what smuggling are we talking about?"

"That boat that blew up off Hurst Point. But there I must draw the line."

"Like that, is it...? Working for Penrose?"

Sophie smiled.

"Who do you actually work for?"

"I hope I work for the good of Britain. But I'd not give a name even if I had one."

"Hmm... Going back over your answers, you only sent out the one sales letter to get in here? Is that right?"

"That's perceptive of you. I shall be more careful in the future. Yes, we struck lucky with just the one sales letter."

Unexpectedly, Morton laughed heartily.

"What's so amusing?" asked Sophie.

"Oh, I don't know. You never seem to get flustered. Got any suspects for the murder?"

"We haven't really got very far. Not Beaton because he's infatuated with Maude Hazlett, and not Rand-Sayers who bribed Gladys, that's Flora, because he was trying to flirt with her in here before he went riding. I suspect he has no alibi for the murder, so he panicked and wanted Gladys to supply one. He preferred her to say he left the Armoury right after she did, but without a mace, of course. He persuaded her by being friendly and apologizing for his earlier behaviour towards her."

Morton wrote down everything she said.

"What was the amount?"

"Two pounds."

"If he's the murderer," said Morton, "two pounds is pathetic unless he's broke. However, twenty pounds and it would be too much to expect a maid not to let on about the money... He wouldn't have messed about with Gladys if he was about to murder Smythe. You've made the right assessment. Gladys, er, Flora, how's she doing?"

"She's fine, thank you. I must inform you, we will be conducting a survey of riding jackets tomorrow morning. We think it is likely the murderer transported the mace under a jacket and not under skirts or elsewhere. The idea is that a heavy piece of metal might have caused damage to the lining of a jacket."

"You should continue with that. If you don't get every jacket, I can always requisition them. And we can always search the house, although I don't fancy that. Did you mention any of this to Talford?"

"No. He interviewed me after you arrived, by the way. He's obsessed with Dr Beaton."

"Has to be, seeing as how he arrested him. Talford and I had a few words. I'm in charge of the case and he resents us being here."

"He arrested Dr Beaton based on a thumbprint and no alibi. He also thinks it required a man of considerable size, such as Dr Beaton, to accomplish the task."

"How did you find that out?"

"I asked him when he interviewed me."

"And he told you? He's not supposed to do that."

"Don't be angry with him. Now, are you going to keep me informed on how the case is progressing?"

"Absolutely not."

"Then you must excuse me. I have to get back to work. May I go, please?"

"Yes. Tell me if you find out anything more."

"No. You've had your free sample. From now on, we will trade information because that's fair."

"No, we won't."

"Goodbye, Inspector," said Sophie with a smile. "It's always informative speaking with you."

She got up and left the room. When she had gone, Morton laughed, then quietly said 'nom de guerre' to himself.

Chapter 20

Dancing divinely

The servants' meal was a dismal affair until the end. Isembard was morose, content only to talk to Daniel. Mrs Williams seemed vexed. Sophie caught her eye and smiled. The housekeeper returned the smile and went back to eating. Sophie understood from her that nothing new had occurred to make matters worse. She glanced at Isembard. When Flora looked up, she winked. Sophie returned the gesture. They all continued eating.

When the meal ended, Mrs Williams left the table, with most of the servants following her. Isembard remained behind as did Daniel, several other menservants, and Flora. It was quiet, as men read newspapers and tried not to think of murder. Flora spoke.

"There'll be another death, won't there, Mr Isembard?"

"What did you say?"

"I can feel it. Ever since I come here, I thought someone would die on the estate. Didn't know it would be a murder. I mean, who'd think of such a thing? But it'll happen again. Another death. Because I feel it stronger than ever and it's closer to the house."

"You silly girl. The police arrested the murderer. He's in jail."

"He didn't do it. Dr Beaton hasn't the right aura for it."

"Aura?" Isembard was quite nonplussed and spoke dismissively.

"I shouldn't have said anything. I'd better get to work." Flora stood up. "Someone in the house is marked. It won't be long coming, neither." She snapped out the words and left the room. The disturbed newspaper readers watched her go.

"What was she talking about, Mr Isembard?" asked Daniel.

"Don't ask me. Females are difficult at the best of times. This lot from London...? Never again. Nothing but trouble-makers and that one's got a screw loose."

While Daniel returned to his newspaper, Isembard looked thoughtful.

"Come on," he said at last. He got up and so did Daniel. The family's dinner was to begin at seven-thirty.

The servants rearranged the furniture in the School Room for dancing after dinner. Mr Benson, at the Victrola, examined the records in the lower cabinet.

"All waltzes and light classical," he said to Vanessa. "It's a good thing I brought my box of goodies."

"That's why you're here, sweetie," said Vanessa, holding a glass while lounging on a settee in a sleeveless, red-orange silk chiffon dress. "This martini you've made is scrumptious. Another of your amazing talents." She sipped again, then exclaimed,

"Maudie, darling! Welcome back to the land of the living."

"Hello, Vanessa."

"Will you dance later, or is it all still too ghastly for you?"

"Oh, I'll shake a leg. I refuse to mope."

"Remember, don't eat too much at dinner. Adrian's brought the latest music from America."

"How lovely. We must have a few waltzes, though. I promised a dance to Uncle Horry."

"So did I. Are you listening Adrian? You'll have to mix it up a bit, otherwise there will be grumbling."

"We can't allow that," replied Adrian. "We'll start off with family favourites, but end the evening with the fun stuff. How does that sound?"

"Super," said Vanessa. "Get Maudie a martini. She's dying of thirst."

"At once, my Lady."

"That's quite the dress," said Maude. "I couldn't carry off something like that."

"You do wear nice things, but you could easily wear something that gets you noticed. We must go shopping together. Say you will, Maude."

"Not until Albert returns to me. Then we'll go."

"You're being a martyr about it all."

"Not really." She studied Vanessa's attire. "I know the sort of clothes you mean, but I don't go to London often, and I rarely go to nightclubs."

"Then we'll do the rounds and we'll have a marvellous time. We'll go before you marry Albert, so we can let our hair down."

"He hasn't proposed."

"Of course, he will. All you need to do is throw your arms around him and shower him with kisses. Do that as soon as you meet Albert next, and he'll pop the jolly old question in a flash."

"You don't think Albert's guilty?"

"Dear Albert? Not on your life. I wish it had been me wrongfully arrested, then I'd get my picture on the front page." Vanessa drained her glass. "Mmm... Another martini over here, darling. My glass is empty. Don't frown, Maude, I'm quite strict with myself. I only have two before dinner. I can't stand hangovers."

The guests and family had congregated before going in to dinner.

"I sincerely apologize for my daughter's rather startling attire," said Helen Scrope to Lady Jane. "Seems more like a chemise to me. I remember explaining to her that one wore undergarments beneath one's dress, not instead of one's dress. She must have forgotten."

"Don't apologize."

"Neither of us approves. If I asked her to change, she would ignore me."

"Please don't make a fuss. We have enough to contend with. I like Vanessa, but she is remarkably different — a symbol of the changing times."

"Regretfully so."

"You possess a very droll sense of humour."

"I maintain my sanity through it. There's Reginald and Amelia."

"How ardent a socialist is she?"

"It amounts to dementia. Surprisingly, her views are relatively temperate, but they are as the Rock of Gibraltar."

"Reginald has always been introspective and I can't recall him ever talking about politics. What do you think the attraction is?"

"I don't know. I'm agreeably surprised, and I've always liked Reginald."

"They're similar, in some ways," said Lady Jane. "Amelia has always been overshadowed by Vanessa, and Reginald by Basil. What if they married?"

"I would be pleased and relieved."

"I hold the same opinion. Now, if only they will release Dr Beaton from prison, we'd have Maude settled down as well. Honestly, I never imagined she'd find a husband and now look what's happened when she finally finds a prospective candidate. We expected a proposal this weekend."

"Dr Beaton's perfect for her. But I think you're counting chickens before they're hatched where Reginald and Amelia are concerned."

"Dinner is served," announced Isembard.

"Perhaps, but it gives one hope to see them together."

The dinner itself passed pleasantly. Although murder had been done the day before, the attention of the table shifted to Dr Beaton's obvious innocence. Constance, realizing she was in a minority, allowed herself to be persuaded into the majority view, which was the only one expressed. Happily, the table chose to ignore the obvious inference that, if Beaton were innocent, then another among their number was not.

Vanessa glared once at Flora and ignored her after that. Lady Jane was looking tired, while Lord James seemed distracted. Colonel Digby took note of them both and decided his sister needed a holiday. He considered how he would conduct himself if a murder had occurred in the back-garden of his four-bedroomed Cheltenham house. Adrian Benson entertained those who sat near him. David Rand-Sayers chatted with Martin Scrope, who was becoming agreeably accustomed to the attentiveness of the younger man.

Daphne Rand-Sayers considered the wager she had with David. She asked herself whether, if he should land a job, and a divorce were averted, she could love him as she once did. Daphne was not sure. She thought of Maria Smythe, who had loved and lost her husband. Once, she would have behaved similarly had David died, but not anymore. Perhaps never again. If he won the wager, she felt she might still lose.

Basil Hazlett considered his parents — one at each end of the table. He determined to talk to them to see how they were. They seldom expressed their inner feelings but, for once, they both were letting slip that something was the matter. His mother seemed worn down. Lord James's self-possession appeared fractured, and something obviously bothered him. Without understanding why, Basil worried for them.

As Ada, Flora, and Sophie served the table, they observed each person as best they could. In the main, nothing remarkable occurred. Flora noticed that Reginald and Amelia were far advanced in their courtship because they spoke quietly and almost exclusively with one another. Only lovers who depend upon one another do that in a general gathering such as at a dinner table.

Sophie knew that Mr Benson's attention wandered towards her on occasion, but not, as far as she could tell, to any other servant, including Flora. This again brought back the memory of seeing him in De Vere Square. As Benson engaged in an amusing conversation which produced laughter, and while Sophie was serving Lord Hazlett, she realized the peer was staring at the young man. He came out of his reverie when he realized she was standing nearby.

Ada occasionally served Lady Jane, who, she noted, was picking at her food. Standing back against the wall, Ada studied her ladyship when her duties permitted. She watched when, for a few moments, Lady Jane's gaze followed Isembard about the room. When Isembard turned and might see her, Lady Jane looked away. There was only the one glance towards Benson that Ada caught, but it was unmistakable. Lady Jane loathed Mr Benson. The spasm of anger that flitted across her features, followed by her heightened colouring, was such as might cause a remark. Lady Jane consequently excused herself from the table, although she returned a minute later with smiling apologies to those on either side of her.

"Why 'ave they both got the hump with Benson?" asked Ada. "Her ladyship 'ates him, that I do know." The agents had met in a quiet passage after dinner.

"It can't just be his manners," said Flora. "He's friendly with everyone, but far too exotic for Lady Holme. There has to be more to it than that, though."

"We haven't much time," said Sophie, looking over her shoulder. "No one stood out to me as a murderer. Did you notice anything in that line?"

Ada and Flora shook their heads. Sophie continued.

"I'm sure the Hazletts are not staring at Benson because he's a murderer or smuggler. I can't think what it can be. Unless he is a blackmailer?"

"Yes," said Ada.

"I vote him a blackmailer, too. How unfortunate for the Hazletts," said Flora, "to have two leeches sucking them dry."

"They're not in the same league. Isembard is straightforward in his way. Benson is more complicated. Maybe he knows about PWP and all that. Maybe he is a part of it and higher up the chain of command." Sophie frowned as she considered the matter. "Then there's De Vere Square with drugs, gambling, and who knows what else?"

"I'd say 'e has something personal over Lady Jane," said Ada. "She looked right embarrassed and angry. But she got over it soon enough because she's a lady."

"I couldn't tell what Lord Hazlett was thinking," said Sophie. "He was gloomy. They must both be aware of Benson's blackmail."

"Ask Lady Jane about it," said Flora. "You're chummy with her now."

"Hardly... Mind you, that's an idea, but one that must keep until tomorrow if I can manage it. For tonight, let's observe the behaviour of the hideous Benson."

"Why not?" said Flora. "Everyone else will - particularly Constance."

"Taken a shine to him, has she? And her husband right there, an' all. Well, I never."

The Victrola remained unemployed for a half hour after dinner while the party conversed in small groups. The smallest group of two sat by themselves in a corner.

"I think we danced once," said Reginald.

"Three times," said Amelia. "We weren't very good."

"I certainly wasn't, but you weren't too bad. Way ahead of me."

"We'll dance tonight. We may as well confirm their suspicions. Mother was being quite maternal towards me before dinner."

"Ah, that's good. My parents seem shaken at present with all the upset. But this dancing business, I'm still not good at it. How about you?"

"Much better. I know, we'll practise upstairs, in the Long Gallery. You can hear the music up there."

"That sounds rather nice... It's a pity about Dr Beaton. We can't have him languishing in prison."

"No, that's so unfair."

"Yes, it is... Do you dance any of those modern dances?"

"Quite a few, including several rather bizarre ones. I prefer the foxtrot with its continuous flowing movement."

"Although I've seen it, I've never tried."

"When I peeked at Adrian's records, I found a couple of tunes to which we can foxtrot."

"Why not, then? I confess to being curious about something, and you need not answer me. Your friendship with Mr Benson?"

"You don't like him, do you? I understand. He doesn't seem quite right - too superficial. Adrian amuses women and annoys men. However, don't underestimate him, because he's a clever boy… and a superb dancer. If he amuses me, dances with me, and can talk politics with intelligence, why would I not like him?"

"I have to think about this."

"Are you jealous?"

"What an extraordinary question."

"It's still a question."

"I suppose I am, then."

"Of him or…?"

"Or what?" Reginald looked at her. "Of his friendship with you…?" Reginald smiled. "Yes, I'm coming to begrudge him that."

"Ah… That's rather nice for me to hear, Reggie. I could never trust him, not now. Besides, the competition for his attention is quite fierce, and he's accustomed to it. I'll only dance with you from now on. Let's slip away and practise. Come on."

"Yes, let's. But afterwards, shall we kiss? I've been wanting to kiss you all day."

"Another surprising proposition, Mr Hazlett. I suppose it can't hurt."

The dancing began. Lady Jane claimed a bad back in refusing all offers to ensure she did not go through the ordeal of refusing Benson alone. Lord James, pressed into service on the ancient boards of Lady Holme that had witnessed so many dances in the past, escaped after a token waltz. He wanted to dance with his wife, but also knew why she would not. As expected, Constance — a competent dancer — melted into the arms of Adrian Benson to the delight of some and raised eyebrows of others. Later, she twirled prettily with her husband, Oscar, and they both seemed to enjoy themselves. Oscar, having finished his last dance with his wife, mentioned to Martin Scrope that a post in Kenya was available to him for the asking. There, he opined, he would run a coffee plantation, and he found the offer a compelling one. Martin observed Constance would probably not like to go to Kenya. Oscar replied it was, of course, out of the question that she should go. There the matter rested. Inwardly, Oscar decided he would go and Constance would not. He wondered if he would cease turning pink over time and instead develop a nice tan.

"Come on, Uncle Horry," said Vanessa, pulling at his sleeve while he spoke to Daphne Rand-Sayers. "You owe me a dance and you cannot escape."

He turned around and faced the eager young woman in her red dress.

"Of course, my dear Poppy... Your dress, what?" He laughed.

"It's not poppy-coloured, it's rose, silly. That's what they called it in the salon."

"Ah, well, then. A rose by any other name would smell as sweet."

"You're quite the clever rogue tonight. Come on, sweep me off my feet."

"With pleasure," said the Colonel, as he was led away, beaming.

The word poppy drew attention. Adrian Benson misstepped while dancing and had to apologize to his partner. Colonel Digby and Vanessa had both spoken the word, but it was Lord Hazlett with whom Benson locked eyes. Both men averted their gaze after only a second. Sophie and Flora, standing by the door, had heard Colonel Digby's distinctive voice and witnessed the exchange of glances between Lord Hazlett and Benson. They turned to each other. Sophie raised her eyebrows. Flora nodded subtly. They turned back to the room — each certain Benson was Poppy or knew him well and, in either case, confirmed he was highly placed in PWP.

Sophie glanced towards Lady Jane, who was deep in conversation with Sandra. She assumed she must have missed or gave no significance to the poppy comment. Sophie reflected that Benson had not looked towards Lady Jane, so it was probable that she was unaware of PWP's existence and the control it exerted over her husband.

"I say, James." Martin Scrope had button-holed him. He often button-holed people. "Saw your neighbour today. Phelps, isn't it? Have much truck with him?"

"Occasionally. He prefers his privacy."

"I should say he does. Saw him across that river. Fellow was on horseback carrying a shotgun. Had two great mastiffs running loose alongside."

"He must have heard about Smythe."

"Then he was out patrolling his borders, I suppose. What's the size of his property?"

"About seven hundred acres."

"As much as that, eh? Of course, it's much smaller than Lady Holme, but even so."

"He's not down all the time. Phelps bought the place during the war and he also owns property in London and the Midlands."

"Lives off the rents, no doubt. A life of ease…? I could never endure that, as I like to keep an active interest in things. Think I'll take a look at his house tomorrow. He's got me curious."

"It's a pretty place, but you won't see it from the road. I've invited him over to dinner several times, but he always politely declines. Claims he has a sensitive stomach and is on a restricted diet."

"Well, I'm not risking those dogs. They look like they'd tear your arm off without thinking anything about it. Why would anyone restrict his or her diet? I don't… as you can probably tell." Martin laughed as he put both hands on his stomach. "Do you think he saw anything?"

"That's highly unlikely. He would have to be offshore or far out on the flats to see where Smythe died."

"Yes, you're perfectly correct, come to think of it."

"Where was he killed, sir?" asked David Rand-Sayers.

"On the shore path below Marley Mound," replied Martin. "What he was doing down there, I cannot say. It's a dead-end. That reminds me, he spoke of smuggling. Do you recall him mentioning it?"

"I'd really rather not talk about it now, Martin," said Lord Hazlett.

"No, of course. Wrong time for me to bring it up."

Lord Hazlett smiled. "Excuse me, I must speak to Janey for a moment."

"We've interviewed the lot and I don't see we're much further ahead," said Detective Sergeant Gowers.

"That's because someone's lying," said Inspector Morton. "They always close ranks and stick together."

"It's odd how they're all vague about the time for everyone else's movements until they come to their own. Then they know precisely where they were."

"They all know when the runaway horse returned to the stables. They've worked out the approximate time of death from that and put themselves as far away from the spot as they can. What a game."

"Amelia Scrope says it was eleven when she saw Smythe last. That doesn't work, because the horse returned to the stables at five minutes past eleven. She's mistaken. Her companion Belinda Beaton can't be exact, but puts the sighting earlier at about ten thirty. Let's say she's right. That's a thirty-five minute gap from the time Smythe was last seen to when they caught the horse. Allowing six or seven minutes for it to gallop two miles, that means the horse was free to run no earlier than ten fifty-eight, because the presence of the other horse would have blocked the path and had him trapped."

"Allowing all that," said Morton, "then Smythe died at about ten fifty or ten fifty-five at the latest. It would take the assailant three to five minutes to do the job and drop the body in the sea."

"All right," said Gowers. "That track's under cover for about three hundred yards. How fast was he going? Couldn't have been that fast because the track narrows considerably further in."

"Smythe was looking for signs of the smugglers. It's likely he stopped once or twice to see how they might work it. Then the poor chap passed the bush and got himself stuck, so he dismounted to turn around. That's where the killer closed in."

"He must have been following close behind - two hundred yards at most."

Morton put his hands behind his head and stretched his legs out before replying.

"Let's give Smythe a quarter of an hour on the track before he's killed. That means he entered the covered section between ten thirty-five and ten forty."

"There you go. Miss Beaton was right in her estimate of ten thirty."

"Yes... Then, why didn't she see the person following him?" asked Morton.

"He was hiding somewhere, avoiding notice."

"That's possible. The murderer waited under cover until Miss Beaton and Miss Scrope moved away and then he trotted after Smythe."

"We'd better take another look in the area tomorrow. We can get the car down there."

"You didn't like the bike ride back?" Morton smiled.

"I know it's only a gentle slope, but it's just so perishing long. I'm sure I'll ache in the morning." Gowers shook his head.

"Look, it's half ten, and we won't make the pubs in Lymington before they close. Then we'd have to scurry back here for the night. Do you reckon we can get beer from the kitchen?"

"If we ask nicely. Lady Holme's home brew is supposed to be quite good, according to Colonel Digby. He's partial to it. And they have bottles of Bass, too."

"Now you're talking," said Morton, getting up. "I hope they've looked after the Bass properly."

Chapter 21

Revolution in the Night

In Sophie's room, the six little maids did not chat, laugh, sing or tell stories. Instead, they plotted and planned. Nelly and Mabel, the agency's two newest recruits, having memorized the parts they would play, returned to their rooms for the night.

Earlier, Flora in the attics, and Fern and Ada elsewhere, had collected some needful things, but there was one item only obtainable after the Scotland Yard men had gone to their bedrooms.

At one in the morning, while a small group of guests still found entertainment in the School Room, Flora, Ada, and Sophie crept along to the Armoury. Flora guarded the entrance of the short corridor while Ada picked the old lock and Sophie held a torch for her to see what she was doing. It took a minute to get the door open. Once inside, Sophie selected a suitable sword by torchlight. She gave it a trial swing and decided it was perfect for the job they had in mind. Sophie wrapped it in a towel. Ada relocked the door, then the raiding party retired with stealth to their rooms, with Flora leading the way to warn of anyone ahead.

Once safe, Sophie sat motionless in a chair while Flora set to work. It took the actress twenty minutes to complete her task. Now the secret agents were ready to start the night's real business. Sophie had been transformed and made unrecognizable. She wore a dark broad-brimmed hat sporting a long feather, a piece of brown curtain arranged as a cloak, and an ancient wig, while her deathly white face was heavily mustachioed and bearded.

"There you are," whispered Flora, handing Sophie a small mirror.

"Good grief!" she hissed. "I look hideous... Why did you give me a giant mole? And what are those smudges?"

"Those give you the fashionably decomposed look. The mole is just a little flourish."

"It is a *huge* flourish."

"That beard makes you look like Guy Fawkes," said Ada.

"It's like you've got a horrible disease, Miss Phoebe," said Fern.

"Good," replied Sophie. "Try it with the torch."

The four agents glided along passages, carrying their equipment. The house aided them by refraining from undue creaking. In silence, they slipped past the Servants' Hall and the kitchen. They turned into the narrow passage which led to the side entrance. Here, Fern took up a position to keep watch. The others approached the door, where Flora slid back the bolts. They all held their breath, fearing the noise. The heavy door protested on its hinges as it swung open, producing pained expressions on their faces in the dark. Once outside, Fern hurried to bolt the door behind them. The waning crescent moon hung over the black landscape. A breeze stirred the dark trees. An owl hooted. Three huddled figures in single file followed the muted torch light. Within twenty steps, they were outside the Pannetry windows. The window to their right was Mr Isembard's bedroom.

Ada found and pulled a length of fishing line. She had attached it to the inside window handle earlier for just this purpose. The handle moved with a grinding noise. Breathless, they waited to hear if the noise had disturbed the butler. No commotion followed, so Ada opened the window wide and removed the line while Flora used a broom to slide carefully open the curtain on its rings. They waited again. From the other side of the bedroom, a steady snore emanated. Sophie got into position.

"Begin," said Flora almost inaudibly.

"Isembard!" Flora spoke in her lowest voice, which came from her lungs but sounded as though it came from a tomb.

"Isembard!" said Sophie in a sharp voice.

"Isembard!" said Ada in her highest register - almost a squeak.

They spoke in rapid succession. Ada then knocked on the window frame, while Sophie tapped it with her sword. Inside, the snoring became uneven. They repeated their performance. The snoring stopped. They spoke his name again.

"Who's there?"

Sophie leaned in closer to the window and shut her eyes. Ada crouched down and switched on the torch, her hand partially covering the beam so that the apparition's face was lit from beneath by a weird glow. Upright by her cheek, held in a gloved hand, the unsheathed sword gleamed next to Sophie's appalling countenance.

Isembard, speechless, sat up and, in horror, turned to stare - the bobble on the end of his Phrygian-shaped nightcap trembling violently.

"Isembard!" Flora, hidden, crouching below the window, poured all the graveyard intonation she could into her speech. Her voice came slow, dark, and deep.

"Beware, butler of Lady Holme."

"Oh, my God." Isembard's choked voice shook with the vibrato of fearful dismay.

"Your days are numbered... You can be butler no more... I will come back for you." As soon as Flora finished speaking, Sophie suddenly opened her eyes.

Ada switched off the torch. They stepped silently away from the window and began a clumsy retreat in the dark, heading for the far end of the servants' quarters. When at a safe distance, they switched the torch back on to guide them, and disappeared around the corner of the house. Fern had the back door open. They entered, then she closed and bolted it behind them.

The jubilant, glittering-eyed, saucy-faced agents assembled in Sophie's bedroom. Flora began removing the make-up while Ada explained all that had happened to Fern, who had trouble stopping herself from laughing out loud.

Flora began scrubbing harder. "Oh dear, it's not coming off," she whispered.

"Where? Let me see," said Sophie, snatching up the mirror. "Oh, really, Flora. You are the limit sometimes." Her face was free of cosmetics. They laughed.

The agents could not return the sword to the Armoury, because Mr Isembard was sitting in the Servants' Hall with the lights on and a large glass of brandy in front of him on the table. It was impossible to pass him without being seen.

On Sunday morning, the wind picked up, clouds rolled in off the sea, and the temperature dropped. Rain was coming, and it was only a question of when. With a lack of direct sunshine, the lowered light within Lady Holme produced a moody feeling. Some passages became quite dark while certain corners lay in deep gloom — the grey light through windows failing to reach them. The staff arose and began its daily labour — activities that had varied little for several centuries.

Nelly was always cheerful no matter what the weather was like outside. As one to look on the bright side of anything, her main purpose seemed to lie in sharing her bright cheer with everyone she met with a pleasant word or smile. She began her tasks, one of which was cleaning lavatories. As there were several used by the guests, she attended to those first before they awoke. When entering each lavatory, she hung a sign on the outside handle which read, Occupied for cleaning purposes. If she had control over the signage, it would say, Knock if you're desperate or come back in ten minutes.

Before seven, Nelly had finished that task and returned to the servants' area by the stairs next to the Pannetry. As she stepped off the last stair, Mr Isembard approached along the passage from the Entrance Hall. Nelly stopped, stared at him, then screamed at the top of her lungs. She turned and ran away to hide in the broom closet next to the Little Pantry.

Isembard stopped in amazement. He had looked terrible before Nelly screamed. He looked dumbstruck afterwards. Sleep deprived and haggard, it came to his exhausted mind that there must be something wrong with him. He must bear some doom-laden mark visible to others, but not himself. He went to find a mirror.

Ada was collecting riding jackets and tweeds off bedroom door handles when Mabel shrieked on the floor below. The quiet maid had also met Isembard. Ada nodded, approving of Mabel's volume and depth of sincerity. She went downstairs to find Mrs Williams looking distracted.

"What are you doing with those?" asked the housekeeper.

"I'm going to brush 'em. We left a note in each guest's bedroom. It's part of the Burgoyne service, Mrs Williams. Guests appreciate the extra touch when they haven't a valet or maid."

"That's thoughtful of you." She hesitated.

"Is anything the matter, Mrs Williams?"

She sighed. "The household. The murder. The ongoing problems with Mr Isembard. And now, this morning, Nelly and Mabel are afraid of him... I must say, he looks terrible, but it's not enough to give one a screaming fit. I can't think what's got into those two girls."

"They're good workers, an' all," said Ada. "It must be something serious. What did they say?"

"Mabel's quiet, as you know. She's just plain frightened of him... I don't blame her. Today, she says she's so afraid, she can't go near him. Nelly said there was death in his face. She also said that if I looked long enough, I'd see it for myself."

"Did you?"

"Well, it's rude to stare. But I did glance at him and he *seems* to be fading away. I know what she means. What am I thinking? We have work to do, Nancy."

"Yes, Mrs Williams."

Ada's inspection of the jackets revealed nothing useful. She wrote down a list of the names of those who gave their jackets to be cleaned. When she returned the jackets later, close to eight o'clock, Reginald Hazlett, having dressed, opened his door holding his olive green plaid jacket in his hand.

"Am I too late?" he asked.

"Oh, no, sir. I can take it now and bring it straight back."

He held out his jacket. Ada observed that his mustard-coloured waistcoat had an inch and a half split in the seam. It was on the right-hand side beneath the armhole.

"Thank you," said Reginald. "I found some dried mud as I was about to put it on. Sorry to trouble you with an extra journey."

"Oh, that's no trouble at all, Mr Hazlett. I won't be a minute."

When she was alone, Ada examined the jacket lining, including its sleeves. She hunted for a poacher's pocket in the back lining, but there wasn't one. Everything was in good repair and unstained. Ada brushed and cleaned the jacket with care. It had a slight odour of mothballs and she discovered a small sprig of lavender in the breast pocket. From that she guessed Reginald had owned the jacket for some years but kept it at Lady Holme, not his London address. She added his name to the jacket list, then returned the garment.

While Ada was doing this, Flora encountered Isembard at the foot of Chapel Stairs. They stopped and silently stared at each other. Flora slowly lifted her arm and pointed at him. Isembard covered his face with both hands.

Lord Hazlett finished his solitary breakfast in the Breakfast Room. He stood up to survey the weather outside, deciding the rain might hold off until the afternoon.

"Excuse me, my Lord," said Isembard.

"What is it?" He turned, amazed by the change in his butler.

"May I have a word, my Lord? In private?"

Lord Hazlett recognized Isembard was under some deep emotional strain, which had sapped his usual confidant, deferential manner. He considered whether this change in the man boded well or ill for himself.

"We'll go to my office."

Isembard bowed and led the way. After Lord Hazlett entered, Isembard shut the door behind them. They faced one another. With effort, Lord Hazlett remained composed.

"What is this about?"

"I, er, I have thought about my situation here, and I'm sorry for the way things worked out. I find I'm no longer able to discharge my duties and should leave soon... Today really... At once, if it could be managed, please. About the month's notice... Something's happened and I can't stay here another month, I can't. No, no, it's best I leave at once. I'm sorry for the inconvenience... and, er, about the other matter. I honestly wish it had never happened." Isembard hastily reassured Lord Hazlett. "Don't worry about that, my Lord. I'll send in excellent reports. They'll be the very best, I promise. They must be, my Lord."

Hazlett's face became blank. He could not fathom the reason for the extraordinary speech, but hesitated to enquire into Isembard's reasons. Doubt beset him, and he worried that if he asked a question, his butler might have a change of heart. These reservations stopped him from letting out a cheer.

"Yes, I'm sorry, too." Lord Hazlett considered the subject of wages and money, which had yet to be broached.

"Very well, Isembard. Where will you go?"

"To Bournemouth first, to stay with my sister. After that, London."

The butler finished with a polite cough.

"About the matter we discussed yesterday. I, er, I don't like leaving empty-handed, so to speak, and I know I'm owed only a few pounds in wages for part of October, and with not working my notice... Well, your Lordship can appreciate my situation, but I have to leave."

"I'll write you a cheque."

"Ah, no, cash, if you please. Not a cheque, my Lord."

Lord Hazlett then realized Isembard was not asking for thousands — he was expecting much less.

"I can manage a hundred and fifty pounds, but that's all."

"That's most generous of you, and more than I deserve."

"Ah, then, that's that. You may pack your things and I'll get your money ready for you."

"I'm already packed, my Lord. If you don't mind, there's a trunk I'll send for later when I'm settled."

"Of course, I don't mind. I'll pay you out at once." He decided not to mention the police investigation and whether the detectives would approve of Isembard leaving, in case it caused Isembard to delay or change his mind.

After they concluded their business and Isembard had gone, Lord Hazlett breezed up the stairs to knock on Lady Hazlett's door.

"It's James." He entered, saying, "Janey, you'll never believe what's just happened!"

"Nancy, did you find anything among the jackets?" Sophie, carrying a bucket, met Ada, her arms filled with towels, in a passage.

"No, not in the jackets. But Reginald Hazlett come to his door wearing a waistcoat with a split in it when he handed me his. Down 'ere, the seam under the arm." She moved her head and lifted her right elbow. "About an inch and a 'alf long, it was. What do you reckon?"

"I don't know. Would he have kept the mace under his waistcoat?"

"Doesn't sound right. It's too tight, 'ardly long enough, and would slip out anyway."

"Maybe the mace caught on it," suggested Sophie.

"Now that's more like it. Although, maybe he just can't sew - and 'e's a bachelor."

"Yes... Not for much longer, I think."

"That's right. I've seen 'em. They're getting right affectionate. The mothers, I mean Lady Hazlett and Mrs Scrope, have noticed the pair, an' all. It's beautiful to see, ain't it?"

"I suppose so." Sophie smiled.

"I like all that. A good romance book and I'm balling me eyes out."

"Is that what you prefer?"

"Oh, yes. I'm reading Trail of the Lonesome Pine at the moment, and it's terrible and lovely. Set in America, and some of their language is right peculiar. I keep 'avin' to stop an' work out what they're talking about."

"May I borrow it when you've finished?"

"'Course, you can. It's me sister's, but she's all right."

After depositing the bucket, Sophie armed herself with a broom and dusters before returning to Great Hall. Flora and she were to clean the Alcove for the coming dinner. She was passing the Grand Stairs in the otherwise empty Entrance Hall when someone hailed her.

"Just a moment!"

With an effortless nonchalance, Adrian Benson descended the stairs. Sophie awaited him at the bottom. She felt most uncomfortable, almost amounting to a dread of being discovered.

Benson smiled. "I've been wanting to speak to you. I shan't keep you a moment." He paused and searched her face. "Yes… You're Phoebe, the maid who had the row with the butler. Tell me, are you happy in your work?"

"Yes, sir, I am."

"Do you ever consider you might like a change? Live a different life?"

"I'm not sure I take your meaning, sir."

"I've noticed you, and your spirit and intelligence. Those are qualities I admire. The thought of helping you crossed my mind. I'd like to take you away from the drudgery of being a maid, so you may enjoy some of the finer things that life offers. Surely you have dreams of how your future would be if only a chance presented itself?"

"Don't know, sir."

"I live in London and have a wide circle of acquaintance. Many opportunities present themselves. For myself, I have done extraordinarily well from those opportunities. Soon, I will buy a house, and I'll need a staff to run it. Someone who pleases me and understands my tastes needs to oversee its management."

"Oh, you mean housekeeper, sir."

Adrian Benson smiled. "You could say that. My idea is that you will be far more exalted than any housekeeper. You might accompany me to France, for example. Then we could go on to the Riviera, or visit Italy." He paused, watching her, while his meaning became apparent. "We'll talk again later when you have more time, Phoebe. Think about what I have said."

He crossed the hall and left by the front door. Sophie hurried away, her thoughts in turmoil.

"I've come to a decision," said Morton, as he and Gowers ate breakfast together in the Servants' Hall. "We'll get Dr Beaton from the nick this morning and put him back into circulation to see what happens. Talford has to lump it."

"He'll complain."

"That's his choice. I'll send him out to check into Beaton's background. He'll enjoy that."

"What if he is the murderer?"

"He might be. I don't see him as one. You read his statement. He was open about handling the mace even before the thumbprint was traced to him. Nobody saw him. If he were the murderer, he'd say he was never in the Armoury yesterday. When confronted by his print, he'd say it's old from weeks ago when he last visited. I'd believe him if he said that, *unless* we can find a motive. That's why I want him back for observation. The merry maids can help us there."

"Funny them being here," said Gowers.

"Hilarious."

"Don't you like Miss Burgoyne? Nearly forgot, she's Phoebe King at present."

"Like her? That doesn't come into it. We're here to do a job."

"She's helpful, though."

"Yes, she is."

"Pretty, too. She has a lovely voice."

"Taken your fancy, has she?"

"Just stating the obvious. I'm engaged, remember, sir."

"That's right."

"How about you?"

"What do you mean?"

"Well, sir, she's very nice, and you're not engaged."

"All right, all right, enough of this malarkey. Let's get to work."

"Yes, sir."

As Inspector Morton returned his plate to the kitchen, Gowers followed, smiling.

When they reached the Armoury and had settled in, Inspector Morton said,

"On the surface, we've got a single motive: smuggling."

"No one strikes me as the type to be doing that," said Gowers.

"What about profiting from it instead of participating?"

"Any of the men might do that. Lord Hazlett for one. I get the impression he doesn't care for the subject."

"Then Smythe was about to blunder in and expose Hazlett's secret business? Possible." Morton tapped a pencil on the desk. "Either of the Hazlett sons is a candidate. Basil, the elder son, is something of a name in the City. Why risk smuggling when you make plenty of money on the Exchange?"

"He wouldn't do it," said Gowers.

"It was what was being smuggled that makes the difference. Weapons and explosives. I can't see any of them wanting those."

"I have an idea about that, sir."

"Go on, then."

"Well, there might be a smuggling network. The man in charge says, I'll bring in your contraband for a price. He deals with different clients and different cargoes. But, of course, as you were saying, it might be someone bringing in their own goods."

"Who is there who might fall into that last category?" asked Morton.

"That's it, isn't it? None of them are about to start a war. Some might fit into the first category. I don't see Beaton anywhere in it."

"Hmm, Reginald Hazlett works for the London Port Authority. He could be part of a network. Telephone the Yard and have someone look into his background."

Gowers wrote a note.

"Martin Scrope's out," said Morton. "You can't be an MP, a revolutionary or gun-runner, and a murderer. However, he might finance others."

"Benson, Rand-Sayers, and Reid. Oscar Reid has overseas connections in Africa."

"We'll check them as well. What do you make of Benson?"

"Difficult to say." Gowers paused. "He's a smooth character who's up to something, I don't doubt. But him carry a mace under those clothes of his? I think he'd rather die before he mucked them up. Of course, he might have been desperate, thinking someone was on to him."

"Add him to the list. Now Rand-Sayers looks jumpy. Put him down, too."

"He seems to follow Scrope everywhere. I'll ask him about that."

"Yes, do. First, we'll put together a comprehensive list of everyone's sightings of everyone else. We'll start with what we've got, then hammer away at any deficiencies until we've got a proper timetable. After that, anyone who needs to explain themselves will get the treatment. Then, it's second interviews all round whether they like it or not."

"That'll be third interviews for them - second interviews for us."

"I'm talking about real interviews. We need to make progress before returning to London... I forgot to ask. How did Fulham do?"

"They lost three-nil. Can you believe it? Cardiff City - who's ever heard of them?"

"You missed nothing, then."

"I suppose." Gowers shrugged. "How are we going to handle them?"

"What do you mean?"

"We have a lot of characters. Is it kid-gloves still?"

"Yes, for all of them. We'll spend more time with those we're interested in. Tell them there's no cause for concern, and we're only clarifying a few points. Usual stuff."

"Except they chatter like monkeys and repeat everything we say."

"Let them talk. That reminds me. I'm not seeing Vanessa Scrope on my own next time. That woman's insane. You can see her."

"I looked over her statement. She came across as a lively sort of person. What did she do?"

"Got on my nerves. Thinks a lot of herself. Right, I'll find Talford and see what he's up to. After you ring up the Yard and Lymington, get cracking on that timetable."

"Yes, sir."

Chapter 22

Getting Through It All

In the Alcove, Flora and Sophie set about cleaning and preparing the room.

"What's the matter?" asked Flora. "You look furious."

"I met Benson. He said something positively outrageous to me."

"Oh, did he, indeed? You must tell your Auntie Glad everything."

"It's unspeakable. I'm not sure I can bring myself to say it."

"Yes, you can. This sounds like a corker."

"He propositioned me. Asked me to live with him."

"My goodness! Did he, *really*?" Flora stopped what she was doing. "Tell me every word he said and what you said."

Sophie recounted the meeting.

"Gadzooks, he's a bold knave," said Flora. "But why are you angry?"

"It's indecent. It goes against all finer feeling and good manners."

"I know it does, but it's jolly interesting. And to think he's a blackmailer and PWP, too. That kind of spoils his charm, don't you think?"

Sophie stopped working. "I'm surprised at you, Flora. You're taking this rather lightly."

"That's because I've had similar incidents."

"Have you…? How ghastly it all is."

They began working again.

"I find them tedious now," said Flora. "The first offer to live in sin made me think that defying all the conventions might be wickedly exciting. For example, think of the glorious notoriety. Makes for a good part in a play, but not in real life. I realized it would soon become insufferable. Not that I was tempted. As you know, I would only ever marry for love. However, I shan't meet the like of your brother again... As for these other arrangements, they often end badly."

"I know you still miss him... You're rather blasé about these unconventional unions. I'm unused to hearing about such things. His behaviour upset me."

"Yes, it did, my poor dear, and it isn't very nice. At first, it upset me, too. As an actress, I get about three or four offers a year. It's quite amazing how a man, an ordinary man, is suddenly convinced he has transformed into an attractive marvel of perfection simply because he possesses money, estates or a yacht. I've had two yacht offers so far and they were nearly identical. So much so, I imagined they were working off the same script, and only changed the name of the boats. The story put to me with professions of extreme smittenness was, we would sail across the seas to exotic lands and into sublime sunsets somewhere or other, while the loving, tender admirer would take care of me forever more. Each promised to shower me with gifts and clothes, and give me my heart's desire. What rot it all was. When I said no, they soon buzzed off to find someone else. It's not about love, it's about control and possession. As soon as one tired of me, he'd be finding someone else to shower upon. Considered from my viewpoint, what would happen if I was on the yacht, and I tired of *him*? I'd have to swim back to shore and I'm not a very good swimmer."

Sophie smiled. "That gives me a more reasoned perspective on the matter. I can't abide bad manners and it was so sudden I didn't know what to say."

"That's good, otherwise you'd have launched into one of your tirades and ended by coshing him."

"No, I wouldn't... That *would* bring about a change in his behaviour, though."

"Don't," said Flora.

"Of course, I won't... In a way it was funny. At first, I couldn't believe my ears. Then, while staring at him, his face seemed to change and become unnatural. Sort of mechanical. He honestly appeared grotesque to me — as though a reptile was speaking."

"Very Garden of Edenish. Mind you, the beautiful, hideous, reptilian Benson's offer is rather awkward for us."

"*Isn't* it? It crossed my mind that he could be lying — setting some sort of trap."

"You mean he recognized you from De Vere Square? Why would he lie to trap you?"

"To get information in case we're on to him or he believes we're working for the police," replied Sophie. "Superficially, I can't imagine he suspects anything. We work for an agency which happened to send staff to two places he happened to attend. As Nancy said, to us it appears dangerous because we know why we were there and are here. Nevertheless, he's a criminal of some sort. Such a coincidence would surely make him suspicious if he recognizes any of us because of *his* guilty conscience."

"It might," agreed Flora, "although it's an elaborate story he's thought up. Remember, some people can be quite unaware of a servant's existence. You may have been pointed out to him because of the row. He started watching you from then on until he became besotted. With some men, that happens with remarkable alacrity, often a matter of minutes. As for him possessing a conscience? I doubt that very much. Fear of being caught, yes; conscience, no."

"We don't know either way, do we, if it's a trap or a proposition? I shall search his room."

"A man like that won't keep a diary and he probably burns letters he receives from women because keeping records of past love affairs would be a present danger. Should you discover such a letter, give it to Constance. She might find it interesting... What will you look for?"

"Just little things. We don't know how he occupies his time, besides being the extortioner we believe him to be."

"If you find a diary, will you read it? I certainly would."

"Yes, because I'm searching for evidence, but I'd hold it with a pair of tongs."

Before the service in the Chapel, Lady Jane offered private thanks that one of her troubles had gone, and she prayed that the others would likewise depart or be dealt with in an equally sudden and miraculous fashion. During the service, which was held early, she was joined by others. Lord Hazlett led in the formal prayers from the book of Common Prayer, while Basil read from the Bible. Together, the household congregation sang hymns.

Afterwards, about the house, Lord James bestowed smiles on everyone except Adrian Benson, finding it difficult in the extreme to forgive someone who was actively persecuting not only himself but his dear wife.

The guests, as yet unaware of Isembard's departure and Dr Beaton's imminent return, chose to ride before the rain set in. Consequently, the stables were busy while the horses were being brought out.

Amelia Scrope asked Ronald to ensure Reginald got a horse first, so as not to be left out as he had been on Friday.

"Don't worry, miss. Mister Reginald's a good rider, so I know he'll take care of Toffee. If anyone asks, I'll say he already asked for Toffee special so they can't have him."

"Thanks, Ronald. You're a good sport," said Amelia.

"Happy to help. Are you riding Kaleidoscope?"

"I am."

"That's good. She's coming out next, or should be. Excuse me, I'll bring Toffee out myself."

"Ronald, you're a marvel."

The little man bowed formally and took his hat off to Amelia.

Several mounted riders waited by the stables. The rest stood talking and laughing in animated groups, watching as each groom brought out the next horse through the ancient stable doors. Along the drive came a taxi. It stopped near the garage instead of continuing to the front door. Someone saw it and made a remark. One or two heads turned to look.

"Albert!" shouted Maude at the top of her voice. Everyone turned to look.

"Maudie!" Dr Beaton shouted back.

Several remarked afterwards that Maude was first in motion by a split second. Every person around the stables turned their attention as the couple ran towards each other, arms outstretched. They ran, they collided, and they demonstrated Love Oblivious To Its Surroundings for everyone's benefit.

"So, it does happen in real life," said Helen Scrope. "It's not an invention of poets and writers."

"Do we continue staring or turn away?" asked Lady Jane.

In laughing bliss, Albert swept Maude off her feet and twirled her in his arms. They showered kisses on each other.

"I wish someone would love me like that," said Vanessa.

"What can Maude be thinking of?" asked Reginald, of no one in particular.

"My brother's behaviour astonishes me," said Belinda. "He's quite unemotional as a rule."

In Lord Hazlett's mind, the phrase Day of Wonders arose.

"Surely, he will ask her to marry him now," said Lady Jane.

"I agree, it's the perfect moment," rejoined Helen.

"Sandra, isn't that just a lovely picture?" said Colonel Digby. "I always said he wasn't a murderer."

"Let us hope you're right for Maude's sake," said Mrs Digby.

When the first gushing effervescence of the lovers' feelings subsided, Albert spoke.

"Maude, Maude, my Maude." He looked into her eyes. "Marry me."

"Yes!" said Maude, almost shouting, her face triumphant with delight.

"We'll go to London and get a ring."

"Yes!"

"Tomorrow?"

"Oh, yes, yes! Let's tell them now. You can talk to Daddy and I can talk to Mummy and it will be wonderful."

"Good heavens. We've got an audience," said Albert, finally aware of the many pairs of eyes fixed upon them.

"It was rather nice, wasn't it?" asked Amelia.

She on Kaleidoscope, and Reginald on Toffee, ambled across the open field.

"Yes, it was. Initially, I was rather shocked at Maude's and Beaton's behaviour. I don't care for public displays of emotion."

"That's the British way, of course. Poor Dr Beaton, he looked so embarrassed at the end. You'll have to get used to calling him Albert."

"Whereas Maude didn't bat an eyelid."

"I'm relieved he's returned to us, and I don't mean just for Maude's sake; I mean for his own."

"So am I… We haven't mentioned it."

"Don't. There's no need."

"But I feel I need to explain the matter."

"It's unnecessary." Amelia looked at him. "Oh, you had better say it then."

"You saw me on the shore path, after poor Toffee here came hurtling out of the cover. Once he passed me, I rode as far along the path as I could go, looking for someone who had lost their horse. I honestly didn't see anyone or anything, so I returned to pursue Toffee. However, I had originally been looking for Richard Smythe. I wanted to talk to him, to hear his ideas about the smuggling. It interested me because of my work at The London Port Authority. Sometimes, I deal with contraband issues. Then it's me who issues the Port's papers to seize goods and cargoes or impound vessels. I liaise with the police and customs officials about what's required. Naturally, I was rather keen to hear him out." Reginald turned in his saddle to face Amelia. "I didn't kill him... Do you believe me?"

Amelia smiled. "Would I be here if I didn't?"

"I must have looked suspicious. It's why I haven't mentioned it to the police."

"I'll give you an alibi. Belinda didn't see you at all. She was riding with Fiona at the time while I was trailing a long way behind them when I saw you and stopped."

"But that's lying, Amelia. You could get yourself into trouble."

"Then why did you seek me out? Why are we contemplating a life together?"

"I didn't seek you for an alibi. Good heavens, no. When I heard Smythe was missing, it seemed to me something more than an accident had occurred. Immediately, I thought, and forgive me for phrasing it this way, good old Amelia saw me. Then it came to me how much I have always liked and trusted you. That made me consider... the things we've been discussing. Everything I've said to you in that respect has been sincere, without a hidden motive.

"When they found his body, I got into a panic. I realized my actions might look extremely suspicious. Although you might trust me, your seeing me on the shore path could be used as damning evidence. By the police and lawyers, I mean. You were the only person I could talk to. I'm sorry if I've brought you into my troubles. It's rather selfish of me."

They rode a little way in silence.

"I understand," began Amelia, "it takes about thirty days to get a marriage licence. You could apply for one tomorrow."

Reginald halted his horse first.

"What did you say?"

"You heard me plainly."

"I don't understand. We agreed to a certain course of action. I must confess I'm looking forward to our program, more so now than when we first spoke. But marriage and so suddenly?"

"I'm sure you are aware of this. A wife cannot testify in court against her husband. You are not a murderer. However, there could be a miscarriage of justice where they convict you of a murder you didn't commit. If we are married, you are safe. I want you safe, so let us marry."

"I'm absolutely amazed… Oh, but I can't allow this. I can't permit you to risk so much on my account. No, it's out of the question."

"That sounds noble, but you can't permit? You can't allow? Why say such things?"

"Because you might come to regret your decision later. Things might not work out between us, and it would be awful for you to be trapped in a marriage you regretted."

"Ah, I see… I wonder, would you be able to get along with *me*?"

"Without a doubt."

"Then say *why* you would."

"Oh, dear, I'm sure this sounds silly and I feel quite embarrassed saying it." He looked towards her. "It's because I've grown to love you over the last two days."

Amelia smiled. "Is that so? That makes it a little easier. Perhaps there was another reason for my suggestion." She pressured her horse with her legs, saying quietly, "Canter." Kaleidoscope picked up the pace, and the distance grew between the two riders.

"Amelia, you don't mean to tell me…? Come on Toffee, after her."

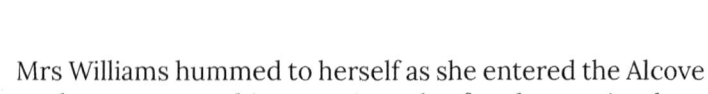

Mrs Williams hummed to herself as she entered the Alcove to make sure everything was in order for the coming luncheon. Satisfied with what she saw, she continued humming while returning to her private office. Isembard was gone and first thing Monday morning she would telephone Burgoyne's Agency to speak to the helpful Miss Burgoyne. Lady Holme required a replacement butler and, according to her ladyship, Miss Burgoyne would send the very best. Mrs Williams rather thought she would.

Just outside her room, she met Miss Burgoyne without realizing it.

"There's something I'd like to ask you, Phoebe."

"Yes, Mrs Williams."

"Would you know if Miss Burgoyne has any butlers on her books at present?"

"I expect she does. I suppose a replacement is wanted?"

"Yes. Are you acquainted with any of them?"

Sophie mentally reviewed her card files and considered the various butlers.

"There's a Mr Boswell who's a kindly looking, older gentleman. I understand he worked at a large house somewhere before. I can't tell you much, I'm afraid."

At that precise moment Sophie could have provided Mr Boswell's age, full name and address, his entire work experience as a butler, and that his references were excellent.

"Mr Boswell... Thank you, Phoebe. I shall mention him when I speak to Miss Burgoyne tomorrow morning."

Mrs Williams walked away, leaving Sophie perplexed. When Mrs Williams telephoned from Lady Holme, she would speak to Miss Jones, who would say that Miss Burgoyne was at Lady Holme, so why not speak to her directly? Miss Jones could manage the request in London, but she would almost certainly give the game away and unknowingly reveal the use of false names. Furthermore, Miss Jones was ignorant of the secret agency and its work. Humiliating discoveries loomed on the horizon at Lady Holme and in London.

"Oh, dear," said Sophie, realizing she had no method of communicating with Miss Jones before she arrived at the office. Even if she could, what would she say?

"Phoebe." Flora had found her in the School Room.

"Yes?"

"Benson is about to go riding alone. I went to the stables and, when I returned, I saw him mounted, talking to Sergeant Gowers. He had his horse pointing towards the gates."

"If he's going outside, where's he headed?"

"Yes, intriguing, isn't it?"

"Right, it's ten past ten. I'll follow him. You search his room."

"Please stop right there for just a moment. You're going to ride after him? They won't give you a horse."

"No, I'll borrow a bicycle."

"Ah, very good. Phoebe, I have done many things, but I have never searched a room before. Can I take Nancy with me? She's clever at that sort of thing."

"We can't all disappear at once. Searching a room is easy, and tell Nancy and Dora to cover for us."

"Don't blame me if I come back with nothing at all or with something ridiculous, like a toothbrush."

"You're not stealing anything. You're searching for clues. Anyway, I must go immediately. You work it out."

"Oh, all right, then. But I'll mess it up. I'm sure I will."

They left the room together. In the Entrance Hall, they encountered Mrs Williams.

"There you are, Phoebe. Lord Hazlett wants a word with you in his study."

"Yes, Mrs Williams," said Sophie.

Flora continued on towards the servants' area, then waited for Mrs Williams to move away. When she could, Sophie turned in silence to mouth the word bicycle. Flora nodded and hurried away.

"You wanted to see me, my Lord, my Lady."

She had not entered the study before. It was his lordship's room with comfortable leather chairs and sofas and all the paraphernalia one would expect to find for the entertainment of men of importance or long-standing friendship. A sumptuous array of leather-bound volumes was arranged on beautifully carved walnut shelves. Decorating the walls were small oil paintings in wide, wooden frames, a few tinted prints, and many watercolours. From where she stood on the red and dark blue Kazak rug, she recognized a Constable and a Girtin on the wall behind Lady Hazlett who sat on the only chair, a pretty painted one, that a woman might prefer. She was to the right of the marble fireplace. Lord Hazlett, on the left, sat behind a simple, lustrous table of great age which served as his desk. He spoke first.

"I've asked to see you because there have been some rather strange, distressing activities in the house of late. I, that is to say, we, hope you and the other maids are not unduly alarmed by what has happened."

"We are saddened but not distressed, my Lord."

"Ah, very good. Excellent, in fact. This murder investigation, it doesn't bother you?"

"It reassures me, my Lord, that the perpetrator is being pursued."

"Does it, indeed? I see. That's what we have observed, Lady Jane and myself. A few servants have required… comforting, shall we say? Whereas, you London maids seem to take it all in your stride."

Sophie did not answer, suddenly realizing that being prepared inwardly for action presented an outward and unconscious self-assurance which was evident to others. In the future, a few crocodile tears might need to be shed at appropriate moments.

"Perhaps it's because we represent an agency and so keep going when we might otherwise let ourselves go."

"Yes, yes, makes perfect sense to me. Does it to you, my dear?"

"No, it doesn't. Rather, yes, it does, but I'm not fully satisfied. I have further questions, Phoebe."

"That's right," said Lord Hazlett. "We thought you might have been nurses during the war. Were you?"

"No, my Lord. I can't answer for the others, but I was in the Land Army."

"Army, there you are. Discipline."

"Lord James," said Lady Jane, "is fudging the questions to get this interview over and done with. I believe you would like this interview to end soon as well. However, I wish it to go on for as long as necessary until we, I, get to the bottom of these matters."

The silence became uncomfortable, particularly so for Lord James.

"I'll help in any way I can, my Lady."

"Yesterday, you spoke of Isembard. Today, the man fled in terror, and good riddance. What did you say to him?"

"I don't recall speaking to Mr Isembard," said Sophie. The memory of Flora's dire warnings through the butler's window came to mind. She suppressed the urge to tell them everything.

"Perhaps the others did."

"Shall I get them for you, my Lady? I can hardly answer on their behalf."

"That's true, Janey."

"No. Out of them all, you are the ringleader. That's obvious. I was astonished by your answers yesterday. You're too clever. I want to know what's going on."

"We arrived last Thursday, my Lady. It isn't possible that we came with the express purpose of removing Mr Isembard from his post."

"I'm not suggesting you did… There's evasion in your answers, but I can't put my finger on what it is you're covering up."

"Ah, Janey, please," said Lord James.

"No. I will have my say. I asked you to tell me the truth. Your background is not that of a maid, I'm certain of it. One does not like to enquire, especially these days with so many families of note in financial difficulties, but I fear I must. In the teeth of a murder and it's investigation you discovered blackmail which trained detectives from Portsmouth and London know nothing about and probably never will. That takes nerve and intelligence. How can I let you leave without an explanation? I appeal to you as a woman of breeding. You see us as we are. We are people of our class. You are familiar with our class. More than that, you are of our class. I'm not wrong, even if you deny it."

"Thank you, my Lady. My Lord Hazlett, may I speak freely?"

He looked cautious and answered with some reluctance.

"You may as well."

"Who I am and what I do, I cannot reveal to you under any circumstance. This is what I may tell you. Mr Smythe was correct. Smugglers are operating along this coast. Someone connected with the operation is likely to be the murderer. I am not attached to the police investigation, but I will assist them in finding the culprit, if possible."

She stopped.

"There's more, isn't there?" asked Lady Jane.

"Indeed, there is, my Lady. I hesitate to speak, and you both can appreciate why and for different reasons."

"How can you know anything?" There was a challenge in his voice.

"Poppy."

"Good Lord." Lord Hazlett sank back in his chair.

"What does she mean, James?" Lady Jane looked from her husband to Sophie and back again.

"How much do you know?" asked Lord James.

"Not much and nothing for certain. Enough to establish a working hypothesis about the organization and your own circumstances. Who is Poppy, my Lord?"

"I cannot tell you. I'm honour-bound."

"We are both honour-bound." Sophie turned to Lady Hazlett. "I need not say the name of the person who troubles you."

"No, you don't. Yesterday, I asked you to tell me if you noticed anything. That person in particular was whom I meant."

"I said I would do so and I shall keep my word. At the moment, I have nothing new to say except I have personal experience of his reprehensible behaviour. As he is also Poppy's agent, one assumes his employer's morality is of the same essence. I would put no trust in what either says."

"I never have," said Lord James. "But then I've had no choice. I suspect I may run the race only to be tripped before the finish line."

"Why don't you explain everything here and now?" asked Lady Jane. "You have nothing to lose."

"I can't."

"Phoebe," said Lady Jane. "Please answer me this time. Did you get rid of Isembard?"

"Yes."

"There, James, we have an ally." Lady Jane wore an expression of immense satisfaction. "I trust Phoebe despite her reticence; you can, too. We won't get another opportunity. This Poppy creature is obviously your enemy, and Benson is that creature's creature. They're determined to do you down. Don't let them win."

Lord Hazlett took his time in answering. He struggled with his decision.

"You're absolutely right. It is extraordinarily difficult for me to break my oath. But I now see that the fraternity I once gave allegiance to has ceased to function in its original form. It has become a tool in the hands of wicked men. Please, Phoebe, sit down."

"Thank you, my Lord."

Chapter 23

Aha!

"To start, I must make myself plain upon one matter. To keep faith with a society that I disagree with has been deeply troubling for me. However, over the years, I became used to the harness put upon me, and I endured my lot. Indeed, I have never known what to do otherwise.

"You have heard of guilds — associations of artisans and tradesmen. They have a long history and flourished in towns throughout Europe. My understanding is that guilds began in Babylon, after the first city-states were organized and built. A species of them was present in the Roman Empire. I'm no expert or historian but, in Europe, after the Roman Empire fell, guilds as one understands them today began to form. Britain, late in so many things, had no guilds until after the Norman Conquest. The new overlords introduced them.

"What is a guild in Britain? Each guild protected and transmitted the secrets of their craft. Masons, silversmiths, wheelwrights, drapers, merchants — there are as many guilds as one can count trades and occupations requiring training. When they banded together in a town, they soon established a monopoly over all business. None could sell in that place without the approval of the guilds. They fixed prices, enforced laws against competition, and stifled innovation. It was impossible to get in unless the local guildhall said so. Their combined strength made the guilds unassailable in their control of the economic life of the town, and it was of their choosing who participated in it. There was no free trade for many centuries."

"This is all very interesting," said Lady Jane, "but how does it concern you?"

"I'm coming to that, Janey. Please bear with me. One common feature of guilds was price-fixing. They wanted raw materials for the lowest cost possible, so their members retained the greatest profits. Suppliers of materials had no chance to form their own associations to protect themselves because the guild members controlling the markets did not permit it.

"About 1320, an enterprising Hazlett expanded salt production in this area. He began sending cartloads to London and towns in the Midlands. It was a profitable business and would continue for centuries to come. The guild-controlled towns — some were much worse than others, you understand — began taxing salt, or fixing its price barely above production costs, or they did both. Suppliers of other materials received the same treatment.

"In the middle of the century, several families producing different materials banded together for mutual aid and protection. Necessity caused them to form their society in secret. This meant guildhall was unaware when members took concerted action against them to beat their taxes and price-fixing. Hazlett was a founding member. The secret name of the society known only to its members is the Pillars Worthy of Praise. A rather pompous name, I've always thought, but it demonstrates the desire to be equal in standing and power to the guilds. Within the society, members are referred to by their resource. Coal, Wool, Iron — I am Salt, as was my father before me. Basil would be Salt, but I shall counsel him against joining. There are levels of initiation, and several offices fulfilling various functions. Some offices are on an annual rotation... I shan't bore you with all of that. The membership is limited to forty-nine families and when a family has failed financially or become extinct, another family is considered and groomed before being brought in to replace them."

"But we have nothing to do with salt," said Lady Jane.

"Ah, but we do. Only today it is through significant shareholdings in British and foreign corporations who manufacture or trade in salt. Otherwise, I would not maintain my standing."

"Sorry, please continue."

"Thank you. A large part of the society's success lay in circumventing the guilds' power through mutual aid. Through joint ventures and pooled profits, funds were created to aid suffering members and to participate in additional opportunities. Sometimes, the society would blockade a particular town, withholding all materials the guilds required for their crafts, but it was subtly done. Wherever possible, society members delivered supplies in the dead of night or at secret locations to avoid guild and city taxes. Not all guild members were content with the oppressive power some individuals wielded within the guildhall, so these often were the recipients of the underground supply.

"There's no excuse for this behaviour, but the society often smuggled goods into cities and to and from the continent. It became a way of life. Sir Walter Hazlett, who built this house, was a great smuggler but never known to be one, not even locally, beyond a few trusted persons. When he sailed, he might do so with three ships, then while at sea, a fourth or fifth ship would join, and these would be the society's ships who often changed their names, flags, and crews to avoid detection. I could tell you many stories. In the distant past, smuggling has been a way of life for the Hazlett family but it has also been a widely used and powerful tool for the society."

"Then that is why you wanted to avoid Richard Smythe's enquiries?" asked Sophie.

"Yes. I've heard those lorries in the night. It's possible the society is involved. That is why I avoided Smythe. I couldn't take the risk. In part, because of the oath, but partly because of jeopardizing my delicate position."

"Then tell us that part, James. Stop waffling on about all those other things."

"They're important to understand the complete picture. I think you grasp the setting now. When I was initiated as a full member in 1879, I learned many secrets and began understanding the full scope of the society's activities. They're immense and have been for centuries. But, as with anything, there have been rises and falls in fortune. The society today is active but much less so than it was in the past.

"I still respect some members, but those are very few and declining in number, and I do not even know the names of the other members. As you can imagine, a secret society must maintain its secrecy and, in common with similar organizations, does so with dreadful oaths of death and destruction upon oath-breakers. These have been enforced in the past, but rarely so because so few would dare to be disloyal.

"I will now speak of Poppy. The hereditary membership for the family known as Poppy is a more recent one, dating to the 1780s. After my full acceptance, I learned their history. Poppy represents opium. When I first discovered this, I assumed it was for supplies to the medical trade in Britain. Later, I found out Poppy was instrumental in fomenting wars in Afghanistan and China. The true trade and source of the monstrous profits the family made, and which benefited the society in general, was the enslavement of people by getting them addicted to opium. Through Poppy, opium was added to ordinary medicines and foods sold in Britain and elsewhere, making those things addictive.

"Cheap production of opium was the mainstay of the business. Although many merchants, including Poppy, were originally supplied from Bengal, Poppy later planted extensive fields around Kandahar in Afghanistan. The best, most populous market for opium was China. Huge profits bought political will at home, resulting in British troops being sent to maintain the security of the trade and continuing profits. It outraged me when I learned of the damage done in foreign nations for the love of money. It's difficult to comprehend the amount of suffering caused by addiction to the drug and the wars supporting its production and trafficking. Poppy and the society do not bear sole responsibility, but they played a crucial role in those affairs.

"Britain won the second Afghan war and, by 1881, all troops were withdrawn. It was during that war that I, recently initiated, discovered the full extent of Poppy's involvement. Father died in 1880, so I took over his full office, a senior one, with much influence within the society.

"The troops had just returned home when Poppy began petitioning the society. He was for sending troops back and needed the co-operation of the society to bring it about if it were possible. There was no reason to send in the army and the nation was tired of such entanglements. Poppy feared the Russians would gain control of his Afghan poppy fields unless British troops maintained a permanent presence in the region. I opposed the motion in a society meeting. I reasoned that, at a minimum, it would provoke the Afghans to insurrection. I further reasoned that stationing the army in the region would raise the likelihood of an incident on the Russian border, precipitating a war with Russia. My arguments fell on deaf ears. Money swayed some while the majority's attitude was one of callous indifference. I lost my temper and struck Poppy, saying I would leave the society for good. I threatened to go to the police. It was this that caused the trouble.

"In the end no troops were sent because the society was unsuccessful in its efforts. But that was it for me. The penalty set down in the society's constitution for my having made such a threat was death in a specified and horrific way. It was no longer a matter of who was right or wrong or the issues being discussed. I had challenged and threatened the society itself, and this amounted, in its view, to treason. Fortunately, cooler heads prevailed. Poppy was baying for my blood. Nevertheless, they commuted my punishment to what you know — confinement to the estate for forty years. If I left the estate, they would kill me. I had no choice but to abide by the decision.

"Being a young man, I found my internment irksome. Horses have always been a great interest of mine. News of an important horse sale at Newbury came to my attention. After a year of idleness, I thought, Why not? I'm not going to London or meddling in anyone's affairs. The way I saw the thing, the risk was upon me and I doubted anyone would notice or care, anyway. I suppose I deceived myself into believing they would do nothing. There was also the chance a successful test might lead to a more normal life for myself. After all, I hadn't actually done anything apart from striking Poppy.

"At Newbury, after dark, they waylaid me and my groom. A man held a gun on me while two others beat my groom unconscious, poured spirits down his throat and over his clothes. They then held his head under the water until he was dead. After putting his body in the river, they marched me back to my hotel in silence. A sergeant arrived to take my statement and the three men remained in the room. The man with the gun approved or disapproved of everything I said while the sergeant adjusted my statement accordingly. The leader pointed a gun at my head, which I might add he had taken pains to first wipe and then hold in his handkerchief. In this way, they forced me to sign the statement. Had I not, I'm convinced the newspapers would have reported my death as a suicide. Once they had my signature, they all left. I came home convinced that, should I ever leave Lady Holme again, another person near to me would die. From that day, I've lived knowing that I caused the death of George Moore, a man I very much liked." Tears came to his eyes.

"You poor, poor dear." Lady Jane, crying, rushed to comfort him.

Sophie sighed and became thoughtful.

"Who is Poppy, my Lord?" she asked in the quiet room.

"I don't know. They have not informed me of any activities within the society all this time. The Poppy of 1881 whom I knew died twenty years ago. He had three children who must be in their fifties or sixties now. Any one of them might be the current Poppy. The position may have passed on again. It's possible the present Poppy may be from another family branch — through a brother or sister, an aunt or an uncle. It's a large family."

"What is the family name?"

"Britten. I know little about them. From Yorkshire originally, they moved to London after the Napoleonic wars ended. They will have properties in many places, but I'm reasonably certain the position-holder will be found in London."

"I don't believe I've heard of them," said Sophie.

"You wouldn't, Phoebe. A chief characteristic of society members is to appear unremarkable to avoid attention. Although several possess titles, most do not."

"What will you do?" asked Lady Jane, turning to Sophie.

"Poppy has to be dealt with, of course," said Sophie. "Thank you, Lord Hazlett. It must have been difficult for you to relate this history. I'm sorry to hear what you have endured. I hope you hit him hard."

Lord Hazlett laughed. "Yes, it was rather a good one, actually." He added, "You must be so careful. There is a year left to run, though I cannot say that even then I would trust the society, and certainly not my enemy, Poppy. I obviously have no desire to provoke them. These people are not to be trifled with."

"Thank you. I shall remember your warning. May I go now?"

"Certainly."

"I'll go, too," said Lady Jane. "We shall talk later, James. I must see to the guests before we go riding."

They left the study. Outside, Lady Jane touched Sophie's arm.

"I knew it was something dreadful, but I did not know it was so bad. Men murdering each other? Secret societies, death threats, centuries of intrigue? I can't believe it."

"It is a shock, isn't it? Shakes one's views, yet it provides underlying reasons for events we thought we knew all about. This situation must be very trying for you."

"Yes, it is, Phoebe. Benson can still cause great harm to his Lordship and me through blackmail. For myself, he holds forged documents of a scurrilous nature that, if published, would be damaging and very embarrassing to refute. The trouble is multiplied because we cannot do anything against him due to Lord Hazlett's precarious situation. You say Benson is connected to this ridiculous Poppy maniac? I can quite believe it of him. But you said something else and Lord James referred to it, too, as though it were the intention of these people. Are you guessing they will further harm Lord Hazlett before it's all over?"

"In part, it is a guess, but this recent activity of theirs seems suspicious. Why blackmail and manipulate with only a year to run in the term? Do they fear Lord Hazlett over something we have not yet heard about?"

"I can't answer. Questions with no answers - I'm sick of them. At least I now know, bad as it is. But poor little George Moore, who was completely innocent…? I remember him. This is all so dreadful… and there's still a year to go. Just carry on, eh, and hope we get through it? That's all we can do."

"Yes, my Lady."

"Did you see Dr Beaton and Miss Hazlett?" asked Detective Sergeant Gowers as he entered the Armoury. "They put on a right show in front of everybody when he returned."

"Did I miss something?" asked Inspector Morton.

"Yes, sir, it was quite the spectacle. They were all over each other. If he's the murderer, he's also a great actor, as good as Douglas Fairbanks."

"That's nice. Now we've got the romance sorted out, we can get on with the case. Let's go over the timetable. There are holes everywhere."

"I know, sir. I jotted down some notes. Here we go." Sergeant Gowers took out his notebook. "Shall I read them?" Morton nodded.

"Persons who can't account for their movements properly or failed to be observed by another party during the vital time period: David Rand-Sayers, Oscar Reid, Constance Reid, Lord Hazlett, Reginald Hazlett.

"Persons who have a cast-iron alibi — Non-riders: Maria Smythe, Daphne Rand-Sayers, Helen Scrope. Riders who sat out: Basil Hazlett, Colonel and Mrs Digby.

"Because those last three swapped horses with..."

"In the same order as they made the swaps, Oscar Reid, Reginald Hazlett, and Fiona Hazlett."

"Right, continue," said Morton.

"Those with wonky stories: Maude Hazlett, Adrian Benson, Dr Beaton, Amelia Scrope.

"Those with verified stories: Lady Hazlett, Martin Scrope, Belinda Beaton, Fiona Hazlett."

"Very good... Are we missing someone?"

"No, I have one more category. Those who possess magic powers and talk nonsense: Vanessa Scrope. She managed to be in two places at once. Lord Hazlett says he saw her in the woods just north of Marley Mound at ten twenty. A mile away, Constance Reid says she saw her jumping a farm fence at the same time. Miss Scrope herself says she was racing along the shore path, trying to catch the runaway horse at ten thirty, which was almost half an hour before the horse bolted. I can't make sense of it."

"I don't know... Jumping a fence is a precise description. Sounds like Mrs Reid saw her, but perhaps her time's wrong. You'll have to question Miss Scrope about all that." Morton stretched out in his chair. "Lord Hazlett, Reginald Hazlett, and Rand-Sayers are the likeliest for opportunity to commit murder. Neither of the Reids could conceal a mace under the jackets they were wearing. Lord Hazlett may have made a mistake, deliberate or not, about seeing Miss Scrope. And by horse's temperament..." Morton consulted his own notes. "His Lordship on Chieftain looks the best bet." Morton tossed his notebook on the table. "Can't use a horse as a witness."

"It'd make a mess of the courtroom if he testified, sir. What do you want to do? Talk to his lordship first?"

"No, not yet. Let's plug these gaps and a different picture might pop out. I reckon Beaton and Maude Hazlett went off somewhere private and got so bashful about owning up to holding hands, they preferred to look suspicious in a murder case."

"They're getting married now, so they'll probably come across with the complete story after a little prompting. She won't want her fiancé in jail a second time."

"Let's start with them first, then Benson, then Amelia Scrope... Why is *she* on the wonky list?"

"She's a precise person, but too sloppy about the times. I don't like that."

"Nor do I. Right, I'll find Beaton while you talk to Miss Hazlett, then we'll see the other two if they're not galloping about somewhere."

Sophie found Ada changing the sheets on a bed in Colonel Digby's room.

"Found you," said Sophie.

"Hello, Phoebe. Anything the matter?"

"Lots, but too long to tell now. Let me give you a hand."

"Oh, thank you. I hate four-posters, I do an' all. The sheets never sit proper and it's murder doin' the corners."

They spoke as they made the bed together.

"Why are they changing linen on a Sunday?"

"No one does, as a rule. The Colonel spilled his nightcap down hisself and got it on the sheets. Do you know he wears pink pyjamas? Mrs Trout laughed so hard she nearly burst her corset when he handed them in."

"They can't be pink."

"No, they are. I saw 'em. Everyone has. I reckon they was red to start but the colour's come out in the wash and now they're pink. Anyway, you came looking for me, miss."

"Can you search Benson's room? I can't at the moment and Glad's following him on a bike."

"Is she really?" Ada looked amazed. "Where's she gone?"

"I don't know. Benson left the estate on horseback and she followed him."

"There's nothing round here for miles. She'll get annoyed if he's just trottin' about. What will she say if he catches her?"

"I hate to think."

"That's right. Though wasn't it funny last night? I couldn't get to sleep because I kep' giggling to meself. Her voice made my hair stand on end."

"It was a great lark, which worked out well." Sophie smiled. "That reminds me, we must return the sword to the Armoury. I put it in the Crow's Nest for safekeeping."

"Has to be late. There's always someone in there, else."

"Yes. Mabel and Nelly did their parts to perfection. It's because of Isembard's departure that I can't search Benson's room. I have to help Mrs Williams make a start counting the wine and spirits inventories in the cellars to verify the records."

"We're nearly done here, so I'll do it straight away. Are we looking for anything in particular?"

"Yes. The name Britten. There's nothing specific other than that. Whatever else looks incriminating or unusual."

"That might be under lock and key. I'll see what I can find... There finished."

"Four-posters do look lovely, though."

They stood back to admire the ancient bed with its carved posts, dark red velvet curtains, and superbly arranged covers, sheets, pillows, and cushions.

"I suppose so. Mind you, 'ave you seen the one in her ladyship's bedroom? Now *that* is really beautiful. You can't imagine a prettier bed. It's all pale blue and gold satin curtains on it, and my goodness, the lace and the needlework. Under the canopy, it's got this dark blue piece with the moon and stars embroidered on it. You'll love it, miss. It's fit for a queen."

"It sounds delightful, so I'll take a peek when I can. Good luck with your search."

Chapter 24

Mutual Aid

The Sunday luncheon of roast beef was planned for a quarter to two. The kitchen was noisy with the busyness of preparation. Mrs Williams, now discharging the butler's duties as well as her own, was anxious for the meal to be a success. While she carefully decanted wine and port, Flora successfully crept past her room without being noticed, having returned from her mission. The agent went in search of Sophie and found her touring the downstairs, watering plants.

"How'd it go?" asked Sophie, as she attended to a massive fern.

"Rather boring. Despite my readiness to spring into action to attempt heroic deeds, the reptile only visited the neighbour's house for about twenty minutes and then came back. Everything looked perfectly normal."

"What took you so long?"

"Returning the bicycle without being noticed. Inspector Morton was talking to Dr Beaton. Instead of standing still like good fellows, they insisted on walking about the lane between the farm and the house."

"Thank you for doing that. What did you make of Benson's visit?"

"Not much. Does he know the people next door? Phelps, isn't it?"

"I believe so. He must know the family, otherwise why would he want a private meeting?"

"Plotting dreadful schemes."

"I don't doubt that for a moment, but which ones?"

"You work that out, Phoebe. I have to make myself apparent to Mrs Williams or she'll think I've run off back to London."

"Oh, yes, do that now while she's decanting wine."

Sophie continued watering while thinking over various things she had seen and heard, trying to make a narrative that led somewhere.

"Well?" asked Morton.

"Miss Maude is in love and very hearty about it, too." Gowers shook his head. "She stated that she and Dr Beaton were together in the forest on Friday. After her initial blush, she freely admitted they had a wonderful time, spent mostly in trying to get away from everyone else so they could be alone. She was preparing to give me all the details. I decided I'd rather not hear them and politely stopped her before she started gushing about her Albert. She's in the clear and provides an alibi for them both. How did it go with Beaton?"

"No chance he did it. Beaton got offended by my questions and became protective of Miss Hazlett. Told me it was absurd if I suspected her for even a single moment. I apologized, and he became matey after that, so I got it all out of him in the end. What about Miss Scrope?"

"I think she's covering for Reginald Hazlett. All the statements have him seen out in open country or near the shore. He disappears early on and reappears when everyone's looking for Smythe. Neither Belinda Beaton nor Fiona Hazlett saw him, so where did he go? I asked her directly if she had seen him after ten fifteen. A little bit of red showed in her cheeks and she hesitated ever so slightly before telling me she saw him a quarter mile north of her at about ten to eleven. She identified a particular tree. She obviously lied about all that because she never mentioned her sighting of him in earlier interviews. And she's the one who was very vague in the first round of interviews about seeing Smythe, which should have been at, er, ten thirty, according to Miss Beaton."

"Hmm, I see. A possible accomplice after the fact, eh?"

"Not surprising, seeing she and Hazlett are courting, as you might say."

"Can we shake her story?"

"It depends on her character and if she thinks it's worth the risk to save him."

"We need more evidence."

"What about Benson?"

"He's a suave beggar. Told me to talk to Constance Reid, so I did. In confidence, she gave him an alibi, but she's not prepared to put it in writing unless absolutely necessary. Said it couldn't possibly be Benson because he travelled in their group between nine and eleven and was in her sight most of the time."

"Where did they go?"

"Marley Mound, and then into the eastern woods. While in there, Benson and she rode off alone, but she refused to go into specifics."

"Of course she did."

"She says they were discussing business matters. I went back to Benson. I got him talking, and he confirmed what Constance Reid had told us about Vanessa Hazlett jumping the fence."

"What do you think, sir?"

"Looks about right, I suppose. He was obviously chatting up Constance Reid and no one's putting him anywhere near the shore at the right time."

"Whereas Reginald Hazlett, by his own statement, was in open country, and now Amelia Scrope says she saw him there. He was close enough to follow, then murder, Smythe, and only her belated statement gives him an alibi." Gowers smiled to himself.

"We'll follow up," said Morton. "I'd like to get his lordship cleared out of the way first."

"Before or after lunch? With the amount of food they have, they'll be sitting down for two hours."

"I can't wait for his dinner to go down. But he's out riding now."

"They all are."

"Let's take the car down to the shore and see what they get up to. We can go over the ground again before it rains."

They were on the point of leaving the Armoury when Sophie entered.

"Good morning, Sergeant Gowers, Inspector Morton."

"Good morning, Miss King," they replied.

"I've popped in to give you our findings on the jackets."

"Please, take a seat," said Morton.

"It's very little, I'm afraid, so I shan't stop. We're all rather busy, at present. We collected nine jackets, and none of them showed any signs of damage. This list is for you to keep." Sophie gave him a folded piece of paper. "The only item of interest concerns Reginald Hazlett. His jacket was examined and found to be in good condition. It was noticed that his waistcoat, a mustard-coloured one, has a seam splitting open on the right, here." She indicated where. "It's an inch and a half long, but we're not sure it signifies much."

"Waistcoat, eh?" said Gowers. "Was it a recent split?"

"I should have said he was wearing the waistcoat at the time, so we couldn't examine it."

"Thank you, Miss King," said Inspector Morton. "That's very helpful."

"Happy to oblige. Now, what do you have for me?"

"Nothing, Miss King."

"Oh, you're not playing fair, is he, Sergeant?" She smiled at Gowers.

"I cannot tell you anything," said Morton.

"Surely you have a suspect or two by now? Come on, Inspector, I *know* you have. Who are they? Tell me, and then we can help."

"If I feel you can assist us, I will definitely ask you, but until then, I am duty-bound to keep all case matters confidential."

"That is so disappointing. I thought we could help one another. So be it. I must return to my labours now. Good day, Sergeant Gowers."

"Good day, miss."

Morton stared after her and then at Gowers. "What?" he asked morosely.

"I didn't say anything. Didn't think anything, either."

"Good, keep it that way."

From the first floor, Ada looked over the banisters into the Entrance Hall below. It was clear. She moved swiftly along the passage, wishing it would not creak so much. At the Chapel Stairs she listened for sounds of approach. Detecting none, she returned to Adrian Benson's door, looking this way and that before entering the room.

She surveyed the room, which had been tidied earlier when the bed was made. Ada could see a few personal effects on the dressing table. She started there by opening drawers. Socks, handkerchiefs, a small, expensive toiletry case, a shaving kit in a separate bag — she rummaged through, returning the items to their exact position. She found a small flapped case containing pens and pencils. This prompted her to examine the wooden stationery box containing paper and envelopes with the Lady Holme address printed on them. While she was examining a sheet for indentations, she heard a noise outside.

The door opened and Adrian Benson stepped in.

"Puss. Puss." Ada was kneeling, looking under the bed and holding up the edge of the coverlet. She turned and screamed. "Agh! You frightened the life out of me! What are you doing creeping about, sir, startling a poor girl?" Ada clutched the base of her throat.

"I'm sorry to make you jump. What are you doing in my room?"

"Looking for the cat, sir, like I was told." Ada's breath was still coming rapidly.

"Oh... A cat?"

"Yes, sir. A big tabby tom. I've been told he nips inside when he can, then goes to sleep on the beds."

"Is he here?"

"He might be. I 'aven't looked everywhere yet."

"Then get on with it. I don't mind cats."

"Neither do I, but this one's a sprayer if 'e gets shut in anywhere. You don't want a cat spraying all over the place, do you, sir?"

"I don't I believe I would."

"He's not on top of the wardrobe. Do you think he's inside?"

"Look for yourself, only be quick about it."

"Yes, sir."

Benson sat in a chair and watched Ada as she poked around the shoes and boxes at the bottom.

"No, he's not here. Sorry to have bothered you." She straightened up and closed the doors.

"Before you leave, tell me something. You're one of the London maids, correct?"

"Yes, sir."

"What's Phoebe's last name?"

"King, sir."

"I take it she lives in London?"

"Yes, Clapham Junction. She often speaks of the noise the trains make."

"South London. Do you have her address?"

"I don't, sir... She's a very nice girl in every respect. Never in *any* trouble off-putting to a gentleman, if you know what I mean."

"Is that so...? Can you catch?"

"Oh, yes, sir."

Benson flipped a shilling towards Ada, who caught it and made it disappear in a single movement.

"That's all, thank you."

"Thank you, sir... If you do see the cat, tell someone so it can be removed."

"I shall do so."

"Thank you." She bobbed.

Ada closed the door behind her. She entered the bedroom next door, which was empty. She called out, "Puss, Puss… Bloomin' moggy, where are you?" for Benson's edification, in case he was listening.

"I wouldn't mind living in this area," said Gowers, viewing the landscape. "Air's clean and it's as peaceful and beautiful as you could want."

The two detectives had not driven all the way down to the shore path along which Richard Smythe had ridden to his dreadful end. Instead, they turned off along the track overlooking the shore path, the track along which Amelia Scrope and Belinda Beaton had ridden on the fateful day. They parked the car where they estimated the two women had been joined by Fiona Hazlett.

"Yes, that might be nice," replied Morton. "That must be the tree Amelia Scrope was talking about."

"Yes, it's the only big tree near here and at the distance from the track that she said. There's another track beyond the tree, by the looks of it."

"Let's say Miss Amelia was right on this spot, then, when she saw Reginald Hazlett on his horse by the side of the tree — if indeed, she did. The point for the moment, though, is that she could have. Now, this track we're on, and that the ladies were on, from this point forwards, rises gently and turns in a north-easterly direction. When Belinda Beaton and Fiona Hazlett went on ahead towards the woods, they would no longer have been able to see to the west of the tree. Neither would they have been able to see the shore path below and around Marley Mound as it's obscured by bushes and brush. So, only one question remains to be answered, and that is why did Miss Scrope suddenly lag behind the other two and then stop altogether?"

"Because she saw and was watching someone whose movements interested her?" suggested Gowers.

"Has to be. Her horse hadn't thrown a shoe or anything like that. Could she have killed Smythe?"

They both turned south and regarded the steady, gentle slope to the sea.

"Yes, she no doubt could have," answered Gowers, "but I can't imagine she could drag the body fifteen feet to roll it into the water."

"Nor hide the mace. She wore breeches and her jacket's too short."

"That's right, sir. But here's the thing. Whoever she was watching, and we believe it was Reginald Hazlett, he had to have seen her, too."

"Oh, yes. Miss Scrope says she saw Richard Smythe, but she also must have seen him ride along the shore path, enter the cover, and become invisible. Even if she didn't, Miss Beaton has seen him heading in that direction. But I reckon Amelia's lying about seeing all of Smythe's movements to protect Reginald Hazlett. Let's say she didn't see Smythe. She hangs back from Mrs Hazlett and Miss Beaton for another reason. That's when Miss Scrope sees Reginald riding along the shore, following what she later learns has been Smythe's course. She watches Reginald enter that cover down there. It's only a hundred and fifty yards away, so she couldn't miss him."

"All right," said Gowers. "Did she see him come out again?"

"Why are you asking that?"

"If she waited the few minutes it took, it was likely she was in on it. The only other reason would be to talk to Hazlett, which she never did do at the time. The difficulty with Amelia Scrope is whether she knew of the murder before or after the fact."

"We'll search the ground here... And now it starts raining. Couldn't have waited, could it?"

"It's still quite mild, though. I'll get our coats from the car."

Hastily donning raincoats, they began inspecting the ground. The rain was light, sufficient to wet everything, but no worse than that.

"What have you got?" asked Morton.

"Nothing, sir."

"Same here. Too much traffic. But you know what? His Lordship's in the clear."

"How do you reckon that?"

"Think about it. All sightings of him before ten and after eleven were behind Marley Mound or into the trees north or east. How could he get from there to the shore and back again without someone seeing him? It's impossible."

"So it is… Then Mr Reginald's our suspect?"

"Looks like it. Just need to find a motive, get him and Miss Amelia to contradict themselves, and we can make the arrest."

"You know, it makes sense, sir. I was wondering why the murderer bothered to return the mace. If it was me, I'd have chucked it in the drink. But with Hazlett, it's a family heirloom, so he took the risk of putting it back."

"I suppose he did. Come on, let's go before it starts pouring."

The servants finished their lunch and immediately afterwards, the secret agency held a hurried conference to exchange information and to plan what they would do next.

"Dora, Sergeant Gowers has created a timetable of events which he constantly refers to. It's quite large, because he's pasted four sheets of paper together. When neither detective is in the Armoury, I assume he takes it with him because I searched for it while they were out. Could you view it with your photographic mind for a few seconds and remember what you saw?"

"I might, Miss Phoebe. I don't know until I try." Fern smiled.

"It will be upside down when you do."

"Oh. I'm not sure, then."

"Sergeant Gowers will also be sitting in front of you."

"I dunno. He's the police. I shouldn't ought to do that."

"I'll go with you," said Ada.

"That's nice of you, but I really don't like to."

"Very well," said Sophie. "Now, the next thing…"

"But I'll give it a go," said Fern suddenly.

"Ah, excellent!" said Sophie. "You and Ada work out when to make your attempt. The next item is to search Benson's room. Ada was interrupted, but wriggled out of an awkward situation with an admirable excuse."

"I can do his room as well, Phoebe," said Fern enthusiastically. "During lunch while you're serving."

"I already did the dresser and underneath the bed," said Ada. "He was watching me when I looked in the wardrobe… Come to think of it, you'll 'ave time, so do the whole room again."

"Funny, ain't it?" said Fern, shrugging her shoulders.

"Now that we've settled those things, there's my mission to discuss. After lunch, I'm borrowing a bike so that I can survey the river-channel by Marley Mound."

"You'll get soaked," said Flora. "Have you seen it outside?"

"I must go. Smuggling is our reason for being here."

"There's the gardener's oilskins," said Ada. "They might be a bit stinky."

"Oh, dear, I don't want to spoil my clothes."

"There are old clothes in the attic to wear underneath," said Dora.

"Wardrobe is my department," said Flora. "I'll find suitable items to match this season's dilapidated tan oilskin look. What about footwear?"

"I haven't seen any wellingtons," said Ada.

"Waders?" suggested Fern. "Ooh, I know. Isembard left an old pair of boots behind to be thrown out. You could wear those. They're quite big, though, so you'll need extra socks."

"I can find those," said Ada.

Sophie sighed. "All right, then. I'll wear Isembard's old boots, but I refuse to wear his old socks."

"No, these'll be nice and clean. I'll borrow 'em."

"From whom?"

"Lord Hazlett's got nice thick woollen ones, but you must take care of them."

"You can't complain at that," said Flora. "You'll be wearing the most aristocratic socks on the estate."

"You're not going to steal his lordship's socks, are you?" asked Fern, aghast.

"No, *borrow* them," said Ada, "and they'll be washed before they're returned."

"Thank you, everyone," said Sophie. "Right, I believe we're all set. I'll be gone for no more than two hours and back without fail before dark. Try to cover for me, but should Mrs Williams notice my absence, tell her to ask Lady Jane about it."

"Have you told her ladyship?" asked Flora.

"No, of course not. We'll just have to risk it. In all likelihood, our false names will be found out tomorrow when Mrs Williams telephones the agency to speak to me, so it doesn't matter much what we do now. Any questions…? Good, let's see to lunch, and best of luck, Dora."

"And the same to you, Miss Phoebe."

Chapter 25

Wet through

The rain came down. It was a persistent, soaking, searching downpour, dropping from a grey cloudy ceiling which perversely looked too bright to hold such volumes of liquid. Sophie struggled through the slapping, watery onslaught. The ancient oilskin coat she wore was too big, but at least being outdoors had dissipated the smell to only a residual odour of ponds, tar, fish, and something nameless and rotten. The matching trousers squeaked and rustled as she pedalled while the black fisherman's hat kept slipping forward over her eyes. Isembard's large boots were cumbersome, prone to sliding off the pedals. Her ensemble kept her from being soaked, but within her oversized armour that warded off a million rain darts, a secondary atmosphere of uncomfortable damp established itself. The fisherman's jersey, riding breeches, superior socks, and the interior of the oilskins were all moist. Her greatest annoyance was having to blink rapidly to see where she was going or to wipe her wet face with an equally wet hand. She cycled with care because the bike tended to skid over the grassy farm track, now turning to mud, which had been dry and firm a few hours earlier. More irritating was the knowledge that she could have journeyed in fine weather the day before.

Under the trees, she followed a woodland track south. As she proceeded, the trees became larger and more magnificent. Despite the weather, the forest was beautiful for reasons not usually apparent. It was a place of solitude, as she had the trees and tracks entirely to herself. In the dim, even light, the woodland was its own world, silent, hidden, and complete — requiring nothing to make it more or less than what it was. As these were unfamiliar paths to Sophie, she felt no sense of possession, but neither was she alien to it. She felt as though she had wandered into someone else's house party, and although not asked to leave, neither was she paid any attention. The woods had a grand indifference to her presence, and this was her chief impression, which produced a minor awe. This forest had always existed, would always exist, and she recalled descriptions of ancient times when Britain had been tree-covered from end to end with no place yet named. Had she not been on a mission, Sophie would still have been glad to be in the dim, wet forest, just this once, for the unexpected depth of indescribable fascination it induced.

Marley Mound lay ahead, but she needed to cut eastward towards the river she had spotted from the top of the Mound on Friday afternoon. She took the next track in that direction. It was promising at first, with more open woodland, now carpeted with leaves. A majestic beech stood in a clearing. Younger beeches close by the track were covered in vivid dark green moss about their roots and lower trunks. Beyond these, the track narrowed with wet, brown bracken closing in, and brushing Sophie's legs as she pedalled. The track continued on and she stopped to look about. She could barely see the path she was travelling and there were no others in sight. All around lay the forest, wet and endless, and she might be anywhere. There must be a path leading to the river. She pushed on, knowing that if she did not turn back in an hour, she would be returning in the dark.

Three hundred yards further, the land changed abruptly to one of new growth. Under the open sky, the path became less choked and began a steady descent. Another path crossed, and she turned south, more or less. Sophie hurried along, conscious that her absence was more likely to be noticed the longer she was away.

At last she found the marsh which lay upon her left. It looked unpleasant in the rain with its dark waters, clumpy tangled growth, and spent reeds. The now undulating, rising path skirted this sullen area. Here, the embedded stones in the ground became larger and more uneven the further she went, forcing Sophie to dismount and push the bike. She had not taken ten steps when she discovered a wide landing area of laid flat stone built upon the bank. It was ancient and unused with grasses growing from the cracks, yet a small patch of open water lay before it. Sophie puzzled over this feature before recalling the marlstone mine which had once been in operation in the Mound itself. She looked across the water and discovered a similar landing opposite. As Sophie understood the layout and extent of Lord Hazlett's estate, the opposite bank was the property of his neighbour, Mr Phelps. She stared at the landing on the far shore as rain pattered on her oilskins. The farther shore was different, and she came to realize in what ways it differed.

The freshwater marsh had silted up over time since the mine had fallen into disuse. Leading from the landing stage on the opposite shore was a wide, open channel of water which turned south to the sea. Sophie had seen this from the top of Marley Mound and thought it was a lagoon. On the further shore, the pale stones of the landing were almost free of plant growth, but the bushes surrounding it grew quite high. At a point well above the water, something log-like, definitely dark brown, protruded from beneath a large bush. It could be a raft or skiff. Then she noticed the end of a heavy rope. She thought it was tied to an iron pin driven into a large stone. The rope ran down into the water, disappearing below the surface. Sophie could not find where it reappeared.

Several hundred yards south, she came to an impasse. On her way, she found horse dung where another path formed a T junction with the one she travelled. That discovery set her thinking. But now, her track ended because it had collapsed into the sea. From where she stood, several interesting features presented themselves. The first lay thirty feet below the path, where the freshwater channel ended by running over a concrete weir with a sluice gate. Here, as she now saw, the submerged rope reappeared, its end tied to another iron ring attached to a platform. As unexpected as was the weir itself, one feature seemed inscrutable at first. A concrete ramp was on the seaward side. It was about ten feet wide, joined the weir at the top, and extended to become a substantial platform on the weir's freshwater side.

Below the weir lay the sea. At that moment, the rising tide lapped three feet below the top. Sophie guessed there was another foot to go before high tide was reached, judging by the tide marks on the concrete wall. The sea's surface in the channel was remarkably calm, with a minimal swell. It lay sheltered by Marley Mound on one side, and the headland, half the mound's height, on the other. Scanning the headland and then seaward, she found nothing else remarkable on the Phelps' property. More tantalizing was what she could now partially see on the Hazlett side of the channel. The top of Marley Mound was bald and dome-like; although Sophie could not see this from her position, she knew it as a fact. What she did observe was the hill running steeply down from the top, which was where she had nearly tumbled over the edge on Friday. This was because, as she could now see, the hill became straight-sided, like a cliff, for some thirty feet. After that, the wall recessed, becoming concave, while also disappearing from view. The undercut and concave arch were too smooth to have been formed by weathering alone. Besides, Sophie thought, this side of Marley Mound was not exposed to the wind and waves of the open sea. It was a sheltered, hidden cove — invisible to passing vessels, a perfect place for smugglers to hide a small, masted boat or land goods from rowing boats. It all depended on how far in the cove extended. Sophie wondered if it connected to the old mine galleries and adits. She returned to Lady Holme, her mind full of possibilities.

"Did you fall in, miss?" asked Ada, who was watching for Sophie's return from the servants' back door. She was relieved to see Sophie come sloshing around the corner in her monstrous gear.

"It feels like it."

"I'm glad you're back. I was gettin' worried you'd be out in the dark. Here, let me 'elp."

"Thank you."

They removed the wet oilskins between them. Sophie looked bedraggled. The fisherman's jersey had grown to the length of a short dress while one of Isembard's old boots had a flapping sole.

"I could do with a bath."

Ada sniffed. "Yes, but you've only got time to dry your hair."

"Why? Has anything happened?"

"Lord and Lady Hazlett and Mrs Williams are all looking for you. She knows you went out."

"Oh, no... Well, it can't be helped now."

"Yes, and Glad has found something tremendous. Dora discovered something in Benson's room. We got the police timetable, although that was a bit dodgy if you ask me, and I've a bit of an idea about it all."

"Wonderful, wonderful. I've had some success, too. We shall discuss everything later, but what happened with Dora?"

"She's potty. Glad and me nearly had a fit writing down what she said. Dora kept leaning over. She was almost standing on her head so she'd 'ave a picture of the timetable right way up in her mind. Couldn't make much of what she saw, except they've got it in for Mr Reginald. That Sergeant Gowers got right shirty about Dora looking at his bits of paper."

"Reginald Hazlett... I wonder why?"

"I think they're going to talk to him and Miss Amelia after dinner. I tried listening in the Chapel again but I couldn't make out what was said. Anyway, it's too dangerous. Mrs Williams is in a very bad mood, so I don't want to cross her."

"I had better see what Mrs Williams wants first. She must be annoyed with me. Then there's dinner to be served. I suppose I'll have to miss mine."

"I'll get rid of these things. You go to your room and I'll bring a towel. Do you have any perfume?"

"I do. Is it that bad, then?"

"Yes, Phoebe, it is. It might be all right when you get out of them old clothes. Must go. Oh, don't forget, give me the socks so I can get them in soak."

"Thank you for your help, Nancy."

Having grown up as the daughter of a vicar in a household that practised Economy, Sophie had always been careful in her use of fragrance to the point of parsimony. A single drop behind each ear when callers were expected was all she allowed herself. By this method, the annual gift of Parma Violet Perfume she received could be made to last almost the entire year. She dried her hair as best she could, washed quickly and put on her maid's attire. Despite these measures, an off odour still clung to her, so she applied perfume until she could detect the smell no more. Her bottle was almost empty and her hair looked damp when she left her room to find Mrs Williams.

"There you are," said an irritated Mrs Williams when Sophie knocked on her door. "Where have you been?"

Sophie sighed before saying,

"Looking for smugglers, Mrs Williams. Only please keep it a secret."

Had Sophie spoken in Hindi, Mrs Williams could not have looked more bewildered.

"You've been doing what?"

"Mr Smythe was convinced contraband was being landed in this area. I don't know if the police are following that line of enquiry, so I decided I would. Please accept my apology for not informing you in advance. I suspect you might have refused my request had I asked. To set matters straight, I shall ensure Burgoyne's Agency deducts the lost time and further compensates for any inconvenience when the bill is submitted."

"No, stop right there. One thing at a time... Smugglers?"

"Yes. Mr Smythe was correct in his assertions."

"You've found something?"

"I believe I have. Did my absence cause any problems?"

"Miss King, I am the housekeeper here and your conduct is my responsibility. I am extremely annoyed that you left the house for *any* reason. In fact, it is intolerable behaviour. That you stand there speaking to me of smugglers is immaterial. I look to you as an example of how a maid should discharge her duties and comport herself. How can I do so now when you leave the house without a word? I'm very disappointed. Shocked, I might add. You represent your agency. What will Miss Burgoyne say when she learns of this incident? I doubt she will be pleased and you may lose your position."

"I am sorry for causing this problem, Mrs Williams. Although it may seem I have no respect for your authority or a disregard for the vexation I've caused, it is not true. I do respect your office and you personally. My apology is sincere. However, I did not leave the house on a selfish whim. As I mentioned, Mr Smythe raised the subject of criminal activity, and it is likely he was murdered because of it. If in some way I can aid the authorities in finding the murderer, is that not worth something?"

"I'm not saying it isn't. Burgoyne's was asked to Lady Holme to fulfil specific tasks. You were not brought here to please yourself as you see fit. You cannot overthrow the order of this house, pleading higher causes as your excuse. No, I am displeased with your headstrong behaviour. No one in the house has a greater desire for the criminal to be brought to justice than I. That such a thing has happened is distressing beyond belief. But that is *not* your concern. I shall speak to her ladyship on this matter, which is something I was encouraged to do by Dora. The cheek of it all. To make that young girl cover for your absence with such an audacious suggestion."

"Then you haven't seen her ladyship?"

"Of course, I haven't. The idea of troubling her ladyship with your ridiculous behaviour never entered my mind. I *shall* speak to her, though."

"Mrs Williams, may I suggest we both see her now? You may find that my excuse was neither flimsy nor deserving of your censure."

"You persist in this?"

"Lady Jane has asked to see me. I will raise the matter of my absence when I speak to her, but I would prefer to do so with you present. Believe me, I have no wish to undermine your authority or position. Instead, I hope to continue the friendly relations we began, but I do realize my actions require explanation if they are to be forgiven. However, I am not at liberty to give further details than I already have."

"You hint at a great deal. Very well, we shall see her ladyship together." She looked at her watch. "There's just enough time before dinner to do so. I believe she is in her room. Come with me."

Lady Hazlett was in her dressing room. When Sophie and Mrs Williams entered, she dismissed her maid, seeing that a troublesome matter was about to be raised. Mrs Williams was invited to speak and did so in simple terms, explaining Sophie's absence.

"Phoebe, it was unfair of you not to inform Mrs Williams of your intentions. If, in the unlikely event something similar should occur again, you are to inform Mrs Williams first, so that she may come and consult with me."

She turned to her housekeeper.

"My apologies for not consulting you before about something that impinged upon household affairs. I ask that you allow some latitude in Phoebe's behaviour, as I have requested that she should attend to certain matters."

"Forgive me, my Lady. I had no idea," said Mrs Williams.

"I know you didn't. No blame whatsoever attaches to you, and I fully understand your reaction. Under normal circumstances, it would be a regrettable incident. Please dismiss the matter from your mind."

"Very good, your ladyship."

"Phoebe, you may go, and I'll speak to you later. I wish to speak privately to Mrs Williams."

"Thank you, my Lady," said Sophie, who bobbed and left the room.

"Do I smell Parma Violets?" asked Lady Jane.

"Yes, my Lady. If it causes offence, I can ask her to remove it."

"Phoebe must have got wet while out. Where did she go?"

"She was looking for smugglers. I believe she has found something she considers useful to the police."

"Perhaps... I owe you an explanation, but you must bear with me for the time being. When the household returns to normal, you and I shall have a long discussion. How are you managing without a butler?"

"It is difficult, particularly at mealtimes. The maids from the agency require no supervision, but our own staff are accustomed to a butler. Several require close monitoring in the dining room, and Phoebe helps with that."

"Well, no one has noticed a deterioration in service and I certainly haven't, but we shall find a butler and you shall have a say in who we select..." A gleam came into Lady Jane's eye. "I know you're put out by her behaviour. Let me tell you something that might alter your opinion. It was Phoebe who got rid of Isembard. Don't ask me how, because I haven't been told, but I'll get the story from her before she leaves. That, I promise you!"

"I'm astounded... How did she manage it?"

"Who knows? So, you see, we are somewhat in her debt."

"Indeed, we are, my Lady. Oh, I wish I'd known."

"She is a very circumspect person and still waters run deep. Has she caused trouble in any other respect?"

"No, my Lady. Indeed, the agency maids are all excellent at their duties. However, a thought has crossed my mind. The youngest maid, Dora, is a pleasant, willing soul, who works hard and, with your ladyship's permission, I would like to offer her a permanent, live-in position, if it can be arranged."

"Do you think she would come?"

"Dora has remarked several times how much she enjoys working at Lady Holme, and the other maids like her, particularly the younger ones."

"See what you can do, Mrs Williams."

"Thank you, my Lady."

Wherever Sophie went, her aura of Parma Violet vied with Lady Holme's inherent scent of lavender. She met Lord James in his study, who was instantly aware of her perfume.

"Ah, Phoebe. I want a word with you," began Lord James. "I've been thinking that if we brought the police into this matter concerning the society, it would do no good. What will you say to them if asked?"

"Only enough to find the murderer if I discover anything in that direction, my Lord. About your situation with the society - nothing."

"Good, good."

"But it has become more difficult now. I located an interesting feature on the Estate of which you must be aware."

"And that is?"

"The weir on the river channel. It can't be seen from Marley Mound, but I found a path leading to it."

"Good grief... you did? You mean, you've been down there?"

"Yes, my Lord. There is a hidden cove on your property. Is that where contraband was brought in?"

Lord Hazlett was still for a moment.

"It's a perfect place and was used for centuries by my forebears. We once owned Phelps' property, so it was entirely concealed to outsiders then."

"Were goods hidden in the mine?"

"They were. I'll explain. The cove is called Underhat and was a natural formation originally. When they extended it to make it more useful, they discovered a marlstone deposit. After that, they mined the hill for marl. They excavated a long tunnel from the dock in the cove to an exit on the north side. About sixty years ago, the tunnel's roof caved in. Before that, and before my father's time, goods were brought up through the tunnel and loaded onto carts. They did that until the mine system became unsafe."

"Have you ever been in it?"

"Long ago, when I was a little boy. When the roof caved in, my father had the mine sealed off by detonating barrels of black powder. That caused a more extensive collapse. It was quite the sight. But you're interested in the cove. That part is safe. There's still a dock and a hundred yards of usable tunnel, although it's very dark inside."

"I believe it's being used, my Lord."

"I know… I didn't until Friday when I inspected the channel. Ever since Smythe first mentioned lorries, I suspected Underhat had been put back into service. Phelps is landing contraband, but whether on his own account or for others, I don't know."

"And you fear the society is involved?"

"I have to assume so. Underhat's existence was known to the society in the past, so you can see why I'm anxious about telling the police. If they enter Phelps' property looking for contraband, the society will assume I'm assisting them. I dislike contemplating what they will do in that case."

"Lord Hazlett, this is vital information. Does anyone else know of Underhat?"

"The family, of course. But it's just an old story. I can't recall ever telling anyone about smuggling… Martin Scrope, perhaps… No one else, I think, although I have been asked about the mine. Smythe certainly knew nothing, and thank goodness, otherwise he'd have brought the police down here from the outset."

"This is extremely difficult," said Sophie.

"Yes, it is. I cannot see how it can be resolved. Can you?"

"No. However, I should imagine that Phelps is lying low at present with the police here. Which makes me think… The police have been scrutinizing the murder scene and surrounding area — would it not seem to the society that the police discovered these things for themselves?"

"That's the risk. If the society thinks I aided them, it will be merciless. To make matters worse, it might seem to the police I had a hand in Smythe's death."

"That's possible. They are looking for a motive, and you will appear to possess one. However, that will be mitigated by the fact that you were in favour of alerting them to the existence of the cove. Surely, is it not better to tell them everything?"

"And face the consequences? If I alone were involved, I certainly would. The society killed my groom and I can't risk another innocent person being killed in retaliation."

"This is strange. I recently met someone in a similar situation."

"Is that so? How did he resolve it?"

"He didn't, but the danger was allayed of its own accord in the end. If Poppy was removed from the situation, what would happen then?"

"I'm not certain... possibly nothing. I have the impression that Poppy is the mainstay of the society these days. In reading newspapers, I sometimes see where the society may be involved but, since the war, from my inexact studies, I believe they do very little these days."

"Expressed as a fraction, what would be the reduction in risk if Poppy were arrested?"

"How can guessing help? But to answer, I would say the risk would be a quarter of what it is now."

"Then, by your own estimation, my Lord, the bulk of the animosity against you is driven by Poppy. Are the rest so dedicated that, if Poppy were arrested, they would continue a vendetta which puts them in jeopardy? Put yourself in one of their meetings. How would it go? How would they vote?"

Lord Hazlett was silent for a while as he considered the matter.

"Support for revenge would collapse. These men are only concerned with business. They do not wish to draw attention from the police upon themselves. What Poppy does currently, I couldn't say, but I should imagine he's breaking the law while the others are quite ordinary investors and business owners. I'm an example of them. As a shareholder, I like stability in business. The people I knew were like-minded. Their children will be the same. The lawless days are behind us, but not so for Poppy. The resource of opium has a long, subversive history. Until you asked to quantify the danger, I'd never considered the matter... Who are you, by the way?"

"A friend. One who hates injustice and secret powers."

"I can see that. Who do you work for?"

"Does it matter, my Lord?"

"I am curious. Last Thursday, you were a maid. It is now Sunday, and you are turning into an avenging fury dressed as a maid. I wonder what I should do...? Allow me to think this over."

"Certainly, my Lord."

Chapter 26

What were you doing?

"Mr Benson, there are one or two points I'd like to go over, if I may."

"Certainly, Inspector."

They sat across the table from one another in the Armoury. Sergeant Gowers worked unobtrusively, studying his timetable and making notes in another part of the room.

"According to Mrs Reid's testimony, you and she rode alone together for some time, but there was a moment when you were separated. Where did you go?"

"Really, Inspector, it was a matter of two or three minutes and we were well into the forest."

"Yes, that's true, but you went off somewhere."

"I did."

"Do you mind telling me where?"

"It's rather embarrassing, but, as you insist, it was a call of nature."

"I see. That's not so embarrassing; it happens to everyone. Was Mrs Reid aware of this urgent call?"

"I don't know. I hope not."

"What did you say to excuse yourself?"

"Oh, something or other, without explaining things… That I'd be back in a moment to catch up with her."

"I understand. Some ladies are very sensitive. Then I suppose you rode out of her sight."

"Well, of course, I did. Really, Inspector, what do you take me for?"

"I'm just interested in facts. Can you be more precise about the length of time you were gone?"

"Three minutes at the outside."

"Now, this would have been about a quarter to eleven. You didn't happen to see anyone else riding about in those three minutes?"

"Thankfully, I didn't."

Morton paused before saying, "You'll be anxious to get ready for dinner. Thank you very much, sir."

"Happy to oblige," replied Benson.

He got up and left the room. Gowers closed the door behind him.

"Those two are up to something," said Morton. "Call of nature... You think he made that up?"

"It sounds plausible, sir. I tend to think they were avoiding her husband and have agreed a story between them."

"Fast worker, isn't he? They only met that morning, as far as we know."

"Mrs Reid's attracted to him, sir, and they both know what they're doing." Gowers spoke in a matter-of-fact voice.

"And they're both going to withhold information to protect their reputations... I don't like it. We'll see the Reid woman again after Hazlett and Amelia Scrope."

"I don't remember investigating a call of nature before. I wonder if it's true... A pint says she backs his story as he told it."

"You should give me odds, but all right, you're on."

"I can taste that beer now."

"So you reckon. We'll take a look at their jackets while they're at dinner. We'll inspect all of them just in case the maids missed anything."

"Phoebe, we have important matters to discuss," said Flora, meeting Sophie coming from the opposite direction in the Entrance Hall. "What's that smell?"

"I hope it's my perfume."

"Yes, and it smells nice. Rather strong, though. Did you empty a bottle over yourself?"

"No, it was those awful oilskins. But enough of that. What are these matters?"

"I found a jacket when... Mrs Williams!" Flora whispered the last part.

The click of the housekeeper's shoes on the flagstones alerted them, even though the woman herself was out of their sight. Flora and Sophie separated to continue with their tasks. After that, the rush to prepare and serve dinner, and the subsequent cleanup afterwards, left no time for an agency discussion.

The engagement of Maude and Dr Beaton had become a major topic of conversation and a source of congratulatory delight around the dinner table. The happy couple often grinned.

"Marriage is a marvellous institution," began Martin Scrope, who went on to air his views on matrimony more fully, while his wife, observing him settle into his subject, struck up a conversation with Fiona.

The agents performed their duties and variously noted dispositions among those assembled. Vanessa, after her initial enthusiasm for Maude's announcement, now looked bored by the talk of engagements and marriage. Lord Hazlett looked pleased and bright when in conversation but when silent, looked careworn. Reginald and Amelia, apparently immune to the changes in seating arrangements meant to provide everyone with a fresh conversationalist at each meal, sat next to each other again. Their smiles were quiet, tempered, and they spoke together almost to the exclusion of others. Lady Jane had forgotten her woes for the time being. Animated, she spoke with interest, her eyes sparkling. Oscar Reid, Belinda Beaton, and the Rand-Sayers formed a group. Daphne Rand-Sayers looked engaged and enthusiastic. Oscar Reid had offered David Rand-Sayers a job in the coffee company and matters, probably as a consequence, seemed to have improved between the erstwhile troubled couple who had been becoming increasingly distant towards each other. Constance Reid spoke with Basil Hazlett and Helen Scrope, but, every so often, her gaze alighted upon Adrian Benson, seated further along the table.

After dinner, Detective Inspector Morton pounced upon Reginald Hazlett. After a few preliminaries, the serious questioning began.

"We've gone over your story several times now. I hate to say it, but there's a hole in it you could drive a bus through. You're telling me you didn't see anyone between approximately ten-forty and eleven o'clock? From other witnesses, we've established your position before and after, but not for those crucial twenty minutes."

"That's correct, Inspector. I wish I could say differently, but I can't."

"Well, this is the problem I have. From where you say you were, you had to have seen Miss Beaton, Miss Hazlett, and Miss Scrope. None of them are saying they saw you, except for Miss Scrope, who suddenly puts you north of where you said you were in your original statement."

"I was by that tree... I must have been mistaken in my original statement."

"Do you wish to change your statement?"

"I had better, I suppose. It was a simple omission or lapse of memory on my part."

"I dare say it was... What's the understanding between you and Miss Scrope?"

"Inspector, I take exception to your inference. There is no understanding, as you put it."

"I was thinking along the lines of an engagement - that type of understanding."

Reginald Hazlett hesitated before responding.

"Oh, that's what you mean... Well, you know, can't count one's chickens and all that, but I'm rather hopeful."

"How nice for you. I'll be speaking to Miss Scrope next. I'm much surprised she didn't ride with you, all things considered."

"What are you suggesting?"

"Well, if you're on the best of terms, shall we say, I'm surprised you weren't riding together. She's with her friends. You're on your own. You didn't see them, she saw you. What's all that about? You say you were down by the shore while she puts you a quarter mile inland. Then, you say you didn't see the murderer or Mr Smythe, but that you saw the loose horse. Chased after it, in fact."

"But... you're making me out to be..."

"I'm not doing anything of the kind. All I do is compare statements and changes to statements from everyone I talk to. That will be all for the moment, Mr Hazlett. Thank you for your patience."

Hazlett left the Armoury after he had amended his statement with the aid of Sergeant Gowers.

"He's rattled," said Gowers.

"Good. We'll give him a little time so that we can learn whether they've put their heads together. We'll know they have if Miss Scrope suddenly remembers something more that's useful for Hazlett's alibi."

"He's sweet on her," said Gowers. "That point you made about them not riding together — If they'd been collaborating, surely they would have made a *point* of riding together and alone to establish an alibi. Whatever it is, they're certainly working the story between them now."

"We'll soon know. She'll be more difficult to trap, because she's got an alibi. But potential charges for false statements and possible perjury might make her reconsider. Miss Scrope knows a good deal more than she's told us so far, I'll warrant."

After dinner, in the School Room lounge, the atmosphere was subdued. The family guests had dressed for dinner. The men in their formal dinner jackets looked crisp and smart, while the ladies in their flowing evening dresses made the ancient room a colourful court of refinement.

"Adrian, what's the matter?" asked Constance. Although in public, she spoke low so as not to be overheard. Benson replied similarly.

"Oh, Connie, it's the strain of these investigations. So much suspicion. I wish we could leave, just the two of us."

"It's dreadful, but it will be over soon… When shall I see you again?"

"Soon, of course. Very soon, darling. How about this? When we get back to London, we'll find a romantic spot to dance the night away, just the two of us."

"That sounds divine. I can more or less meet you anytime you say. I just need some warning to make my excuse."

"I'll telephone you, then."

"Only do so during the day when Oscar's at his office."

"Naturally. When we meet again, we'll make our plans for a weekend together. I'll find an idyllic cottage somewhere where nobody knows us. Here comes your uncle." Adrian Benson spoke louder. "So the silly man lost everything he had on the turn of a single card."

"Gambling story, eh?" said Colonel Digby. "Know a few of that sort myself. I never could understand the attraction of it. A penny a point makes it interesting, but what makes some of these fellas risk their entire fortunes is beyond me."

"The casino at Monte Carlo does well by them," said Benson.

"That's true. Monte's a beautiful place and it would *never* be the same without the casino. People have different vices, and I'm glad to say gambling is not one of mine." He laughed.

"Vices? What are you talking about, Uncle Horry?" asked Vanessa, who drifted over. "Come on, tell us your terrible secret."

"I was just joking, my dear. Don't you worry about that," said Colonel Digby. "Gambling's not one of your hidden vices, is it?"

"It's never interested me," said Vanessa. "My vice is speed. I can't wait until they make faster cars. Then you'll see me flying around Brooklands."

"I don't know how you do it," said Constance. "What if you crashed?"

"Then I'd be gone, but at least I would have lived first."

"Yes, I can understand that," said Constance. She had a great urge to glance at Adrian just then. "Excuse me a moment."

"Blimey," whispered Ada to Flora a little later, as they stood ready to serve in the School Room, "it's all going on, ain't it?"

"Yes. It's remarkable how one gets attuned to catch these little things."

"That's right. But the desperate look on her face is something to behold. And all the furtive looks, and hidden little smiles between the pair of them. I bet Phoebe's seen 'em, an' all."

They watched as Sophie served a drink to Dr Beaton. She was standing at another station but joined Ada and Flora when she saw them looking towards her.

"Unbelievable, isn't it?" whispered Sophie, her eyebrows raised.

"Do you think her husband has noticed?" asked Flora. "No one else seems to have done — they probably assume they're talking about the weather."

"I'm not sure," Sophie replied. "I know Mr Reid's going to Kenya after he's sorted something out about a replacement."

"Coffee plantation," said Ada.

"First week of November," said Flora. "His replacement is David Rand-Two-Pounds-Sayers."

"Then Mr Reid must realize what's going on between the Reptile and Constance and he's clearing out," said Sophie. "I wonder if Benson has an ulterior motive. His behaviour seems excessive, what with his proposition to me, and now this with Mrs Reid."

"He obviously has a deviously deficient brain, is devoid of decency, and his reptilian behaviour is disgustingly disgraceful. But good for Oscar Reid," said Flora. "Kenya sounds lovely by all accounts."

"Burgoyne's could open a branch office there," said Sophie.

"That's a marvellous idea! Ooh, sorry, too loud. Just imagine the warm weather and relaxed way of life."

"'Ere we go. I'll get this one." Ada answered a summons.

When she returned, she said,

"Why don't we 'ave our meeting here? They all look cosy for a bit. If we keep our voices low and stand in a line, we should be all right."

"Good idea," said Sophie. "Reports. I found where the smugglers land their contraband and it's seen recent use. I'll give you all the details later."

"Well done. I'm so pleased for you," said Flora. "In the attic, I found a riding jacket that not only looked fairly new but also had the lining cut out of it. It has a small bloodstain on the inside in the right sort of area."

"You didn't!" exclaimed Sophie.

"Keep it down or they'll notice us," warned Flora.

"She did, miss. We put it somewhere safe, don't worry."

"Whose jacket is it?"

"Can't tell, but it's expensive," said Flora. "The labels were removed."

"But we 'ad an idea," said Ada. "Dora searched the Reptile's room, but she didn't find nothing. So when Glad found the jacket, and we thought about it for a bit, we sent her back to have a butcher's in the fireplace. Sure enough, he'd lit the fire that was laid in 'is room. Anyway, she come back with some ashes in an envelope. There's not much to see, but there was a few ends of burnt thread in it. We reckon it's silk like what the jacket lining is 'cause we sort of matched it to the raggedy bits left on it."

"So, you're saying Benson is the murderer?"

"I'd like to, miss, but Dora said no fires were lit last night, she knowing on account of being friendly with the sculleries. Which meant it was lit during the day. So we thought to look in other rooms and found three where there had been fires. Guess what? We found the same threads in each of them."

"Her ladyship is looking thirsty. I'll attend to her," said Flora.

"What *is* going on?" asked Sophie.

"I dunno. The other rooms belonged to Mr Basil, Mr Reginald, and his lordship."

"Why the preponderance of Hazletts?"

Sophie considered what she had heard.

"Is it a new jacket, did you say?"

"Yes. Very well made. Must have cost a packet."

"Then it wouldn't belong to Reginald Hazlett."

"That's right, of course, it wouldn't," said Ada. "It can't be 'is lordship's neither, come to think of it. 'is clothes are more old-fashioned."

"Right," said Sophie. "It means someone knows what they're doing by destroying the evidence. He couldn't manage to burn the whole jacket at once without being noticed. But neither could he get the laundress to clean it without it being traced to him. So he destroyed what he could - the most incriminating part. By tearing out the lining, he determined to plant evidence on others, should the police discover the importance of the jacket. Then he hid it." Sophie surveyed the lounge. "Just think, the murderer is in this room right now... When could he have destroyed the lining?"

"This afternoon, but 'ad to be after lunch, while everyone was downstairs, otherwise the scullery maids would have cleaned the fireplace in the morning like I was saying. Also, he might've been caught in the act before lunch, as some people were still in their rooms. It could have been any one of this lot."

"That's true, but the jacket must fit the man who owns it. If we give it to Inspector Morton, he can trace it to the correct person."

"I suppose so. I'd like us to catch 'im, but we can't have Scotland Yard getting upset. They wouldn't give us no more jobs."

"Perhaps we should inform Inspector Morton now. Where's it hidden?"

"I don't know. Glad put it somewhere after we looked at it. She found it in a trunk in the attic. She remembered seeing a jacket when she was rummaging, but didn't think nothing of it at the time. That was when she was sorting out clothes for you to wear when you was a ghost." Having said this, Ada had to stifle a laugh which threatened to escape.

"Shh. Or go outside," said Sophie. "You'll start me off... Oh, my turn." Sophie served the guest and afterwards they were all busy and remained so for quite a while.

Chapter 27

Unbelievable

"Miss Scrope," began Inspector Morton. "I apologize for going over this again, but you were the best placed person to have seen the murderer. Sergeant Gowers and myself inspected the ground and there's little cover for anyone to hide in except at the foot of the hill. Do you recall seeing anyone in that direction between ten-thirty and eleven?"

"Had I seen anyone, I would have mentioned it."

"Very good, miss. Now, Miss Beaton and Mrs Hazlett were riding together and facing approximately northeast. The lie of the land there and their direction makes it difficult for them to see anyone on the shore or the shore path. If anyone was under cover at the bottom of the hill, they would miss them, too. At the point you remained, you could see both those areas. Is that correct?"

"I suppose it must be if you say so."

"Why did you stop and dismount?"

"I was admiring the view."

"It's one you're familiar with, so what was so special about it that you let your friends ride on without you?"

"Is there anything *wrong* with doing that?"

"No. But there had to be a reason for you to remain alone."

"They were talking of things I took no interest in. I preferred the beauty of the scenery."

"Yes, I can appreciate that." Inspector Morton leaned back in his chair. "What were they talking about?"

"Is that important?"

"It's a simple question."

"They were speaking of Dr Beaton and Maude Hazlett."

"And you didn't find that subject interesting?"

"Miss Beaton and I had already discussed it before Fiona joined us."

"How far away were they when you decided you would catch up with them?"

"Oh... I'm not sure."

"An approximation would do."

"Two or three hundred yards."

"Are you sure? It wouldn't have been half a mile, let's say?"

"No, it wasn't that far."

"When you saw Mr Hazlett, how far away were they then?"

"I didn't measure it, Inspector."

"Fifty yards?"

"No, they were further away."

"Eight hundred yards?"

"It was nothing like that."

"Four hundred?"

"I don't know."

"Three hundred?"

"Why are you insisting on this point?"

"When you saw Mr Hazlett north of you, did you remount immediately?"

"Ah, soon after, I believe."

"How soon, please?"

"I don't remember."

"From your statement, you stated you were alone, dismounted for about ten minutes. Miss Beaton and Mrs Reid say they walked their horses at a slow pace and didn't stop. Let's allow them three miles per hour. In ten minutes, they should have been half a mile away. You say it was a lesser distance. That means either the time you were alone or the distance your friends travelled is incorrect. I'm simply trying to find out which it is."

"Perhaps they were further away than I realized. It was probably half a mile, then."

"Would you say it was three quarters of a mile?"

"No, of course not. That distance would put them almost into the forest."

Morton wrote a note. He took his time over it.

"Now the next point I'd like to clear up concerns Richard Smythe. Both you and Miss Beaton are riding slowly. She observed him cross the path at ten-thirty heading towards the shore, whereas you didn't. A man on a horse a short distance away and you didn't see him? Do you have anything more to say about that?"

"No. I missed seeing him. I can't be a very observant person, I suppose."

"Perhaps not. For Mr Smythe to be killed, the murderer had to do one of two things. He was already waiting under cover of the trees and scrub at the foot of Marley Mound, or he followed after him."

"He must have been waiting. That makes sense to me."

"Except it's impossible. We've compiled everyone's statements and nobody was out of anyone's sight long enough for them also to be waiting for an indeterminate amount of time to ambush Mr Smythe."

"Then why did you suggest it?"

"It's a possibility. If you amended your statement, for example, then we could reconsider the matter."

"I'm not likely to do that."

"So Reginald Hazlett definitely wasn't waiting under cover for Richard Smythe?"

"Of course he wasn't. I told you, I saw him by the tree."

"No one else did."

"But he was there."

"I spoke to Mr Hazlett, earlier."

Inspector Morton stared at her. Amelia did not answer, momentarily dropping her gaze.

"He said some very interesting things. Why were you and he not riding together?"

"That's because we agreed we would keep things from our respective parents until we are more certain about what we intend to do."

"Oh, of course, that makes perfect sense. So that's why Mr Hazlett was hesitant about mentioning your understanding?"

"Yes, Inspector."

"I'm glad to have cleared up that one. Charges of perjury and conspiracy to commit murder have very nasty consequences attached to them." He paused, then added, "I think that's all for now, Miss Scrope. Thank you."

Sergeant Gowers opened the door for her to leave and closed it after her. He approached Morton at the table.

"They've worked it between themselves."

"Looks like it," said Morton. "We'll return to London tomorrow and let all this lot go about their business."

"That will please them. Do you think she's in on the murder or just providing an alibi?"

"Can't say at the moment. Alibi, at least. We need a lot more on Hazlett for the charges to stick. And I'm sure we'll find evidence for a motive in London." Morton put his hands behind his head. He had a satisfied air. "I reckon we can call it a night and get away early."

"No, sir. We have to interview Constance Reid to ask about the call of nature story. And, although I've put it off, I don't mind seeing Vanessa Scrope so much now. Might be interesting."

"You're right. Let's get Mrs Reid in here first. I'm not staying for the other one."

It was now almost ten, and the gathering in the School Room lounge was fragmenting and winding down. Oscar Reid had gone to bed, telling no one. Vanessa Scrope was entertaining Sergeant Gowers in the Armoury. Adrian Benson and Basil Hazlett were elsewhere, while Amelia and Reginald were having a brief discussion before leaving.

"They're going to arrest you if they can find a motive," said Amelia, almost under her breath.

"Are you sure?" whispered Reginald.

"As certain as I can be."

"Then I'll tell them everything."

"You can't. We're committed to our course of action. Licence tomorrow and, afterwards, we'll just tough it out whatever happens. If we change our stories now, it will be as good as putting a noose around your neck. They'll say I'm an accomplice, too."

"Let's go somewhere else and talk this over. I can't bear the thought of anything happening to you. Whatever happens, that shall not be."

"We can talk, but I'd rather you just held me."

"What on earth did Inspector Morton say to Amelia?" asked Sophie in a whisper as they surveyed the room and the depressed-looking couple in particular.

"I've heard the term ashen-faced before," replied Flora, "but now I've actually seen it. Look at Reginald, he's getting the same look."

"They must 'ave something on him and 'er. Couldn't you ask the Inspector, miss?"

"Perhaps, when we take the jacket to him. Which reminds me, I still must get the sword from the Crow's Nest. I can return it when we see the Inspector."

"You wouldn't catch me going up there at night," said Ada. "That's where Lady Holme died… At least, it's where she caught the chill that took her off."

"Phoebe doesn't believe in ghosts," said Flora. "Or have you changed your mind about that?"

"No, I haven't. I need the evidence of my own eyes. However, when Nelly was telling us that first dreadful story, I didn't feel so certain. It was easy for me to imagine it was all true."

"Mrs Williams is coming," said Ada.

"You either have eyes in the back of your head or a sixth sense," said Flora.

"Her shoes," said Ada, who smiled.

Seconds later, Mrs Williams entered, quickly scanning the room.

"Phoebe, you may go. There's no sense in three maids being present."

"Thank you, Mrs Williams."

Since entering Lady Holme, for the first time Sophie was at a loose end. She entered the Servants' Hall and would have read a newspaper had she not remembered the sword needed to be returned to the Armoury. Knowing it would be dark in the attics, she got her torch from her room. Tiredness from her duties and from cycling in the rain was catching up with her.

She climbed the Chapel Stairs and, although the School Room was in another part of the house, she could hear noises emanating from there. In climbing higher, she noticed the incipient, complex smell of lavender and ancient house returning. The first floor was quiet, and she met no one. Upon reaching the attics, she searched for a light switch, found one, then switched it on. A single, unshaded light bulb provided dim illumination on the landing, but little into the passage. The gabled rooms around the landing had their entrances lit while their interiors were a black void. No light from the moon or stars entered through the windows.

The zig and zag of the main passage soon shut out the glow from the landing light. Sophie knew her torch battery was recent, but she was concerned the bulb would burn out, which they often did at inconvenient moments. As she cautiously worked her way forward across the creaking boards, she checked for other light switches and bulbs but found none. She knew an oil lamp would be more practical, but decided against getting one. Having come so far, she may as well continue.

Soon, the passage branched. Straight ahead lay the attics above the oldest part of the house, while to her right the passage continued its eccentric way through the rest of the maze above the main building. Sophie turned right and soon came to the landing above the Grand Stairs. At least here she found another light switch and determined her return journey would be by these stairs even if she met family or guests. Such meetings servants were required to avoid when possible.

As before, only the landing area was lit and soon she walked with a hand extended so she did not hit her head or have anything brush against her face. Her hand touched something, which gave her a slight start. It was a bunch of dried lavender sprays. The lavender perfume became more noticeable to the extent that Sophie thought her mind was playing a trick on her by associating the touch of dried lavender with its fresh scent.

The Crow's Nest was in the middle of the house at the back. She got to its strange, square door. Further along lay Great Hall Stairs. She saw no light in that direction, but heard noises which she assumed came from below. She opened the door and stepped over the high threshold. Sophie searched for a light switch, and to her surprise, found one. When she threw the switch, three shaded lights came on. She shut the door.

This was supposed to be a quick errand, but, having stepped into the room and in many ways back in time, the story of Lady Holme came to mind. It was the true story that vividly presented itself with no thought of the other. Sophie went to the window by the side of the telescope. She thought it had to be the window out of which Lady Holme had leaned. She touched the handle and thought of the painting downstairs; Cicely Hazlett, who died young of a broken heart, waiting for her husband to return. Then, when he did return, he died soon afterwards of the same malady. She had believed the story when Nelly told it. Subsequently, Sophie had forgotten the tale through the demands of work and investigation but, here, with her hand at the window, it returned forcibly, more real than when told to her. She opened the window and leaned out.

Like Cicely before her, she could see nothing through the dark. The tang of salt air was on the wind. No light showed except for a few pinpoints on the Isle of Wight and a cluster of brighter lights in nearer Lymington to the west. She sighed, realizing that poor Cicely could never have seen the Falcon sailing in the night upon the Solent. Sophie had already known that, but she had to look. After closing the window, she heard the noise of someone in the passage. The slow, shuffling sound, accompanied by creaks, came closer. They ceased nearby, and the house became silent. As Sophie watched, the door slowly opened.

Chapter 28

Showdown

"What are you doing here?" asked Benson peremptorily.

"Ah, it's the ubiquitous reptile. I knew it would be you. Have you lost something?"

"What do you mean by this insolence? How dare you speak to me like that?"

"I dare anything where you're concerned. I've been thinking about your atrocious behaviour and have concluded you are an oily snake."

"Ah, I don't know what has disturbed you, but, um, snakes are not oily, don't you know."

"Then you are unique in the world of reptiles."

Benson took a step towards Sophie. When she moved, he made a grab for her, but she avoided his clutches by darting around the table. Sophie snatched up the heavy pot of salt and held it menacingly.

"Come, come, what is the matter with you, my dear?"

"Don't you *dear* me. You didn't find your jacket because I've hidden it somewhere. Your game is over."

"I don't play games." Benson looked irritated.

"What are you doing with Constance, then? Is she providing you with an alibi? Make her besotted with you so you can have her lie to protect your scaly skin."

Benson laughed in a conceited way. "Really, you go too far. Put that down and be reasonable."

"Don't drivel. You should not have tried that same tactic on me. Of course, you recognized me."

"What, a plain, uninteresting woman like you?"

"How venomous we are, but you betray yourself. You may not have noticed me, but *everyone* remembers Gladys. I've been observing you. I saw you looking at her, recalling where you had seen her before. Arrogant creature, you dropped your guard and gave yourself away. Anyway, none of that matters now. You're finished."

"Think so?" Benson drew out a knife. "It's nice and quiet up here." He was smiling.

Sophie hurled the pot at him but missed because he ducked. She snatched up the small telescope on the table.

"You should have minded your own business." He started inching towards Sophie, moving around the table, careful to keep himself between her and the door.

"You said it was quiet up here." Sophie jumped in the air and landed as heavily and loudly as she could. "Not anymore!" She jumped again. "Everyone has heard that." She started stamping. Benson made a lunge and succeeded in cutting her arm even as she twisted away to avoid his attack.

"You've cut it." She threw the telescope at him, then dived for the corner of the room. Benson began closing in on her.

Sophie grabbed a long object standing in the corner and stripped away a towel. She flourished the sword at Benson. The smile left his face when he saw the long blade with its basket hilt.

"Oh, I say, you won't use that thing?"

"I'm going to chop your blasted head off, you vile creature! You've ruined my dress!" She began moving threateningly towards him.

Benson saw by her look she might fulfil her word, so he ran out of the door. Sophie went after him, heading towards the Great Hall Stairs at the far end of the attics.

The darkness swallowed them both. Not ten feet from the lighted doorway of the Crow's Nest, Sophie could see nothing in the dark, and the attic was silent. If anything, she was at a disadvantage, being silhouetted by the dim light behind her.

Benson was hiding somewhere, motionless, but where was he? She suspected he would spring out as she crossed the entrance of a room.

Ahead, Sophie's torch revealed two closed doors with all the others open. Try as she might, she could get no sense of where Benson hid. A few moments later, a board creaked - he was further away than she had expected, but she still did not know in which room. Inching forward, she was careful to make as little noise as she could. Her pulse raced. Step after slow, careful step, she held the sword pointed in the direction of each open doorway as she approached, flashing her torch and glancing inside. Every room so far had been empty. Sophie stopped when her torch revealed Great Hall Stairs ahead. Four rooms with their doors open lay between her and the landing. Beyond the landing lay three gables. Two were rooms and one was the open area at the end of the passage. Benson was in one of the six remaining rooms. There were also several dark corners where he could be lurking. She looked behind her and felt she was safe from attack from that quarter. She switched off her torch.

Sophie considered what she was doing. She intended to drive Benson downstairs so that the men of the household could deal with him. But she asked herself what she would do and how would she react if they came face to face? She hoped to avoid such a confrontation, deciding it was now a waiting game with time on her side.

It was quiet. There were few sounds from the house below and none in the attic. Sophie began to think he might have escaped her. She decided to press on with her search of the remaining rooms. Just as she took a step forward, the smell of lavender intensified. It seemed to come as an invisible puff — a cloud — much richer and more intensely pungent than anything she had experienced before. Instantly there followed a slight noise, issuing from the second room on her left, which was followed by a curse and many sneezes. Benson came hurtling out of the dark. She switched on her torch. Dazzled by her light, and alarmed at her close proximity, Benson turned and fled to the staircase.

"Aha! I've got you now!" Sophie ran after him.

Running pell-mell down the stairs, she noticed fragments of old lavender sprays scattered everywhere on the treads. Benson had obviously walked into a bunch of dry lavender. He was less than ten yards ahead of her and moving fast.

On the floor below, he turned into the Long Gallery. Here their footsteps made the house boom as though a team of shire horses was galloping through. Benson, running while gripping his knife, rushed past Reginald and Amelia. They were too stunned to do or say anything, and more so when Sophie appeared, fierce-faced, holding up her skirts with one hand, and brandishing a sword with the other.

"Police!" she managed to shout as she hurtled past them.

Benson, being faster and less encumbered, increased his lead in the gallery. He got to the Grand Staircase but did not check his speed, and so stumbled down several steps before regaining his balance.

Sophie reached the stairs and realized he was going to outdistance her. She bellowed, "Murder! Police! Murder!" as she ran down.

Benson leaped from the stairs, heading for the front door. At that moment, Ada dashed across the hall and managed to trip him so that he fell and rolled across the flagstones. He got up and, as he opened the front door, Flora threw an ice bucket that caught him between the shoulder blades. He thought he had been stabbed with the sword and stopped to see his injury. Upon turning, he found Flora and Ada with their blackjacks in hand while Sophie charged down the last few stairs. Others were coming from the School Room. In panic, still clutching his knife, he got the door open. The agency followed him outside.

"What's all that row?" asked Martin Scrope of his wife.

"It sounds like a herd of buffalo," said Colonel Digby to himself.

"I'll send a maid to find out what's going on," said Maude. "Oh, where have they all gone?"

"This doesn't sound right," said Lord Hazlett, who got up and left the room, followed by Basil and David Rand-Sayers.

In the Armoury, Inspector Morton had been interviewing Constance Reid.

"There's one more point I'd like to clear up. Mr Benson left you on your own for several minutes and you waited for him. Is that correct?"

"Yes, it is, Inspector."

"What was he doing?"

"Well, I don't know."

"Where did he say he was going?"

"I can hardly bring myself to repeat it..."

"What's that!?" cried Morton.

The continuous sounds from the distant Long Gallery reached the Armoury.

"Sounds like thunder, sir," said Gowers. He got up and crossed to the window behind Morton. "Can't see anything. It's not raining."

"It sounds like it's coming from the Gallery," said Constance.

"Oh, it's stopped... What's that noise?"

"That's people running down the Grand Stairs. Something peculiar is going on."

"Excuse us," said Morton. "Come on."

The Scotland Yard men hurried from the Armoury.

"Drop the knife and surrender," said Sophie.

She was pointing the sword at Benson, holding it with two hands — a great rent in the sleeve of her dress. Flora was on her left clutching a rake and Ada, on her right, was ready to throw a brick. Benson had been brought to bay in front of the garages. Someone had switched on outdoor lights around the house. The stables and garage were in darkness. The countryside beyond and the sky overhead were a continuous black dome. Benson had nowhere to go.

"Adrian, what's going on?" Vanessa came as close as she dared. She saw the knife he held. She sounded disappointed, as though she had lost something valuable.

"He murdered Richard Smythe," said Sophie.

"Where are the police?" asked Martin Scrope, walking towards the group on the edge of darkness.

Lord Hazlett approached Sophie to ask kindly, "Excuse me, may I have my sword?"

"Oh... Not until he drops the knife... If it pleases you, my Lord."

"The police have arrived," said Lord Hazlett. He added in a softer tone, "Best leave it to them."

"Very good, my Lord."

Sophie offered him the hilt, and he took it from her.

"This was Sir Walter's sword. A good choice."

"We'll take over now, thank you," said Morton. "If you could all move right back, please."

"Come on, son," said Gowers. "Put down the knife and let's have a chat."

"You've got nothing on me," said Benson. A twig of lavender was stuck in his hair. "I was trying to escape that mad woman with the sword when these others attacked me."

"We have your bloodstained jacket!" called out Flora.

"Wiv the lining cut out!" shouted Fern, who was standing with a group of servants.

"And you tried to blame others by burning bits of it in their fireplaces!" shouted Ada.

"Stop shouting," said Morton. "Is that right? You've got evidence?"

"We were going to bring it to you, but we had to serve dinner and then drinks," said Flora.

"It's not *my* jacket," said Benson.

"If that's true," said Gowers, "then put down the knife. You've got nothing to worry about."

Benson hesitated. "Very well." He dropped the knife and stepped forward. Morton and Gowers moved in on him.

"We'll need statements from everyone," said Morton.

"Take mine first," said Amelia Scrope, addressing Morton but facing Benson. "Adrian, I bought you a jacket a year ago. You wore it on Friday, but you haven't worn it since. What did you do with it?"

"Amelia... I don't know what you're talking about."

"You have forgotten, then."

Benson did not answer and turned away from her.

"'Ere, he's cut Phoebe's arm," said Ada, examining Sophie's wound.

"Where? Show me." Morton strode over.

"You all right?" he asked with concern in his voice.

"It's not deep," said Sophie. "I'm more worried about my dress." She lifted her arm to display the damaged sleeve but, in so doing, also revealed the gash in her arm.

"Ooh, nasty. Go inside and let Dr Beaton see to that right away. Excuse me."

Inspector Morton returned to Gowers and Benson.

"Adrian Benson, I'm arresting you on the charge of aggravated assault with a weapon..."

When he had finished, Adrian Benson said,

"You'll find you've made a terrible mistake. She attacked me."

"Do you think there's a risk he might escape?" asked Morton, turning to the sergeant.

"Oh, yes, he looks like a runner," said Gowers.

For some reason, when they put handcuffs on him, Benson yelped loudly several times. Several men seemed to find it amusing. They all returned to the house, discussing the astonishing events of the night. Constance Reid, walking by herself, may have been crying. Lady Jane was thoughtful.

Reginald took Amelia to one side, away from everyone else.

"Before you talk to the police, will you please tell me what it is you'll say?"

"I very nearly did tell you some of it. Do you remember when you said we would not discuss former loves? You had two, and I had one. Mine was Adrian. I mentioned what the attraction was for me. It didn't last, because I soon realized he had lost interest. He was always pleasant whenever we met, but I never meant anything significant to him. I got over it, of course. Instead of hating Adrian, I find I've always had a soft spot for him and still do... or rather, did.

"As I said outside, I bought him a jacket. He was wearing it and I thought he was doing so for me. In recognition of... I had hoped... It doesn't matter now. He's forgotten me and he's forgotten that I gave him the jacket." She was silent for a moment.

"I saw Richard Smythe, and you, of course, but in between, I saw Adrian. He was keeping to cover below Marley Mound, but I didn't think anything of it at the time. He was unaware of my seeing him. I watched while I could until he disappeared from view. It seems obvious now that he was going after Richard. But it didn't appear that way then. I think he had spotted Richard from higher up the hill or just under the trees before following him by the most concealed route.

"When it was announced that Richard had been murdered, I could not bring myself to accept that Adrian was his killer. It didn't even cross my mind at first. It was so unlike the man I knew. From then on, I decided I would protect him because there must have been a mistake. I fudged the time of Richard's sighting and said I hadn't seen him when Belinda did, when, in fact, I had. Then, to complicate matters, you came to me, and I saw at once that you were in the same predicament.

"I trusted I could save you both, and that you and Adrian were going through the same ghastly type of mistaken situation. I had hoped to get away with it, assuming the police would discover the real murderer.

"Tonight, I noticed Adrian and Constance. It crossed my mind that he had put her up to providing him with an alibi. Please remember, Adrian is no longer important to me... You are. When I saw the two of them talking and the way they spoke to each other, I guessed he was deliberately using her, playing with her feelings to save himself. She, however, is seriously attracted to him. He means a lot to her. I now understand Adrian is good at that — worming his way into a woman's affections. I've heard one or two stories, besides. Vanessa says whatever comes into her mind, so I hear her talk about Adrian sometimes.

"Anyway, that is more or less my sorry little story. I loved him. He liked me for a while. That's it. His spell is broken. What finished it was when that maid ran past us with the sword. It was incredible, but I instantly knew that whatever had happened, she was in the right. Do you think she would have killed him?"

"I don't know... Perhaps not."

"You realize he tried to kill her, don't you?"

"I suppose he must have."

"That's what decided me. I'll tell the police all they need to know to convict him. With Richard's murder, I didn't see it happen, and I fooled myself into believing that it couldn't possibly have been done by Adrian. Seeing him chased and him carrying a knife left me with no doubt that he not only murdered Richard, but tried to kill that maid... Where did she get that sword from?"

"It should be in the Armoury; how it ended up in the attics I don't know."

There seemed nothing more to say and Reginald stared in front of him, becoming introspective and fidgety. Amelia watched as he arrived at his decision. He turned towards her.

"Even though I'm no longer a suspect, I'll go into Lymington first thing in the morning for the marriage licence, unless you've changed your mind."

"That is a splendid idea."

"I'm so thankful and relieved you said that. Amelia, we have a month to cram in all our courting with as many outings and romantic dinners as we can manage. Do you mind?"

"Not at all, you dear man. Where shall we go first?"

Chapter 29

You can't do that

It was gone one in the morning in the Armoury.

"I'm finding this room a bit depressing," said Sergeant Gowers.

"Bang goes our lovely theory," said Inspector Morton. "Miss Scrope's still holding back something, not that it matters now. We've got him on her evidence alone. Then there's Mrs Reid, the jacket, the threads, the assault on Miss Burgoyne... Could we up that to attempted murder?"

"What...? No, I don't think so. The defending counsel would make mincemeat of our case with her swinging a sword about. We should keep her out of it, anyway."

"Something the matter, sir?"

"All that work and we were wrong."

"Not so far wrong, when everything's considered. Miss Scrope was busy steering us away, but we were on the right track. How could we know that Mrs Reid was covering for Benson as well?"

"Pretty clever of him, though, saying he'd go and look for her husband so that, when he returned, they could do a bit of undisturbed necking. Then he leaves her for the quarter hour she reckons he was gone. He kills Smythe, returns, and then they're all over each other. And even when she just gave her revised statement, she was still annoyed with him for keeping her waiting so long. It's like her mind works in different compartments. She loathes him for using her and killing someone. Then she's also put out because he got caught and took so much time in killing Smythe. Most peculiar... I think she loves him."

"It's hard to credit how people behave, isn't it, sir? Although she said they'd met socially twice before and that nothing happened between them, I get the impression he must have said something encouraging to her."

"That's what I thought. It's almost like Benson marked the women of the Hazlett and Scrope families for deliberate attention."

"Could be. But here's the thing. By my calculation, it only took Benson about an hour to get her to fall for him here at Lady Holme. Looking at it from Mrs Reid's perspective, it only took an hour to get Benson to fall for her. They didn't hang about, did they? Might be a world's record... Here, why don't we ask him how he did it? Then we could write a book explaining his methods. There'd be money in that."

"Are you serious?" asked Morton.

"No. It just strikes me as funny in an odd way."

"Yes, highly comical."

"Look on the bright side, sir. We've got the case wrapped up, Benson's in jail, the little he's told us doesn't hang together, and he won't get off because we have two witnesses. Motive is almost immaterial."

"Still got to investigate this smuggling lark. Mind you, they'll hand that over to someone else. If there's one good thing about this case, at least it isn't as complicated as the last country house show."

"That's true."

There was a knock on the door before it opened.

"I'm not disturbing you, am I?" asked Sophie.

"No, not all," said Morton, who stood up, as did Gowers. "Come in. Sorry, it's not a more cheerful place." He seemed delighted to see her.

"Thank you. I know it's late, and you've been so busy with interviews. I hope they were satisfactory."

"They were." Morton smiled. "We'll be leaving tomorrow... How's the arm, by the way?"

Sophie held up her bandaged left arm.

"Thank you for asking. Dr Beaton did a neat job on it. It required several stitches, but he said it should heal without a problem. Not so my dress. He could not stitch that up so easily." She laughed lightly, and the men smiled more broadly.

"I won't keep you long. I tried to rest, but couldn't sleep until I had spoken. You can't prosecute Benson."

There was a long silence before an answer came.

"I'm almost afraid to ask... Why would that be?"

"At present, I'm not at liberty to explain everything. If you prosecuted him, there would be another murder. Perhaps more than one, and these would be innocent victims."

"More?" said Gowers.

"Yes."

"Would you care to tell us why, Miss Burgoyne?" asked Morton. All hint of a smile had gone.

"Benson is the agent of a powerful person. This person has organized a smuggling network, and I know how they bring in the contraband. This network will resort to violence to achieve its aims and maintain its secrecy. Benson is an example of one of their agents, but you'll get nothing from him, because he fears retribution from the network."

"Do you have any names?" asked Morton.

"Yes, but I can't tell them to you just like that unless you hear my proposal and a detailed plan is worked out."

"You're joking?"

"No. I suggest you keep Benson in jail for a few weeks while efforts are made to bring about the downfall of this network and then, after that, you may prosecute him to your heart's content."

"We can't do that, miss," said Gowers. "There are legal limits to how long we can detain people before charging them. After being charged, we have to bring them before a magistrate. Then they can ask to see a solicitor at any time."

"I assumed it would be something of the sort. But in this case, it's so serious, can't you just ignore all of that and put him under lock and key in a place where nobody can find him?"

"No, we cannot," said Morton.

"That's a pity... Oh, I know. Couldn't the Royal Navy press-gang him?"

"That's illegal and hasn't been done for a century," said Morton.

"That's that, then. I suppose you could talk to Superintendent Penrose about this."

"I thought you would mention him."

"Only because I'm not aware of anyone else who could deal with such a matter... You're disappointed, and I'm sorry to be so troublesome, but this network must be dealt with first or there will be more murders. That's all I came to say for the moment. Good night, Inspector, Sergeant Gowers."

"Goodnight," they said.

Sophie closed the door behind her. Neither man spoke for several seconds.

"I don't believe it!" exclaimed Morton. "She's done it again!"

Monday morning began with rain. Early on, Sergeant Gowers approached the table where Morton was sitting, carefully carrying the mace used to kill Richard Smythe.

"Can I point something out to you, sir?"

"What have you found?"

"This object's been bothering me, so I took another look at it. Can you see here? You might need your glass."

Inspector Morton took out his magnifier.

"What am I looking for? Oh, I see what you mean."

"This thing was forged," said Gowers. "You can see the hammer marks. A tiny thread has caught on that small, sharp lip of metal. Some twerp sprinkled fingerprint powder on it, but I believe it's a thread from Benson's jacket. Looks the same to me. Needs a microscope, to be sure."

"So, it is... I think you're right... That's excellent. We can tie the mace to the jacket and the jacket to Benson. Well done... Why the sudden interest?"

"I asked myself, why did Benson return the mace? Makes no sense for him to do that. The only answer I came up with was to put the blame on someone in the house. Now, if he's the agent Miss Burgoyne says he is, then what have these people he's acting for got against the Hazlett family?"

"Yes... And Lord Hazlett's a recluse. Can you imagine being stuck here for thirty-nine years?"

"I don't know, might not be so bad... Not in this room, though."

"Right. So Hazlett is avoiding someone, you reckon? Only they've come down here to cause him trouble. Smuggling's the thing it's tied to, and as soon as Smythe starts talking about it, Benson decides to whack him. After he's done that, he reckons he can put the blame onto Hazlett because he knows we'll look at the maces due to the type of injuries."

"He wanted to blackmail his lordship."

"You always say blackmail. Sometimes, I think you've got it on the brain, but this time you might be right."

"And it fits with burning the lining in different fireplaces." Gowers nodded sagely.

"Yes, by why his own fireplace?"

"Benson has the cast-iron alibi of a woman in love with him. For Mrs Reid to testify against him, she'd have to not only overcome her love for him but also endure the embarrassment of admitting her infidelity in public. Obviously, he was going to keep her sweet until it was all over. That meant she wouldn't speak against him, and he knew it. Therefore, the threads in the grate make it seem like he's an innocent party who's being framed along with the others. Now it's either that, or Benson started burning the jacket, realized it was too much of a job to do all at once in a small grate and so thought to spread the evidence of the burned lining remains among the Hazlett family."

"Could have been either."

"Yes," said Gowers. "I reckon he started burning the lining in his own grate first, realized the silk didn't burn unless in direct flame, so he put it on the three Hazlett men. For himself, he was confident his alibi was unshakable. Evidence in several grates might make us think a Hazlett male was putting it on to him. The two sons don't live here, so it's not likely to be them Benson's against. It must be his lordship. The mace and the burnt lining points to someone living in this house."

"That's all very likely." Morton put his hands behind his head. "But as it stands with Mrs Reid, her statement now has Benson heading to the shore, at the right time, gone long enough to commit the deed, and returning in a highly excited state unrelated to any passion for her. If he hadn't been caught last night, she would never have given us such a statement. He should have played his cards right and left Miss Burgoyne alone. Once he'd disposed of the jacket, nothing would trace back to him.

"And another thing, Lord Hazlett must have told Miss Burgoyne all or part of his story. Otherwise, where is she getting her information from?"

"Must be him. His lordship hasn't told us anything and I doubt he ever will. So how did she get it out of him? That's what I'd like to know… Coo, she's a one, isn't she? Her and that blinking sword."

"She gives me a headache," said Morton. "What a worry she is."

"Whoever marries her is going to have a *lot* of trouble on his hands."

"Is she seeing somebody, then?"

"I don't think so, but I wouldn't really know."

"Oh… No, I didn't think she was, either." Morton sighed, then looked at his watch. "I'll call Penrose and see what he says. After that, we'll go to Lymington to lay charges against Benson, and then we can go home."

A change of heart came over most guests. With the police business finishing up, there was no good reason for anyone to stay who had a mind to leave. The first to depart was Dr Beaton, who had patients to see. He was soon followed by Oscar Reid, now fully determined to live in Kenya, and David Rand-Sayers. Reid headed for his office in London. Rand-Sayers would join him there later, to train as Reid's replacement, but first he needed to return to his Lymington home to get some clothes for the coming week. Daphne Rand-Sayers and her husband were affectionate towards each other when he left. Constance Reid did not rise when her husband departed, and so he left her undisturbed.

At ten o'clock, Reginald Hazlett obtained a marriage licence and could not stop smiling as he returned to Lady Holme. Not until tomorrow would he go to his office at the London Port Authority, therefore Amelia and he could spend the rest of the day together. The Scrope family was not travelling to Southampton until the next day.

Lady Hazlett summoned Sophie to the office at ten. She invited her to sit.

"I don't believe I can take any more excitement," began her ladyship. "How is your arm, my dear?"

"It is quite comfortable, thank you, my Lady."

"Good... It is strange. Although my enemy is in police custody, I have yet to feel any relief from knowing that fact. I suppose I will in time. Lord Hazlett and I have spoken at length. He is concerned the matter has yet to finish and these Pillars of Wisdom people shall still cause him grief. What did you tell the police?"

"I simply referred to them as a smuggling network and that I have information on how their network operates. By the way, we call them PWP."

"That's much more sensible. What will the detectives do next, do you think?"

"Inspector Morton has to report the matter to his superiors, but I'm sure he will not be involved in the business because it lies outside his jurisdiction. I expect to be questioned about what I know later on today."

"Ah, yes, of course."

"My hope is that PWP, and Poppy specifically, will become the subject of a successful police investigation."

"That is our hope, too," said Lady Hazlett, who paused before continuing. "Upon another matter, I prevented Mrs Williams from calling your agency this morning."

"Oh. About the butler, you mean?"

"Yes. There seemed no point in her calling London to speak to Miss Burgoyne, when you, Phoebe King, are she."

"My goodness."

"I was awake for much of the night, as you can appreciate, when it struck me that the pleasant and efficient Miss Burgoyne I spoke to on the telephone could hardly be ignorant of your, shall we say, secretive behaviour? At first, I decided she must be aware of your activities. Then it occurred to me. You are Miss Burgoyne."

"Did I give myself away? My voice, for example?"

"No, not that so much. It's rather difficult recognizing a voice speaking on the telephone. It's your manner. You are rather a decided sort of person… especially for a maid." Lady Hazlett smiled.

"I apologize for the subterfuge."

"Don't apologize. We are glad you came because heaven only knows what we would have done without you… I don't know any Burgoynes, although I believe Lady Shelling is a Burgoyne. I've met her in the past."

"She is my aunt."

"Is she really?" Lady Hazlett smiled. "And is she keeping well?"

"Yes, she is in the best of health, thank you."

"Excellent. Tell me a little about yourself. Are there any titles in your family?"

"Lord Bledding is a distant relation, although his family name is Drysdale."

"I met old Lord Bledding, but not the son who has the title now."

"We had an English baronetcy once, but Sir Giles Burgoyne was forced to abandon it in 1636."

"That happens to the best of families."

"It does, but with the Burgoynes, it's a positive mania. We also lost the original duchy of Burgundy in 1361 when our claim of succession was denied because our branch lived in England. The duchy reverted to the French crown. Then there were two lesser titles taken away in Normandy and Aquitaine during the French Revolution."

"Goodness gracious me. That means you must be able to trace your lineage right back to the original kings of France. Then, if it were possible, who in your family would have the duchy now?"

"My father is next in line. He's a vicar, and even if the duchy were offered to him, he'd refuse it." Sophie laughed at the idea of her father as a duke. "But if they had changed the French laws of succession instead of abolishing them, allowing women to inherit titles, then Lady Shelling would be first."

"Most interesting... Now, we have a few matters to discuss. Mrs Williams does not know you are using a pseudonym and I shall not tell her or anyone else because it is obviously important to you and your work. That means you will keep our secrets and we shall keep yours. Are we agreed?"

"Yes, your ladyship."

"Then that's settled. I understand there is a butler on your agency's books who may be suitable for Lady Holme. Is this correct?"

"It is. I can give you his particulars now, and should he seem suitable, I can ring the agency and arrange for him to come for an interview at your convenience."

"That is excellent. If it could be arranged at the earliest opportunity, so much the better - this week if possible. Um, may I ask if he comes with a hidden agenda?" Lady Jane asked her question with a perfectly serious face.

"Not one of which I am aware. If he does, my Lady, it will be his own and not mine."

"That is how I would expect Miss Burgoyne to answer." She smiled.

Sophie smiled, too. "Shall I write the details down for you?"

"If you please."

Lady Hazlett moved a pen and a sheet of paper to the corner of the desk for Sophie to use. As she began writing, Lady Hazlett spoke again.

"The other matter concerns Dora, the between maid. Mrs Williams has taken a liking to her and would like Dora to stay on here if she is agreeable to such a proposal."

"I think she might like that. Shall I speak to her?"

"Yes. Would Dora be her actual name?"

"Her real name is Fern. She aided in the ejection of Mr Isembard, but she is not involved in any other matters worth mentioning. Fern is as she appears - a between maid - and a nice young girl who wishes only to find a secure position. I'm glad Mrs Williams likes her."

"Yes, that's important. Ring the bell for tea please, Phoebe."

Sophie got up and tugged the tassel.

"While we are waiting, you shall tell me of your escapades. How did you get rid of Isembard and why were you chasing Benson through the house with a sword?"

"Which escapade would you like to hear first, my Lady?"

Lady Hazlett was immensely satisfied with everything she heard from Sophie, laughing with greater abandon than she had for many years when told of the apparition at Isembard's window. Sophie left the office shortly afterwards, leaving Lady Jane in high spirits. As she neared the Armoury, she met Detective Sergeant Gowers.

"Good morning, Miss Phoebe. Might we have a word with you, please?" He stretched out a hand towards the Armoury door.

"Good morning, sergeant. I'll be happy to see you."

Inspector Morton stood up when she entered the room. His face was expressionless. Gowers closed the door.

"Good morning," said Morton. "I won't keep you long. I, um, I spoke to Superintendent Penrose and he would like you to ring him at once. This smuggling network greatly interests him and others. To cut a long story short, we're to keep Benson under arrest, but not lay murder charges yet. You can use the telephone in the servants' area."

"Certainly. Do you have his number?"

"I do. Shall we?" He gestured towards the door, which Gowers opened for her.

They were silent as they walked. Gowers' placid face betrayed no emotion. Morton seemed tense. Sophie felt an inward horror because she was about to speak on the telephone while others would hear what she said.

Chapter 30

Roughly on the Same Page

Penrose heard the entire story from Sophie, except for her naming PWP and explaining Lord Hazlett's predicament. As she spoke on the telephone in the ancient passageway, she got the distinct impression that Morton and Gowers listened all the more intently when she was recounting the difficult or more delicate parts. This attention made her feel uncomfortably warm. The two impassive Scotland Yard men learned of the matchbook that connected Benson to the Lymington area and which had brought Sophie to Lady Holme, the lorries exiting on or close to Phelps' property, the smuggler's cove which lay between the Hazlett's and Phelps' estates, and of the Britten family name.

Towards the end, Superintendent Penrose told Sophie she was not to leave Lady Holme before he arrived, and further explained that others would be there soon to take charge of things. Then he asked to speak to Morton. They conversed briefly in the manner of determined men deciding important matters.

"We're all confined to barracks," said a displeased Morton after hanging up the receiver.

Gowers nodded, as though expecting such news, although his expression had not altered. Sophie, relieved her ordeal was over, was now stuck in the passageway with two unhappy detectives.

"I'm sorry, but it can't be helped," said Sophie.

"No, I suppose you're right," said Morton.

"I have work to do," said Gowers, and disappeared with alacrity before Morton could say anything to him.

Inspector Morton and Sophie glanced at each other awkwardly.

"I, um, I should apologize for being curt," said Morton. "I don't mean it towards you personally and you've done a lovely bit of work. It's the job, I suppose. Often, I get a sense of urgency to crack a case and resolve it quickly, so anything that looks like a delay has me fuming."

"Inspector Morton, I quite understand. You are a professional detective and I appreciate the drive you must possess to catch criminals. Then I intrude, in my amateurish way, and put a spoke in your wheel. You must find me very annoying." Sophie smiled.

"Well, yes... that's part of it, although it's not you, yourself." Morton returned her smile. "The other part is that you're putting yourself in danger and, er, you could get hurt. Benson meant to kill you."

"Thank you for your concern. The fact is, I didn't go looking for trouble, but found it nonetheless. We were coming to see you, but I had to go to the attics first. At the same moment, he came to retrieve his jacket to dispose of it. It was by pure chance we met and I could tell immediately by his attitude he meant to harm me."

"I understand. I can appreciate why you're not telling me the complete story. All the same, you must be careful."

"I shall endeavour to be. But please answer me this. I would never have suspected Benson of murdering Mr Smythe. To me, he just *doesn't* look the type. Extortion, blackmail, and fraud - I can see those as being more his line of work."

"Yes, that's true, going by looks. However, there's many a murderer who never planned to be one. What happens is they get themselves into a scrape — usually it's money or sometimes infidelity — and they have a blind faith in themselves that they can work things out if they could just get rid of a certain person. Often the victim is a spouse or a relative with money. What's more, the killer thinks he can get away with it because he's been successful with smaller crimes in the past. I don't doubt Benson has committed many crimes but, because we haven't apprehended him, he believes he's some type of golden boy who can get away with anything he sets his mind to, including murder."

"I see what you mean. That fits him perfectly, I should think. I'm very sorry, I would like to talk further, but I really must get back to work. Thank you for explaining the matter to me."

"Oh, you're more than welcome," said Morton, who smiled. "I must see his lordship to inform him about the new batch of impending visitors."

Sophie did not serve at lunch in the Alcove. Lady Jane thought it prudent to avoid distracting her guests and family with a servant who might produce a sword at any moment. Constance was indisposed and kept to her room. Lady Jane was suspecting there was trouble between her daughter and her son-in-law, Oscar Reid. She believed Benson was the cause.

The conversation around the table dwelt at first upon the imminent arrival of the various important new visitors. Lord Hazlett, forced to say something, volunteered that it appeared Richard Smythe had indeed been correct in his assertions. They did then, however, explore the events of the preceding night.

"Who is Benson, anyway?" asked Colonel Digby.

The question hung in the air, as cutlery faintly clattered on plates.

"This is the problem when one doesn't know a person's family," said Martin Scrope, taking advantage of the quiet. "If we'd known his antecedents, we might have had a better gauge of the man... To *think*, we had a murderer in our midst and did not recognize the fact." He paused, hoping for a response but, finding none, he ploughed on, disregarding

Lord and Lady Hazletts' reserve and his daughters' anxious glances. Martin was unaware that Vanessa was close to tears, Amelia seemed irritated, and that his wife, Helen, was trying to catch his attention before he said any more.

"What I want to know," continued Martin, "is why the police took so much time interviewing Constance and Amelia? I mean to say, what could they possibly have to do with Benson?" He turned to Amelia to pose his next question. "What was it all about, eh?"

Helen shut her eyes as if by so doing she could remove her husband to somewhere else - some other place in the world. She was about to say something when Reginald spoke.

"I think, sir, it's best we drop the matter entirely as it is quite disturbing the ladies, as well as myself. On another matter, may I see you after lunch? There is something important I wish to discuss."

Martin stared at Reginald as though only just realizing he was at the table. His brow furrowed as he struggled to guess what the younger Hazlett could want to see him about. "Yes, of course you can."

Lady Jane, Helen, and Sandra Digby telegraphed significant looks between one another. Maude stared at her brother, Reginald, before looking at Amelia. Then she knew.

"I say, how perfectly ripping!" she announced.

"What is?" asked Colonel Digby.

Fiona Hazlett and Daphne Rand-Sayers now also knew. Amelia looked up to find Fiona smiling warmly at her. Then she noticed Ada and Flora standing by the wall beyond Fiona, looking well pleased about something. Maude, now recognizing the semaphore passing between the other ladies, realized that she may have jumped the gun.

"Everything, Uncle Horry, absolutely everything," replied Maude.

"Well, you would say that. When are you thinking of tying the knot, hmm?"

"We haven't worked out the details just yet but, as soon we do, you'll be the first to know."

"Look forward to hearing that bit of news. Beaton's a lucky dog, that's all I can say," said Digby.

When Sophie spoke to Fern about staying on as a maid at Lady Holme, the little Londoner jumped at the chance. Among Fern's numerous reasons for staying were these: she got on very well with Mrs Williams, had become friendly with several maids, particularly friendly with Nelly and Mabel, there were Guernsey cows on the home farm, and she hoped to meet the ghost of Lady Holme. The one proviso Fern hoped could be arranged, and to which Sophie readily agreed, was that, if in the future the secret agency required her photographic memory skills, she should be allowed time off to go on the mission, because, in her own words "I ain't never had so much fun in all me life."

Before leaving, Sophie spoke to Lord and Lady Hazlett in private. She related Fern's willingness to accept the position of maid at Lady Holme and of the proviso. The workaround Sophie suggested to cover Fern's absence was that Burgoyne's would supply a replacement maid gratis while Fern was away. Lord and Lady Hazlett stared at Sophie after she made her unusual request.

"Could you tell us why?" asked Lord James.

"Because I promised her some police work which I have yet to fulfil."

"It concerns Phoebe's work into which we'd best not inquire," said Lady Jane to her husband.

"Ah, I see," said Lord James. "As long as you're satisfied with the arrangement, my dear, I have no objections."

"This won't occur too often, I hope? It might unsettle the rest of the staff."

"No, Lady Jane. Several times a year, at most, I suppose."

"If it's no more than that, then it should be satisfactory. I'll tell Mrs Williams to find a permanent room for Fern. Of course, she'll need to return to London to get her things. She can start Monday of next week."

"That will be excellent, Lady Jane."

The first visitor roared in on a Norton Big Four motorcycle after lunch and after the rain had stopped. Clad in a long brown leather coat, gauntlets, goggles, and aviator's hat, he set his bike on its stand outside the front door. He looked like a dispatch rider, and a travel-stained one at that. He strode up to the door and gave it a loud knock. When he saw there was a bell, he pressed it several times, then lifted his goggles.

After almost a minute, Old Joe opened the door. He scowled at the man.

"Trades and delivery around the side, if you please," said Old Joe.

"Neither, my good man. I'm here to see his lordship. Is he in, or out riding? I saw activity about the stables."

Old Joe looked the visitor up and down. He saw the scar along his jawline. "Who be you?"

"Yardley's the name. If he's in the house, I'll give you my card. If not, I'll find him myself."

"He be out on his hoss."

"Thank you." Mr Yardley returned to his motorbike and kick-started it. He drove it slowly, as quietly as the noisy machine could manage, to the stables. The only person he encountered was Maude, who stared at him in amazement as he came into view.

"You'll frighten the horses," she bellowed.

"No, I won't," bellowed Yardley in return. "I'm looking for Lord Hazlett. Do you know where he is?"

"Who the Dickens are you?"

He cut the engine and got off his motorcycle.

"The name's Yardley, and I'm here on government business. Urgent, I might add."

"Well, he's not here... That's no way to introduce yourself," said Maude, noticing his public school accent.

"Rather rude, I agree. Excuse me if I've offended you. I'll start again. Good afternoon. To whom do I have the honour of speaking?"

"I am Miss Hazlett."

"May I enquire into his lordship's whereabouts?"

"That's better. He's out riding now because he thought the visitors were arriving later. I suppose you're one of them."

"Correct, and it is a pleasure to meet you, Miss Hazlett."

Maude smiled. "What's it all about?"

"Abject apologies, but I can only give name, rank, and serial number."

"Oh... Then you'll have to wait until he returns."

"I can't waste time, so that's not possible. This is a big estate. Any idea where he's likely to be?"

"You're not riding that thing all over the place, scaring animals and people."

"Come, come, it's not that bad... Here's an idea. I realize I'm not properly dressed for riding, but could you lend me a horse, please?"

"Tch! I don't know who you are?"

"Government business, and all that. Upon my honour, I promise to take care of the horse first and foremost."

Maude sighed. "Oh, very well, then. Follow me."

They entered the stables and after some discussion about horses, Yardley saddled Falcon, led him out, and swung easily into the saddle. To Maude's relief, he proved to be an experienced rider. She watched him gallop from the stable yard. When he had gone, she idly examined the Norton, wondering what it would be like to ride a motorcycle.

"Lord Hazlett?" asked Yardley as he brought Falcon to a halt. The two men met to the north of Marley Mound. "Sorry to be a bother, but may I speak to you?"

The peer had followed the young man's progress as he galloped towards him along the woodland path. He could not imagine what type of person he was or what his business could be.

"Yes."

"The name's Yardley, my Lord. I've come about the smuggling business. Unfortunately, you will soon have more strangers turning up on your doorstep and no doubt behaving badly, but we'll try to be brief and keep everything as unobtrusive as possible."

"Who do you work for?"

"I'm a freelancer and do odd jobs for the Home Office and Scotland Yard, that sort of thing. My job is to take care of unpleasant situations such as the one you find yourself in at present. I arrived first because I happened to be closer, but there'll be a gaggle of serious-minded London chappies turning up in a couple of hours."

"I think it best I wait and speak to them when they arrive."

"Quite right, my Lord. Don't trust anyone. Perhaps this will make a difference. Less than two hours ago, I learned that contraband is being brought ashore here and temporarily held in a disused mine before being taken away by lorry, and that neighbour Phelps plays an integral part in the scheme."

"Ah, as I see, you understand the situation. Yes, it does make a difference. I was expecting a visit, but you have moved faster than I anticipated."

"Then let me reassure you on one point, my Lord. Our intention is to take out the entire network from top to bottom. I have been informed the Britten family is involved and they should be under observation as we speak."

"Is that so? Are you familiar with them?"

"Up to a point. They are, or were, very big in the opium trade. This is the third time I've encountered their involvement in illegal activity. And this time, they shall not escape."

"You say 'were'. What do you mean by that?"

"The Brittens have suffered a reverse in their fortunes. They lost their holdings in Afghanistan three years ago and other severe financial losses followed soon afterwards. They're rather desperate to rebuild their drug business and seem now committed to criminal activities."

"My goodness... You wouldn't happen to know the present head of the family?"

"Johanna Britten. She's widowed and in her sixties. Her husband and son went down with the Lusitania, but she has three daughters."

Lord Hazlett was quiet for more than a minute. "Let me show you the place you're interested in."

An hour later, Lord Hazlett and Yardley returned to the house, deep in conversation.

"Can I offer you something to drink?" asked Lord Hazlett.

Yardley was removing his leather coat to reveal an infantry officer's jacket without insignia over a blue jersey, cavalry officer's trousers that were stained and patched, and an expensive pair of high boots that were scuffed and scarred. He put his clothes in the cloakroom.

"That's kind of you, my Lord, but I do not wish to disgrace the rooms of your beautiful house with my unseemly attire. However, a mug of tea in the kitchen would be most welcome." He removed his leather helmet to reveal a head of thick, yellow hair.

"Nonsense, man. You obviously came dressed for rough work. I garden sometimes in clothes fit for a scarecrow." Lord Hazlett smiled. "They're the most comfortable ones I've got."

"Then, by all means, my Lord."

"We'll go into the office so we won't be disturbed."

They settled themselves, and Lord Hazlett rang the bell.

"That's an uncommonly fine horse you have, my Lord," said Yardley. "Do I detect a touch of the Byerley Turk in him?"

"You do, indeed. He's named Chieftain and I like to imagine he's a complete throwback to the Turk. Where do you ride?"

"Mostly on my father's estate or the surrounding country. He has some pleasant bridleways and trails, but they pale in comparison to the ones here."

"And where is Lord Ranemore's estate?" While riding, Lord Hazlett had enquired into his companion's family.

"South Downs between Arundel and Littlehampton. It was belting down when I left, then I hit brilliant sunshine around Chichester, rain again around Portsmouth, and had just missed whatever you got here when I arrived."

"It was solid rain earlier, but it slacked off late morning."

"Good. You know, that channel you showed me is very interestin'. With the right craft, the blighters could land a couple of tons at a time. I'd like to see that hidden dock before I leave. Do you have a canoe or a rowing-boat I could use?"

"There are several old skiffs you can choose from. Surely you won't want Phelps catching sight of you in the channel?"

"No, I'll avoid that by going at dusk. I'll get a couple of chaps to act as lookouts and I'll approach it from inland, then haul the skiff over the weir. If anyone comes from seaward, a lookout will warn me from above, and I'll beat it upstream, then up the landing ramp and back over the weir."

Lord Hazlett smiled. The door opened and Sophie entered.

"You rang, my Lord."

She recognized the man in the unusual garb from their previous meetings. The astonishment she felt registered only by a slight raising of her eyebrows. Yardley spotted her surprise, subtle though it was, and grinned at her.

"Yes, Phoebe. A pot of tea for two... Would you like anything to eat?"

"I never say no to food," replied Yardley, looking pleased with himself. "What have you got that's handy?" he enquired of Sophie.

"Mrs Chiverton hasn't finished baking for this afternoon's tea, but there is some excellent Madeira cake, and I can cook toast or make a sandwich, if you wish."

"Are you eating, my Lord?" asked Yardley.

"I'll eat some toast to keep you company. And bring us the damson jam, Phoebe."

"Yes, my lord." She turned to Mr Yardley.

"I don't want to put you to any trouble. Toast and jam for me, too, please. And some of that cake you recommended." He grinned broadly at her again.

Sophie bobbed towards Lord Hazlett and then left the room. His lordship became thoughtful for a moment.

"Perhaps you already know this, but that young lady caught our murderer last night. We've had some remarkable goings on here just of late."

"So I understand. I had heard of Benson's capture."

"She had him at sword point, with nowhere to run, if you can believe it."

"My word, how daring of her. I saw her torn sleeve was stitched. He didn't wound her by any chance?" Yardley asked his question with a concerned look.

"Yes, a knife wound to the arm. We had a doctor staying who said it was nothing to worry about. He took care of it... I'm thankful she was here... Do you think Johanna Britten will be arrested?"

"Too early to say. The trick is to seize her quickly while smashing the smugglers at the same time. Hopefully, we'll get evidence against Mrs Britten that will stand up in court. The legal aspect is rather outside my jurisdiction."

"I see... Hello, who's this?" Lord Hazlett looked at a car pulling up close to the window outside the office.

"Ah, confound them. The reinforcements are here before we've had our toast, my Lord."

Three plain cars arrived in short order. Apart from the drivers, Superintendent Penrose, Archie Drysdale, and Detective Sergeant Daniels were in one car; the second car contained an army colonel and lieutenant in civilian clothes, while the third contained representatives from the Home Office, Admiralty, and Customs and Excise Department.

Lord Hazlett ushered the newcomers into his study, where after a few preliminaries, the group got down to business. Soon the table became littered with maps and notebooks. Yardley gave his report on the hidden dock and a general lay-out of the channel and its weir. In half an hour, they all had a firm grasp on the situation. Within an hour, they had a plan. The telephone was used to initiate proceedings, implementing the plan within the various institutions. Then, as quickly as they had come, two cars departed, taking with them the army, navy, and government representatives.

"I say," whispered Archie, when he caught Sophie alone coming from the servants' area. "I want a private word with you."

"Take the stairs by the chapel and I'll meet you in the attics in ten minutes."

"Penrose is also looking for you."

"Should I see him first?"

"Certainly not."

"Are you annoyed?"

"Very."

They met in the attics as planned and went to the Crow's Nest.

"You must keep your voice down," said Sophie. "Sound carries in this house."

"Sophie, you told me you were coming down here for research. How is it you were swinging a sword about like a maniac while chasing an armed killer?"

"It… just fell out that way. There was nothing I could have done differently."

"There were two capable Scotland Yard detectives in the house. Did it not occur to you to inform them and allow the police to do their job? No, instead you get yourself slashed by a lunatic."

"Archie, I met Benson up here by accident. We were on our way to inform the detectives of everything we knew when he surprised me."

"*We* again. If you are to work for the Foreign Office in future, you can't bring all your friends along to make a party of it."

"I take exception to that. Burgoyne's was doing no such thing, Mr Drysdale. We have been serious about our business ever since we came. You should remember that we must work as domestic staff *and* gather information."

"I understand you perfectly well. Please remember that. There was no conceivable way you were not making a lark out of the whole thing. I understand four of you arrived here.

I am aware of Flora and Miss McMahon. Who is this fourth person?"

"Fern, but she thinks we're just gathering information for the police. She knows nothing about spying and is only nineteen."

"Please use the word espionage. It's really too, too bad of you. Agents aren't supposed to get involved in whatever they please. If you blow your cover... Well, just don't."

"Seeing as we are having this rather frank and unpleasant discussion, let me tell you one or two things, so that you can come down off your high-horse. You gave yourself away as a spy to Auntie Bessie. There, what do you have to say for yourself now?"

"How is that possible?"

"You passed yourself off as a vacant, foppish man about town and you tried that on Auntie. Well, she knows you from when you were a little boy. She knows you're not vacant, although you acted as if you were. So you see, you blew your own cover. I have yet to blow mine."

"I don't think I come across as vacant, do I?"

"A little."

"Oh. Thanks for the warning... Hold on, do you mean that Bessie knows you're a spy?"

"She guessed, all because of you. Now she's helping me... I couldn't stop her, you know what she's like."

"Oh, good grief. I'll see her as soon as I get back to town."

"And another thing while we're at it. Although you paid me for one spying job, I am not being paid regularly, and yet I am being bullied by you. If you wish to bully me, even though I must say that I don't care for your tone or attitude when you do so, you should consider making regular payments so that I, as an employee, know precisely where I stand. I'm new to all of this. Where did I get my training? Not from you. I'm having to work it out as I go along. If there are mishaps, then there are mishaps, and you must expect them until further notice."

"Those are valid observations, ones of which I am cognisant. My bullying, if that's what it is, is caused by my annoyance with you going off half-cocked without informing anyone, particularly me. These matters are risky. Put yourself in my place for a moment. I read in the newspaper of Mr Smythe's fatal accident. Mr Smythe was the lawyer who first informed the authorities of possible smugglers."

"I discovered that since we last spoke."

"Yes, now please follow closely. He dies, tragically. Do I hear from my research agent on the spot? No. The accident becomes a murder. Doctor Beaton gets arrested and is then released. Do I receive a telephone call about these things? No, no, and no. This is not how professional agents behave. What would you do in my position?"

"Pay me a salary, train me, and tell me why the pretend gardener is here."

Archie laughed with little humour. "He's just as bad as you are. I can't do a thing with either of you. He's not even supposed to be at Lady Holme, and neither are you when it comes down to it."

"Is his name Yardley? Ada overheard the name in a conversation."

"Yes, I'll introduce you to him. He's a decent chap and a friend of mine, but he's as hare-brained as you are."

"I'm not hare-brained."

"And I am not *foppish*... Stop laughing."

"Come on, Sweet Boy, let's not argue." She took him by the arm. "I'll do much better next time."

"Ah, I'm sure you will..." They began walking towards the stairs. "I can't believe cousin Bessie has got herself involved in all of this."

"One thing Auntie's good at and that's keeping secrets. Also, she knows many influential people."

"But it's all so unprofessional, Soap," Archie sighed. "It's like we're muddling through."

"That's our British way. How we ever got an empire is beyond me. But you never know, perhaps other nations are in an even bigger muddle than we are."

"Now that is a sobering thought." He halted at the top of the stairs. "Better not be seen together anymore."

"What is going to happen to the smugglers?"

"An operation is being put together for when the next shipment arrives. I can't give you any details until it's all over."

"That sounds exciting. By the way, the Brittens belong to a secret society called The Pillars of Wisdom. Have you heard of them?"

"No. What do they do?"

"This is just between you and me. The police cannot hear of it or it will break the promise I made."

"I promise not to repeat a word of what you say."

"PWP has a long history of circumventing the law. Initially, it was only a supplier-of-resources club which wanted to obtain better prices and fair access to markets for themselves. Within the society, the representatives of powerful families are called by their resource name, such as Iron, Coal, and Wool, and they hand down their position within PWP from one generation to the next. So, centuries ago, some families joined forces to protect themselves from the predations of the guilds. To do this, they tried many things, including smuggling, which has been a part of their operations ever since. The Brittens represent a particular resource and, in their case, it is opium. They call themselves Poppy, or the head of the clan does. Benson is an agent of Poppy although I don't know in what capacity he was acting. He killed Smythe because PWP's smuggling operations were at the point of being exposed, but he must have acted unilaterally. Mr Smythe's information was not common knowledge, and Benson could only have caught wind of it within an hour of his arrival. That means he had no time to get authorization, so he must be quite high up in the scheme of things."

"Most fascinatin'. He might be involved in the smuggling himself and so decided it was too dangerous to allow Smythe to continue making a fuss... I take it he has some type of hold over Lord Hazlett... Not going to tell me, are you?"

"I gave my word. I shouldn't really have said anything."

"Then I'm honoured. I'm not familiar with the Brittens, but Penrose says their name crops up occasionally in connection with drug-trafficking. The Inspector's quite excited at the prospect of catching them. Apparently, it's Mrs Johanna

Britten who is the brains of the family, although her name is new to me."

"Good grief! A woman?"

"Does that surprise you?" asked Archie.

"Yes. I suppose it's because I've been visualizing a man all along. Where does she live?"

"No, you don't. There'll be a bit of a show soon and it might be rather ugly. Stay well out of it."

"You mean I can't do even the tiniest amount of research? That seems rather unsporting of you, Archie. I did help, and I'd like to be in at the end."

"The information you've provided is invaluable. But, as you said yourself, you're not trained in these things."

"Archie, for a spy, you are positively hurtling towards middle-age."

"Please stop calling me names."

"Very well, no more personal comments, as long as you do the same and stop treating me like an accident-prone ninny who is running about asking for trouble."

"You must have been a holy terror at school. Your poor teachers."

"Oh, they didn't suffer. I got reasonably good marks, which made up for a lot. But don't go changing the subject. I want to be involved in this. Surely, there would be no harm in my delving into the Britten's background?"

"More research, eh? You do realize that the police are presently investigating them? How would it look if a Foreign Office agent started poking about in and interfering with their enquiries? Not very good, let me tell you."

"I wouldn't do that. How about... a little asking around and some light observation from a distance? I'm curious to see what sort of house she lives in. It's nothing more than that."

"If I could believe you would stop there, I wouldn't worry." He looked at her. "You're going to do it anyway, no matter what I say. Please, for your own sake, and for mine, don't get into any trouble. This is all so unofficial, it's unofficially unofficial. That means I shall *never* hear your name crop up in any awkward conversation in the future. Do I make myself clear?"

"Your caution is duly noted."

"Good afternoon, Miss King," said Superintendent Penrose, who temporarily had the use of the office.

"Good afternoon, Inspector."

"Please make yourself comfortable and we'll have a little chat."

Sophie sat down. Penrose observed her for a few moments.

"Had a talking to, have you?"

"Yes, thank you."

"I won't add too much to your burden, then. Poor old Inspector Morton... He's a good chap and I like him. He's serious-minded, you know that, but he has to be. My suggestion is this — should you work with Morton again, just tell him everything as you're going along, particularly anything to do with a prime suspect in a murder case. You're not competing with the force. However, Morton's under no requirement to tell you anything. In fact, the opposite is the case, as we've discussed before. He asked me who employs you. What could I tell him? That you work for Mr Drysdale? No, can't say that. That you were acting as a private individual? Well, you were, you know. Remember, it was your own idea that you and your agency should come to Lady Holme to explore the area. So, in effect, you misled him because he thought you'd been sent here by someone officially. He also told me you and a person named Gladys Walton gave false statements to Inspector Talford. We policemen take a very dim view of such goings on. Just say you won't do it again and it's one less thing for me to worry about."

"I won't do it again. But, Inspector, what if Mr Drysdale *had* sent me?"

"Different matter entirely. You'd be authorized to deflect revealing questions because of the nature of your work. Nothing wrong with that. Doing so as a private individual opens you up to prosecution. Now the matter won't be going anywhere this time, but you can't always count on people's goodwill."

"Thank you, Inspector. As you can see, I'm still learning the ropes."

"I read through your statement concerning your meeting with Benson and I'd like to ask you a serious question. Would you have killed him if you had caught him?"

"I've asked myself that, and I wish I could give you a definite answer."

"Well, try this. What was it you wanted him to do?"

"To stop running and drop the knife. I rationalized my actions. By waving the sword, I believed I could drive him downstairs to be captured."

"Ah. What if he had turned and attacked you?"

"Run him through, of course, but only if he went for me."

Penrose nodded. "The police have to walk a fine line. When we carry firearms, which is rare and only under special circumstances, we can't fire first but can only return fire once shot at. It was actually this rule which contributed to the deaths of three officers in the Sydney Street Siege. But that's another matter. Despite all this, you'll find nine out of ten officers prefer to keep it the way it is. We don't want guns and gun-play on our streets. Why I was asking about your intentions regarding Benson was because, a little while ago, you enquired of Morton about obtaining a permit for a pistol."

"I did. Do you think I shouldn't have one?"

"It's got nothing to do with what I think. If you want a permit, that's your affair, and it's your legal right to apply for one. But if I may, I'll make an observation. If that there sword hadn't been handy, you'd be dead, but if you had had a pistol, Benson would be dead. Afterwards, you'd have to live with the consequences of your actions. There might have been legal repercussions, but certainly there'd have been mental ones. Do you see my point?"

"Yes, and I thoroughly appreciate your taking the time to explain matters. It does give me pause for thought. Now I'll ask you something. There is a gentleman in this building whom we both know but do not name. What is his position vis-à-vis the use of firearms?"

"I've no idea who you are talking about. I'm sorry, Miss King, but I'm short on time and I need one more question answered about this affair."

Sophie sighed. "And what is your question?"

"It seems plain to me that Lord Hazlett knew smuggling was going on but, for personal reasons, chose not to address the matter. Your knowing the name of Britten can only have come through him. How's he connected with Johanna Britten?"

"I cannot say."

Penrose smiled. "She must have some kind of hold over him. I'll ask again if the situation warrants it. Believe me, I shan't hesitate to haul you and Lord Hazlett over the coals if I have to. I've given you fair warning."

"I'm certain that if you studied the salient points of Lord Hazlett's life, everything would become apparent soon enough."

"Thank you, I'll do just that. I believe that's all... You're leaving today, I understand."

"That's correct. It has been quite the experience, although I feel so sorry for Maria Smythe. She was devastated by her loss, you know."

"I'm sure she was and tis a pity that the greatest weight of this business falls upon her. I believe she has littl'uns."

"A five-year-old boy and a three-year-old girl."

"Breaks your heart, doesn't it?"

"Indeed, it does."

"Yes, yes... Right, I think that's all. Thank you, Miss King. And may I take this opportunity to say how much I appreciate your bit of work."

"Thank you, Inspector. Has any of it helped in your counterfeit banknote investigation?"

"A little, but now it's my turn to keep secrets. Goodbye, and I'm sure we'll be meeting again soon."

"Ooh, how nice. I look forward to it. Goodbye."

In a small, private sitting room on the first floor, Archie, with deep misgivings, introduced Sophie to Yardley.

"Sophie, may I introduce Mr Ralph Yardley to you...? Ralph, this is my cousin, Miss Sophie Burgoyne."

"I am delighted to meet you, Miss Burgoyne." Yardley bowed slightly.

"And I am likewise pleased to meet you." She also gave a slight bow.

"Do you think it will rain later?" asked Yardley.

"Possibly," replied Sophie. "one never knows this time of year."

"That is so true. What do you think, Archibald, old man? Will it rain later?"

"I think I shall buzz off and leave you two wags to play your games. Remember, don't be seen talking to each other." He left the room and closed the door.

"I heard him refer to you as Sinjin earlier," said Sophie.

"That's what my friends call me. A variation on St John, one of my middle names. Do you have a nickname?"

"Yes, it's Miss Burgoyne."

"Oh... Are you annoyed with me?"

"Yes. You were rather rude earlier on. In fact, both our meetings have been marked by your impolite behaviour. The first meeting I can forgive, because of the circumstances. But for today's episode, you owe me an apology. As soon as I entered Lord Hazlett's office, you started to grin at me in a very unseemly way which might have undermined my position in the house and blown my cover. I will not be grinned at while I'm working. I don't know if you were laughing at me because

I work as a maid, or what else might have caused you such amusement, but I found your behaviour objectionable."

"Did you really? Oh, I say, I'm awfully sorry. I didn't intend it like that at all. I did just find the situation amusing, our meeting incognito again, but now, of course, I don't. It had nothing to do with your working as a maid, I assure you. I'm very sorry."

"I accept your apology. I was worried that Lord Hazlett might have noticed we had met before."

"Miss Burgoyne, you are perfectly correct, and it was ill-mannered of me. All I can say in my defence is that I have wanted to meet you again."

"Oh... How do you know Archie?"

"We met in a trench while Fritz was lobbing shells at us. He had a cosy dugout, so we brewed some tea and had a chin wag."

"Were you in the same regiment?"

"No. I had gone for a stroll during the night and couldn't get back to my own trenches, so I popped in to see our friendly neighbours, Archie being one of them."

"You make it sound like a tea party. I'm sure it was anything but."

"That is all in the past now. You and I are currently working to secure a future where it doesn't happen again."

"I wholeheartedly agree with you there... May I ask a question, Mr Yardley?"

"Certainly, Miss Burgoyne."

"How is it you shot a man the last time we met, and yet the police shield you from enquiry or prosecution?"

"Yes, well... that's a tough question for me to answer truthfully. I'm afraid I must decline to answer."

"I understand your reticence. The world seems to be full of secrets these days."

"Thank you. And, ah, please excuse my outfit. I didn't know I would meet you today."

"Not at all. I was marvelling, actually, at the way all the different services are represented in your costume - army, navy, and flying corps."

Yardley grinned. "Does your arm cause you any trouble?"

"Not at present, I'm glad to say."

"That's very good. May I ask a question?"

"Certainly you may ask, and I might even answer," said Sophie.

Yardley smiled. "You run an employment agency and do odd jobs for the government. How do you mange it? Doesn't it take up all of your time?"

"It does, but as I'm thoroughly enjoying myself, I don't mind. The management side of things isn't too much trouble. What do you do when you're not... you know, creeping about?"

Yardley glanced at her. He saw she was not mocking him, but if she was amused, she hid it well.

"Tinker with things that have engines. I have a few other interests... Miss Burgoyne, I'd very much like to continue our conversation, but I must attend to several pressing matters, so now is not the time. What would you say to a spot of lunch at the Savoy?"

"I'm afraid I must decline your kind offer, but thank you all the same, Mr Yardley."

"Oh... May I know why?"

"We have just met. I am quite old-fashioned in some respects, and we neither of us knows one another's family or friends apart from Archie. Also, there is the added complication of two agents becoming acquainted. We both know that such connections are frowned upon."

"It's nothing personal, then?"

"Dear me!" Sophie laughed. "No, it isn't. But if it were, how on earth could I reply to such a pointed question?"

"Yes, rather awkward of me... What do you propose I do?"

"My goodness, whatever next? You are so direct."

"I ask simply because I would like to meet you again. Do you have a suggestion about how I might accomplish that?"

"I'm not averse to the idea, but any meeting can only be in a larger social setting, Mr Yardley."

"Ah, excellent, excellent. I was, perhaps, a little too forward."

Sophie smiled.

"I shall go," said Yardley. "May I communicate with you at your agency?"

"Yes, but please write if you choose to do so. I work for a living and my agency is new, requiring constant attention. Interruptions, no matter how well-intentioned or interesting, can be quite distracting."

"I understand your wishes perfectly. Au revoir, Miss Burgoyne."

"Goodbye, Mr Yardley."

"You had better leave first," he said, reverting to the role of agent. He held open the ancient, carved wooden door.

"Thank you," said Sophie.

Sophie left the sitting room, and Yardley watched her walk away. When she had gone, he went in the opposite direction.

Chapter 31

Kensington

At ten o'clock Monday morning, Johanna Britten was at home in 36 Vienna Gardens, Kensington. The attractive, substantial yellow brick house was entirely suitable for an upper class family. In the parlour, which overlooked the street at the front, the housemaid drew back the dark blue velvet curtains in the bay window to reveal net curtains in the gap created. She measured the width of the gap and adjusted the curtains until it was a foot wide, measured again, and then proffered the ruler to Mrs Britten. Johanna measured the gap herself before handing back the ruler, which the maid placed on a small occasional table next to them.

"What's the weather today?" asked Johanna.

"The papers say it'll be gloomy and chilly, with a chance of rain this afternoon," replied Thora, her housemaid. "The wind strength is light to moderate."

"I could have told *them* that much. It's October. That will be all, Thora."

"Yes, Mrs Britten."

After the maid left the spacious room, Mrs Britten stepped forward to put her head between the velvet curtains. She scanned the street and then the windows of the house opposite. She picked up a pair of opera glasses to study each individual window. Every curtain appeared undisturbed and in order. Number fifty-three had a window opened six inches on its third floor. Mrs Britten trained the glasses on that opening for a long time. A street cleaner came into view, so she turned her glasses upon him. She recognized the man with his long moustache. A nurse trundled into sight, pushing a perambulator along the farther pavement. "Number 43," said Mrs Britten. She returned to her chair after putting down the glasses.

Victorian reception rooms had tended towards overcrowding through the owners' desire to display curios, ornaments and paintings as evidence of their wealth and knowledge. The high-ceilinged drawing room at number 36 excelled in such a fashion, being stuffed with furniture and knick-knacks. Where this drawing room triumphed over its competitors was in artwork. There was barely a square inch of red painted wall to be seen beneath the artistic façade. Heavy gilt frames touched one another, crowding the wall space between the high wainscot up to the crown moulding. Every shape and size, and every conceivable subject was represented — from cows to castles and portraits to battles. It was a fortune hanging on hooks, as many of the oils were by notable artists. Visitors to 36 Vienna were not to be impressed by the householder's taste or eye for beauty. They were to be stunned into disbelief at the sheer quantity and cost, while unintentionally made to marvel at the loss of dignity each work suffered by such compaction.

Johanna had dressed in old-fashioned yet well-cut, expensive clothes. A solid woman in her sixties, she wore no cosmetics and her long hair was completely grey, bordering on the untidy although it was restrained in a bun. Mrs Britten had plenty of servants, but she detested the idea of a lady's maid. She approached three ornate brass bell pulls arranged in a row on the wall by the fireplace. She pulled one knob and waited a couple of minutes.

"You rang, madam?"

"Yes, Humphries. Did Mr Benson telephone on the house line?"

"I'm afraid not, madam." Humphries was her tall, thin secretary, about forty years old.

"It doesn't matter. He will visit here tomorrow. Tell me at once should he ring."

"I shall certainly do so... Was there anything else?"

"What is the price of Imperial Medical today?"

"Unchanged from Friday at fourteen and six."

"Begin selling it in small parcels. Stop if the price goes below twelve shillings."

"Very good, madam."

"I will need cash come January. I refuse to touch the paintings, but we must sell or mortgage the remaining properties. What do we have left?"

"The house in Pimlico, the two semis in Cricklewood, and there are eight terraced houses remaining in Battersea."

"Eight? That's all...? Very well, Humphries, mortgage Pimlico and sell the rest. How much will that bring in?"

"Difficult to say, madam. If we can get a mortgage on Pimlico for seven thousand, then roughly twelve thousand in all."

"Do the best you can."

"At once, madam."

He left the room quietly. When he had gone, Johanna walked about, inspecting the curios, antiquities and paintings. In her mind, she reckoned the value of the room's contents, and arrived at a figure of forty thousand. But she well knew that in the current economic climate, the artwork would only realize twenty-five thousand on a good day. However, she was loath to sell. Vienna Gardens, and this room in particular, represented the high-water mark of the Britten family's success. Once, in their heyday, the conservative and unobtrusive Brittens had been worth millions, yet they had never sunk money into a large mansion. Now, should she sell everything, she might realize a hundred and twenty thousand on her remaining possessions. She had been forced to sell many properties already because of losses on the stock market and the failure of schemes to realize their early promise. Still, she had irons in the fire; she told herself this as she toured the room. New schemes were presenting themselves and a little capital could bring in a solid twenty thousand a year, perhaps more, when the smuggling business was fully re-established. Then she could buy out Phelps to be next door and on the spot when Hazlett came to his final grief. She flushed with a surge of anger when she thought of Lord James Hazlett. Johanna shook, because she hated him so.

The insult that loathsome man had offered to her family was outrageous. But since then, there had been one setback after another for Poppy and the Brittens. She remembered her father-in-law, whose declining mental capacities had him storming about the house almost to the day he died. He raged over Hazlett even though the peer had been confined to Lady Holme for fifteen years by that time. Britten senior stormed, convinced Hazlett had cursed him and the family, and that only the peer's death would lift such a plague from the Brittens. Despite the nonsensical rages, Johanna saw a kernel of truth in them. She noted the change, the downward slide in fortune, from the moment tPWoP had censured Hazlett. Johanna, then a new bride, had throughout her married life and subsequent widowhood despised the name Hazlett.

Then came the deaths of her husband and son. They had gone to America with hopes of expanding the opium trade because Asian markets were now denied them, while the home market had declined substantially through competition. But they hurriedly made plans to return upon receiving reports from agents in Afghanistan and Persia. Her husband had received information concerning the efforts of German emissaries who were trying to destabilize India and Afghanistan through diplomatic missions while the war in Europe was being fought. Upon learning this, Mr Britten had made haste to return, intent upon lobbying the British government directly and through his contacts, for troops to be sent into Afghanistan even while war raged in France. Johanna's son had accompanied his father to America to learn the ropes of the Britten business. They had died, both husband and son, when a U-boat torpedoed the Lusitania in which they sailed in May 1915. Johanna saw the tragedy with great clarity. She believed they need not have gone to America, nor returned in a hurry, if only Britain had maintained troops in Afghanistan. That there were no troops in Afghanistan was Hazlett's fault. Her logic was simple. She need not look for another reason for being singled out for bereavement before her time. Hazlett had killed her husband and son as surely as if he had launched the torpedo with his own hands. This, added to the deep distress her father-in-law had experienced during his declining years, affected her deeply, causing her thoughts to become darker. Hazlett's existence spoiled all things Poppy. That the Brittens had lost their Afghan fields and the cheap supply of opium from them was Hazlett's fault, too. Now, as the remnants of the Britten fortune ebbed away, Johanna was determined to reverse that flow no matter what it took. If only the eminently useful Adrian would call her. He had yet to report on the progress of the blackmailing scheme at Lady Holme. Johanna wanted the Hazletts to suffer in every conceivable way.

Mid-afternoon, Johanna received a visitor — a thickset, powerful man about fifty, expensively dressed in a dandified way, sporting a top hat and spats. The maid showed him into the parlour.

"Afternoon, Johanna."

"Hello, Ferrers. What's brought you here?"

"Your man didn't meet my man at two o'clock like he was supposed to. Anything wrong?"

"There shouldn't be. I've been expecting a call from him. But all arrangements are in place on the Lymington end, so he's not needed to manage any shipments."

"That's all right, then. We'll go ahead as planned. If he's messing about, cut him loose. You can only work with people you can trust. But he must keep his trap shut if he knows what's good for him."

"There's no need for concern. I can run my own affairs, thank you."

"Of course you can, otherwise I wouldn't be here. But a little reminder about basics never hurts." Ferrers looked at several paintings. "I like this room of yours. You've got a lot of class artwork. That one with the elephants and maharajah is nice. It looks so foreign."

"That's a favourite of mine. Can I offer you something?"

"No, I'm fine, thanks. I only came round to see how things stood. Nice seeing you again, Johanna. I'll find my own way out."

At five o'clock, Ronald drove the secret agents to the station. He was chipper and seemed genuinely pleased when informed that Fern would return to stay in a week's time.

While the car was still travelling along the drive, Sophie turned to look through the small, oval rear window. The beauty of the Tudor house struck her afresh. It was not just the house she wanted to see one last time. She had hoped she might glimpse someone at an attic window — a white figure, a figure in a silvery dress with pearls in her hair, waving goodbye. It saddened her a little that the pretty windows were empty. This was something she had not mentioned to anyone — that in the attics, the house or Lady Cicely herself, had come to her aid. It was true Benson had blundered into an old bunch of lavender in the dark, causing him to sneeze and reveal his hiding place at a critical moment. That was a physical fact. What was also a fact, according to Sophie's certain knowledge, was the intense smell of lavender filling the air in the attics just prior to his sneeze. She likened it to a strong, gushing jet of lavender perfume streaming through the darkness. There was no accounting for the phenomenon in natural terms and it was Lady Cicely Holme's presence or the house itself exuding the pronounced scent just when needed.

"You look thoughtful," said Flora.

"I find I'm sad at leaving. There's something magical about these old places."

"That is so true. You don't find the same atmosphere in London houses. Everything there is so orderly and scraped clean. That's useful and welcome enough in its way, but it takes away one's imagination and willingness to believe in extraordinary things."

"What makes you say that? Just now, I mean."

"I don't really know… Perhaps, I do. Being inside Lady Holme had me feeling as though I were living in the fifteen hundreds. Subtract a few modern conveniences and it could have been so. Now that we're leaving, I doubt I'll ever have that feeling again. I'd like to keep this precious mood in a little bottle and savour it from time to time. How about you, Nancy?"

"It's funny you should say that. As soon as we get back to town, I'm buying a big bottle of lavender perfume… Here, you're lucky, Dora. You get to come back."

"I felt right at home as soon as I stepped in the place," said Fern. "It's funny. Old Isembard didn't really spoil it with his moaning and groaning."

Ronald tapped on the partition window, which Sophie slid back.

"Excuse me, I couldn't help overhearing a bit of what you were saying. That's how it hit me when I first arrived. Like I was coming home."

"Have you ever seen the ghost?" asked Fern.

"No, I haven't. You said ghost singular. Does that mean you believe Mrs Williams' story and not the other one with the murders?"

"Oh, yes," replied Fern. "Nelly told us it. She had us all in tears."

"You've made the right choice. As soon as I heard it, I said to myself, Ronald, that's a true story. So if you ever see her Ladyship, tell her I said thanks very much for letting me stay in her house."

"I'll do just that," said Fern, more than pleased with Ronald's request and attitude.

"And tell her I said thank you, too," said Sophie.

"About what?" asked Flora.

"Nothing to speak of, really, but she'll know what I mean."

On Wednesday, October 20, Flora arrived at Sophie's office with news just before lunchtime. She had been offered the part she had auditioned for, but which had been given to the producer's lady-friend. The lady-friend had mysteriously failed to show up for Monday's performance. Among the cast, the rumour was there had been a blazing row between the producer and his lady-friend, concluding with a parting of the ways. Many hoped the rift would be permanent. As the current stand-in was not doing justice to the part, Flora got the call.

"I'm honestly in two minds about it," said Flora. "Can't you drum up more spying business, Sophie? Then I could make a clean break from the theatre."

"It's a precarious situation, and who can say with any certainty when work will come in?"

"Acting is precarious, too, unless you have a name or get into a touring company. The show might close in two weeks, although the notices aren't bad. It's not exactly a brilliant play, but my part's quite respectable."

"What will you do if the run gets extended and another Scotland Yard job comes in?"

"Toss a coin and see what happens. You could take me on your books and I can do what Ada does... Where is she today?"

"Her nan is poorly again, so she took a day off."

Elizabeth knocked on the door before entering.

"I'm not disturbing you, am I? The post has arrived, Miss Burgoyne."

"No, of course not, Elizabeth. Did you find out anything about Johanna Britten?"

"Not much, I fear. She is a very private person." Elizabeth entered further and placed a stack of a dozen envelopes on Sophie's desk.

"Thank you. Please bring me what you have."

Elizabeth nodded and left. Sophie and Flora then heard her speaking to Ada immediately outside.

"Good morning, Ada."

"Good morning, Elizabeth. Did the castor oil work?"

"Yes, thank you. I gave Ferdinand the dose you recommended, and it went through him like a charm. He had a thorough cleaning out. But now he's grumpy because he has to stay in the garden until further notice. The onslaught when it came was rather sudden."

"Oh, dear. At least he's sorted out now."

Flora looked enquiringly at Sophie, who mouthed the word "Cats". Flora nodded.

The door opened and Ada came in. They exchanged greetings.

"I can come back if you're busy, miss."

"No, please stay. This is your day off. Is something the matter?"

"I'd say there is. My Nan's an old crook."

"Oh, dear. What's happened now?"

"Do you remember my telling you how she's bedridden and can't get about? Well, she pleaded with me to spend time with her so that we could chat and I'd read to her. She complained I 'ardly ever see her, which is not true, but there you go. Ooh, I brought Trail of the Lonesome Pine with me, but it's in my bag. Don't let me forget, miss. Anyway, I told her I would stop in and take the day off for 'er sake because her spirits were low.

"So, as you know, we all live in two side-by-side houses. I went in next door where Nan is, and, for once, I took my slippers with me. Well, with all this spying we've been doing, it's got me into the habit of being quiet when I walk in the 'ouse. Then, when I come to her bedroom door, I didn't knock in case she was asleep. So me Nan hasn't 'eard me coming, right? I put me head round the door and guess what? She's not in bed. Oh, no! The old fraud is standing on a chair, getting a book down from the pile on top of the wardrobe.

"She turns, sees me, has a little jump, and then goes as red as a beetroot. But that only lasts two seconds. You'll never guess what she said to me. 'Oh, Ada,' she says, 'It's a miracle! I got the use of me legs back all of a sudden not 'alf an hour ago. Only don't tell anyone or the miracle won't stick.'" Ada crossed her arms, looking furious.

"That's rather a good one when caught in the act, don't you think?" said Flora.

"I suppose," said Ada. "How can she go treating me like an idiot? Anyway, we had a big ding dong and now we're not talking. So it's on me to tell the rest of the family that she's been lying about her legs not working. There'll be ructions tonight, I can see it now... Some of them will believe her and not me. She's so stubborn, she won't back down. What do I do?"

"That's a difficult one, because I know you love her," said Flora.

"If it were me," said Sophie, "I would let those of your family who *believe* your nan have the care of her. If anyone asks why you're not doing your fair share, tell them the truth. You can still be friendly towards your nan. Are you certain that there's nothing wrong with her legs?"

"She was on tiptoes on the chair! She looked like a flaming ballerina... A biggish one, mind you. And she got down sprightly enough. Me own Nan, an' all."

"That's too bad," said Sophie. "I'm sorry this has happened... Excuse me a moment." Sophie picked up an envelope. "This has a Lymington postmark," she said. Sophie slit open the envelope with a paper-knife and found it contained two pieces of paper — a brief note and a cheque. She read the note. "It's from Lord and Lady Hazlett... a small token of their appreciation... Ah, that's nice of them." Sophie unfolded the cheque. "Well, blow me down!" It was for seven hundred and fifty pounds. She looked up at Ada and Flora with her mouth still open. "Don't move an inch." Sophie turned her chair to the safe she referred to as Milly and opened its door. She took out some notes from the cash box.

"I'll go to the bank for the rest. Here's twenty pounds for you... and twenty for you."

"Twenty pounds, miss?" said Ada in astonishment.

"I can face my landlady with head held high... Thank you, thank you, you darling creature. But why?" asked Flora.

"You can thank the Hazletts for this bounty. And you have another thirty pounds coming to you."

"Streuth," said Ada. "Fifty quid?"

"Ditto," said Flora.

Elizabeth knocked on the door. "Pardon me, but a Mrs Green has arrived with your replacement dress, Miss Burgoyne. She would also like to see you for a moment."

"She must be from Green and Weitz, who supply our servant dresses. Please show her in... Don't go," she said to Ada and Flora, "I'm sure she'll only be a minute." They put the office back in order and all monies disappeared.

"Good morning, ladies," said the visitor as soon as she entered. "I apologize for interrupting your important conference," continued the cheery woman. "Do I have the honour of addressing Miss Burgoyne?" she asked Sophie.

"I am she. It's a pleasure meeting you, Mrs Green. Please sit down."

"Thank you, I shall, but first, here is the dress you ordered. I'm sorry I didn't meet you after you had placed your original order, but I was that busy at the time. I always like to meet my customers in person." She put a brown paper parcel on Sophie's desk before sitting down. Mrs Green was about forty with dark curly hair. Sophie liked the blue gaberdine coat she was wearing. Ada thought her nice shoes must be expensive. Flora wondered if her own long, thick hair would fit into a cloche hat such as Mrs Green was wearing.

"I won't keep you. There's nothing like building cordial relations in business. Miss Burgoyne, I hope the garments you received were satisfactory."

"Very much so. We have discussed their excellent fit and quality."

Mrs Green beamed. "I always say quality speaks for itself. It gladdens me to hear you mention such things. But I'm not here for praise. I'm here to propose... let's call it a business proposition. But don't worry, there's no money involved. It's all about goodwill between businesses. Yours and mine. And let me say this, I find it most encouraging to see a lady running things. Most enterprising of you."

"That's kind of you to say. What is the nature of this proposition?"

"I'll come to the point. As you know, we manufacture a better class of uniform and domestic servant wear. However, we have other lines. I'm sure you're familiar with the West End salons, where they don't put prices on the dresses."

"I'd be afraid to go in one," said Flora.

"That is my point. And, mind you, they always charge in guineas, not pounds. That's all right if you can get away with it. That's their business, and good luck to them, too. I say that because who do you think supplies many of those dresses?"

"You?" asked Ada.

"Yes, my dear."

"But I thought they came from France?" said Sophie.

"Ah," said Mrs Green, raising her eyebrows. "That's the impression they like to give. Some of it does, of course. A lot of it comes from West Ham and Whitechapel. I'm on Brick Lane, where we make the twenty-five guinea dresses you'll see in the salons. We also do everyday wear but it's all most exclusive and excellent quality suitable for the upper classes of every level.

"Anyway, my dears, the salons do not sell everything they receive from us. We must accept a number of returns. A few we can rework and send out again, but I'm stuck with many garments because I'm not allowed to sell to the public. You see, if I do, I'll lose my exclusive trade with the salons. And these are not the articles to be sold from a barrow. Far from it. But it may interest you to learn that I can sell privately to a select few.

"Now, here's my proposition. This is all you need to do. When you can, recommend my uniform business to your clients. Just a mention, that's all I'm asking. For anyone interested, I can send out samples throughout the empire. You're my satisfied customers and word of mouth is the best form of advertising. The very best. In exchange for this little service, you are welcome to join our private club. That's where you can buy the finest quality ladies' clothing at a fraction of the retail price. A fraction. My goodness, if my prices were any lower, I'd be giving the garments away. And we can do alterations and custom pieces if you wish."

Mrs Green fixed each of them in turn with a stare.

"Think of it, my dears, Paris creations... West End quality... East End prices... Perfect for young ladies who must spend money wisely upon their wardrobe these days. All I ask in return is when any of your clients or connections need to outfit their staff, you just point them in my direction. We're adaptable and can fulfil all requirements. Now, is that a fair exchange, I ask you?"

"Eminently so," said Sophie.

"Then I'll trouble you no longer. Here's my card to get you in. When you arrive at this address, they'll issue you a membership card for you to keep. It's all exclusive. The fitting rooms are clean and serviceable, and the staff has a lot of experience. We're open between one and six o'clock Wednesday and Thursday afternoons for club members. Funnily enough, today is an excellent time to go because a lot of nice garments have just arrived. Some lovely things. I'm sure they'll soon be gone."

"Thank you for telling us this," said Sophie.

"Don't mention it, Miss Burgoyne. It was my pleasure entirely. I must be going, and thank you for giving me your valuable time."

They all said goodbye, and Mrs Green closed the door behind her. The young women looked at one another.

"Paris creations," said Sophie.

"West End quality," said Flora.

"East End prices... I know Brick Lane like the back of me 'and," said Ada.

"Shall we have a quick lunch and then go and see what it's like?" asked Sophie.

Flora nodded. "Oh, yes. We have to."

"I think we should get there before the doors open, miss."

Chapter 32

Smugglers

"Keepin' a house under surveillance 'as to be the most boring job in the world," said Ada. "An' it's cold." It was late Wednesday afternoon, with the light fading.

"Stamp your feet," said Sophie, stamping her own. "At least it isn't raining."

"Not yet, it ain't, miss."

The two secret agents had been walking but now stood talking once more. They were standing at a corner of Vienna Gardens looking towards number thirty-six.

"At least we've learned something of how the police operate when they keep a place under surveillance."

"You mean that fella there, the world's slowest street cleaner? I'd 'ave the whole street done with a toothbrush in the time he's taking over that little patch. If he was right outside 'er house, she'd spot he's a copper in a second."

"Yes, but he's careful to stay clear of her windows and has a legitimate excuse for loitering on the street."

"I think the two policemen in the car down the end of the road 'ave the cushier job." Ada stared along Vienna Gardens before speaking again. "Do you like them houses?"

"Yes, it's a distinguished area. It's curious how close Mrs Britten lives to De Vere Square... I think I prefer the stuccoed ones."

"Pardon, miss. What did you say?"

"Stucco... It's a man-made mud applied to walls and ceilings. I don't know what it's made from, but they've put a layer on the house fronts so they can get that smooth finish when they paint."

"Oh, I see. There's none of that round where I live. Looks nice though... I wonder what it's like living in one of these? Do you think the neighbours get along all matey with each other?"

"They're probably polite when they meet, but distant otherwise."

"Yes, they'd be like that... In Poplar, you either love your neighbours or you 'ate them. Makes it lively sometimes. I'll never forget when the Browns, they live four doors down, had a wedding reception for their eldest daughter, Joan. They was all drunk, minister included, so someone said. You've never seen such a punch-up as there was that night. 'alf the street got involved. They was all shouting and carrying on, because not everyone likes the Browns. The old bill came, so it didn't last long. Poor Joan, 'er in 'er wedding dress, an' all. She was in tears over the shambles. I felt sorry for her, but then I did see her bung a bottle right before her father got arrested. *And* she tripped up a copper as he went after 'er mum. But it was alright. She got away. I can't see anything like that 'appening around here."

"No, I cannot imagine it ever would."

"Blimey, here 'e comes again," whispered Ada. "Bet you 'e asks what we're doing this time."

Along Victoria Street, a policeman on his rounds approached them at a stately pace. He seemed at ease with the world while his gaze took in houses, traffic, pedestrians - everything and everyone, except Sophie and Ada. When his slow, measured step brought him within five yards, he apparently noticed them for the first time, even though he had passed them by before.

"Good afternoon, ladies. Waiting for someone?"

"Yes, and most uncomfortable it is, too," replied Sophie.

"Oh... Who might you be waiting for?"

"I'm not allowed to say. We're reporters for the Daily Banner's gossip column and we're here trying to scoop a story. Have you noticed anything unusual going on in the vicinity?"

"Nothing out of the ordinary, miss. Which, um, which house are you interested in?"

"Just between us, and please, *don't* let this go any further, number twenty-nine."

"Ah, I see. Very good, miss. Sorry to have troubled you and I hope you're not kept waiting much longer. Have a good evening."

"Good evening, officer."

Sophie and Ada smiled at each other as he walked away.

"That street cleaner must knock off soon. What will the police do to keep an eye on things when he's gone?"

Ada's question soon received an answer. A man in a shabby suit and a heavy, even shabbier, overcoat pushed a cart along the side of the road. He stopped right next to them.

"Chestnuts, how lovely," said Sophie. "When will they be ready?" she asked the man.

"I've got to stoke up the brazier... About a quarter of an hour."

"We'll come back," replied Sophie.

"You waiting for someone?" asked the chestnut man.

"We were, but they haven't shown up. We ought to ring them. Do you know if there's a public telephone nearer than the High Street?"

"I, er... No, there isn't."

"Thank you so much," said Sophie

They walked away, and when they were out of earshot, Ada said,

"He's a copper if ever I saw one."

"Yes, and doesn't know the area, which is an entirely wrong choice for a proper chestnut seller."

"Are we going back? They're the first I've seen this year."

"We should. I rather fancy some, and I've never bought roasted chestnuts off a cart before."

In the gathering dusk, a freighter slowed to a halt two miles south-west of the Isle of Wight. Soon, the crew were busy lowering a launch by boom over the side. Once the craft was in the water, the deckhands lowered crates in a cargo net by boom, depositing them into the open space of the launch. Someone on the launch released the net from the hook, which was winched back in. The launch motored clear, allowing the freighter to resume its passage eastward along the Channel.

The launch headed towards the Isle of Wight. When several hundred yards offshore, it turned west, keeping parallel with the land. Although there were few boats about, the launch now blended with the inshore traffic. It worked its way around the Needles lighthouse at the western tip, before turning sharply northeast, holding a course towards the middle of the mile-wide gap between Hurst Point Lighthouse on the mainland and Cliff End on the Isle of Wight. Here, the launch cut its speed to dead slow.

Evening was coming on, and the boats at sea had switched on their running lights. Now almost invisible upon the water, the launch waited in the near dark. After some minutes, a small craft with lights entered the gap from the east. Someone aboard it flashed a signal with a torch. The darkened launch picked up speed, heading towards the oncoming vessel, then some half a mile distant.

As they neared one another, the two vessels began a curious dance. The small craft switched off its running lights and, a second later, the launch switched on its own. They drew closer to one another and stopped — dark shapes against the day's last glow of light.

"You're on time, John. It's all clear as far as Southampton," said a voice from the darkened small craft which proved by its shape to be a fishing smack.

"Thanks, Ben," said a man on the launch. "See you in the pub later?"

"That's my second home. Where else would I be?" Ben laughed.

"I dunno... You happy about this job?"

"Pay's worth the risk. I reckon them London gents know what they're doing. It's better how they've got it arranged now."

"We'll see. It's boxes of Moroccan dates this trip. No explosives, so we should be all right."

"You were right lucky before. Who's on board this time?"

"Shrimp. He wants to get the job done, so he's not very chatty."

"Hello, Ben," said Shrimp.

"Don't you know me no more, Shrimp? Sorry to hear about your old man."

"Thanks. Comes to us all, dunnit? Anyway, I gets nervous on a job. The sooner it's all over, the better I like it."

"Yeah, you're right. Let's push on. First round's on you, John."

"Ha, so you reckon. We'll see you later."

The launch set in motion again and the smack fell in some thirty yards behind. The launch now switched off its lights and, within a moment, the smack's running lights came on as they preserved the semblance of their being one boat instead of two sailing through the gap. They passed Hurst Castle to enter the Solent proper. Now the two vessels steered closer to the mainland. After a mile, the smack turned to port, heading for Lymington, while the launch, still not showing any lights, continued on, moving closer and closer inshore. It cut its speed again. The two men aboard scanned the shore.

"There it is," said Shrimp, tapping his companion on the shoulder.

A tiny speck of light shone at just above sea-level, picking out the tops of waves in the swell. The launch turned towards it, while Shrimp turned on a torch to see where they were going.

On the top of Marley Mound and from within the shelter of some bushes, Ralph 'Sinjin' Yardley swept the horizon with his field-glasses in the last light of the day. There was nothing remarkable to be seen, as had been the case over the last two days. He turned north and, keeping to cover, moved cautiously towards the trees. Pitched just in front was an army tent, housing a radio and its operator.

"See anything, sir?"

"No, corporal. Any news since the lorry entered Phelps' property?"

"Nothing, sir. The other station says it's all quiet on Spanish Lane, although we can both hear the cows mooing and they're a mile away. Amazing how sound carries at night."

"That's true. Listen, I'm going down to the weir to look around. I'll get as close as I can. Tell the sergeant when he returns that there must be complete silence from now on. I'll make sure the cliff lookout is wide awake."

"Yes, sir."

Yardley left the tent. He joined the hidden lookout on the cliff, almost slithering forward on his stomach for the last few yards.

"Report," he whispered.

"Nothing, sir."

"I'm going to the weir. Any noise on this side of the river channel in the next ten minutes will probably be me blundering through the undergrowth."

"Yes, sir."

"Stay alert and silent. I expect activity tonight... You're an old soldier. Is the safety off on your rifle?"

"Yes, sir. An old habit from the trenches. I'll switch it on." There followed a faint click.

"Good man... Still a private, though?"

"I've made sergeant twice and been broken twice. Next time, I'll make sure I keep my stripes, sir. Third time lucky, as they say."

"I hope you do. Did you go through the lot?"

"Yes, sir. I was in the BEF at the Battle of Mons and many actions afterwards."

"Ah, an Old Contemptible. I take my hat off to you."

There was a sound of rustling as Yardley reached inside his coat.

"Get yourself a drink." Yardley thrust a five-pound note into the man's hand.

"God bless you, sir."

Yardley left to descend by various paths to sea level. He worked his way along the side of the marsh in the increasing gloom, to arrive at the point from where he could observe the weir had it been daylight. The shadow from Marley Mound made it much darker. The lookout above listened for sounds of Yardley's progress but, although on one occasion he detected a faint noise, he lost him in the shadows below.

About fifteen minutes later, Yardley could not miss the sound of a big engine approaching in the quiet dark of the countryside as a vehicle crossed Phelps' property from the east. Soon he saw the glow from its headlamps lighting up trees on higher ground. The vehicle, a lorry, came to a halt some hundred and fifty yards from his position. Within a minute, two glowing lanterns, bobbing erratically, came closer to the accompaniment of a clattering, squeaking noise. The lorry began a three-point turn.

The small party descended towards the landing, which lay less than a hundred yards away from Yardley. There were four men, including the lorry driver after he turned off the engine and left the vehicle. Yardley clearly heard a voice say, 'Get a move on.' It was an upper class accent. The gang took a few minutes to remove a raft from cover and get it into the water, where they ferried it by rope towards the weir. In the light of their lanterns, Yardley discerned that all four men were on the raft. Someone switched on a powerful torch and aimed it out to sea, holding the light steady. The men secured the raft before stepping onto the concrete platform built on top of the weir. All the while, the signal torch shone out in the same direction even when a man placed it on the iron framework of the sluice.

"Are we late?"

For a moment, a shadow blocked the torch beam as someone consulted their wristwatch by the light.

"A mere five minutes," replied the more refined voice.

"What a time to get a puncture."

"These things happen... We should remain quiet."

The men did so. Two of them smoked cigarettes.

"Here we go," said the leader, perhaps ten minutes later.

Yardley fixed his attention on the launch as it inched into view on the lower water of the weir's seaward side. He could barely distinguish the figures on the craft, but could tell when the rope was cast. They tied the launch fore and aft. The unloading began.

In silence and darkness, Yardley watched six shadowy men unload. He counted some fifty good-sized boxes being transferred from the launch into waiting hands. The contraband was then carried up the ramp, across the platform, and carefully stacked on the raft. Among the cargo were three long wooden crates, each requiring two men a-piece to carry them. Other boxes and crates of different shapes and sizes soon followed.

"How much can the raft carry?" asked someone on the boat.

"Two trips should do the lot," said the leader. "Are you aware of the shipment next Thursday?"

"Oh, yes. Do we do everything the same?"

"More or less. We'll stow that shipment in Underhat instead. I'll be here to guide you in and out, and someone will help you unload."

"Right you are, governor."

Yardley surmised the leader was Phelps. While examining Underhat on Monday, Yardley had found litter proving the hidden dock saw regular use. A fragment of burnt newspaper dated January 1919 hinted at when the activity had begun. Another interesting find was evidence of people using Underhat as a temporary hiding place. Yardley discovered a small hut containing a thin, dirty mattress and other bedding. The fireplace in front of the hut was a ring of stones containing an iron griddle which bore traces of recent use. The hiding place was excellent for smuggling people into the country, if they did not mind the dark, dank surroundings, or the sea always slapping against the dock's concrete seawall and slurping in the stairwell leading down to the restless water.

The boat shoved off, heading out to sea, leaving the receiving party to ferry contraband back to the landing and to load the lorry. Yardley, deciding he had seen enough after learning the squeaky object was only a hand trolley, retreated from his position in stealth.

Chapter 33

Convoy

It was after three in the morning. In Lady Holme's Great Hall, nine men had gathered and sat in chairs. Yardley came in, going to a table behind which was a large map of southern England on a stand.

"Good morning, gentlemen." He spoke as he walked. "As you all know, the show should begin within the hour." He came to a stop. "Now, where do we stand on certain matters? The freighter?"

A navy officer replied. "It's waiting to dock at Antwerp. We can seize it once it's in port."

"Excellent. The local help?"

"We identified the suspected fishing vessel entering Lymington after the rendezvous, sir." answered Detective Inspector Talford. "The owner and his associates are known to us. We've an idea who was present on the launch from your observations. Officers are ready to make the arrests when requested."

"Good, and we can haul in neighbour Phelps any time we choose... Johanna Britten?"

"She's under surveillance at her house," said Detective Sergeant Gowers. "Additional officers were added to the cordon earlier tonight."

"Right. We believe two or three men will accompany the shipment. Now, as discussed, we expect the lorry to head for London. Hopefully, they'll lead us to their weapons cache if they maintain one. I saw three cases of rifles being unloaded from the launch and some disassembled light machine guns. However, our fellows might surprise us by going in a different direction, which is why every constabulary surrounding Hampshire and between here and London have officers stationed at major crossroads. They are on the alert for our lorry. Should they spot it, they'll phone in the sighting to Scotland Yard. All of you have its description and registration number. It's an unmarked Leyland seven-ton with wooden sides and a tarpaulin over the top. The blighters have switched number plates, so we're no further ahead on that score.

"Now, from here, we will follow the Leyland with our convoy at a sufficient distance so we don't scare our pigeon. We'll keep them in sight if possible, but at no point should we be more than a mile behind. The South Hampshires have kindly lent us a squad in case the party gets interestin' along the way." He nodded and smiled at a lieutenant. "Above all, this is a police matter, but as the army has the latest radio equipment, a radio van will accompany the pursuit to keep Scotland Yard informed of our position and relay sightings of our quarry back to us. Let's hope we don't lose the beggars. Any questions?"

"Which route is the likeliest?" asked a Customs and Excise man.

"Can't say for certain. If it were me, I'd use the Portsmouth Road to London, to blend in with the commercial traffic going to and from the docks. The usual timing of their departure lends credence to this theory."

"They'll hit London when the traffic's getting heavy," said Inspector Morton. "They won't be driving through the city. It would take too long."

"A valid point... Anyone else...? Splendid." He looked at his wristwatch. "I have... three-twenty-five. We expect their departure by four. You all know what to do, so good hunting."

The meeting adjourned, and the men moved to their vehicles.

Lord James stared into the darkness of his bedroom. He wanted to sleep, and had for two hours earlier but, once awakened, worrying what the coming day's events might bring made sleeping impossible. He heard the front door bang shut, followed by the sounds of men getting into vehicles. The night stillness returned. He waited.

Silence reigned until an obtrusive sound pervaded Lord James' bedroom. He listened to that which he had heard twenty times before. He now *knew* it was Poppy's agents in the act of smuggling, only having suspected the truth before. The lorry was traversing Phelps' land, before turning northwards to enter Spanish Lane near Frog's Hole. This cross-country jaunt took several minutes. He could tell when the vehicle approached Lady Holme as the noise increased. Tonight, the vehicle seemed louder, as though it might come into his very room. The crescendo came, then the racket decreased. Almost as soon as the lorry had passed, engines started close by, some beneath Lady Holme's windows. Lord James got up to look. Below him, a small stream of dark shapes - some with minimal lights and others with none - proceeded along the driveway. They drove slowly, ensuring the noise from their engines did not surpass that which the lorry made, so that neither Phelps nor the lorry driver would be alerted to this activity. Lord James smiled at the ruse.

When they had gone, he returned to bed. Closing his eyes, he sincerely hoped the day would go well.

A convoy of pursuit vehicles travelled the Hampshire stage of the Portsmouth Road. First in line was the army's radio van, which was kept informed by Scotland Yard of the lorry's whereabouts and so could guide the vehicles following it. Second came a Scotland Yard car, a Morris, containing Morton, Gowers, a driver and another detective. Third was Yardley's Vauxhall Velox. Bringing up the rear was the army lorry carrying sixteen soldiers, including a lieutenant who sat in the front with the driver.

Yardley sat in the back while an immense man drove the Velox. They were both dressed as labourers.

"Len, this jacket's tight across the shoulders... Smells a bit, too," said Yardley.

"It's all I could get. There wasn't much in the second-hand shop. Lymington's not what you'd call a big place." Leonard Feather was Yardley's chauffeur — Bradford born, ex-boxer, ex-army, a socialist, and the man who once saved Yardley's life.

"It was short notice, I know. What speed are we doing?"

"Thirty on the nose. They're keeping it there on the open road and about twenty through towns."

"Feels like a funeral procession... Sunrise at seven-thirty... We left Portsmouth at four-forty, and it's about seventy miles to London. Let's give them an average... Hold on. When you say 'they', who do you mean?"

"The radio van. It can't go over thirty on account of the equipment it carries. I thought you knew?"

"Nobody told me. Good grief, the Leyland could be anywhere. Pull alongside the van."

On a straight stretch of empty road, the Velox left the line to drive parallel with the lead vehicle. The driver noticed the car's lights beside the van, but could not see Yardley in the dark.

"No good, Len. He can't see me waving. Drive on to the next village and we'll flag them down."

The Velox rapidly pulled ahead until it was half a mile in front.

"Petersfield coming up," said Len.

"Good, they'll have street lamps."

Len slowed the car while Yardley signalled with a torch, alerting the convoy to halt on the outskirts of the small town. The Velox stopped. Yardley got out and waited in the road for the van to reach him. The front passenger, a corporal, opened his small window.

"Where's the Leyland?" demanded Yardley.

"We believe it's about five miles ahead, sir," replied the corporal. "The police here in Petersfield saw it pass through ten minutes ago."

"Tell me, if we are ten minutes behind when we reach London, how shall we find it?"

"Oh... er... I don't know, sir."

"Why have we stopped?" asked Inspector Morton. Gowers also approached.

"The radio van cannot exceed thirty miles per hour and so the Leyland is miles ahead of us somewhere," replied Yardley.

"Streuth... Where did you see it last?" Morton asked the corporal.

"Just past Southampton."

The men outside made various unpleasant and pointed remarks.

"What's going on?" asked the lieutenant, walking from the army lorry.

"We're near to losing the Leyland. We can fit two of your men in my car. How many can *you* take?" he asked Morton.

"Just the one."

Yardley turned to the lieutenant. "I'm aware you must accompany the radio van, but I want three good men, including your best shot and the old soldier. I don't know his name."

"That's Atkinson. He is our best shot. I'll send them at once."

"Follow on as best you can!" called Yardley after him.

"Right you are, sir!"

"Driver!"

"Yes, sir."

"Can you get any more out of this crate?"

"There's a speed governor on the engine. Won't go over thirty."

"Remove it."

"I'll see to it, sir."

"Good man." Yardley smiled and banged lightly on the door with the edge of his hand.

The driver jumped out and lifted the bonnet. A radio operator put his head through the partition. "Sighting reported by Scotland Yard, sir. On the Portsmouth road, entering Guildford, two minutes ago."

"Thank you."

Three soldiers came running up the road with their rifles.

"Smallest in the front with me," boomed Len from the Velox. A soldier approached, soon aghast at the space he was expected to occupy next to the big man. He handed his rifle to the soldier in the back, then squeezed into the front.

"Cosy, isn't it?" said Len. "Don't look scared. I'm not thinking of marrying you."

With the Velox leading, the cars soon set off once more. Beyond Petersfield, they picked up the pace.

"Don't lose them," said Morton. It was dark and cramped inside the Morris.

"Their car is a lot faster than our'n, sir," said the driver.

"*Don't* lose them."

The Morris hurtled through the night, lurching around corners on overworked springs.

"I should have asked before, really," said Gowers, as they slewed around a sharp bend. "What state are the tyres in?"

"A new set, sergeant," replied the driver.

"That's a relief. Then we've half a chance of coming out of this alive."

"Who's this Yardley chap? Anyone know?" asked Morton.

"He be a lord or summat," said the soldier. "Leastways, that's what the lieutenant was sayin'."

"Is that right?" said Morton.

"His driver's a big fella," said Gowers. "You seen the size of him?"

"I was talking to him," said the driver.

"You just concentrate on what you're doing," said Morton. "What's his name?"

"Leonard Feather. He was a boxer from up north before the war."

"I remember him," said Gowers. "A heavyweight who showed great promise. Had a few knockouts. The start of the war must have ended his career."

"What's he doing with Yardley?"

"You mean besides driving like a lunatic?" replied Gowers. "Well, sir, I imagine he'd be a handy person to have in a tight corner."

"Precisely."

Gowers tried to divine Morton's meaning in the dark interior of the car, but failed to do so.

At Guildford, police officers waiting in a car became incensed by the speed of the two cars passing through their town. They gave chase, but soon abandoned the pursuit as a lost cause.

"Have you come into some money?" enquired Lady Shelling while seated at the breakfast table at White Lyon Yard. It was just after seven. "I ask, because that is a very smart new dress you're wearing."

"Not exactly, Auntie. I received an unexpected dividend connected with the last case," replied Sophie.

"You're very annoyin'. Why don't you confide in me?"

"It's the nature of the work."

"Utter tosh. I helped you and so I'm owed an explanation."

"You helped, thank you."

"From the little you say, it wasn't of much use."

"It was useful up to a point."

"Then you should give me more important things to do."

Sophie gave her aunt an old-fashioned look. "Why are you up so early?"

"Blasted cousin Archie insists upon seeing me this morning. Even imposed the time upon me. Young squirt, what does he think he's going to tell me I don't already know? The spies today have no panache and lack romance."

"Oh, come off it, Auntie. You're going overboard about all of this. He's concerned you learned he's a spy and just wants to sound you out on how you may both proceed in the future."

"It is so infantile and civil servant-like. Of course I'll keep his precious secret. The boy's becoming institutionalized in his mind." She tapped the side of her head.

"Whatever do you mean?"

"He's all process, procedure, and everything by the rules. The older he gets, the worse he'll become. When in advanced years and lolling about as a senior civil servant, his brain will be in such an utter state of decay it will have the consistency of thin porridge."

Sophie smiled. "He's coming to tell you off and you're annoyed he dares do it."

"So? I can be as annoyed as I wish. And another thing, you owe me a proper account of everything that happened at Lady Holme. Don't palm me off with scraps and evade my questions."

"I can relate much more this time, but don't expect me to tell you everything as a *right*. It's not you who chooses what I will say. It is my choice because some information is sensitive."

"I don't know whence you get this barracking attitude. It certainly isn't from Henry, your father. My brother was always so easy to manage and even to manipulate when we were young."

"I get it from you, of course... If you critique me, then you are, in essence, critiquing yourself."

"Oh, is that so...? Very clever of you. Your point, I believe."

"May we have some peace while I'm eating?"

"Very well, dearest niece, but I'm not letting you off the hook. Kedgeree... no, I don't fancy that."

Aunt Bessie rang a small bell on the table. A maid entered the room.

"Iris, bring me scrambled eggs and toast."

"Yes, my Lady." Iris left the room.

"Auntie, there *is* something you could help with."

"Oh, yes. What would that be?"

"Flora and I know some people. Neither is married. She is Anne Ponsonby-Forbes-Miller, and he is John Winslow-Pickett-Ayres-Caernavon. We are certain they haven't met, but we wish them to marry."

"It would be a calamity if they did."

"We believe they would have the world's longest surname."

Aunt Bessie laughed. "Go on, I'm interested."

"The idea is this. They would come to dinner here among a small, select group and we lock the doors so they can't leave until they're engaged."

"I beg your pardon?"

"We arrange it so that they are exclusively in each other's company. If either seems to flag in their attentions, we'll jolly them along, implying they are perfect for one another."

"Are they mindless?"

"Suggestible and shy. When you meet them, you'll realize why they are both unmarried. They'd make a good match, though."

"You're serious about this, aren't you? I must say, it sounds amusin'. But a dinner here would be a rather staid affair for what you're proposing."

"Ha ha. We have a secret weapon who goes by the name of Bubbles Golightly."

"Gracious me, what an extraordinary name. A stage name, perhaps?"

"Exactly so, although she has never been on the stage. A friend, Ada, will masquerade as an upcoming music-hall entertainer who goes by the soubriquet, Bubbles Golightly. We will all sing music-hall songs together, while Flora accompanies Bubbles on the piano. Ada's already practising and putting her heart into it. She's rather good. We're hoping the camaraderie of a singalong produces the desired romantic effects in Anne and John. For example, they will hold the same song sheet."

"It has possibilities. Two subterfuges on the go at the same time... Hmm."

"Oh. I thought you'd be more interested."

"I am, Sophie, I am... You may have forgotten, but I plan to go to Italy in early December and I can't see how I can fit in such an evening, what with the engagements I already have until that time."

"Yes, of course. It slipped my mind. How long are you going for?"

"Three months, perhaps longer. I had thought you might come with me but, of course, you can't, what with your agency and other work."

"Auntie, I distinctly recall your saying you didn't want me tagging along."

"I'm finding you more tolerable than expected. I can talk to you and you never simper. Once, I took a companion to the South of France. After a week, I wanted to throttle her."

"I'm glad you didn't."

"I was speaking figuratively, of course... Now, if you could be more amenable in other areas, I might reconsider my plans."

"Ooh, like that, is it?"

"Yes, it is."

"Let me think this over."

Sophie finished her breakfast. The scrambled eggs arrived. Sophie waited while her aunt cut off a small square of toast piled with egg and watched as it was neatly packed onto her fork. Before it reached her mouth, Sophie said.

"I'll make you a full-fledged spy," the forkful hung in mid-air, "on one condition."

"You timed that deliberately," said Aunt Bessie, who took her first bite. When she had finished, she said, "You have my undivided attention, my dear."

"If I give you an order or a request, it cannot be countermanded, varied, adapted, or derailed. Is that understood?"

"I understand. Am I permitted to disagree with it?"

"No. The work is serious and not a matter of games between you and me. You must understand, I am on probation. What I am being asked to do goes beyond me entrusting you with a secret or two and letting you contribute when you feel like it. If you are to help, I cannot have my authority undermined, even if it is unintentional on your part or you feel you have good reason to do so. I welcome recommendations and suggestions, but I have the final say in all matters."

"These eggs are very good," said Aunt Bessie. "You should try some if you're not too full." She paused for a moment. "Do you think it wise to challenge and berate your wealthy old aunt, who might cut you out of her will?"

"Not the will again, Auntie. To answer, normally, no. In this matter, I am forced to oppose your wishes. I intend doing this unusual work as long as I can. Auntie, I love you for yourself and because you are my aunt. But in these affairs, I must suspend the influence of those feelings."

"Why?"

"Because of the danger. I have discovered appalling things in the last few weeks."

"I see. You're perfectly right, of course. Remember, you haven't actually told me *all* about your escapades, so I'm partially ignorant of what it is you do. I know you spy and work for the police. Now you are hinting at a more serious aspect I hadn't considered."

"It's true I have kept much from you, but then these events are of a type where I tell you all or nothing."

"I can appreciate the difficulty... You must find me very tiresome sometimes."

"You're challenging, but not tiresome. What are we to do?"

"I'm not sure... Perhaps, if you explained some small thing to help me understand a little better."

"Let me see... Yes, I believe I have it. Do you recall a discussion we had about Lord Stokely, and how he was involved in a murder?"

"Yes, I do."

"That story is true. I could add another, more recent account, which also includes murder. This is not hearsay, but evidence, from my own certain knowledge of him and his agents."

"Good heavens... It's as serious as that? Honestly, my dear, I hadn't realized... What a blundering fool I've been."

"Auntie, of course you're not."

"But Archie must know all this, too... I was going to give him such a lovely broadside when we met. I can't do that now."

"Cheer up. Think over my proposal."

"Sophie, I'm not usually a timid person, but from what you say, I would expose myself to some risk."

"Not unduly, but there's always a chance. For example, suppose you were talking to an acquaintance while attempting to get information. Let us further suppose, unbeknown to you, that the person has a connection to someone else, a criminal, who will stop at nothing. A slip on your part and what happens? Either a mission is compromised or you might put yourself in jeopardy. Are you willing to take on that type of responsibility?"

"I like to think I would. I'm not so sure now it comes to it... You're so aggravatin' when you're in the right."

"Then why don't we leave it as it stands? I'll ask for your help when possible, and I'll relate such anecdotes as I'm able."

"Very well. I'll think over everything you've said, and I shall be like a little lamb when I see Archie."

Sophie got up and kissed her aunt on the cheek. "You are a darling and I understand how galling it must be for you. I'm the same, remember? I must *know* what's going on."

"Run along to your blasted office." Aunt Bessie smiled at her. "How's it doing these days?"

"It's ticking over nicely, thank you. One thing puzzles me, I'm not getting very many staffing requests for large events and parties, or even placements for London houses. I thought that might change with the London season approaching."

"A lot of families are hard up, my dear. They can no longer afford to keep a property open in town, or the staff to maintain it, for the whole season. However, if I were arranging something, I probably wouldn't contact your agency before early December, and if not then, I would leave it until after Christmas. It's likely you'll be inundated come the first week of January."

"Yes, of *course*. That makes perfect sense. Thank you, and I shall keep your observation in mind."

"Will you dine here tonight?"

"No, I won't, because I'm going out. Something is nagging me and I must see it through."

"You're not putting yourself in danger again, are you?"

"Oh, no, Auntie. Absolutely not."

Chapter 34

Old Paradise Street

The two speeding cars finally caught up with the Leyland lorry between Cobham and Esher. More vehicles were now on the Portsmouth road, travelling in both directions. The Leyland slowed as it entered the lighted, more heavily populated areas on the outskirts of London. The Velox was behind it, followed by the Morris.

"We can breathe again," said Gowers, when they first caught sight of the lorry.

"Can I smoke, sir" asked the soldier.

"No, not in the car," replied Morton. "It's against regulations."

"I used to live around here," said the detective.

"This is still Kingston, isn't it?" said Gowers.

"That's right. I lived near Fairfield Park."

"Hello, the Leyland's turning off," said Morton. "Where's he going?"

"Kingston Hill," said the detective. "If he doesn't stop, we'll pass south of Richmond Park, heading for Wandsworth."

"Pass the map back here," said Gowers. "If he's crossing the Thames, he won't use Wandsworth Bridge. It's no good for heavy traffic. If he crosses by Putney Bridge, then he's likely headed for west or north London. Let's have a look." With difficulty, Gowers consulted the map by torchlight. "No, I can't narrow it down better than that. For all we know, he might head for Tower Bridge."

"Sunrise is about half past seven... Twenty minutes." Morton peered at the brightening sky. "Not a cloud anywhere."

"I could do with a bit of breakfast," said the detective.

"Oh, come on," said Gowers. "You never mention food when everyone's hungry. It's too upsetting."

The traffic slowed in Battersea and policemen on point-duty became a frequent sight. The sun crested the horizon.

"Go on," said Morton to the driver. "Yardley's giving us the lead."

"That's thoughtful of him," said Gowers.

The Velox pulled over to the kerb, allowing the Morris to move ahead, and then pulled out to fall in behind. There was now a single car between the Morris and the Leyland.

"Get your warrants out," said Morton. "We're following the Leyland through all crossroads. If that car in front gets stopped by an officer on point, drive around it."

"Yes, sir," replied the driver.

At the next crossroad they had to do just that. With windows down and police warrants held up, they shouted a hurried explanation. The point-duty officer waved the Morris and the Velox through.

Sophie walked along Bishopsgate carrying two empty shopping bags and made a detour into Leadenhall market to get supplies for the office. There she bought some loose tea, cakes, biscuits, sugar, and fruit, among which was a perfect bunch of bananas. She was pleased, because the fruiterer did not always stock them. Havering-under-Lyme's only shop had never sold bananas, so they were an exotic rarity for Sophie. It was a pleasant triumph with which to begin her day.

"Good morning, Elizabeth, you're here early."

"Good morning, Miss Burgoyne. Yes, I wanted to see you first thing. Yesterday afternoon, I discovered something interesting about Johanna Britten."

"Did you really? Tell me as soon as I put these things away. We have bananas today for the fruit bowl." Sophie looked excited as she imparted her news.

"Oh, how lovely," said Elizabeth.

After Sophie had spoken to Miss Jones and the two typists, and put away her purchases, Elizabeth came to her office armed with a map and a sheaf of papers. She put down the papers and held the map in readiness.

"May I?" asked Elizabeth.

"Please continue."

The older lady spread the large-scale map on the desk, orientating it towards Sophie.

"This is Kensington... Here is Vienna Gardens, and that is number 36. The road to the south is Montcrieff Drive. The gardens back on to each other and there's no lane between them, as you can see. Directly opposite the back of number 36 is a small, detached building - number 58. According to the scale, the approximate dimensions are eighteen feet wide by twenty-five feet deep. Perhaps you have seen it?"

"No. Ada and I didn't go along Montcrieff." Sophie continued studying the map.

"Ah, pity. At first, I imagined it was a small shop, but then I remembered Kensington is almost entirely given over to residences except along the major roads. I visited the Land Registry to look it up... I hope you don't mind. The office wasn't particularly busy, you see."

"No." Sophie looked at Elizabeth. "That is why you are here. You are not to be *busy*, but have ideas and follow up with research."

"Thank you... I discovered that the property is in fact a small, two-storey residence, built in 1868. The original owner was Mr Samuel Britten. He transferred it to his son, Charles Britten, in 1899."

"He was Johanna's husband. Sorry, I interrupted you."

"That's quite all right," said Elizabeth awkwardly. "According to Charles Britten's probated will, he bequeathed 29 Montcrieff to his wife, Johanna. Then in September 1915, the title was transferred again to the eldest Britten daughter, Alexandra."

"Does that seem odd to you?"

"Not necessarily so, except it was registered under her married name of Alexandra Pink. She was married in 1912, so it hardly seems appropriate for a wedding gift, although the transfer may have been recorded later."

"Doesn't Alexandra live in Manchester?"

"She does. Alexandra has four children, and Mr Pink is the wealthy owner of several textile mills. He's also quite a big name in wool, I understand."

Sophie leaned back in her chair. At the mention of wool, the other PWP names, such as salt and iron, came to mind. She considered her words before she spoke.

"A wealthy mill owner with a large family could not make use of such a small property. Why would Johanna give her already married daughter a property Alexandra doesn't need and cannot, would not, use?"

"Exactly, Miss Burgoyne."

"I shall examine this property today. The Brittens would undoubtedly have sold it if it hadn't a use for them. There is the possibility that household staff have their quarters in the building."

"I hadn't thought of that," said Elizabeth.

"But even if my suggestion explains the use, it doesn't account for the transfer to Alexandra. Do you have any ideas?"

"Not really, Miss Burgoyne... Do you?"

"The only two that seem possible are that it is a hideout or an escape route from 36 Vienna Gardens. The change in titleholder distances the connection from the Britten name while keeping the property value within the family... You have done excellently well, Elizabeth."

"Thank you... I hope your examination of the property bears fruit."

"So do I, but it won't be bananas." They smiled.

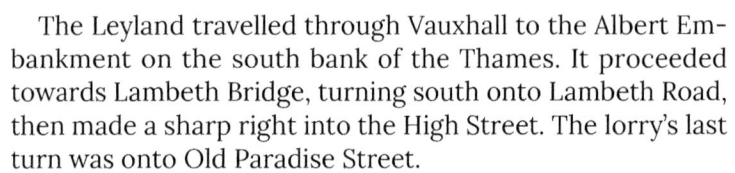

The Leyland travelled through Vauxhall to the Albert Embankment on the south bank of the Thames. It proceeded towards Lambeth Bridge, turning south onto Lambeth Road, then made a sharp right into the High Street. The lorry's last turn was onto Old Paradise Street.

"Coo. Don't come down here alone of a night," said Gowers.

The police watched, parked at a distance, as the Leyland backed into a yard on the far side of a railway arch.

Inspector Morton turned to the detective. "Quick as you can, find a telephone and inform the Yard where we are and make sure the army doesn't come barrelling down here. They may have lookouts, so tell them to park along the Embankment. Make sure they understand that last part."

"Right you are, sir."

Yardley, dressed in workman's clothes, approached Morton's side of the car and tapped on the window.

"I'll do a tour to see if there are other exits and what we're up against."

"That'd be helpful. Don't let your soldiers out of the car and no rifles in sight. We can't have their uniforms giving the show way."

"Quite right, Morton. I'll tell them and then toddle off."

"I've asked for the radio van and lorry to park along the Albert Embankment."

"Yes, that's a good idea. Looks more natural. The Yard is sending reinforcements?"

"It should get busy here soon. I'm off the job, though. They gave the smuggling case to someone else, higher up. Just so happened we were on the spot in Lymington to pitch in when asked."

"Oh, that's a pity... Give me your room number at the Yard and I'll drop by when it's all over. I'll tell you how it turns out. After, I've had a bath, of course."

Morton smiled and gave his number.

The detectives in the Morris watched Yardley saunter away with his cap pulled down, and hands thrust in his pockets.

"Friendly sort of chap," said Gowers.

"Seems so," said Morton.

"Mucks in on anything and everything."

"That's what I noticed about him." Morton turned to Gowers. "I think he's the man we wanted to talk to in the Dorking case."

"Oh, you mean the helpful gentleman... Quite likely."

The day wore on at Sack Lane, Old Paradise Street, and Vienna Gardens. Sophie attended to agency business and, by two in the afternoon, she found herself at a loose end. Miss Jones dealt with all the typing assignments. Elizabeth interviewed applicants for domestic positions. Sophie decided upon two things. First, she would increase Elizabeth's wages. Second, she would go alone to Kensington. Ada was serving at a dinner that evening, while Flora would perform her new part.

By now, a line of police vans and army vehicles had formed on the Albert Embankment. Although within a few hundred yards of the old, four-storey warehouse, situated in the middle of its square yard, the constables and soldiers stationed by the river appeared to have no connection with anything on the other side of the tracks. These were the reserves in case there was shooting.

The yard's only entrance was secured by iron gates covered in rusting sheet metal. These also prevented a passer-by from seeing anything within. The police had set up several observation posts. A hut beside the tracks on top of the railway embankment afforded an imperfect view of the warehouse's top floor, but it was distant, requiring the use of binoculars. As yet, the observers had seen no movement.

Despite the noise of trains going to and from Waterloo Station, Yardley, Len, Atkinson, the old soldier, and an army radio operator had chosen that hut for their post.

Elsewhere, plain-clothes detectives waited in cars. The plan was to wait for a vehicle to enter or exit the premises, then rush in and seize suspects. Since the Leyland had gone through the gates, nothing had moved, except every few minutes, a smoke-belching train clattered over the tracks high up on the railway embankment.

It was equally quiet in Vienna Gardens, where half a dozen detectives, eight constables and two police matrons waited. Several were in a house adjacent to number 36, requisitioned for the purpose. They waited for the signal that the police had entered the warehouse on Old Paradise Street.

"Do you think the Superintendent has it in for us?" asked Gowers, as he and Morton sat in a car at the end of Vienna Gardens.

"Yes, I do. He knew we'd been up all night and hadn't been home for days. He sent us straight here from Lambeth. There's already another inspector in charge, so why send us here?

"And he's nice and cushy in the house... Why'd the Super do it?"

"I've no idea, and I don't care anymore."

Gowers yawned. "'Scuse me. You and him always seem to get along alright... We've had some nice cases in the past... What would you do if you weren't on the force?"

"Sleep... Have a life."

"As an occupation, I mean."

"Do we have to talk?"

"It's the only way I can stay awake... sir."

"A bit late with that one, weren't you? Go on, have a doze. I'll nudge you when anything happens."

At a quarter to four, Sophie stood across the road from 29 Montcrieff Drive, pretending to consult a map. The small building was a symmetrical bijou cottage with a tiny stone-paved forecourt. Once, it must have been pretty, perhaps serving as a summer house. But the Brittens had not adequately maintained the cottage for many years. It was unlike the surrounding houses in size and style — someone had especially requested the builder to erect this particular house. As house building was also an exercise in economics, Sophie assumed the builder received a heavy premium, and Samuel Britten was the one who had paid the overcharge in 1868.

The house possessed an uninhabited air and a blank look, with all its curtains drawn at the windows. On either side, the prosperous, well-kept houses threw into relief the cottage's neglected, scruffy appearance. The grime on the windows attested to the fact that no self-respecting servant attached to a wealthy family had anything to do with the place. Sophie crossed the road and glanced at the forecourt. No weeds, even dead ones, were to be seen between the stones of the forecourt. At least someone gave a little attention to the lower portions of the place. She started along the pavement so as not to attract the attention of the neighbours.

It occurred to Sophie to enter through the gate in the low wall, but she decided against this. She would attract needless attention, and to what purpose? There was no answer to this, and she was uncertain why she was there. Sophie glanced up at the front once more. Her new position gave a view of the upper windows from a more acute angle. By this, she noticed a sagging curtain, gathered in the middle, as though the rail it hung upon was bent, causing the heavy material to press into the rail's deformation of several inches in depth. But it was what the bent rail revealed that interested her. She could dimly see, for Sophie now disregarded the threat of prying eyes, a few inches of an upright object against the dark interior of the upper room. Without a doubt it was a bar — the top of a round, vertical bar. She ceased staring to move right away from the front of the house, excited by this minor discovery. The pretty, forgotten cottage had bars at the upper storey window and a Britten had installed them. Were they installed at every window?

Sophie did not leave. The thought she might have missed something drew her back. From the opposite pavement, she stared, drinking in the house. There was no smoke from the chimney. The worn roof sagged slightly. Paint on the upper window frames had blistered in their southern exposure to the sun. Leaves protruded from the eavestrough. These things contributed to the unkempt look. She studied the door and its worn brass handle. The sun gave a slight shine to its surface. It shone not from polishing but from use. The plain brown door was heavy and had three locks. She crossed the street again, to open and shut the gate. It barely squeaked. She stared at the four steps leading to the front door and observed the dust, which was apparent everywhere, except on the clean central section of each step. She hurried away. Someone used the cottage, but not as a residence. This was Poppy's secret place, and Sophie sought a policeman.

At five minutes to four, one of the two entrance gates on Old Paradise Street began opening inwards. An old man in an army greatcoat and in no hurry pushed the gate back, to hook it to a post with a piece of wire. This unveiling revealed to the road a four-storey Victorian warehouse with loading doors on each floor and winches to haul up goods straight from the back of a flatbed lorry. The closed main doors were hung in a tall arch. To one side of these doors, a short flight of steps led to a front door of ordinary proportions — the entrance to an office. The yard was not empty. There were two cars parked in the front and, abandoned next to the fence, was an inoperable steam lorry. In the open space in front of the warehouse stood the Leyland. The driver started its engine. The passenger shouted something to the old man, who waved back dismissively. Then the watchman moved even slower in opening the other gate. He fastened it before plodding towards the road where he checked for traffic.

Finding none, he motioned the lorry forward, moving to one side to let it pass.

Once on the road, the driver made noisy gear changes in the tunnel under the railway lines. The old man returned to unhook and close a gate. Before he did, three full police cars shot through the entrance, bumped over the uneven, rutted ground, and screeched to a halt, forming a line in front of the warehouse. At that moment, the Leyland was issuing from the tunnel where it became surrounded by fast moving cars and running constables, intent on barring its way. The driver, looking for a way out, saw behind him two cars now blocking the lorry in that direction.

The army vehicles on the Albert Embankment began moving. Yardley, Len, carrying a rope, and Atkinson ran alongside the elevated railway tracks in that doubled-over, keeping-your-head-down lope familiar to those who had been through the recent war. A Scotland Yard detective, with a paper in hand and accompanied by a constable, climbed the front steps. They pounded on the front door, shouting for admittance. They stopped and waited. At that moment, the yard was quiet and still, without any passing trains. From overhead came the sound of breaking glass. Someone pushed the muzzle of a light machine gun through the broken pane and began firing upon the police below. They scattered, diving for cover wherever they could find it. A few revolvers had been issued to the police but, while these officers returned fire when they could, it was too dangerous for them to take careful aim. The incessant machine gun fire paused every so often while the invisible attacker expertly loaded a fresh magazine.

Yardley, Len, and Atkinson scrambled down the railway embankment in their approach to the side of the warehouse facing the tracks.

"Stay here and cover us," said Yardley to the soldier.

Atkinson nodded and moved behind a telegraph pole, his rifle at the ready. Len secured the rope and let fall the free end over the twenty-foot drop. He climbed down. Yardley followed. At the bottom, they took out their revolvers and ran towards a side door with wooden stairs leading up to it. Len tried the door, but found it locked. All the while, the machine gun chattered at the front of the building.

"We'll get in through a window," whispered Yardley.

They had just turned away when the door behind them burst open, knocking Len off balance. The first man escaping had no weapon and, avoiding Len, ran down the stairs, but he collided with Yardley, who grabbed him. They fell sprawling. Yardley rolled over and leapt on the man. The second man out carried an automatic. Len seized him and they grappled, unable to use their pistols at such close quarters. For several seconds, the various combatants struggled and strained. Yardley's opponent went limp, ceasing to fight.

"Stop, I give up. I don't 'ave a gun, honest. I'm just a warehouseman and do what I'm told."

Yardley sprang up and trained his revolver on him. "Don't move." He glanced up at Len. He had his man trapped in a headlock with his gun hand immobilized. The opponent was fast succumbing to the pressure of the hold. All the time, the machine gun kept firing.

Without warning, a third man, pistol in hand, sprang through the door and ran like a hare towards a fence at the back. Yardley aimed his revolver, but then hesitated. He called to Atkinson, who was still behind the telegraph pole.

"Tricky shot! Can you wing him!? My responsibility and all that!"

Atkinson dropped to one knee and, over open sights, aimed his rifle. He paused a moment and then fired. The sprinting man made two hops, clutched his leg and fell to the ground.

"Will that do you, sir!?" asked Atkinson.

"That was perfect, my friend!"

The machine gun continued firing, and a train rumbled by.

Chapter 35

Double-decker

Vienna Gardens had few pedestrians. From the south corner at her end of the road, Sophie could see no street cleaner, chestnut seller, or any other person with a legitimate reason to loiter. She wondered if the surveillance had been called off. She crossed the road to the north corner. From here, she had an oblique view of the front of number 36. Nothing looked any different. She supposed that if she peered into parked cars, she might find a policeman. As she contemplated the risks of her inadvertently exposing hidden officers, if there were any, a glossy Lanchester limousine passed her, gliding to a halt at the south corner. It struck Sophie as a strange, rather awkward, place to park. She stepped back to appear less obvious to the occupants. Her hand rested for a moment on her pocket where she kept her blackjack. They had to have seen her from behind as they entered the road and as she had been staring along Vienna. She turned to walk north up Victoria Street, worried that someone had seen her investigating the Montcrieff cottage and had come now to question her about her extraordinary interest.

As she walked, a car door slammed shut, and she heard the car driving off. Sophie looked back. A man wearing a top hat and an expensive overcoat with a fur collar had entered Vienna Gardens. After waiting a moment, she returned to the north corner. Sophie had a good view of him and he had not noticed her. He was a heavyset man with a peculiar gait. His legs moved, but his body seemed inflexible. He wore spats and carried a heavy cane. She crossed to the other corner to view him from the back. Without a doubt, he waddled. His shoulders were the broadest Sophie had ever laid eyes on. To date, he was by far the most extraordinary person she had seen in Vienna Gardens, and there was a chance his destination was number thirty-six. Then the man stopped abruptly, hesitated for a split second, before turning about and hastening away. Sophie darted around the corner and then ran down Victoria Street towards Montcrieff.

From the next corner, she cautiously observed the man proceed north on Victoria towards Kensington Gardens. He hailed a passing cab and got in. The taxi continued on towards Kensington Road. Sophie returned to Vienna, assuming the man's sudden change in plan was due to his having recognized police officers in position, watching the house.

A grenade tossed from the upper storey warehouse window landed among the police. Soldiers had advanced through the yard gates and their accurate, sustained rifle fire made it impossible for the machine gunner to fire upon them. When the grenade exploded, a constable fell, wounded. The warehouse became silent and the firing stopped.

Yardley climbed the stairs inside to the floor where the acrid smell of cordite hung heavy in the smokey air. The floor was one large room, half filled with crates and mountainous stacks of fabrics on rolls. Len joined him. They moved from pillar to pillar, advancing upon the large, raggedly shattered window at the front. The machine gunner's firing position lay within a floor-to-ceiling wire crib containing crates of weapons and ammunition. A man lay stretched out on the floor beneath the window.

"Three wounds," said Yardley, as he examined the body lying among hundreds of shell casings. "You were a stubborn beggar. Let's find out who you are." He began going through the man's pockets.

"All clear!" bellowed Len, keeping away from the opening.

Mrs Johanna Britten was worried, not in a fearful sense, but by the annoyance of unanswered, repetitive questions. Where was Adrian? He was not under arrest as far as her agents knew, but where was he? Why was there a new street cleaner? A servant had purchased chestnuts on the corner of her road. Why was that? They never came to this area. From her vantage point at the curtains, she scanned windows, doors and cars. Someone had pulled a curtain back on number sixty-two.

She rang the bell, and the maid subsequently appeared.

"Thora, it is three minutes past four. Mr Ferrers is always prompt, but now he is late. Has he telephoned?"

"No, Mrs Britten. He only ever uses your private line, never the household line."

"Thank you." As they stood facing each other, the telephone for the private line started ringing.

"That will be him. You may go."

"Yes, madam."

Johanna picked up the receiver. "Hello."

Ferrers' deep voice replied, "No time for goodbyes." He hung up.

Johanna glanced around the room at the paintings. She sighed and called Thora, informing her not to answer or open the front door under any circumstances for the next hour. Before going upstairs, Johanna locked the front door and slid several bolts across. On the top floor, she produced a key to unlock a spare bedroom door. Inside the room, she opened a wardrobe and removed a small battered suitcase, a capacious but ordinary handbag, and an old and rather cheap overcoat. Leaving there, Johanna descended a floor to go to her own bedroom. She shut the door. From a safe behind a picture, she removed three long cotton bags of some weight and placed them in the handbag. Johanna opened the centre drawer of her dressing table and found an empty cotton bag.

She opened a lower drawer, extracted a tray of jewellery and then tipped its contents into the empty bag, before adding the earrings, necklace, and several rings she was wearing. Pulling the draw-string tight, she put the bag with its companions in her handbag. Then she went downstairs. From the servants' closet, she removed the cook's hat. As she opened the cellar door, someone began banging loudly on the front door, shouting, "Police, open up!" She put the hat on her head.

She descended into the clean, old, but well-lit cellars — bordering on the immaculate. Johanna entered the rear section. There, she unlocked a door built into the back wall. She threw the light switch just inside, and a string of bulbs illuminated a narrow, orderly tunnel. She closed the door behind her and relocked it. The underground passage had a plank walkway, brick walls, and smelt damp. She swung an iron-barred gate closed and also locked it behind her. At the other end, Johanna could see the door leading to the cellar of 29 Montcrieff.

As Sophie re-entered Vienna Gardens, a great commotion was breaking out around number 36. A constable rushed past her.

"Excuse me!" she called, but he ignored her in his rush.

She walked towards the house, where knots of policemen had gathered at the entrance and around the gate. The street reverberated with the sound of a heavy hammer hitting the front door. It occurred to her that, as nobody was opening the door, either there was no one in the house, they were deliberately not answering, or else they were escaping. Of the three choices, Sophie could only act upon the third possibility. She hurriedly retraced her steps to Montcrieff.

In the cottage, Johanna emerged from the cellar door under the stairs into a short hall. The downstairs had two small reception rooms. One was part filled with a pile of furniture under dust sheets, while the shelves and cabinets in the remaining space contained neat rows of small bottles. Johanna picked up three bottles of heroin tablets and put them in her handbag. She entered the other room. It was dirty. Long scores marred the wooden floor. She looked at six heavy, rope-handled crates, which she knew were full of raw opium. Johanna remembered a time when the room had been so full of such crates the floor had required shoring up with additional supports underneath. She put on her coat and arranged a scarf around her neck. In a once expensive but now cracked gilt-framed French mirror, she adjusted the cook's hat on her head. Johanna looked at her reflection in the filmy glass. The woman looking back was respectable, erect in posture, and looking very well for her age. She smiled, then cast an eye over the place before unlocking the front door.

Sophie was puzzled and, in an unguarded moment, put her hands on her hips in amazement. Montcrieff was empty save for three parked cars. There was not a policeman in sight. Where were they? Quite close and coming towards her was an older woman, probably a servant — a cleaner or cook. The police swarmed one street over while here there was nothing amiss. She imagined Johanna Britten might have already escaped by car. Perhaps the police had taken her away. It was annoying not to know. She put her hands down, remembering she was in a public place.

The woman drew near and, although she was obviously a domestic servant, Sophie prepared to be polite by smiling or offering a 'good afternoon'. Instead, when the woman passed, she did not acknowledge Sophie in any way. Sophie knew it took all sorts to make the world, and that some people bore extraordinary burdens which made them indifferent to others. She walked away in the same direction as the woman who was rounding the corner into Victoria Street.

Sophie stopped to stand at the corner of Vienna Gardens for the last time. She had noticed two significant things. Despite the crowd, the police, people carrying things, and the staff of number 36 being ushered into vans under escort, the domestic servant Sophie had been following did not so much as glance at the obvious noise and uproar. Sophie believed it was nigh on impossible for any British-born person to ignore such a sight as a police raid. The second notable fact was the woman's costly shoes and silk stockings — items well beyond a domestic's financial reach. Sophie followed her.

Gowers was awake, sitting in the car. Morton stood outside smoking.

"Start the car. They're knocking on the door." He threw away his cigarette and got in.

"At last," said Gowers.

"Look at them all! They don't need us there. Drive to the next street over in case someone takes to his toes through the back."

Gowers did so.

"There's no one here. What's that inspector up to?" asked Gowers.

"Now, now... He might have someone posted and we can't see them. Don't hang him yet... You see that cleaning woman? Park just about where she is now."

"Yes, sir." Gowers drove on. The detectives scanned the houses and the gaps between them. "Will this do... by this little place?"

"Good enough... In fact, it must be almost directly behind number 36."

They sat quietly for a few moments.

"I think my eyes are playing up," said Gowers.

"What do you mean?"

"I'd swear I just saw Miss Burgoyne."

"Oh, come off it. Is that a joke?"

"No, straight up. Honestly I did, sir. She was standing over there with her hands on her hips, and then she followed the cleaner around the corner."

"Can't be her. She's a lady. She'd never put her hands on her hips."

"What never?" asked Gowers.

"Never in public, then. It's unladylike."

"A pint says it was her, standing on the corner, with her hands on her hips."

"All right, you're on. There's only one way for us to find out, and nothing much is doing here."

They pulled away from the kerb.

The bus stop outside the southern gates of Kensington Gardens is an exposed one. In the extensive park, the October colours looked inviting, although the temperature was now dropping along with the sinking sun. The domestic servant with the expensive shoes stood first in line. Sophie was second, and there was no one else. A breeze skimming across the park's open spaces made itself felt. A number 9 double-decker bus drove towards them. The woman put out her hand for the bus to stop. The number 9 was doing anything but speeding, yet its brakes squealed abominably as it more or less lurched to a halt.

"Room inside," said the conductress.

They always said the same to avoid extra climbing of the stairs to collect fares. There were twenty-two seats on the lower deck, ten of which were occupied. Johanna Britten took the empty double seat on the right-hand side behind the driver's compartment. Sophie sat beside a woman with parcels on one of the three-person bench seats next to the platform. The bus left the stop. Before it had gone any distance, a young man sprang onto the platform and went upstairs, which meant the conductress must follow him up to collect his fare.

As the bus picked up speed, the solid tyres transferred every irregularity of the road surface into the springs, where the disturbing effect partially dissipated, before transmitting the residual oscillations into the seats of the passengers. Sophie felt as though she was being shaken to pieces.

While being involuntarily swayed in the bus at turns, stops and starts, or bounced over larger bumps, or just shaken, no passenger spoke to another. They travelled in silence while in continuous motion in every direction, additional to the valuable forward direction for which they had paid their fares.

Sophie thought that the woman with the shoes had to be Johanna Britten. With this assumption laid as a foundational stone for all further thought, she could not imagine what she was supposed to do next. Where was Mrs Britten going? Did she realize she is being followed? Sophie could not answer the first question. The answer to the second, she admitted, was 'very possibly', although at no point had they looked each other in the eye. The bus worked its slow way past the Royal Albert Hall.

At what point should she inform the police? Sophie wrestled with this problem in many ways. If Johanna was in disguise, she might also have another identity. When confronted, might she deny and then disprove Sophie's charges? What to do? It was absolutely impossible, Sophie felt, to make a scene on the bus. It was just not done. But the circumstances would not improve at a station or in the street. This was London. A crowd would gather. Sophie would entertain the onlookers in a dreadful spectacle of bad behaviour. She shrank from the idea, almost blushing at the thought of a public display. If Sophie was to act, it was here and now, in the semi-privacy of the bus, otherwise she may as well follow Johanna to Dover, and wave her off, allowing Poppy to sail safely to the continent.

At Hyde Park corner, the conductress' seating recommendations became useless. From the lower deck, six people alighted, including the woman with the parcels, to be exchanged for nine new passengers downstairs, and eight who stamped their way upstairs. Johanna, she noticed, had slid well beyond the middle of her two-passenger seat to prevent another person from sitting next to her without being forced to say, 'Excuse me. Is this seat taken?' This petty, ungracious behaviour annoyed Sophie. The bus entered Piccadilly Road opposite Green Park.

"Excuse me," said Sophie in a commanding voice, clearly audible to every person on the lower deck. "Is this seat taken?"

Johanna looked up fleetingly before looking away. "There are other vacant places," she said. Her case was on the seat next to her by the window. She would have to move it for Sophie to sit.

While she stood over her, Sophie could smell expensive perfume.

"I want to sit here, Johanna."

They glared at each other. Johanna moved her case and sidled across. Sophie sat down.

"Where are you going?" asked Sophie in a low voice.

"I do not converse with strangers on public conveyances."

"Perhaps I should introduce myself. I'm the person who captured Adrian Benson."

"You did what?" hissed Johanna.

"Quiet. Don't make a scene," said Sophie, not daring to glance at the other passengers.

"What have you done with him?"

"He isn't dead, but he's safely hidden where you'll never find him."

Johanna hesitated, then tossed her head. "I don't care what happens to him. Who are you?"

"That doesn't matter. Although not from the police, I think it time you surrendered to them."

"What are you talking about? You've got nothing on me. Just because they knocked on my door?"

"And the cottage on Montcrieff? Come, come, why even suggest your innocence? We both know you're as guilty as sin."

"Did Hazlett put you up to this? Is this his game?"

"Who is Hazlett?"

Johanna said nothing, but pursed her lips.

"This is most upsetting," she said at last, with a catch in her voice. Johanna sniffed several times and seemed to sag. "Excuse me."

She reached into her handbag. Instead of taking out a handkerchief, as Sophie had expected, she produced a small automatic pistol.

"You have one of those?" Sophie sounded surprised and unexpectedly experienced a twinge of jealously. The dainty object did not look intimidating but was, as she knew, lethal.

"Get out of my way," said Johanna through gritted teeth.

Sophie stared at the pistol inches from her stomach, and then at Johanna Britten. She could see she would shoot by her determined look.

"Very well."

Sophie inched slowly back. She noticed the muzzle swaying and pitching in every motion of the bus. The driver braked but did not stop. The muzzle swung away, forward. Sophie lunged at it.

The women struggled. Johanna desperately fought to turn the gun on Sophie and used both her hands in trying to raise it. Sophie forced the muzzle towards the floor, and was surprised by the woman's strength. She had thought the task of overpowering Johanna would be simple, but it had now turned into a protracted struggle. Unused to such exertions and knowing no wrestling tricks, Sophie could only hope that Johanna tired before she did. But trapped in a corner and frantic, Johanna faced imprisonment and poverty. She strove with all her might in one last effort to get free from the only person obstructing her path.

People in the bus were watching, commenting, jeering, and some were standing. Sophie heard the words 'cat fight.' As the reluctant conductress approached, the pistol went off. The bus screeched to a halt, causing passengers to be thrown about.

The loudness of the report checked the efforts of the combatants while the bus rapidly emptied of passengers. Sophie wondered if she had been shot. The women stared at one another, both still holding onto the gun. Sophie's mouth was open in astonishment. Then it snapped shut, and she punched Mrs Britten in the eye, before wrenching the pistol from her grasp. She stood up.

"How *dare* you fire a gun in public! You wretched, wretched woman!"

And that was how Inspector Morton and Sergeant Gowers found Sophie on the bus — dishevelled, hatless, clutching an automatic pistol, and shouting — right in Piccadilly Circus.

"May I take that?" asked Morton, his hand out to receive the pistol.

"Arrest her! This vile creature is Johanna Britten!"

For a reason known only to himself, Sergeant Gowers was smiling.

Epilogue

"I am so thoroughly ashamed of myself," said Sophie. "I never meant to cause such a row on the bus. It was the farthest thing from my mind."

She was sitting in Superintendent Penrose's office in New Scotland Yard on Friday morning.

"Arh... Well, it happened, didn't it? And at Piccadilly Circus, of all places. At least your name didn't get in the papers."

"That was all thanks to Inspector Morton... He was very kind and considerate. I thought he would detain me. Instead, he had Sergeant Gowers get me away from the bus. Could you thank him for me, please?"

"You should do that for yourself."

"No, I can't possibly face him. Not after my dreadful behaviour." Sophie's face flushed. "It's ghastly enough talking to *you* about it."

"Don't upset yourself. You were lucky it was Morton and not a constable in the area... Fleet Street would have had a field day. They would have descended on Havering-under-Lyme and troubled your family. May I suggest a few headlines to you?"

"No, please, it's all too, too ghastly for words."

"The publicity might have been dreadful, but you're wrong otherwise. Johanna Britten would have escaped if you hadn't followed her. She had a fake passport and twenty-five thousand in notes and bonds in that case of hers, plus another ten thousand in jewels."

"Did she?"

"Yes, and in that there cottage, we found a tidy sum in illegal drugs... Did you read the papers?"

"I daren't look at them, but I saw the headline, 'War in Lambeth' and 'Maniac killed in police raid.' Was anyone else hurt?"

"Three police officers and a soldier were wounded. One constable got hit in the back by shrapnel. He'll live, so he'll get a desk job after a few months of recuperation. The others were bullet wounds, but they're walking wounded, as you might say."

"Oh, dear, dear, what a dreadful business."

"It is that... You're not quite so chipper today, Miss Burgoyne, but you will be soon. Then you'll have questions, so I'll answer what I can for you now. We got their weapons cache. Over four hundred rifles, fifty machine guns, three hundred pistols, mortars, grenades, ammunition... No high explosives, though... Have a guess what else we found."

"I don't know... I'm not sure I'm thinking straight today."

"My smile should give you a clue."

"Ooh. Forged notes?"

"A hundred and twenty thousand pounds' worth of them. They had just been delivered yesterday morning. What's more, we now know who's printing them and where the press is operating. The Belgian police are probably taking care of matters while we're sitting here. That's why I'm smiling... I'm also smiling because, in a large part, it's all thanks to you."

"I don't feel I did very much. Things just seemed to turn out the right way without my planning them. It was luck."

"Don't dismiss luck as a factor. You can't count on it, but it's there. I know a farmer in Somerset who has been struck by lightning twice while on his cart. It was on the exact same stretch of lane, and with the same horse in harness. He fell off his cart the second time and guess what happened? Well, you won't know, of course. He found a gold watch in the tall grass by the side of the lane. It was a very good one and hadn't wound down. There was no inscription on the case, so it couldn't be traced. No one came forward to claim it, so he got it. Now he wishes he'd fallen off his cart the first time as well."

Sophie smiled. "It feels rather like that for me... I don't seem to be able to think everything through."

"Who can? Parts of it get easier in time. If you don't mind my saying this, your problem is you don't tell anyone what you're up to."

"But that's difficult. I tried to tell a constable about the cottage, but he was busy. Then I believed I had identified Johanna Britten... What would you have done if you were me?"

"Do exactly as you did, but inform the conductress on the bus. She'd get the driver to stop the vehicle as soon as she saw the next policeman."

"Oh. That never even occurred to me... What if I knew Mrs Britten had a gun?"

"Do the same, only tell the conductress to get the passengers off." Penrose smiled at her. "You had a pistol in your hand. What went through your mind?"

"Nothing in particular, really. All I wanted to do was get the gun away from her and make everything safe. I had no thought of shooting her, if that's what you're inferring?"

"No, I didn't mean to infer that. I wanted to hear your answer, that's all."

"And what are you thinking now?"

"Ladies always like to know what a person's thinking. Mrs Penrose can be quite persistent with me sometimes."

"You're not going to tell me, are you?"

"Of course, I shan't... Have you told me everything you've been up to at Lady Holme?"

"I've told you everything you need to know." Sophie smiled. "We must leave it like that, then. I have a few things to do, and I'm sure you're busy. Goodbye, Inspector."

He stood up. "Goodbye, Miss Burgoyne... Oh, yes. There's a little job coming up in a couple of weeks. I can't say anything about it just at present. Might you be interested?"

"Burgoyne's Agency is always interested in helping the police. I look forward to hearing from you."

"I'll telephone you nearer the time, then."

Upon hearing of the capture of Johanna Britten, Lord Hazlett fell ill, spending two days in bed in a state of chronic fatigue. Dr Beaton put it down to nervous exhaustion. Lord James was reluctant to explain his history to anyone, especially his future son-in-law. After a week, he was better physically, but struggled with a fear of leaving the estate. The first time he left Lady Holme was to visit Maria Smythe. Lady Jane accompanied him, and they were driven to the Smythe's residence by Ronald. He waited outside, wondering what it was that took them so much time to discuss. Ronald did not learn any details that day, but later came to understand that Maria Smythe and her children never wanted for anything.

After that, the Hazletts stayed in a London hotel. Lady Jane is looking forward to the arrival of the next Royal Invitation and Lord James has given his word they shall go.

Amelia and Reginald married quietly in November, as soon as the licence arrived. Lord James substantially increased Reginald's allowance and the newlyweds have their own place in London. There is talk of them moving into an unused wing of Lady Holme, but Amelia and Reginald are unsure if that would be a wise choice to make, although it seems attractive to them in many ways.

Fern, alias Dora, has settled in nicely at Lady Holme, and Mrs Williams is very pleased with her work. Another person is also pleased with Fern, or so the rumour goes. It is the view of some that should Ronald pop the question one day, well, it would hardly come as a surprise.

Constance lives in London, alone. She worries Oscar will get sunburned in Kenya. Several times she has put pen to paper, but the right words never quite seem to get written and the paper with its crossings-out and false starts ends up in the basket. Constance wishes Oscar would write to her — perhaps he will one day.

This secret is only known by a few people. Penrose recruited Detective Inspector Morton and Detective Sergeant Gowers for Special Duties. They will remain working as CID detectives, but will receive unusual cases from time to time.

Speaking of recruits, Aunt Bessie has deferred her Italian tour indefinitely. She had to or, she felt, she would never find out what her niece was doing. It now appears that to perform in public Bubbles Golightly will have her chance, while Anne and John of the long names will have theirs, too, although they do not know this yet.

Johanna Britten is facing a long list of serious charges. Adrian Benson suddenly ceased being 'in transit' right after the police raids. His solicitor holds little hope for the outcome of Benson's forthcoming murder trial. Since PWP was already invisible, no one has remarked on its passing; the society has more or less collapsed, now that its prime mover is under lock and key.

Ferrers smouldered with an inward rage. No sign of his violent thoughts was to be seen on his face or in his manner, but rage was there all right. He sat in Lord Stokely's Kensington house, which was situated close to Vienna Gardens.

"I find this setback rather tiresome." His lordship had been speaking for some time, but now he arose and began to pace the study slowly. "In future, we should bring in bigger shipments, as I first suggested. It's not the loss of the weapons or the cost that bothers me so much as the loss of time."

"There's still the small cache of arms in Manchester," said Ferrers. "None of those arrested know of its whereabouts, so it's safe."

"For what I envision, that is hardly enough, old thing."

"A big shipment means a lot of greased palms, and a lot of people who know too much."

"Well, look where your methods got us? You said Johanna Britten could get the job done with no problems and now she's under arrest."

"Yes, she's a friend of mine and somebody's going to pay for that, make no mistake. But, before we go any further, let me ask you a question. How do you reckon you're going to bring in your *big* shipments?"

"That's not my problem. It's yours."

"Fair enough. There was nothing wrong with the arrangements we had. Johanna's services had been tried and tested for years before we ever used them, and there was never a problem. So don't start coming it with me as though I'm at fault. I don't like what's happened any more than you do. Having settled that... All right, big shipments it is. How big are we talking?"

"Let's say, for each shipment... a thousand rifles with ammunition, pistols, etc., etc."

Ferrers was silent for a moment as he considered the problem. "That's got to be better than ten tons and more like fifteen, so we'll need a gang or cranes to unload. We can't drop that lot on an English dock unless it's well camouflaged, like in a grain or iron ore shipment. That would also mean a very careful picking of the continental port where the cargo is to be loaded." Ferrers scratched his chin and then began to wag a forefinger in Stokely's direction. "Of course, we could get a tramp steamer to run the cargo up a river at night... Scotland or Cornwall would do for that, but it means buying off the locals wherever we unload... You leave it with me, I'll sort this out."

"I'm sure you will. The next item we should discuss is the suppression of troublesome political opponents. Any suggestions?"

"Knock 'em all off. If we can't do that, then ruin their reputations. Got a list?"

"I have it here."

Lord Stokely passed a handwritten paper to Ferrers, who put on gold-framed spectacles to read it. He was silent as he considered the names.

"Reads like a who's who of political life," said Ferrers. "You want to just work down the list or do you have a plan?"

"My plan is to deal with the Liberal party first so they lose the next election. Then we will work on the Tories once they are in power. You can keep that list and give it some thought till we talk again in a few days."

"Right you are. I'll be going. I want to find out who it was who did the dirty on Johanna so they can get what's coming to them."

"You're a man after my own heart," said Stokely.

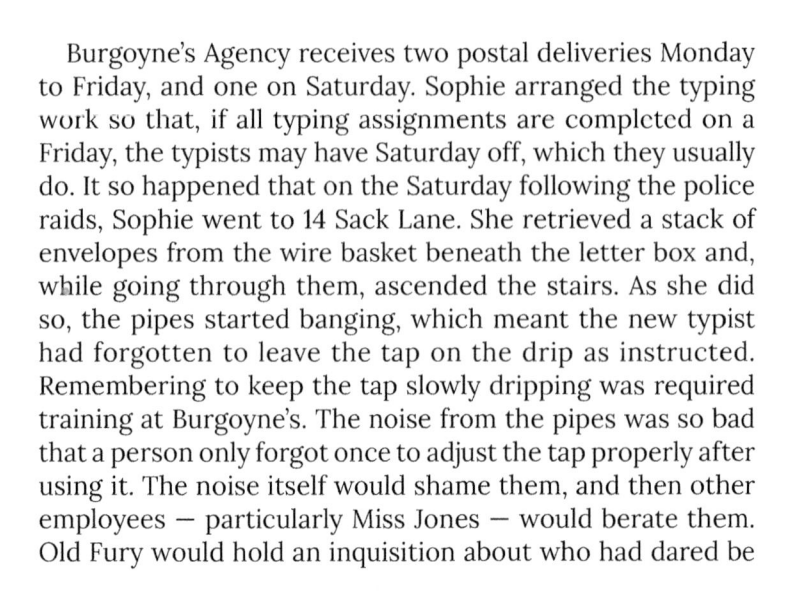

Burgoyne's Agency receives two postal deliveries Monday to Friday, and one on Saturday. Sophie arranged the typing work so that, if all typing assignments are completed on a Friday, the typists may have Saturday off, which they usually do. It so happened that on the Saturday following the police raids, Sophie went to 14 Sack Lane. She retrieved a stack of envelopes from the wire basket beneath the letter box and, while going through them, ascended the stairs. As she did so, the pipes started banging, which meant the new typist had forgotten to leave the tap on the drip as instructed. Remembering to keep the tap slowly dripping was required training at Burgoyne's. The noise from the pipes was so bad that a person only forgot once to adjust the tap properly after using it. The noise itself would shame them, and then other employees — particularly Miss Jones — would berate them. Old Fury would hold an inquisition about who had dared be so stupid as to do such a thing. Today, as the office was empty, Sophie dealt with it.

Two letters among the pile held her interest, and she lingered before opening either. One, written in an untidy, yet legible scrawl, was from Mr Ralph Yardley. In it, he expressed pleasure and delight at having met her, and apologized again for his rather cavalier attitude. He inquired after Sophie and her family, and asked what sort of places and things she liked. Yardley mentioned several upcoming social events where they could meet in public in the company of others if she so wished.

The second letter was from Inspector Morton. He wrote with a slight awkwardness of expression in stiff and formal handwriting. Morton also expressed a desire to meet Sophie at a social event. The largest departure from Yardley's missive in Morton's was his very full apology for his behaviour towards Sophie while in his capacity as a police officer. He re-iterated that there was nothing personal in his conduct towards her. So effusive was he at one point, his admiration for her shone through.

Sophie re-read both letters. Two letters of apology from two very different yet able men, expressing hopes of meeting her again outside of any work — surely, her cup runneth over. She certainly smiled as though it did.

ALSO BY G J BELLAMY

If you have enjoyed this book, please help by leaving a good review. It is greatly appreciated.

SOPHIE BURGOYNE SERIES
Secret Agency
Lady Holme
Dredemere Castle
Available now in the US at   https://www.amazon.com/dp/B0BQ6PLP4Y
and in the UK at   https://www.amazon.co.uk/dp/B0BQ6PLP4Y
Chertsey Park
Primrose Hill

BRENT UMBER SERIES
Death between the Vines
Death in a Restaurant
Death of a Detective
Death at Hill Hall
Death on the Slopes
Death of a Narcissist

Printed in Great Britain
by Amazon